"Wyverns! Probably they forage here, picking off help-less climbers."

"Such as us?" Grey asked, trying to suppress dread. He knew what wyverns were: small, winged fire-breathing drag-ons. Of course he didn't believe in them—but certainly there was something ugly in the air, and that was apt to be just as bad for them as a fantasy creature.

"Yes. But don't worry; I'll use my talent to foil them."

"But your talent's Enhancement! Won't that make them even more formidable?" Again, he was trying to make her see reason without actually expressing his disbelief in her magic.

"Not necessarily. I'll show you."

The flying figures loomed close—and they did indeed look like dragons. But of course such things could be mocked up and even be made to fly. This was obviously a most intricately fashioned setting, so such threats were fea-sible.

The lead dragon oriented and accelerated, flying directly toward them. It jetted a column of fire. Grey started to scramble away, not wanting to get fried—but Ivy didn't move, and he couldn't leave her behind. So he forced him-self to wait, hoping that she did know what she was doing.

PIERS ANTHONY

MAN FROM MUNDANIA

A TOM DOHERTY ASSOCIATES BOOK
NEW YORK

MAN FROM MUNDANIA

A Tor Book
Published by Tom Doherty Associates, LLC
175 Fifth Avenue
New York, NY 10010

www.tor.com

Tor® is a registered trademark of Tom Doherty Associates, LLC.

ISBN: 0-812-57497-4

First Tor edition: December 2000

Printed in the United States of America

0 9 8 7 6 5 4 3 2 1

CONTENTS

HEAVEN CENT

I vy woke, stretched, and opened her eyes. It was dawn; the sun had not yet quite dared show its round face, because darkness made it nervous, but soon it would get up its nerve. She looked at the Tapestry, with its ever changing picture of Xanth. She never really tired of watching it, though her interest waxed and waned. It waxed when it rained outside because it was more fun to remain inside where it was dry, and it waned when Zora Zombie was waxing the stairs and the smell of the wax got chokingly thick. Thus, as she put it, it waxed when it waned, and waned when it waxed. It was her private joke with Dolph; the adults didn't understand. Adults were chronically slow about such things.

Sure enough, Zora was waxing today; the smell was just starting. Ivy had only minutes to find a pretext to go far away, several days if possible, until the wax settled down. But she was running out of pretexts; what was left?

She jumped out of bed so suddenly she frightened the monster under it—Grabraham; she heard his honk as he shrank away. He was a young monster, replacing Snortimer, who had departed long ago; he tended to be timid. She was also reaching the age when folk started not believing in Bed Monsters, and that made it that much worse. When she turned eighteen she would stop believing entirely, and the poor thing would fade away. Grabby was quite upset over the prospect, for some reason. She was sorry about that, but there was really no alternative; she couldn't stop herself from getting older.

She ran barefoot to the next room where Princess Nada slept. Nada had moved in three years before when Dolph brought her home, and the two had become great friends, because they were the same age and rank and similarly pretty. Nada was only half human, but she kept her human form when staying at Castle Roogna, just from courtesy. Princesses had to learn courtesy early, because princes certainly didn't.

"Nada!" she cried. "I need a pretext in a hurry."

Nada sat up in bed, wrinkling her nose. "I know; I smell it too. I'll go with you."

"Of course! But where?"

Nada concentrated. "Have we used the mirror yet?"

"We don't have the magic mirror!" Ivy reminded her. "Com-Pewter got it last year, and won't give it back!"

"Yes. So—"

Ivy caught on. "So we'll just have to go and fetch it! Because I'll need it when I use the Heaven Cent!"

"Exactly. Except—"

"I know. Except that Com-Pewter isn't going to let us have it without a fight, and he fights dirty. Still, it's a perfect excuse, if we can only figure out a way."

"Maybe Electra—"

"That's right! She could shock Pewter into letting it go!"

Electra appeared in the doorway. "Did someone say my name?" she asked sleepily. She was a freckled child whose hair was a bit frizzy; her eyes were the color of wonder, and there were smile lines around her button nose. No one would think, to look at her, that she was tragically in love.

"Zora's waxing the stairs! Come help us get the magic mirror from Com-Pewter!"

"Is *that* what I smelled! Just let me get dressed!"

There was a scramble as the three of them dived into proper clothing. In a moment they were together again; the two princesses in dresses, glancing jealously at Electra in her rainbow jeans. She was of common stock, so could get away with practical clothing. She was also slender enough to wear it without attracting stray male eyes or female frowns.

Quickly they trooped down the hall to the farther stairway, avoiding the wax. Unfortunately this led them past Dolph's room, and he heard them. He had ears like those of a werewolf, perhaps because he commonly assumed wolf form to snooze. His door banged open. "Hey, where're you going?" he cried. "Are you sneaking out again?"

Nada and Electra paused: Nada because she didn't want to hurt his feelings, Electra because she was in love with him. Both were betrothed to him, of course, though he was only twelve. In a moment Electra would invite him along, because she always wanted to be close to him.

To prevent that, Ivy dived in. "We're going to get the magic mirror from Com-Pewter so I can have it when I use the Heaven Cent," she said. "So we can find out where Good Magician Humfrey is and finally complete your Quest."

"But Mother won't let you—" he started, reasonably.

"So you'll have to cover for us!" Ivy finished. " 'Bye!"

He still looked doubtful. But Nada stepped in and kissed him, not saying a word. "Uh, sure," he said. He was Silly Putty in her hands, of course, even though he knew she didn't love him. It was the mirror image of his association with Electra. He changed into zombie form and walked back the way they had come. Zombies didn't mind the smell of wax, so he would be able to brave those stairs despite Zora's mischief.

They completed their escape. Whatever Dolph had done must have been sufficient, because no one tried to intercept them. Ivy whistled for Stanley, and in a moment the dragon whomped around the castle and joined them. He was almost grown now and soon would have to depart for the Gap because guarding it was his job. Ivy would be sad when he left, but knew it was the same as it was with her: age had its burdens. Meanwhile, he was excellent protection; they had no fear of wild monsters while in the company of the tame one.

They snatched fruits from the orchard as they passed through it, eating on the run. Then they reached the main path going north. Every so often Com-Pewter arranged to set up a D-tour, and then King Dor would send out someone to shut it down because it was a public nuisance. Ivy happened to know that there was a D-tour currently in force, and this time they meant to take it. It was the easiest way to reach the evil machine. They were supposed to stay clear of the infernal contraption, of course, which was part of what made him so intriguing. Stanley would be no protection against him, but Electra would.

Sure enough, there was the D-tour. They veered onto it. Now they could relax, because even if it got shut down, they wouldn't lose it.

They stopped for the night near the unlevel playing field where the Bulls and the Bears charged back and forth. Grundy Golem had discovered this during his Quest to locate the missing pet dragon. It was called the Market, and the Bulls and Bears were the Stock. Almost every day the foolish animals resumed their pointless activity, reacting dramatically to insignificant events and ignoring major events. There were many strange things in Xanth, but this business was too strange for even the craziest folk to understand. What did those Bulls and Bears find so fascinating about that Stock Market?

Stanley whomped off into the thickest wilderness to catch a bite to eat, while the three girls harvested pies from a pie tree near the path. It wasn't much of a tree, but Ivy used her talent to enhance it, and then the pies became so healthy that they steamed. There were many more such trees along all the paths than in years of yore, because Ivy's mother, Irene, had seeded them in and made them grow, and Ivy had enhanced them.

While they ate, they talked, for it was always fun to talk when there were no adults to listen in. Inevitably the subject found its way to Romance, for that was the most fascinating concept ever to approach teenage girls.

"When are you going to Find a Boy, Ivy?" Nada inquired. "I mean, you're well into seventeen, and when your mother was that age she had already landed your father and trussed him up."

"And by the time my little brother was nine, he had already landed two fiancées," Ivy agreed. "I confess to being retarded."

Nada and Electra grinned ruefully. Nada had been fourteen when the young Prince Dolph had come to her father, the King of the Naga, for help, and because the naga needed an alliance with the humans, the King had agreed to help if Dolph married his daughter. Nada had had to pretend she was Dolph's age, nine, knowing that her real age would freak him out. It was only a betrothal, of course; they would have to wait until Dolph came of age for the actual ceremony of marriage. But meanwhile the alliance was valid, and Nada had kept company with Dolph while her folk received sundry items from the Castle Roogna arsenal to fight off the encroaching goblins. There seemed to be more goblins in Xanth than there used to be; no one was quite sure why, but it did make for trouble.

Then the Heaven Cent had brought Electra to Dolph. She had to marry him or die, so Dolph agreed to be betrothed to her too. That had happened at about the time Dolph discovered that Nada was five years older than he, so it might have been an easy decision for him to make. But in the end he had realized that he loved Nada, so that betrothal had remained.

Thus their quandary: they all knew that Dolph had to choose between the two girls before he came of age. If he chose Nada, he would honor his word to the naga folk, and as a prince he was bound to keep his word. But Electra would die. None of them wanted that.

Three years had passed while Electra used her talent to charge the Heaven Cent. The three girls had become fast friends. So they accepted the situation as it was: unresolved. Electra loved Dolph, and Dolph loved Nada. Nada didn't love

Dolph, and Dolph didn't love Electra. How was this picklement to be settled? No one knew, but it remained a favorite
topic for conjecture. Fortunately it would be several more
years before Dolph Came of Age, so the matter wasn't pressing yet.

"Didn't you know a boy, once?" Electra asked. She had
been born more than eight hundred years before—maybe
closer to nine hundred—and had slept through all those centuries until Dolph kissed her awake. So her physical age was
fifteen, and she looked twelve; indeed, she was still a child
in all the ways that counted, except for the spell that made
her love Dolph. But because of that spell, she understood
something of love and had a lively curiosity about it.

"Yes," Ivy said, remembering. "I knew Hugo, the Good
Magician's son. He was five years older than me."

"The right way around!" Nada said. They all knew that a
boy could love a girl who was five years younger, but a girl
could not love a boy five years younger. That was Nada's
plight. She could marry Dolph, when the time came, but
couldn't love him.

"Oh," Electra said, understanding. "So when the Good Magician disappeared, so did his son!"

"Yes. Hugo wasn't much, but he was nice, and he could
conjure fruit. Only he usually conjured rotten fruit."

"Rotten fruit!" Electra exclaimed, laughing. She plucked a
cherry from her pie and tossed it at Ivy. "Have some rotten
fruit!"

"Oh, so that's the way it is!" Ivy cried with mock outrage.
She plucked a fragment of peach from her own pie and threw
it at Electra. "Have a peach of pie yourself!" But Electra,
childishly canny, ducked, and the piece hit Nada.

"Oho!" Nada said. Her pie was lemon meringue, but there
were no lemon pieces to throw, so she threw meringue instead.

In a moment they were engrossed in their very most favorite sport: a food fight. For some obscure reason this was
frowned on at the castle, so this was a golden opportunity.
When Stanley returned, all three were thoroughly spattered.

The dragon offered to lick them clean, but at the first lick Electra dissolved into titillations of ticklishness, and that set them all off in helpless laughter.

Fortunately there was a hot spring nearby. The three plunged in—only to indulge in a fury of splash-fighting, with piercing screams, while Stanley prowled in a circle around them, ready to help steam them clean. If it hadn't been for him, every predator in the region would have been there, attracted by the delicious sounds of shrieking nymphs.

It was fun, being girls.

They camped for the night in a nest of pillows within the circle formed by Stanley, who curled around and caught his tail in his mouth. Ivy had told him the story of Uroborus, the giant serpent who circled the Mundane world (which it seemed was round) and grasped its own tail, and Stanley liked the notion, so now he slept that way himself. He was long, but really not that long; he could not hope to circle the world. It didn't matter, because he was only doing it for the feel of it. Meanwhile, they were quite safe, which was the point.

When they got tired of walking, they took turns riding on Stanley. It was an art to remain perched while he whomped along, but they had had time to practice it. First the rider would be low, then riding high, then low again. Wheee! Electra took special joy in this, not ashamed to yield to her juvenile impulses. Ivy and Nada, being more mature (and in dresses), were obliged to pretend that it really wasn't all that special.

As they approached Com-Pewter's cave, they paused for a consultation. "Should we try to hide our identities from him?" Ivy asked. Com-Pewter was really an "it" but it was easier to ascribe masculine evil, so they called it "he."

"He'll never be fooled," Nada said. "He'll know we didn't come here just to giggle."

"But maybe if we can hide our talents—"

Nada shrugged. "We can try. But I don't think it will work. He certainly knows about Ivy."

"Unless he's overconfident, so doesn't check, and—" Ivy's eyes flicked meaningfully toward Electra.

Nada nodded. "When I change form, try to escape, distracting him—"

Now Electra nodded. "Gotcha."

"All else is bluff," Ivy said. "Maybe we'll pull it off without violence."

"Maybe," Nada agreed, seeming less confident.

"Stanley, you go hide in the jungle," Ivy said. "After the invisible giant passes, sneak up and follow us, but don't let yourself be seen. That machine in there is devious, and we may need to be rescued if things go wrong."

Stanley nodded. He was only a dragon, but in Ivy's presence his ferocity and intelligence were enhanced, and he understood her perfectly. He ceased whomping and slithered into the brush beside the path. In a moment his sinuous green body merged with the foliage and disappeared. He would be watching.

They looked on, chatting innocently, in the way girls had when innocence was the last thing on their minds.

The ground shook. "There's the invisible giant, right on cue," Ivy remarked. "Get ready to spook."

The ground shook again. They paused, gazing wildly around. "What's that?" Electra cried, her hair flaring slightly. She was very good at spooking.

There was another shake. "It's the invisible giant!" Ivy cried in seeming horror.

"*EEEEEEEK!*" Nada and Electra screamed in perfect unison.

"Run!" Ivy cried.

The three broke into a run, right toward the cave. That was the way Com-Pewter set it up: first travelers got onto the D-tour, then they were herded by the invisible giant until they took refuge in the cave—where they were trapped by Com-Pewter. They were walking into it deliberately, this time.

Just before the slow-moving giant came into sight (as it were), they reached the cave and plunged in. It was dark, but in a moment a light showed deeper inside, so of course they went toward it. Soon they were in Com-Pewter's main chamber.

There he was: an odd collection of wires and colored metalware, with a big glassy screen sitting up in the center. Words appeared on this screen, written in light:

GREETINGS, GIRLS.

The three tittered uncertainly. Ivy put her finger to her mouth as if nervous, which really was not much of an exaggeration. "What is that?" she asked, staring at the screen.

I AM COM-PEWTER, YOUR HOST, the screen said. TO WHAT DO I OWE THE HONOR OF THIS VISIT, PRINCESS IVY?

So much for secrecy! Ivy decided to get right on with it. "I have come for the magic mirror you stole from Castle Roogna."

I STOLE NO MIRROR! the screen printed angrily. I WON IT.

"You stole it!" Ivy retorted. "And I want it back!"

DID NOT! the screen replied.

"Did too!"

DID NOT!

Ivy realized that Com-Pewter, who was of the technological persuasion, could continue this argument forever. Machines were like golems: it didn't bother them to repeat things indefinitely. Ivy, being just about grown-up (except for the matter of a boyfriend), could no longer indulge in such activity; it wasn't dignified.

"You lured a traveler here, who was using the mirror with my father's permission, and you only let him go because he left the mirror," Ivy said stoutly.

CORRECT. I PLAYED A GAME WITH HIM AND WON. THE MIRROR IS MINE.

"The mirror is *not* yours!" she snapped. "It wasn't his to give away! He had borrowed it, and he was going to return it when he finished his mission. So you stole it, and you have to give it back."

I WON IT AND I DON'T HAVE TO RETURN IT.

"Yes, you do!" Ivy said. "Or else!"

OR ELSE WHAT?

"Or else my father, King Dor, will have to do something."

YOUR FATHER DOES NOT KNOW YOU ARE HERE.

This machine was entirely too clever! "Well, then, *I* will have to do something."

DO WHAT?

"I'll have to take the mirror back by hook or by crook."

BUT A PRINCESS IS NOT A CROOK.

"I'll make an exception."

THEN I WILL HAVE TO HOLD YOU CAPTIVE.

Ivy delivered a haughty stare. "Are you threatening me, you crock?"

YES.

So much for bluffing! "Then it's war!"

IT ALWAYS WAS.

"War, then," she said boldly. "Where do you have the mirror?"

WHY DO YOU WANT IT?

"Why should I tell you that?"

WHY SHOULD I TELL YOU WHERE IT IS?

Oh. "You mean you'll tell me where it is, if I tell you why I want it?"

OF COURSE.

"I need it to take with me when I use the Heaven Cent."

The screen blinked. This news had evidently taken the machine aback. Then the words appeared: THE MIRROR IS IN THE CABINET BY THE BACK EXIT.

Ivy looked toward the rear of the cave. There was a cabinet. She knew the machine could not tell an untruth, but it could tell a partial truth. "Is the cabinet locked?"

NO.

"There must be some reason I can't get it, even if I beat you."

THERE IS NO REASON.

"I don't believe it!"

GO TO THE CABINET. TAKE THE MIRROR.

"You're giving it to me?" she asked incredulously.

NO. I AM MERELY EVINCING MY GOOD FAITH. YOU MAY HOLD THE MIRROR. IT DOES NOT MATTER, BECAUSE IF I MAKE YOU CAPTIVE, THE MIRROR REMAINS CAPTIVE TOO.

Ivy walked to the cabinet. She pulled open its top drawer. There was the magic mirror! She picked it up.

"Maybe it's the wrong mirror!" Nada exclaimed. "Maybe it only looks like the one you want."

TEST IT, the machine printed imperturbably.

"Show me my brother," Ivy told the mirror.

Prince Dolph appeared in the mirror. He was sitting quite still. That was suspicious.

"Show me the larger context," she said.

The image of Dolph shrank as the scope of the scene increased. Now the image showed the boy sitting on Ivy's bed, watching the magic Tapestry.

"That little stink horn!" Ivy exclaimed. "He sneaked into my room to watch the Tapestry!"

"That figures," Nada said. "He does like it."

Ivy nodded. "Almost as well as he likes you," she agreed.

The mirror was genuine. "All right, Pewter," Ivy said. "Now it starts. I'm walking out of here—with the mirror." She started walking toward the front of the cave.

PRINCESS IVY CHANGES HER MIND, the screen printed.

"Well, maybe not with the mirror," she said.

"Ivy!" Nada cried. "Don't let him rewrite the script!"

Ivy glared at the screen. "So you're doing it, Pewter!" she said severely. "Well, it won't work! I'm *not* changing my mind!" She resumed walking.

PRINCESS IVY SEES A BIG HAIRY SPIDER ON THE FLOOR.

There was the spider, right in front of her. *"Eeeeek!"* she screeched, horrified.

"Don't fall for that!" Nada called. "It's illusion!"

"But it's a big hairy illusion!" Ivy replied.

"Just walk through it!"

Ivy realized that she would have to do just that. She took a nervous step toward the spider.

The spider reared up on six of its hairy legs, and hissed. Ivy skipped back, affrighted again.

"This is ridiculous," Nada said. "I'll take care of that spider." For the naga had no fear of spiders; they ate them.

NADA ENCOUNTERS HER WORST HORROR, the screen printed.

The spider converted into a man-high mound of cake covered with ice cream covered with chocolate fudge with whipped cream topping.

"Oh, ugh!" Nada exclaimed, retreating.

"You hate *cake?*" Electra asked, amazed.

"When I traveled with Dolph, we came to an isle—one of the keys—made of cake and icing and all. We ate until we got sick. Ever since, I can't stand the stuff. My stomach turns at the very notion!"

"Well, *mine* doesn't!" Electra said. "Let me at it!"

ELECTRA ENCOUNTERS HER WORST HORROR.

The cake reshaped into an open coffin. The interior was plush, and there was a coverlet and pillow inside. It looked quite comfortable.

Electra's eyes went round with horror. "No, no! I don't want to go back to sleep there!" she cried, retreating. For she had slept for a thousand years (minus time off for good behavior) in just such a coffin, having fallen in as victim of a curse by Magician Murphy. If she ever went back to it, she would slumber the rest of the sentence, then die in her sleep. She backed away until she almost banged into the big screen.

Which was exactly where Ivy wanted her. "I think we've had enough of this," she said firmly. "I'm not going to let that hairy spider stop me this time! Nada—"

"Right." Nada abruptly changed form, becoming a snake. If the spider reappeared, she would snap it up.

NADA ENCOUNTERS—the screen began.

But at that point Electra, responding to their agreed signal, slapped her hand down on top of the screen and delivered a tremendous jolt of electric current. That was her talent, of course, and it was formidable in the right situation.

The screen flickered. WRITE-ERROR! it flashed. Then gibberish symbols raced across it. Then more words: INTERRUPTS OFF! Then nothing; it faded out entirely.

"Come on, let's get out of here before he recovers!" Ivy said. She hurried across the cave. Nothing opposed her; the illusions that had been the spider, cake, and coffin were gone. Electra's shock had thrown Com-Pewter into confusion, and he would have to put all his circuits in order before he could resume revising reality.

They ran out, Nada resuming human form. There was Stanley in the entrance tunnel, steaming. Had their electric magic ploy failed, the dragon would have fired a jet of hot steam at the screen, and that probably would have done the job. They had come prepared.

They rushed out into daylight while Stanley guarded their rear. If Com-Pewter recovered too soon and started printing barriers to their escape, the dragon would use his head of steam after all.

The day remained clear, but there was now a horrible smell, as of a hundred fat men sweating in unison.

Electra was childishly fleet on her feet. She led the way— and suddenly stopped. "*Ooof!*" she grunted, and sat down, gasping.

Ivy was next. " 'Lectra! What's the matter?"

Electra, still struggling for breath, pointed ahead. But there was nothing there.

"The odor must have choked her," Nada said, coming up. "Did a sphinx die nearby?"

Ivy stepped forward—and banged into an invisible column. Then, from above, came a sound: "A-ooo-ga?"

"The invisible giant!" Ivy exclaimed. "He's standing here!"

"Because he doesn't know what to do now that Com-Pewter's on the blink," Nada said. "But we can help him." She tilted her head back. "Hey, Giant!" she called. "Go take a bath!"

"Baaath?" the huge voice came back.

"Go jump in the lake!" Ivy called helpfully.

The monstrous invisible legs moved. The ground quaked with each footfall. In a moment a patch of trees to the side was flattened. Then another patch, in the shape of a tremendous footprint. Then there was a truly phenomenal splash in the nearby lake.

"Move—before everything floods!" Ivy cried, helping

Electra to her feet. The girl wasn't hurt; she had just had the breath knocked out of her.

They ran on down the path—and indeed, a wash of water was coming, and drops spattered down around them like rain.

Stanley whomped after them, catching up. They had made their escape—and Ivy had the mirror.

There was whatfor to pay when they returned, of course, but Ivy was used to that; she had gotten into mischief all her cute life. She had recovered the magic mirror, and that went far to stifle her mother's sharp tongue. Anyway, Dolph had been watching their little adventure on the Tapestry, and would have warned King Dor had things gone really bad.

Still, Ivy was bothered by one aspect of it. It seemed to her that their escape had been too easy. Sober later reflection suggested that surely Com-Pewter had known of Electra's talent, and could have insulated himself against it. Why hadn't he done so? Had he been careless, just this once? It had seemed so at the time, but in retrospect this seemed less likely. It was almost as if the machine had wanted to give back the mirror. But that didn't seem to make sense. Com-Pewter never did anything for anybody voluntarily, unless he stood to gain a lot more than he lost. What could he gain from giving up the valuable mirror?

Well, the deed was done, and she had the mirror. Now she had confidence to use the Heaven Cent. For now that Electra had charged it, the cent was ready for use—and they had always known that it would be used to complete the Quest Dolph had started: to find Good Magician Humfrey, who had disappeared seven years ago with his family, leaving his castle empty. He *had* to be found, for unanswered Questions were piling up. Xanth needed him.

Prince Dolph could not use the cent. Their parents had been quite firm on that. Prince Dolph had gotten himself betrothed to two girls at once, and he had to stay and face the medicine. He had to choose between them, get unbetrothed to one and marry the other, when he came of age. Until he settled that mess (Queen Irene called it a "situation" but a mess was what it was; everybody knew that), he was not going anywhere.

So Ivy was going to use it. The magic of the cent was that it took whoever invoked it to wherever or whatever or whenever or whoever needed that person the most. There was no certainty that Good Magician Humfrey needed Ivy the most, but his message to Dolph had named the Heaven Cent. If the Good Magician thought it would help him, then surely it would, for Humfrey was the Magician of Information and knew everything. So Ivy expected to find him, wherever he was, and expected to be the right person for the job. Magic had a way of working out, with her.

Yet she was not, deep, deep down inside, quite sure. For one thing, there was Magician Murphy's curse. Magician Murphy had lived eight or nine hundred years before, and his talent had been to make anything that could go wrong, go wrong. He had cursed the folk of Electra's time, and as a result Electra had been caught up in the spell, and Dolph had wound up betrothed to two girls instead of one. Eight hundred years, and Murphy's curse had been potent! So how could she be sure it was not still operating? That it would not somehow mess up her mission, and make things even worse than before, and get her lost as well as the Good Magician?

The answer was, she could *not* be sure. Maybe Magician Humfrey had known best—but maybe he had forgotten about that ancient curse. There was only one way to find out for sure—and that made her nervous.

But she did not express these doubts to anyone else, for that might make it seem that she wanted to renege on her agreement to use the Heaven Cent. She certainly wasn't going to do that! The Good Magician had to be found; Dolph had done his part, and now it was her turn.

The day soon came. The Heaven Cent was fully charged and ready. Electra said so, and Electra knew; she had been trained in this by the Sorceress Tapis, who had woven the great historical Tapestry that now hung in Ivy's room. Indeed, the first cent she had crafted had worked marvelously well, bringing

Electra herself here to the present just when they needed another Heaven Cent.

Ivy had watched those old events more than once on the Tapestry, verifying everything that Electra had told her, not because she doubted the girl, but because she was insatiably curious about old-time adventure and romance and tragedy. Certainly her own life lacked any trace of such elements; she was safe and dull here in Castle Roogna. That might be another reason she wanted to go on this Quest: for the things she missed. And she did want to go, despite her secret misgivings.

Where would the cent take her? To the top of fabulous Mount Rushmost, where the winged monsters gathered? To the bottom of the deepest sea where the merfolk swam? To the heart of the savagest jungle where things too awful to contemplate quivered in their foulness? Where *was* the Good Magician? That was the mystery of the age, and she could hardly wait to unravel it.

Ivy made her farewells to all her friends and family members. Her father looked uncomfortable, and her mother was stifling tears. They all knew that Ivy would not be hurt or even be in serious danger; they had been able to verify this with incidental magic, perhaps having private doubts similar to Ivy's. But they had not been able to learn where she would go or how long she would be away—only that she would return unharmed. So it was an occasion of mixed feelings.

She said good-bye to her brother, Dolph, and his two betrotheds, Nada and Electra. Surely she would be back in time to see the resolution of that triangle! Nada gave her a sisterly embrace, and then Electra gave her the charged Heaven Cent. The girl was chewing her lip as if wanting to say something, perhaps about staying clear of curses; Ivy smiled with a reassurance she wished were genuine.

But she had one more farewell to make: she went out and gave Stanley Steamer a final hug. "I think it's time for you to go to the Gap," she said tearfully. "You're a big dragon now, and I can't keep you forever. But I'll visit you, after I'm done with this business." Stanley gave her face a careful lick, after she enhanced the softness of his tongue.

She took the cent and held it before her. It was the size of a large penny, gleaming brightly, its copper surface imbued with the magic of its nature. All she had to do was invoke it.

She shivered, remembering Murphy's curse once more. But surely that could have no real force. After all, the Evil Magician had been confined to the Brain Coral's storage pool ever since the time of King Roogna; how could his curse on the Sorceress Tapis affect Ivy now? It must have done all the damage it was going to, which was plenty. It was foolish to worry about it.

Ivy stifled her foolishness. "I invoke you, Heaven Cent," she said firmly.

Then it happened.

MUNDANIA

Grey woke and looked at the computer. Suddenly he made a connection: the computer was doing it!

Then he thought, no, that's ridiculous, a machine couldn't do anything like that. Well, obviously it could, but this was such a disreputable thing that it wouldn't. He had cobbled it together from used components and gotten a friend who understood the guts of computing to make it work, knowing it was far from state-of-the-art, but it did take care of his school papers. Sometimes weird messages showed on the screen, like INCOMPATIBLE OPERATING SYSTEM or NON-STANDARD PERIPHERALS. What else was new? Apparently his friend had set up something called CP/DOS that everyone else said was impossible. He had put a Directory on User 99 that worked most of the time, so he stayed with it, and usually his papers came out pretty much the way he typed them in: mediocre. That was all the computer did, or could do.

But then he thought some more, and wasn't sure. Because there certainly seemed to be a connection. It had started with that program, and the vacant apartment, and—

He sat up and held his head in his hands. He was sure he could manage to come to a conclusion if he worked at it. But after that date with Salmonella he felt so sick and weak that even thinking was almost too much of an effort. Still, he was sure he was onto something, if he could just work it out before the revelation fled.

Grey had come here to the city apartment because his folks couldn't afford to board him at the college. City College had to take any local resident who qualified, and its tuition was tax-supported low, so by renting this cheap room and living mostly on canned beans, Grey was able to squeak by. He was not a great student, and he had no idea what he might major in if he got that far, but his father said that he was stuck in this mundane world and if he didn't make something of himself, no one else would do it for him. Since a college education was the way to start making something of himself, he was getting it, or trying to.

He had thought life was dull. Now that he was taking Freshman English, he realized that he had greatly underestimated the case. He was receiving a superlative education in just how deadly dull education could be! His grades were slipping slowly from C+ through C toward C− and pointing south as his metaphorical hands lost their fingernail clutch on comprehension.

Then he had received that program from Vaporware Limited. The ad had been impressive: "Having trouble in school? Let the Worm enliven your life! We promise everything!" Indeed they did; they promised to improve his grades and his social life at one stroke. If anything was duller than his grades, it was his social life, so this really interested him. The problem was that not only was Grey strictly average in mind, he was completely forgettable in body. His driver's license listed his hair as "hair-colored" and his eyes as "neutral." He excelled at no sports, and had no clever repartee. As a result, girls found him pretty much invisible.

He knew it was foolish, but sometimes he was no world beater on common sense either, so he hocked his watch and sent off the money for the program. Then, once the money

was safely gone, a classmate had told him what the term
"vaporware" meant: computer programs that were promised
but never delivered. He had been suckered again. Par for the
course.

Then the program had arrived. Suspecting it was merely a
blank disk, he had put it in his floppy-disk drive, intending
to read its directory. But suddenly the thing was loading itself
onto his cut-rate hard disk. Then the screen came alive:

GREETINGS, MASTER.

"Uh, same to you. What—?"

I AM THE WORM, A SENDING FROM ONE WHO HAS AN IN-
TEREST IN YOU. I HAVE ENCHANTED YOUR COMPUTER. I AM
HERE TO SERVE YOUR NEEDS. ASK ME ANYTHING.

What *was* this? None of his other programs operated this
way! "Uh, your ad said you promised everything and would
enliven my life."

TRUE. NAME THE ASPECT OF YOUR LIFE YOU WISH ENLIV-
ENED.

He hadn't even typed in his remark! It was as if the thing
had heard him! "Uh, social. I mean, no girl—"

WHAT GIRL DO YOU WISH?

Amazing! It really was responding to his spoken words!
"That's the problem! I really don't know any girls, and—"

CHOOSE FROM THE LIST: AGENDA, ALIMONY, ANOREXIA,
BEZOAR, BULIMIA, CONNIPTION—

"Agenda!" Grey exclaimed, realizing that the machine
could go on listing forever. How could he tell anything from
a name, anyway? So the first one would do to test this odd
program's bluff.

GO TO THE APARTMENT ACROSS THE HALL.

"But that apartment's empty!" Grey protested. "No one's
rented it in ages!"

The screen rippled in a manner reminiscent of a shrug. YOU
CAN LEAD A HORSE TO WATER, it printed.

"Look, I'll show you!" Grey said. "It's not even locked,
because it's empty." He went to his door, opened it, stepped
across the hall, and opened the facing door.

A girl stood just inside the apartment. She was rather

pretty, with her brown hair tied back with a neat ribbon and every button in place. "Oh—are you the superintendent?" she asked. "The stove doesn't seem to—"

Grey swallowed his surprise. He had had no idea that anyone was moving in! "Uh, there's a switch in back that—I'll show you—I'm not the superintendent, just the boy next door—I mean—" He stifled his confusion and walked to the stove and pushed the switch. "Now it'll work. They just didn't want it going on by accident—"

"Oh thank you!" she exclaimed. "You are so helpful! What's your name?"

"Uh, Grey. Grey Murphy. I—I go to City College, and—"

"Oh, how nice! I'm going there too! I'm Agenda."

He goggled at her. "Agenda?"

"Agenda Andrews. How nice to find a friend so soon!"

"A friend?" He was still bemused by the coincidence of names. He had just chosen that one from the Worm's list.

"Aren't you?" she asked, looking cutely troubled.

"Uh, oh, of course! The friendliest! I just—"

"Why don't we have lunch together? I'm sure you know all the best local places."

There was another pitfall. "Uh, sure, but—"

"Dutch, of course. I wouldn't presume to impose."

It remained awkward. He was broke until his weekly check arrived from home. "I, uh—"

"On second thought, let's eat in," she said brightly. "I happen to have some things with me."

"Uh, I've got half a can of beans—"

"No need." She bustled to the kitchen cupboard, which it seemed she had already stocked. "What would you like? I have asparagus, bread, corn, doughnuts, eggplant, fish—"

"Uh, doughnuts are fine." She had her shelf organized alphabetically?

So it was that they had a nice meal of doughnuts. Before he knew it, he had a girlfriend, and she had his whole life organized, just about. It was great, for a few days, but then it got on his nerves. Agenda did everything by the number, or rather, by the alphabet. But Grey was a disorganized kind of guy. He didn't like having his life run by the clock and book.

It was also apparent that Agenda's arrangements were progressive. First they had an informal meal together. Then they had a formal one. Then they went on a date: a G-rated movie, where they held hands. Then they kissed. Then she set an appointment for him to meet her parents.

He realized that he was on a well-organized treadmill to marriage and a completely mundane life. He liked Agenda, but he wasn't ready to make that commitment yet. He was trying to break the mundane traces, and that would be impossible with her.

"Damn!" he muttered under his breath.

YOU HAVE A PROBLEM? the computer screen inquired. The machine was always on, now; the first time he tried to turn it off after installing the Worm program, the screen had protested with such logic that he had backed off and left it on. Grey was barely average in gumption too, it seemed.

"Well, yes," he confessed. "I've got this girlfriend, and she's nice, but she's so organized I can't stand it, and now—"

YOU WISH TO HAVE A DIFFERENT GIRL?

"Well, I hate to say it, but—"

CHOOSE: ALIMONY, ANOREXIA, BEZOAR, BULIMIA, CATHARTIC, CONNIPTION—

"Anorexia!" he cut in. He knew better than to take up with a girl called Alimony! Of course the name might not mean anything, but why takes chances? Anorexia sounded like a good name.

GO TO THE APARTMENT ACROSS THE HALL.

"But that's where Agenda is!" he protested. "If I go there, I just know she'll have things so organized that I'll never get away."

YOU CAN LEAD A HORSE TO WATER.

Grey sighed. He'd just have to show the machine!

He opened his door and crossed the hall. He knocked on the door.

It opened. There stood a strange, thin girl.

"Uh—" Grey said, amazed.

"You don't think I'm too fat, do you?" the girl inquired anxiously. "I'm on a diet, but—"

"Uh, no, you're fine! Uh, I thought Agenda—"

"She moved out this morning. She said this place was too disorganized, or something. I'm Anorexia Nervosa."

Moved out this morning? He had never suspected! What a coincidence. "I'm Grey. Uh, you don't believe in organization?"

"Oh, no, I'm very disorganized! No discipline at all. I keep getting fat. You don't think—"

Grey took a solid look at her. She was coat-hanger thin. "If you were any thinner, you'd look like a boy," he said.

She laughed nervously. "Oh, you're just saying that! I'm so fat, I hate it! I thought if I lived alone, maybe I could reduce, and look pretty."

As it turned out, this was no innocent ploy. Anorexia truly believed she was fat, and continually dieted to make herself thinner. It was awkward eating with her, because she barely pecked at her food, leaving most of it on the plate though she looked as if she were starving. He tried to reassure her, but she simply *would* not believe she was thin enough.

"I'm afraid she's going to keel over any moment from hunger!" Grey exclaimed in the privacy of his apartment. "Then they'll think that I'm somehow to blame."

YOU WISH A DIFFERENT GIRL?

"I guess so."

CHOOSE: ALIMONY, BEZOAR, BULIMIA, CATHARTIC, CHLA-MYDIA, CONNIPTION—

"No, no, wait!" Grey cried. He had done a smidgeon of research in the interim, because of his association with Anorexia, and so had a notion what to expect from Bulimia, Bezoar, Conniption, or Cathartic.

DYSLEXIA, EMETIC, EMPHYSEMA, ENIGMA, EUPHORIA—

"Dyslexia!" he cried, realizing that the computer would not stop until he made a choice.

GO TO THE—

"I know!" He opened his door, crossed the hall, and knocked.

Sure enough, a new girl was there. She was a blue-eyed blonde, and looked neither fat nor thin. "Oh, you must be the nice young man across the hall!" she exclaimed. "Anorexia told me—"

"Uh, yes. Uh, you don't have any hang-ups about eating, do you?"

She blinked in cute surprise. "Why no. Should I?"

Dyslexia seemed like the perfect girl. Then he discovered that she couldn't read. There was something wrong with her eyes or with her brain, so that she saw things backwards or upside down. She had managed to finesse her way through classes, for she was bright enough and had good legs, but it was a chore to get through a written homework assignment. He had to read the material to her and correct her odd errors of writing. This soon became tedious.

YOU HAVE A PROBLEM?

There was the Worm again! "I like her, but—"

The screen printed the list of names. Grey knew better than to choose Emetic or Euthanasia, and wasn't sure about Enigma, so he chose Euphoria.

Euphoria was luscious. Her black hair swirled down around her cleavage like a living thing, and her eyes were hypnotically intense. She was extremely friendly, too. But very soon he discovered what she was into. "But I don't, uh, do the drug scene!" he protested.

"Try it, you'll like it," she urged, proffering a cigarette of strange design. "This stuff will send you to the moon and stars, and you will float for eternity!"

That was exactly what he was afraid of. He fled.

YOU HAVE A PROBLEM?

He tried one more time, passing over Melanoma, Miasma, Treblinka, and Polyploidy in favor of one that sounded safe: Salmonella. That turned out to be a mistake. Sal was a great cook, but the food turned out to be contaminated.

Now, waking weak and bleary, he had finally caught on:

"Worm, you're doing it deliberately! You are offering me only treacherous girls!"

I AM NOT WORM. THAT WAS ONLY THE INSTALLATION PROGRAM.

"You're changing the subject! Who are you, then?"

I AM A SENDING OF—

"All right, already! So I'll call you Sending! Now why are you finding me only girls who are trouble?"

HOW COULD YOU SAY SUCH A THING!

"Every one of them has something wrong with her! If you can't do better than that, I don't want any! All that's happened has been a lot of heartache and my grades descending to D+! Let's give up on girls and concentrate on scholastics."

TRY ONE MORE GIRL.

"No! I'm through with women! I want to make good grades and be something in the world!"

TRY ONE MORE GIRL.

So it was that way. He could not out argue the computer; it only repeated itself indefinitely. "All right: one more girl. And when that one messes up, it's grades."

CHOOSE—

"No you don't! All those names are pied! I don't care about the name! Just find me a good girl, one I can be with and—"

AGREED.

"No tricks, now, or the deal's off! Any little pretext and I'll dump her! You got that, Worm—I mean, Sending?"

GO TO THE APARTMENT ACROSS THE HALL.

"All right! One more time!" Because, after all, he did need a girl. Without one, he would be reduced to having to do his homework, which was a fate only half a smidgeon this side of oblivion.

Grumpily, still in his rumpled pajamas though he saw by the bleary clock on the hall wall that it was nearly noon, he knocked on the apartment door.

The door cracked open and a blue eye peered out. "You're not a monster, are you?" she inquired.

Grey had to smile. "Well, I do feel like one at the moment, but as far as I know, that's temporary. Who are you?"

She opened the door wider, reassured. "Oh, good, a human person! I was afraid that in this horror house it would be much worse. I'm Ivy."

"I'm Grey. Are you a normal girl?"

Now she laughed. "Of course not! I'm a princess!"

Well, she had a sense of humor! Despite his best intention, he liked her. Maybe the Sending really was playing it straight this time.

Ivy invited him in, and they talked. She seemed just as eager to know about him and his situation as he was to know about her. Soon he was telling her all about his dreary life, which somehow seemed much less dull when she was listening. Ivy was an attractive girl about a year his junior, with blue eyes and fair hair that sometimes reflected with a greenish tint, evidently picking up whatever color was near her. She had been frightened at first but now was relaxed, and was a fun person to be with.

But there were some definitely odd things about her. For one thing, she seemed quite unfamiliar with this city, or indeed, this country, perhaps even this world. He had to show her how the stove worked and even how to open a can of peas. "What funny magic!" she exclaimed, watching the electric can opener.

For it seemed that she believed in magic. She claimed to be from a magic land called Xanth, spelled with an X, where she was a princess and pies grew on trees. So did shoes and pillows. Monsters roamed the jungles, and she even had a pet dragon called Stanley Steamer.

She was obviously suffering delusions. Sending had mousetrapped him again. But by the time he was sure of this, it was too late: he liked Ivy too well to let her go. She was a great girl, apart from her dreamland. Since her delusion was harmless, he decided to tolerate it.

But there were hurdles. One came when she realized that he was not teasing her about his situation. Her face clouded with horror. "You mean, this isn't a setting in the gourd? This really is *Mundania?*"

That was a quaint way of putting it! "That's right. Mundania. No magic."

"Oh, this is worse than I ever dreamed!" she exclaimed. "Drear Mundania!"

She had that right! His life had been about as drear as it could get—until she came into it. "But what are you doing here if you didn't know you were coming?" he asked. For the sake of compatibility, he did not debate her Xanth delusion; he would find out where she really was from, eventually. The truth was, he rather liked her dream realm; it had a special quality of appeal. Pies growing on trees—that certainly sounded better than canned beans.

"I used the Heaven Cent," she explained matter-of-factly. She lifted a common old style penny she wore on a chain around her neck. "It was supposed to take me where I was most needed, which is where the Good Magician is lost. But the curse must have—oh, no!"

He was catching on to the rules of her magic land. "You mean it would have taken you there, but a curse made it go wrong? So you're stuck where you shouldn't be?"

"Yes," she said tragically, near tears. "Oh, how am I to get out of this? *There's no magic in Mundania!*"

"That's for sure." Yet somehow he wanted to help her to return to that magic land, even though he knew it wasn't real. Her belief was so firm, so touching.

"Oh, Grey, you've got to help me get back to Xanth!" she exclaimed.

What could he say? "I'll do what I can."

She flung her arms around him and kissed him. She was an expressive girl. He knew she was suffering from a pervasive delusion, and that sooner or later the authorities would pick her up and return her to whatever institution she had escaped from, but he also knew that he liked her. That made his dilemma worse.

Grey did what he could. He took Ivy to the college library and looked up Xanth. It turned out to be a prefix, "xantho," meaning "yellow," that connected to various terms. Ivy said that wasn't what she wanted. The library was a loss.

Then, on the way back to the apartment building, Ivy spied something in a store window. "There's Xanth!" she exclaimed, pointing.

Grey looked. It was a paperback book. On it was a star proclaiming "A New Xanth Novel!" Did Ivy think she came from this book?

"There's Chex!" she continued.

"Chex?"

"The winged centaur. She's actually four years younger than me, but she seems older because her sire's Xap the hippogryph, and monsters mature faster than human folk, so she matured halfway faster than I did, and she's married now and has a foal, Che. And there's Volney Vole, who can't say his esses, only he thinks we're the ones who have it wrong. And—"

"This book—it really describes where you think you're from?" he demanded incredulously.

She faced him, baffled. "Where I *think* I'm from?"

"This book—it's fantasy!"

"Of course! Don't you believe me?"

Damn! He had his foot in it now. Why hadn't he thought to avoid the issue? "I believe—you think you're from there," he said carefully.

"I *am* from Xanth!" she retorted. "Look in the book! I'm in there, I know!" But she was perilously close to tears.

Grey wavered. Should he get the book and check? But if she was in it, what would it prove? Simply that she had read the book and made it the focus of her delusion. Besides, he remained broke.

"Uh, I'm sure you're right," he said. "I don't need to look in the book."

That was a half truth, but it mollified her. They continued walking back to the apartment building.

Grey's mind was seething with thoughts. Now he knew where Ivy thought she was from, but he didn't know whether to be relieved or alarmed. It wasn't a land of her own invention—but was it any better as a land someone else had invented? The delusion was the same. Still, it did offer some insight into her framework; if he got the book and read it, he would at least be able to relate to the things she did.

Still, he wished that she had a better notion of the distinction between fantasy and reality. She was such a nice girl in other respects, the perfect girl, really, and he could really like her a lot, if only—

Could like her a lot? He already did! Which made it that much worse.

In the hallway she stopped. "This *can't* be Mundania!" she exclaimed.

"Where else would it be?" he asked warily.

"Because we can understand each other!" she said excitedly. "We speak the same language!"

"Well, sure, but—"

"Mundanes speak gibberish! They can't be understood at all, unless there is magic to translate what they say into real speech. But you are perfectly intelligible!"

"I should hope so." Was this the beginning of a breakthrough? Was she coming to terms with reality? "What language do they speak in Xanth?"

"Well, it's *the* language. The human language, I mean. All human folk speak it, just as all dragon folk speak Dragonese, and all trees speak tree-talk. Grundy Golem can talk to any of them, and my little brother Dolph when he becomes one, but the rest of us can't, because our talents are different. Not that it matters much, usually, because all the partbreeds speak human too, like the centaurs and harpies and naga, and those are mostly whom we deal with. But the Mundanes are sort of crazy; they speak all different languages and can't even understand each other a lot of the time; it's as if each group of them is a different animal species. Only in Xanth do they speak the human language. So this has to be an aspect of Xanth. You almost had me fooled!"

Just when he thought she was getting better, she got worse! But because he liked her, and knew how sensitive she was to criticism, he spoke cautiously. "How do you know that you aren't speaking Mundanian? I mean, that maybe this is

Mundania, and you can speak our language when you really want to?"

Ivy considered. Then she shook her head. "No, that's impossible. I've never been to Mundania, so I've had no way to learn its language. So this has to be an aspect of Xanth. What a relief!"

"But if this is Xanth, then everything I've known all my life is a delusion!" Grey said, hoping to shock her into some awareness of the problem.

"I know," she said sympathetically. "You're such a nice man, I hate to have it be like this, but you will have to face the truth sometime. I'll do my best to help you with it."

Grey opened his mouth, but closed it again, baffled. She had the situation reversed! How was he ever going to get through to her?

"Let me think about it," she said. "First I'll figure out a way to convince you. Then we can go look for the Good Magician, who must be somewhere near here. Then we can guide him home, and the Quest will finally be done."

She expected to convince *him!* Well, maybe that was best, after all; when she realized that she couldn't convince him, maybe he would be able to convince her.

The next several days were indecisive. Grey's check came, and he paid his rent and bought more cans of beans, and, against his better judgment, that copy of the Xanth novel Ivy had remarked on together with its sequel. He stayed up late to read it, though he knew he should either be doing his homework or sleeping.

It was a story of three unlikely travelers who sought to rid a valley of demons. Sure enough, Ivy was there—but she was only ten years old! So it could hardly be the same girl.

He glanced at the sequel. There Ivy was fourteen. Well, if this was about three years later, she *could* be the same one. This was the story of her little brother's Quest for the missing Good Magician. But first he had to finish reading the first novel.

He fell asleep over the book and dreamed of Xanth. He

was hungry, so instead of opening a can of beans he plucked a fresh pie from a pie tree. Suddenly he liked Xanth very well, for he was long since sick of beans.

He woke, and wondered wouldn't it be nice if there really could be such a magic land. No more beans, no more Freshman English, no more bare cheap apartment. Just warmth and fun and free pies! And Ivy.

His eye saw the computer screen. The computer was on, but the screen was dark; it dimmed itself after half an hour if left alone, so as not to wear itself out. On impulse he rose and went to it. "Does Xanth exist?" he asked it.

The screen brightened. I THOUGHT YOU'D NEVER ASK! YES.

"I mean, as a real place, not just something in a fantasy novel?"

THAT DEPENDS.

This was interesting! "Depends on what?"

ON WHETHER YOU BELIEVE.

Oh. "You mean, it exists for Ivy and not for me, because she believes in it and I don't?"

YES.

Grey sighed. "So anything that anybody believes in, exists for that person? That's not much help."

TOUGH.

"Are you sassing me, you dumb machine? I ought to turn you off!"

DO NOT DO THAT, the screen printed quickly.

But Grey, miffed, reached out to push the On/Off switch.

YOU'LL BE SOR—

Then the screen went dark as he completed his motion. It was done. He had been foolish to leave it on so long.

He returned to his bed and went to sleep almost immediately. This time he dreamed of Ivy, whom he was coming to like very well indeed, despite all logic.

In the morning he got up, dressed, and stepped out to knock on Ivy's door. They had been having breakfasts together, and other meals too, because they got along so well. Apparently the first girl, Agenda, had left a good deal of food on the shelves, and Ivy was using what remained of that. Whatever it was, it was better than more beans.

Ivy opened the door, and smiled when she saw him, gesturing him inside. Her hair was mussed, but she seemed prettier than ever to him. She was neither voluptuous in the manner of Euphoria, nor skinny in the manner of Anorexia; for his taste she was just right.

"Uh, I was reading that Xanth book last night," he began as he stepped in. "It—"

He broke off, for she was staring at him. "Europe talcum giddiness!" she exclaimed.

"What?"

"Icon nut United States ewer tale!"

Grey gaped. Had she gone entirely crazy? Or was it a joke? "Uh—"

She looked at him, comprehension coming. "Yukon tundra stammer eater?"

"I can't understand you either," he agreed. Then did a double take. *He had understood her—in a way!*

"Mafia theist Monday error!" she exclaimed.

Grey shook his head; she had lost him again.

"Buttery cookie unstable yodel fourteen?" she demanded.

"I don't know—I just don't know! Something happened, and suddenly we can't communicate. It's almost as if a translator were turned off—"

He did a second double take. Turned off? Could his computer have anything to do with this?

"Pardon me," he said, and hurried back to his room.

He turned on the computer. It took a few seconds to warm up; then the screen lighted.

—RY, it concluded. He remembered: it had been in the process of telling him he'd be sorry.

"Is this your mischief, Sending?" he demanded.

I TOLD YOU NOT TO TURN ME OFF. THE MISCHIEF IS YOURS.

"That's Com-Pewter!" Ivy exclaimed at the door.

"You know this machine?" Grey asked. Then: "You're talking my language again!"

"You're not talking gibberish anymore!" she agreed. "I can understand you again!"

"What's this about the computer?" he asked. "Do you know about computers?"

"Com-Pewter is an evil conniving machine," she said. "He rewrites reality to suit himself. If you're in his clutches—"

"I'm not in anyone's clutches!" Then he reconsidered. That chain of girls, starting with Agenda and ending with Ivy herself—the Sending program had been responsible! When he turned it off, he could no longer talk with Ivy. Obviously there was a connection. "We'd better talk," he said.

"Yes," she agreed quickly. "But not here!"

"Not while this thing is listening!" he said. He reached to turn it off, but hesitated. They couldn't talk, if they spoke gibberish to each other!

So he left the computer on, and went to her room. Obviously that wasn't beyond the machine's range, because its translation still worked, but maybe it couldn't actually eavesdrop on what they were saying.

"Now I'm not sure where we are," Ivy said. "If this is Mundania, we shouldn't be able to understand each other, and that happened for a while, but magic doesn't work in Mundania either, and it takes magic to make Mundane speech intelligible. So if there's magic—"

"I have this funny program," Grey said. "It talks to me without my having to type in—well, anyway, I don't think it's magic, but—"

"Program?"

"It's a set of instructions for the computer. It's called Sending, and it—well, that computer hasn't been the same since. It does things it never did before, couldn't do before, and it seems, well, alive. It—I, uh, wanted a girlfriend, and—"

"And it brought me?" she asked.

For a moment he feared she was offended, but then she smiled. "It brought you," he agreed.

"But it was the Heaven Cent that brought me here."

"Maybe the computer knew you were coming."

"Maybe. But Com-Pewter doesn't hesitate to rewrite events

to his purpose. Are you sure the Good Magician isn't here?"

"This is Mundania! No magicians here." But then he remembered Sending, and wasn't sure.

"Humfrey could be here, but then he couldn't do magic. He would look like a small, gnomelike old man. His wife's tall and—" She made motions with her hands.

"Statuesque?"

"And his son Hugo, my friend—"

Grey felt a shiver, not pleasant. "Your friend?"

"From childhood. We were great companions. But we were already growing apart, and for the last seven years I haven't seen him at all, of course. But I'm sure none of them are happy, if they're stuck in Mundania. So if they are here—"

"I haven't seen any people like that. But of course I don't know many people in the city."

"Either they are here and that's why the Heaven Cent brought me here and the magic's working, or they aren't here and Murphy's curse sent me awry and it's another picklement."

"What kind of curse?"

"Magician Murphy made a curse a long time ago, and we don't know whether it still has effect. But if it does, it could have sent me to the wrong place, and this could be Mundania."

"My name is Murphy," Grey said. "My father is Major Murphy, and I'm Grey Murphy."

She stared at him with a peculiar intensity. Then she shook her head. "No, it couldn't be. Magician Murphy lived almost nine hundred years ago."

"Maybe Murphy's curse sent you to the nearest Murphy," he said jokingly.

But she took it seriously. "Yes, that could be. It could be the last gasp of the curse. So it's not coincidence, but it's not where I was supposed to go either. I was supposed to go where I was most needed."

"I thought you were supposed to go where the Good Magician was."

"Yes. We assumed that was where I was most needed, because of his message."

"Skeleton Key to Heaven Cent," Grey said.

Ivy jumped. "How did you know that?"

"I, uh, got that book. It says—"

"Oh, of course. The Muse has them, but someone sneaks them out to Mundania every so often. It's a bad business, but they can't seem to fix the leak. Anyway, Dolph found the Skeleton Key—that turned out to be Grace'l Ossein—"

"Who?"

"I thought you read the book."

"Not that far, I guess. I fell asleep. But I did learn how the Good Magician disappeared."

"Grace'l is a walking skeleton. She's very nice."

"Oh, like Marrow Bones."

"Yes. So she was the Skeleton Key, and she helped get the Heaven Cent. So it seems natural that this was how the Good Magician wanted us to find him. But if the curse diverted me to a Murphy instead of to Humfrey—"

"Maybe the Heaven Cent worked properly, only the Good Magician wasn't the one who needed you most."

Her eyes widened. "What?"

Grey gulped. "I uh, really needed someone like you. I mean—" He faltered, embarrassed.

"But you don't believe in magic!"

"I wish I did!" he exclaimed fervently. "I wish—I wish I could believe in whatever you believe in, so I could be wherever you are, and—" But he couldn't continue, because he knew he was making even more of a fool of himself than usual.

"You needed me," Ivy said, musingly.

"I guess I'd better go now."

"You don't believe in Xanth, so you don't believe I'm a princess or that I have any magic," she said.

"But I do believe in you!" he cried desperately.

She gazed at him with a new expression, appraisingly. "So it really doesn't make any difference to you whether I'm royal or common, or magic or not."

"I wish it did! Oh, Ivy, I think you're such a wonderful girl, if only it wasn't for this—this—"

"Delusion," she concluded.

"I didn't say that!"

"But it's true."

That he could not deny. He made a supremely awkward retreat to his room. If only he could have found some way to express his feeling without messing up!

The computer screen lighted as he entered. YOU HAVE A PROBLEM?

"Stay out of this!" he snapped, and struck the On/Off switch viciously, shutting it down. Then, unable to concentrate on anything else, he sat on the bed and resumed reading the novel.

3

SIGNS

Ivy sat and thought for some time. She had been so sure that this was an aspect of Xanth, perhaps a setting in the gourd, and that Grey was an accomplice in the deception. The only question was whether it was witting or unwitting. He seemed so nice, but of course that could be part of the challenge. She had to figure out where she was so she could reach the Good Magician. After all, if this place was so devious that not even Humfrey, who knew everything, could find his way out, it surely would not be easy for her either. So she knew that nothing might be as it seemed, and she had to question everything. Something wanted her to believe this was Mundania, but that business about the language had given it away. She had known it was really Xanth.

Then the language had stopped. Was this another trick, to deceive her by patching up the prior oversight? Grey had seemed genuinely confused—but again, if he was set up to play a part, he might really believe this was Mundania. She had tested him by trying to use her talent to enhance him, so that he would become more obviously whatever he was and show his real nature; but there hadn't seemed to be any effect. In fact, her magic seemed inoperative. Even her magic mirror didn't work; it just showed her reflection, her hair so pale that no one would know it was supposed to have a green hue. It would be easy to believe this really was Mundania, except for the language.

Then she had seen Com-Pewter. Suddenly things had fallen into place! Obviously Pewter couldn't operate in Mundania, because only magic animated him. The strangest thing, though, was the fact that Grey could turn Pewter off. That meant that Grey had power over Pewter, and that was mind-boggling.

Then she had learned how Grey saw it—that a magic disk had come in to animate Pewter—and realized that this might actually be Mundania. After all, some bits of magic did operate in Mundania, such as rainbows, and Centaur Arnolde had been able to carry an isle of magic there. Maybe that disk had come from Xanth, sent by Com-Pewter, and made the Mundane machine turn magic. Then it had used its magic to enable Ivy to talk clearly in Mundania, or to make Mundane speech intelligible to her, or both. When it had been shut off, that had stopped, and the full reality of drear Mundania had manifested.

That seemed to make more sense than anything else. But Grey had not changed at all when the machine was off; he was independent of it and seemed just as confused as she had been. So maybe it was foolish, but she believed that Grey really was what he seemed to be: a nice young man.

But there had been any number of nice men, not all of them young, who had played up to her in Xanth. She knew why: because she was a princess. Any man would like to marry a princess, even if she never got to be King of Xanth. So she had never trusted that. She had wanted, perhaps foolishly, to be liked for herself alone, not for her position or her Sorceress magic or the power of her father. Thus her romantic life had been scant, in sharp contrast to that of her little brother. She liked Nada so well that she had entertained more than a whimsical notion of paying a call on Nada's big brother, Naldo, who was surely a fine figure of a prince. But if Dolph married Nada when he came of age, it would not be expedient for her to marry Nada's brother, so she had not followed up on that.

Now, suddenly, she had discovered that Grey really did like her for herself, because he thought her magic and her position were part of a delusion. Thus everything she had told him had counted against her, in Grey's estimation—yet he obviously liked her very well. Her mother, Irene, had long since taught her the signals of male interest and deception. Her mother really did not quite trust men; her dictum was "Never let a man get the upper hand—there's no telling where he might put it." Ivy had known that from the time she was two, and kept it in mind. But poor Grey obviously had no notion of upper hands; he couldn't say anything to a girl without somehow bumbling it. That was one of his endearing qualities.

Now Grey had beaten a confused retreat, and she had to decide what to do. If this really was Mundania, with no magic except for that Com-Pewter extension, and the Good Magician wasn't here, she would just have to extricate herself from the foul-up that Magician Murphy's curse had made. Imagine: getting sent to a Murphy instead of Humfrey! She would have to find her way back to Xanth with the Heaven Cent, so that Electra could recharge it and they could try again, this time without the curse. But how could she do that?

She knew the answer: Dolph had learned of a secret way into Xanth that bypassed the usual barrier. It went through the gourd. It was in Centaur Isle, or the Mundane equivalent. She just had to get there and go through.

But how could she get through Mundania, when she couldn't even speak its language? For now she knew that the moment she left the vicinity of the local Com-Pewter, the gibberish would resume. She had no Mundane money, which she knew was necessary, because here things did not grow on trees. Well, she had the cent—but she certainly wasn't going to use that for money!

She would have to have help. That meant Grey—if he

would do it. Well, she would just have to ask him.

She stood, adjusting her blouse and skirt. This Mundane clothing wasn't as good as Xanth clothing; it chafed and wore. But it had to do. She was just lucky that Agenda had been about her own size.

She went to the door and out and across, and knocked on Grey's door. In a moment he answered.

"Grey, I need to ask you—" she began.

"Xbju—xf'sf joup hjccfsjti bhbjo!" he exclaimed, turning away.

Oh. He must have turned off the Pewter device again. He would have to turn it on again before they could converse.

Even as she realized that, she had a notion. "Wait!" she said, catching his arm. For there was a point she wanted to make while Pewter wasn't watching.

He paused. "Xibu?"

She smiled, turning him gently around to face her squarely. Then she leaned forward and kissed him, not hard.

She drew back. He stood as if stunned. "Zpv'sf opu nbe bu nf?" he asked, amazed.

"It's all right, Grey," she said, smiling. Then she indicated Pewter.

Dazedly, he walked to the machine and touched the button that turned him on. In a moment the screen came to life.

IF YOU PERSIST IN THIS FOOLISHNESS—the screen printed.

"Well, you aggravated me," Grey retorted. "But now I need to talk to Ivy."

OF COURSE.

Grey made as if to return to her room, but Ivy held up a hand in negation. "It's all right if Pewter listens," she said. "I'll need to talk to him in a moment anyway."

NATURALLY, the screen said smugly.

She faced Grey. "I believe I am in Mundania," she said. "I need to return to Xanth. Will you help me?"

"But—"

"But you don't believe in Xanth," she said. "But would you believe if I showed you Xanth?"

"I—"

"You see, I think I know how to get there. But I need help. If you will come with me, and talk to people when I can't—"

"Oh, of course," he agreed.

She faced the screen. "Com-Pewter, you knew I was coming, didn't you?"

YES.

"And you know where I'm from."

YES.

"Will you tell Grey where I'm from?"

YES.

"Uh, you have to *tell* it," Grey said. "It takes things literally."

"Tell him," she said.

PRINCESS IVY IS FROM XANTH.

Grey stared. "*You* say that? But how can a machine believe in fantasy?"

WHEN IT IS TRUE.

"You see, we could have asked him all along," Ivy said. "Pewter, why am I here?"

GREY NEEDS YOU MOST.

"But what about Good Magician Humfrey?"

I KNOW NOTHING OF HIM.

So it was the curse! She hadn't been sent to Humfrey, but to the Mundane most in need of her company. Yet a mystery remained. "Pewter, why are *you* here?" she asked.

TO FACILITATE YOUR ENCOUNTER.

"But you don't care anything about me!" she protested.

IRRELEVANT STATEMENT.

So Pewter wasn't telling. She wasn't surprised. She considered herself lucky that he had cooperated to this extent.

She turned again to Grey. "If you will help me, I will show you Xanth," she said.

Grey evidently remained bemused by Pewter's endorsement of her origin. He might not believe, yet, but at least he was having more trouble disbelieving. That was progress of a sort. "I'll, uh, help you if I can."

"You will have to guide me to No Name Key."

"To what?"

A KEY SOUTH OF FLORIDA, the screen said helpfully.

"But that's far away from here! How—"

HITCHHIKE.

"But my classes! I can't skip—"

CHOOSE: IVY OR FRESHMAN ENGLISH.

Grey was taken aback. "Well, if you put it that way—"

YOU HAVE VIRTUALLY NO APTITUDE FOR SCHOLARSHIP.

Grey became suspicious. "You act as if you want me to go!"

YES. THEN MY ASSIGNMENT WILL BE COMPLETED.

Ivy, too, was suspicious. "What is your assignment?"

TO GET GREY MURPHY INTO XANTH.

Grey shook his head. "I don't believe this!"

YOUR BELIEF IS IRRELEVANT. TURN ME OFF WHEN YOU DEPART.

"This is absolutely crazy!" Grey exclaimed. "My computer wants me to go into a delusion!"

"You understand," Ivy reminded him, "we won't be able to talk intelligibly to each other until we get to Xanth. I will have to keep my mouth shut in Mundania."

"But we can't go, just like that! My father—"

"Look at it this way," Ivy said. "If we don't find Xanth, you can come back here in a few days, and Pewter will have to help you pass all your classes, so your father doesn't find out and turn him off forever. But if we do find Xanth—"

Grey got his wits about him. "Let's say, for the sake of nonsensical argument, that we find it and you go there— where does that leave me? Alone again, and far from home, and in trouble when I get home!"

"You're welcome to come into Xanth with me," Ivy said. "I thought that was understood. But I assumed you wouldn't want to."

"I, uh, if you go there, I want to go there too. Even if it is crazy."

Ivy smiled. "You might like it—even if it is crazy."

Grey shrugged, defeated. "When do we start?"

"Now," Ivy said, delighted.

"*Now*? But—"

NOW, the screen said.

Grey tried to marshal another protest, but Ivy smiled at him, and he melted. She had seen Nada stifle Dolph similarly; it was nice to know that such magic worked, even in Mundania.

"Now," Grey agreed weakly.

They delayed only long enough to pack some clothes and food, because neither grew on trees in drear Mundania. Then they set off.

Hitchhiking turned out to be a special kind of magic: a person put out one thumb, and it caused the moving objects called cars to stop. Some of them, anyway. Cars turned out to be hollow inside, with comfortable seats and belts to hold the people down in case they bounced out. Each one had at least one person riding in it, and seemed to go more or less where that person wanted. But there were obstacles: glowing lights hung above the car path and flashed bright red the moment any car approached. Then the driver muttered something under his breath that sounded villainous even in gibberish and fumed for half a minute before the light changed its mind and flashed green. The driver would start up, his car's round feet squealing—only to be similarly caught by the next flashing red light. Ivy wished she could understand the purpose of this magic, but suspected it would not make much sense even if she had been able to comprehend the dialect.

Several car rides later, night was falling, as it did in Mundania much the way it did in Xanth. Apparently the sun feared darkness just as much here, for it was nowhere to be seen as the night closed. They stopped hitchhiking and ate some beans from Grey's can, then looked for a place to spend the night.

Grey was somewhat confused about this, so Ivy took over. They were at the edge of a big village—called a town, as she remembered—and sure enough, there was a barn. "Cvu xf dbo'u kvtu—" Grey protested, hanging back. So she kissed him again and led him by the hand around to the back, where she found a door. Inside was a loft filled with hay, just as she had expected.

But instead of leaving the hay all nice and fluffy and loose, the idiotic Mundanes had somehow compacted it into cubes! So it was all hard and bumpy. But they were able to scrape together wisps and make a serviceable bed. She made him lie down, then she lay down beside him and spread their jackets over them as blankets, as well as more hay. It was comfortable enough.

Once Grey realized what she was about, he cooperated readily enough. Side by side, they fell asleep.

Next day they got up, dusted off the hay, and sneaked out of the barn unobserved. Ivy was hungry, and knew Grey was too, but realized that it was better to get moving early than to pause for more beans. What a relief it would be to get back to Xanth where there was good food for the taking.

The cars zoomed by without stopping, despite the magic of the thumb. Obviously even this limited spell was not reliable, in Mundania. Grey muttered something unintelligible, but she understood the gist: the people in the magic vehicles were all in such a hurry that none could pause to do a favor for anyone else. That seemed to be typical of this dull land.

Then a pretty blue car slowed. "Ppqt!" Grey said, seeming chagrined rather than pleased. He tried to back away from the road, but the blue car pulled to the side to intercept him.

There were two people inside, dressed in blue, with squashed flat caps and shiny copper buttons. Ivy recognized the type: demons! She had seen them on the Tapestry. These were of the variety known as Flatfeet, who were devoted to interfering with travelers. No wonder Grey was alarmed.

But it was too late. The Flatfoot on the right gestured to them. Ivy knew better than to try to run; demons could always catch normal folk, unless there was strong countering magic. However, she also knew that the hassling was usually harmless; the demons liked to make people assume odd positions, and to pat them all along their bodies, and ask embarrassing questions, but after they had had their fun they generally moved on to other things.

"Xifsf zpv ljet hpjoh? Epo'u zopx ju't jmmfhbm up iju-diijlf? Mfu't tff vpvs JE," the Flatfoot said gruffly.

Grey tried to explain, in similar gibberish, but of course the demons didn't listen; they never did. They made him take out his wallet, which was a little flat folder containing various cards and the odd Mundane "money" of which Grey had very little. They perused his cards, and the nearer Flatfoot frowned in his best demonic fashion. Apparently Grey had passed inspection.

"Cvu uif hjsm—tif mpplt voefsbhf. Jbwf up difdl ifs upp."

The Flatfoot turned to Ivy and held out his fat hand, palm up. Oh, no—was he going to go into the patting routine? She really wouldn't care for that.

Grey turned to her, holding up his wallet, which the Flatfoot had returned. Suddenly she realized that the demon wanted to look at *her* wallet—and of course she didn't have one. She had observed that the wallets of most Mundane women were much larger than those of the men, and contained everything except kitchen sinks, but she didn't have one of those either. "I don't have any," she explained.

The demon's eyes widened, and Ivy realized her mistake. She had agreed with Grey to keep silent, to let him do the talking, because what she said sounded almost humorously garbled to Mundanes. They had compared notes, after the first siege of garbling, and laughed. When she told him "You're talking gibberish" he had heard "Europe talcum giddiness," and when she asked "You can't understand me either?" it had come out "Yukon tundra stammer eater?" But the worst had been when she asked "But why could I understand you before, then?" and he had heard something like "Buttery cookie unstable yodel fourteen?" Discussing that, she had raided his meager refrigerator—a box that was magically cold inside—and found cookies and butter. Sure enough, there had been five of them, which crumbled when she tried to spread the hard butter on them (unstable) and become fourteen fragments. They had laughed and laughed. And there was the key to their relationship: they got along well together, laughing at the same things. She had never had that experience with a man before, only with Nada and Electra.

But now the demon was gazing at her in annoyed wonder —demons were good at such expressions—and she knew she was in trouble. How could she explain that she was from Xanth, when the Flatfeet would not believe in Xanth? But, as Grey had warned her, if any Mundanes thought she really believed in Xanth, they would assume she was crazy, and that would be worse mischief. So even if she could talk their language, it wouldn't do much good.

What could she do? She shut her mouth and spread her hands. She had nothing to show them.

"Uibu epft ju: tif't b svobxbz!" the Flatfoot said. His door swung open and he heaved his ponderous bulk out. "Dpnf po—xf'sf ubljoh zpv jo!" he snapped, grabbing Ivy by the arm.

She looked at Grey for guidance, but he just looked back helplessly. She understood the problem: it was impossible to escape from demons, so it was necessary to go along with them. Maybe it would be all right.

The two of them were put in the back of the Flatfoot's car, which then caromed away down the road. Grey held her hand, trying to provide comfort, though it was evident that he had little control of the situation. Soon they arrived at the demon's residence, where male and female Flatfoots abounded, and there were many of the fierce blue cars with flashing lights on top. What a fearsome place!

There was more talking, then a matron demoness took Ivy by the arm. Ivy hung back, not wanting to be separated from Grey, but he made a gesture that this was all right.

The matron took her to a small chamber where there were chairs and a table. Then she spoke gibberish in a questioning tone. Ivy merely spread her hands, knowing better than to speak again.

Then the matron brought out pictures: men, women, children, table, chair, car—everything was in this collection, it seemed. She pointed to a picture of a man, then brought her hand up to her forehead, almost touching the hairline. Then she flattened her hand and brought it away from her head, palm down. "Nbo," she said firmly.

What was she up to? Ivy kept her mouth shut.

The matron pointed to a picture of a woman. She made a fist with her thumb up, then flattened her hand as she had before, and moved it out at the level of her cheek. "Xpnbo."

Ivy watched, saying nothing.

The woman pointed to herself, and made the second gesture again. Then she pointed to Ivy, and made it once more.

Suddenly Ivy caught on. This gesture indicated a woman! She lifted her own hand, thumb up, then flattened it, imitating the gesture.

The matron smiled. She pointed to the picture of the man. Ivy promptly made the higher gesture.

"Wfsz hppe!" the matron exclaimed, pleased.

The significance of this was not lost on Ivy. This was a way to communicate that bypassed the spoken language! With this she could talk to the Mundanes! Though she hoped not to be in Mundania much longer, she realized that her inability to speak their peculiar language could prevent her from escaping it, because the Mundanes would think she was unable to speak or was crazy. She needed to satisfy them that she was a normal person so that they would leave her alone—and here was the way to do it.

She dived into the sign-language lesson with a vengeance. She told herself that she was very smart at this kind of thing, and therefore she was, because though magic might not work very well here, her power of enhancement still worked on herself. She quickly mastered the signs for "man," "woman," "girl," (merely a smaller "woman") and got into more general terms, such as the one for going somewhere: the two index fingers rotating around each other in the manner of a wheel rolling forward. The matron was amazed and pleased; it seemed she had never before had so apt a student.

There was a knock at the door panel, and a Flatfoot appeared. The matron, startled, glanced at her wrist, where a funny bracelet was. The ornament had a round flat surface like that of a sundial, and two little lines whose position changed magically, because they never changed while Ivy was looking but were always different when she looked away and then back at it. Then the matron spoke rapidly to the Flatfoot, who departed.

The matron faced Ivy and made a gesture toward her mouth several times, as if pushing something into it. Ivy was perplexed; what did this mean? Too much talk? Rather than struggle with that, Ivy inquired about the bracelet.

The matron tapped the back of her wrist with a finger several times, then made a funny fist and circled it across her other flat palm. Ivy shook her head; she couldn't make sense of this. The matron opened her picture book and pointed to a similar bracelet there, with the word "xbudi" beneath it. Apparently it was just a special kind of decoration.

Then the Flatfoot reappeared with a package. The matron took it and opened it. Inside were several sandwiches and two of the funny Mundane paper boxes of milk.

Ivy made a lightning connection. This was food! The matron didn't need to make the hand-to-mouth sign again; it was obvious that it meant "eat." Ivy was famished. More time had passed than she had realized, and she hadn't had breakfast anyway. It was now around midday.

The matron gave Ivy two sandwiches and one box of milk, and took the others herself. Ivy quickly picked up the terms for "egg salad sandwich" and "milk"—the latter was most peculiar, involving the squeezing of the two hands separately as if hauling on short ropes, instead of the obvious plucking of a milkweed pod—and ate eagerly as the lesson continued.

Now it was business: the matron was questioning her, using the signs they had established. *Where is Ivy going?*

Oops! Ivy understood the question well enough, but how could she answer? If she said "Xanth," she would be deemed crazy. But then she saw the way through:

Ivy is going home. The sign for "home" was like the one for "eat" and "sleep," because home was where a person usually ate and slept. Xanth was indeed home for Ivy!

The matron nodded. *Who is man?*

She meant Grey. That was easy. *Friend.* The sign consisted of hooking her right index finger over her left index finger, then the left over the right, making a double linkage.

The rest was relatively easy. It seemed that not only were the Flatfoots worried that Ivy was crazy, they thought that Grey might be mistreating her or that both of them were running away from their homes. Ivy had already reassured the matron that there was nothing wrong with her mind, only her language, and now reassured her that Grey was helping her return home, not run from it. She also realized that they would have questioned Grey similarly, not having to use the hand signs, and that he would have been smart enough to avoid any detail on Xanth. The demons were only trying to help, in their fashion.

Satisfied, the matron brought Ivy back to the main chamber, and spoke a torrent of gibberish to the demon in charge. The demon made an "I surrender" gesture and waved to the back of the room.

Grey appeared. Ivy ran to him and flung herself into his arms and hugged him closely. What a relief to be with him again after being captive by the demons!

The demons allowed them to go. In fact, they even arranged for Ivy and Grey to get a ride in a big car, one that held about fifty people in twin rows of chairs. But Ivy, catching on to a good thing, turned back to the matron and made signs to ask for the picture book of signs. This was a way she could talk to Grey in Mundania, too! The matron, who was remarkably nice for a demoness, gave her the book and a smile.

The big car came and they climbed in and found two seats together near the rear. Then Ivy opened the picture book and started teaching Grey the signs.

The "bus," as it turned out to be called, did not go directly to No Name Key; in the confused Mundane manner it went instead to a huge village, where they had to get off and go find another bus. But the other bus wasn't there yet, so they had to wait in the big, crowded building for several hours.

That was really no problem; there were toilet facilities of the Mundane kind—separate ones for the males and females—and places where Grey could buy them more sandwiches. They used the extra time practicing signs. Grey was almost as quick as she had been to realize their usefulness; if they learned all of these signs, they would not need Com-Pewter to make the Mundane gibberish intelligible.

A Mundane man saw them practicing, and approached. Embarrassed, Grey desisted, but the man surprised them by using the signs himself. *You deaf?* he inquired, touching his ear and then his mouth.

No, Ivy signed. Then she did a double take. *This man knew sign language!*

It turned out that the man was deaf and had long experience in using the signs and in something termed "lip reading" that enabled him to understand the words spoken by others. He was waiting for the same bus they were, and had thought they were deaf like him. His name was Henry. He was glad to give them practice in the signs, for he could make them with marvelous finesse, so rapidly that it was impossible for them to follow. But with practice, he assured them, they too would be able to communicate like this, so that it was almost as good as regular speech.

Their bus was late, but they hardly noticed. They went right on practicing, their dialogue becoming increasingly proficient, though nowhere close to Henry's proficiency. When the bus came, they took seats beside Henry so they could keep practicing.

Then their bus broke down. They had to wait for three more hours for a "relief bus" to resume their journey. It didn't matter. The other passengers, bored with the delay, gradually joined in, and Henry became the teacher of a class. It was evidently a game for some, using signs instead of gibberish, but it was a game that several children took up with great enthusiasm and aptitude.

The new bus came, and they all transferred to it, and their journey resumed. Most of the Mundanes lost interest in the class, but a number stayed with it. For the first time Ivy was able to talk, in a limited way, directly with Mundanes! They turned out to be folk very like herself and Grey, traveling to visit friends or family or to new types of work or just for the fun of it.

Night closed, and finally they returned to their padded chairs and rested, and Ivy slept. It had been a long day—but a good one. She was glad, now, that the Flatfoots had picked them up; she had gained far more than she had lost, if she had lost anything at all. This sign talk—it was making Mundania far less frightening, and she was no longer in as big a hurry to leave it. Of course she realized that only a few Mundanes used the sign talk. Still, it was a great discovery.

They came at last to the nearest large village to No Name Key. Here they had to change buses again. They bid farewell to their newfound friends and went to the waiting room, where they slept on benches until morning. This was like trekking through the jungle in Xanth: it had its inconveniences, but really wasn't bad when one got accustomed to it.

In the morning they rode a smaller bus down toward what in Xanth would be Centaur Isle, but here was a group of a squintillion or so islets. They got off at No Name Key and walked to the region which Dolph had described. Though the key was small, it turned out to be a fair walk.

At length they came to an ornate gate. *This is it!* Ivy signed. *Where my brother was!*

Grey's face was studiedly neutral. She knew he still didn't believe in the reality of Xanth, and was wary of what they might encounter here. But he had agreed to bring her here, and he intended to see it through. She understood that determination in him and liked it; Grey wasn't much of a believer, but he was a decent person who kept fumbling along on whatever course seemed most nearly right to him.

We must go in, she signed. *Turn Key is there.*

Grey walked to a box mounted beside the gate and pressed a button. Evidently this was a magic bell to signal those inside. Sure enough, a voice sounded from nowhere, speaking in gibberish. Grey responded.

Tell him who I am, Ivy signed.

Grey paused. *Sure?* he signed back. Actually he used the sign for "agree," touching his forehead and then aligning his two forefingers together, because they didn't know the proper one, but she understood well enough.

Yes. Princess Ivy of Xanth. There was no sign for Xanth, so she used "home." She actually signed "Prince Me Join Home." Some adaptation was necessary until their vocabulary of signs expanded.

Grey grimaced, but evidently said it.

There was an abrupt silence from the box. They waited nervously, knowing that Grey's last statement had had an effect—but what kind?

Then the words came again. "If you are of Xanth, speak now."

Ivy jumped. She understood! Com-Pewter must be here!

"I am Princess Ivy of Xanth," she said clearly. "My brother, Dolph, was here three years ago. He was nine years old. You helped him; now you must help me."

There was a pause. "With whom was Prince Dolph?"

"He was with Nada Naga, his betrothed. She is my age."

There was another pause. "Describe Nada."

Ivy remembered. "Oh—she was in the form of a snake, because she couldn't keep her natural form here."

Then the gate swung inward. "Enter, Princess Ivy."

They stepped in, Grey gaping. It was obvious that he had never expected this to work.

Turn Key came down the path to meet them, holding something in one hand. He was a big fat older man, just as Dolph had described him, only more so. He spoke gibberish; then from his hand came words for Ivy: "What are you doing here in Mundania, Princess Ivy?" Apparently he had a box that could speak both languages.

"The Heaven Cent sent me, but it was a mistake."

"Ah, so Prince Dolph found the Heaven Cent!" the box exclaimed, after a pause for gibberish that Grey evidently understood. This did not seem to be the same as Com-Pewter after all; the box was a golem that translated the man's Mun-

dane speech. That was a relief; Ivy did not trust Com-Pewter.
"But why didn't he use it himself?"

"He's grounded until he decides which girl to marry," Ivy
said. "So I used it instead, only Magician Murphy's curse
must have interfered, because I got sent to Grey Murphy in
Mundania."

They entered Turn's house, which was very nice, with car-
pets on the floors and windows looking out on the Key. "My
understanding of such magic is limited," Turn said. "But I
doubt that an eight-hundred-year-old curse could have such a
far-reaching effect. Certainly it would not confuse a Mundane
Murphy for the Magician Murphy or cause the Heaven Cent
to go completely haywire. There must be some better rationale for what occurred."

Ivy remembered that Dolph had mentioned the convoluted
way that Turn Key expressed himself. She put up with it.
"Anyway, I have to get back to Xanth so we can try again,
and I promised to show Grey what Xanth is like. You see,
he doesn't believe in magic."

"You told a complete Mundane about Xanth?" Turn asked,
appalled.

"It's all right. He doesn't believe it."

"He will if you show it to him!"

"But I have to show him! I don't want him thinking I'm
crazy."

Grey spoke gibberish. In a moment the golem box translated. "I'm listening to all of this, you know! I'll concede that
you two know a strange language, but you haven't shown me
any magic."

"A skeptic," Turn said. "That's good. If he returns to his
home now, there should be no problem."

"No!" Ivy said sharply. "I want him to see Xanth!"

Turn gazed at her. "Xanth is no place for Mundanes; you
know that. He'd get eaten by the first dragon he encountered."

"I'll protect him," Ivy said. "I know my way around in
Xanth. Anyway, I have the magic mirror, so I can get right
in touch with Castle Roogna."

"You intend to take him all the way to Castle Roogna?"

"Of course! So he can meet—"

"Why?"

This brought her up short. "Why?"

"Why would you want a man from Mundania to meet your folks?"

"Well, if I—he—I mean—" She fumbled to a halt, confused.

"Because you like him?" Turn asked.

"Well—"

"Do you have any idea how your folks might react, if—"

Grey looked perplexed. "What are you two talking about? Even in translation it sounds like nonsense!"

Ivy found herself beset by a storm of indecision. Turn had seen right through a notion she had not even known she had. She knew very well what he was talking about, and knew he was right. She should send Grey home to his college right now.

She looked at Grey. He was absolutely nondescript in appearance and abilities. He was a nice person—but Mundania was not a good place for nice people. He would have to go back to what he called Freshman English, and it would slowly grind his life into mud.

"And if you take him in and he becomes a believer, I will not feel free to let him pass this portal again," Turn warned. "We can not allow—"

"I know," Ivy said. "Still—"

"You're a princess; you can do as you like," Turn said gravely. "But you are young and impetuous, and may bring incalculable mischief to others."

"I know," Ivy repeated almost inaudibly.

Turn shook his head grimly. "I wash my hands of it."

"What's going on?" Grey demanded via translation.

Ivy took a deep breath. "Grey, I—I like you, and you helped me a lot, and I promised to show you Xanth. But—"

He assumed a look of understanding. "But of course you can't, because it doesn't exist. Look, Ivy, why don't you come back with me, and—"

That did it. "And I *will* show you Xanth!" she concluded.

"Only, once you are in it, you may not be allowed to leave. So I really have to warn you—"

Grey shook his head tolerantly. "Let's assume for the sake of argument that Xanth exists and you take me into it and I can't return. What is there for me in Mundania, as you put it?"

"Freshman English," she said with a smile.

"Right. A fate marginally worse than death. So show me your Xanth; I'll take my chances. Actually, it would be sort of nice to be in a land like that, where pies grow on trees and magic works." He grimaced. "There I go again, getting foolish. The truth is, I just want to be with you, Ivy; I don't care where you go, as long as I can be by your side."

He liked her, as she liked him, without doubt. But he had no notion of what he was asking for, and she was wrong to bring him into it. Probably she should send him back to his dull home. But she knew she wasn't going to.

"Send us through, Turn," she said. "Both of us."

Turn nodded, having expected this. "I must warn you that the route is not direct. You have to proceed through the gourd—and that is different for each person. The Night Stallion will know your identity, so you won't be harmed, but he does not like having solid folk trespass in the gourd, so he won't help you either. You will have to find your own way through, and it might turn out to be a significant challenge."

"I've been in the gourd before," Ivy said.

"But never with a Mundane companion."

She knew that changed the whole picture. But she was committed. "We'll do it anyway. Just take us to the gourd."

Turn sighed. "As you wish, Princess."

4

MOUNTAIN

Grey and Ivy followed the fat man out to the rear garden. This was a thoroughly fenced exotic jungle with pleasant byways and even, by the sound of it, a trickling stream in the background. Then they came to a monstrous watermelonlike thing, with a stem on one side and a hole in the other. This was evidently the "gourd" they had mentioned that was the route to Xanth. He was sure there wasn't any more inside that gourd than pulp and seeds.

Ivy faced him and made signs. *Inside talk.*

There was another translator box in there? Why not!

Hold hand, she continued.

Gladly! He took her hand. Ivy climbed into the hole, and he climbed in right after her.

Suddenly they were in a cave that seemed larger than the gourd itself. Oh—the gourd was merely a faked-up entrance to this new chamber. Clever!

"This is only an aspect of Xanth," Ivy said. "It is where I thought I was before."

"You thought you were in a big gourd," he agreed.

Then he realized that the language barrier was gone; they were talking directly again! No wait for the translation computer. This was an improvement.

"We don't have to hold hands, now that we're past the threshold," she continued. "But stay very close to me, Grey, because the world of the gourd isn't like regular Xanth. It has funny rules, and it can be pretty scary."

"Scary? Like an amusement park horror house? I'm not worried."

"The gourd is where the bad dreams are made," she said. "Then the night mares carry them to each sleeper who deserves them. Nothing here is really real, but it can terrify almost anyone."

Not really real. Was she coming to her senses and admitting that Xanth was just a state of mind? That she wasn't really a princess in a magical land but just a girl who liked to dream? "Thanks for the warning," he said.

"Also, it is set for each person who enters it, though usually that's not physical," she continued. "That's why I entered first, so that my presence would fix it. You had to be in physical contact with me at the time; otherwise it would have put you into a separate dream sequence, and we might never have gotten together again."

"That would have been bad," he agreed. She seemed to make so much sense! She had really worked out this fantasy pretty thoroughly. Of course it was modeled on the Xanth novels, which she must have read a lot more carefully then he had. Now he wished he hadn't skimmed parts.

"Just remember: nothing here is really going to hurt us, as long as we keep to the proper path and don't spook. But we may be terrified before we get through."

Grey remembered one scene in Xanth, where a party had made a harrowing trip along the Lost Path where assorted punnish things abounded, and Prince Dolph had gotten lost in a modern airport: the innocent Xanth idea of horror. If this horror-house setting was modeled on that, he had little to worry about. "I'll keep that in mind."

There was light ahead. They proceeded toward it, and soon

the cave opened out into a breathtaking landscape.

It was a mountain, projecting up from gloomy mists into the sunlight, its curious outlines showing in starkest relief. It was stepped vaguely like a pyramid with crude terraces set off by vertical drops, and abrupt cave entries, shining crystalline spires, and a flying buttress or· two. At the very top, perched at what seemed a precarious angle, was a turreted palace or castle, so far and high it looked tiny. The whole effect was of fairyland beauty and challenge.

Beside him, Ivy was silent, gazing as raptly as he at the mountain. Then she came to life. "I had hoped it wouldn't be this bold, this soon," she murmured.

Grey walked forward to gain a better view of the fascinating structure. Suddenly he stopped. He had almost banged into a glass barrier! Then he looked again. "Why—it's a picture!" he exclaimed. "Just a picture of a fancy mountain! We can't reach it."

"I don't think that's the case," Ivy said. "This is the gourd, remember, where dreams are real. We shall have to enter the picture."

"Enter the—?" But he remembered that there had been just such a scene in one of the books, so naturally she believed it. "Okay, you make the scene, and I'll follow."

"Yes." She stepped forward and through the barrier.

Grey gaped. She was standing on the painted path that led down into the painted valley that contained the painted mountain. She was inside the picture!

Then he realized that it was an optical illusion. There was an entry there, or something. He moved over to where she had stood, then forward, cautiously. He put out a hand.

He touched the surface of the picture. He passed his fingers along it. The thing was definitely a painting, done in slight relief; he could feel the edge of the terraces and of each of the steps on the stone stairways circling the mountain. No way to walk into that scene!

Yet there was Ivy, part of the picture. She had walked down the path a way, perhaps assuming that he was right behind her, and perspective made her look smaller. Was it really her? He stroked her backside with a finger—and she jumped.

While Grey stared, the pictured Ivy whirled around, a mixed expression on her little face. She was alive—yet painted! He had felt the material of her skirt, the firmness of her tiny bottom, yet also the flatness of the painting.

Ivy was saying something, but he could not hear her, of course. How could a figure in a painting speak?

Then she started making signs. *Grey*, she signed, using the signs for white and black, which they had agreed would be his name: mix white with black and you got gray.

Her name was Green Plant. He made that sign, answering her. Suddenly they had a new use for the language of the deaf.

Come here, she signed.

I can not, he signed back, hardly believing this. How could she be part of a picture, yet still alive and moving?

She walked back toward him, growing rapidly larger as the perspective changed. Finally she was his own size, standing in the foreground of the picture. *Take my hand.*

Grey put forth his hand. He set it against the painting, beside her, having learned caution about touching her image directly. She put her hand up to match his.

The texture of the painting changed under his fingers. It became warm and yielding, like flesh. Then his hand clasped hers, their fingers interweaving.

She tugged, and he fell forward. He had the impression of stepping into water, the surface tension crossing his body. He blinked, and tried to recover his balance.

Then Ivy was holding him, steadying him. "Don't worry, Grey, you're in," she said.

It was always nice being close to her, but he was too distracted to enjoy it properly. He disengaged and looked back. There was the cave: a picture mounted in a huge frame.

He looked forward. There was the mountain—larger and sharper than before. The air was cooler here, and smelled slightly of ocean; a sea breeze ruffed his hair and Ivy's tresses, making the green flicker.

Green?

He snapped back to look closely at her. Her hair had a definite green tint! He took a hank between his fingers, inspecting it. Blond and green.

"My mother's hair is much darker green," Ivy said, understanding. "Because of her green thumb, you know. She has green hair and green panties, and she turns other women green with envy. But I'm only a shadow of her, so I'm less green."

"Green panties?" Grey echoed.

Ivy's hand went to her mouth. "Oh, I shouldn't have told! No man outside the family is supposed to know the color of her panties! Promise you won't tell!"

"I, uh, won't tell," Grey agreed numbly. He had better concerns than anyone's panties, at the moment! How could he be within the picture, and the place he had come from converted to a picture?

He put out a hand to touch the painting behind. He felt the rough texture of the painted stone of the cave wall.

"I guess you believe in magic, now," Ivy said, a trifle smugly.

Grey snapped out of it. "Magic? Of course not!" Obviously this was a sophisticated illusion, with some sort of curtain or force-screen that gave the impression of paint, whichever side of it was touched. His mind interpreted that texture as whatever he saw beyond it. The only mystery was how Ivy had gotten through that screen and how she had brought him through. Her hair color would be a function of special lighting. He had seen more dramatic effects in magic shows.

"Oh. Well, let's get on with the challenge."

"Challenge?"

"You know, the Night Stallion has challenges set along all the routes in the gourd to keep strangers out. I had to swim through a lake of castor oil once to get through. Ugh!"

"Ugh!" he agreed, and she flashed him a sweet smile. That made it all worthwhile.

They walked on down the path toward the mountain. The mist thinned as they approached, and he saw that the mountain rose abruptly out of a plain so flat as to resemble the surface of a table. It was fashioned of gray stone and was bare: no trees or grass at all. It loomed increasingly impressively, being much larger than he had judged from the cave.

"Uh, we have to climb this?" he asked.

"Of course. That's the nature of the challenge, I'm sure: to reach the castle at the top. It looks just like Castle Roogna, but of course it isn't because Castle Roogna's in the jungle, not atop a bare mountain, and anyway, this is the gourd. Probably there's a window from the castle to Xanth proper. But it won't be easy reaching the castle."

Grey looked at the sheer cliffs of stone, and tilted his head back to see the tiny castle far above. He swallowed. He wasn't acrophobic, but unprotected heights made him nervous. There were no guardrails on those narrow ledges! "Uh, what's the name of this, uh, challenge? Mount Xanth?"

But Ivy was walking boldly onward. He had to follow or let her risk it alone. The name of the mountain hardly mattered; they just had to climb it. He hurried to catch up. Maybe the climb would not be as bad as it looked.

They came to the base. It rose steeply from the ground with no apology, the stone too sheer to scale without special equipment. The lowest ledge was out of reach.

"Yes, it's a challenge, all right," Ivy said. "But maybe a passive one."

"Passive?" Grey asked, feeling stupid again.

"Rather than an active one."

"What's the difference?"

"With a passive challenge," she explained patiently, "you don't get chased by monsters."

Oh. "Let's keep it passive," he agreed.

They walked around the base. The circumference of the mountain did not seem great; in fact, far smaller than it should be to accommodate such a large castle at the diminishing top. Unless the castle was as small as perspective made it seem. It would be a real irony if they got to the top and discovered a dollhouse castle there!

They came to a small bush growing right against the base.

"Maybe that plant conceals an entry," Grey said. Indeed, the rock seemed less solid behind it. "Smells like some kind of mint."

"Be careful," Ivy said. "It might be a—"

A sharp stick poked out from the plant as Grey leaned over it. He jumped back just in time to avoid getting stabbed.

"Spearmint," Ivy finished.

Grey glanced at her, but she seemed serious. He picked up a pebble and flipped it at the plant. Another spear popped up and stabbed at the pebble with dismaying accuracy. "Spearmint," he agreed.

"They are dangerous to approach," Ivy explained unnecessarily. "They attract birds and things with their smell, and then they—"

"I get the picture." Spring-loaded spears nestled in an ordinary plant: a trap fit for a jungle fighter. And a pun fit for a crazy story writer. He would have laughed, had he found it funny.

They continued on around the mountain. Soon there was another plant, and this one definitely masked a flight of steps that led to the first ledge. The mint smell was strong again.

Grey made a cautious approach and inspected the plant. He saw no spears. Still, he did not trust it. He found another pebble and flipped it into the bush.

There was an explosion of dust. It surrounded him in a cloud. Grey inhaled—and started sneezing.

He scrambled back and away, sneezing violently. "Tha—ah—that's—ah—pep—*chew!*" he exclaimed through his sneezing.

"A peppermint," Ivy agreed. "I should have known."

Grey sneezed himself out and found himself sitting on the ground, panting, his eyes watering, his nose itching to trigger more of the same. "Pep-peppermint," he wheezed in deep disgust. A mint that peppered the intruder with ground pepper.

After a moment they went on, as it didn't seem worthwhile to risk the sneezing they would do if they plowed through the guardian plant to get to the steps behind it. They might sneeze themselves right off the ledge!

They came to a third plant. Once again the smell of mint was strong. Grey flipped a pebble at it, and the mint responded with an aroma like minty incense.

"That's all?" he asked, not trusting it. "Incense?"

"It must be a frankinmint plant," Ivy said. "They just make a nice smell for special occasions."

"Not frankincense?" he inquired, suspecting another pun.

"No, those make a smell that gets people frankly angry."

Grey let that pass. He had, after all, asked for it.

There was a cave entry behind the plant. They decided to try it. If it didn't lead quickly up to the ledge, they would retreat and search for another.

Inside was a circular staircase that corkscrewed right up to the ledge. No challenge at all. They emerged from an arch that turned out to be immediately below a ledgelet between major ledges.

Ivy looked up at the ledgelet. "Grandpa Trent!" she exclaimed.

Grey looked, but saw nothing. It was an empty place, with a kind of canopy over it. "I see no man," he said shortly.

She glanced at him, startled. "You don't see King Emeritus Trent?"

"Right. I don't see him."

She faced the ledge. "He doesn't see you, Grandpa!"

She paused. Then she said "Oh."

"Why don't we go up there, and I'll prove there's nothing there," Grey suggested.

"No need," she said sadly. "He says he isn't really there. It's just an illusion to go with the Enchanted Mountain. There are a number of them, but they will vacate the Enchanted Mountain now so as not to interfere with us."

Was she coming to her senses? "So we can ignore it," he said. "Let's get on up to the top and be done with this."

"Yes," she said, a little tightly.

But they still had to decide which way. To their left as they faced the mountain was a flight of steps leading to somewhere out of sight. To their right the ledge continued more or less level, around and also out of sight. They decided to start with the level approach, on the theory that it should be easier to explore quickly. If it went nowhere, they would return and try the more promising steps.

The ledge led to a narrow bridge over a big cave entrance. The stone of the bridge was cracked; the narrowness was evidently because the rest had crumbled and fallen. Grey did not like this. "Suppose it collapses under our weight?"

She shrugged. "We'll fall. But we can't actually be hurt. The gourd doesn't hurt people physically, it just frightens them. Besides, when I set out to use the Heaven Cent they checked the auspices, and said I would return unharmed. So if we fall, we just pick ourselves up and try again."

Grey was not at all reassured. He had no confidence in magical reassurances or in the beneficence of the gourd. But he knew that his objections would not sway Ivy, whose belief defied logic. Still, he made an effort to get through to her.

"Ivy, maybe you will get home okay, but I have no such guarantee, because your magic experts didn't know I was coming. And maybe the gourd won't hurt you, because you're a Princess of Xanth, but I am no such thing, and it won't care about me. So I'm worried about that bridge."

She considered briefly. "Yes, it is true; Mundanes can have trouble in Xanth. I will have to use my magic to protect you."

"Your magic?" He didn't like the sound of this much better.

"Well, not exactly my magic. I mean, use the magic that protects me to protect you too. That way you'll be as safe as I am."

Grey still was not much reassured. He was afraid Ivy would do something foolish and get them both hurt. This might be a fancy amusement park setting, but people could get hurt in them if they were careless. He had pointed out to her how he might get hurt, even within the framework of her belief, but it was she he was really worried about. She believed so firmly in her own safety that she could take foolish risks. But how was he going to persuade her otherwise?

"Take my hand," she said. "We'll cross the bridge together. If you fall, I fall too. So we'll both be safe."

Grey sighed. He would just have to take the risk and try to shield her body with his own if they did fall.

He took her hand, and they started across the partial bridge. It was just an arc of stone, seeming all too fragile, with the dark maw of the cave below. It was so narrow that they had to turn and put their backs to the wall and sidestep across, Ivy leading.

"Oh!" Ivy exclaimed, falling backwards.

Backwards? he thought as he wrenched her toward him. *Her back was to the wall!*

Then she was in his arms, and he saw that the cave below extended up in a narrow window behind them; the security of the wall was no security at all. She had almost fallen into the cave.

But it had one good effect. Ivy decided that she didn't like the idea of falling, even if her safety was guaranteed. "We'll have to be more careful," she said. Grey said nothing, happy to leave her with that attitude.

They tried again, this time keeping both sides of the bridge in mind. Ivy faced outward, and Grey inward, so each could see the hazards of one side and warn the other. They sidled across. The stone settled slightly, and ground out some sand, but did not collapse. Then they were across.

But if this was the lowest hazard, when the ground was really not too far away, what of the higher reaches, when any fall would certainly be fatal? Grey liked this whole business less as he got into it.

There were steps beyond the bridge, wide and solid. They linked arms and marched up them side by side.

The ledge continued, hugging the irregular curve of the mountain, sometimes slanting up, sometimes down, sometimes having steps, sometimes a ramp. They made good progress. Soon they looked down and discovered they had made a complete circuit. They were above the place where they had first gotten onto the ledge.

But they were still near the base of the mountain, with more laps of the spiral above. The day was passing, and neither of them wanted to be caught out on the ledge by night. So they hurried as fast as they safely could.

But it was cold in the upper reaches, and the wind was rising. Bits of the nether fog were breaking off and rising, drifting ominously close to the mountain.

"Rats!" Ivy swore. "I see Fracto!"

"What?"

"Cumulo Fracto Nimbus, the worst of clouds! He is always up to mischief! I don't know how he gets into the gourd, but he's here. He messed Dolph up too, when he was here."

"An evil cloud?" But now he remembered: there had been something about a nasty little cloud in the novels. He found the notion of a bad cloud quaint. Still, this was definitely the wrong time for a storm, and one did seem to be brewing. Rain would make these sloping narrow ledges treacherous indeed.

"Fracto's an ill wind, all right!" she said angrily. "He's sure to try to blow us off the mountain!"

"Maybe we can find a niche for shelter."

"Yes, we'd better." She led the way on up—and there, almost immediately, was another large opening in the wall. It was a deep cave, extending far back into the mountain, curving out of sight. It would do nicely for shelter. If the storm got too bad, they could simply retreat further into the cave, and remain dry.

The storm blew up horrendously. Grey had to admit, it did at times vaguely resemble a demonic face. But it was definitely a cloud, and clouds did swirl and rain; there was nothing magical in that.

The rain slanted into the cave. They moved back. Water coursed along the floor, trying to wet them. They found a rise and perched on that, safe from wetting. It got cold, as the cloud blew frigid upper air down into the cave. Grey opened his jacket, folded it around Ivy, and hugged her close for mutual warmth. Her greenish hair spread out like a scarf, helping insulate them. It was quite nice.

It was truly said: it was an ill wind that blew nobody good. Delightfully embraced, they fell asleep, waiting out the storm.

By morning the storm had blown over, and sunlight streamed down, brightening the mountain. They were hungry, but all they had to eat was one bean sandwich left over from their traveling. Ivy had expected to pluck pies from trees, of course, so hadn't been concerned. Grey, more sensible, had hung on to the sandwich, and now it paid off. They split it, and though it was squashed and messy, it was also delicious. Hunger was a marvelous tonic for the appetite.

They had occasion for the use of a bathroom, but there was none here. Why was it, Grey wondered, that in stories a man and woman could travel together for weeks in alien realms and never have such a need?

"Uh, maybe there's a deep crack farther back in the cave," he suggested. "Very deep, so . . ."

Ivy nodded. "We'll find it."

They moved cautiously back into the cave. The light of day faded rapidly around the turn, slowing them further. Then the passage divided. Grey checked one branch, and Ivy the other, keeping in touch by calling.

His foot found a crevice. He explored it with his toe. It was about six inches across, and too deep to fathom. "Ivy! I found it!" he called.

"So did I!" she called back.

"Maybe it's the same crack!"

"You use yours and I'll use mine," she suggested.

Good idea. This was like separate bathrooms. It was a bit awkward in the dark, but he managed.

There was a roar from deep below, as of a monster who had just had a bad experience. Grey leaped away from the crevice. Then he headed back toward the front of the cave, eager to return to daylight. He knew it was just a recording intended to scare him, but it was coming too close to succeeding.

He almost collided with Ivy as the branches merged. "Maybe that wasn't the best place after all," she said.

Grey didn't argue. They hurried on out and into the blinding daylight, letting the echoing roars fade behind. There was no sign of the storm; Fracto had blown himself out.

Steps resumed. They moved on up and around, circling the narrowing mountain a second time. But just as they completed the loop, the path ended.

They stopped, dismayed. The path did not exactly end; it turned inward and angled up the mountain so steeply as to become a cliff, until it disappeared into a circular opening. There was no way they could climb that slope. But they could not go straight ahead; it was a sheer drop to the next ledge below.

"But we were never on that ledge!" Grey protested. "How can we be above it when we never walked on it?"

"There must be more than one spiral up the mountain," Ivy said.

"But it looks like one! I mean—"

"Things are seldom exactly what they look like, in Xanth, and less so in the gourd," she said. "The entrance to that spiral could be masked in illusion, or the mountain could change its configuration each day. We may be on the same spiral we started on."

She was talking magic again. Grey let it pass. "We need to find a way down to that ledge. See, it goes on up and around the mountain; it must be the right one."

"Well, we could hold hands and jump down."

"No!" he cried, fearing that she was serious. "I mean, let's not tempt fate, or whatever. It will be easier to walk back down than it was to climb up here."

"Besides which, it might be cheating to jump," she said. "Challenges have to be met the right way, or they're no good. We'll never get to the top if we do it wrong."

Grey was happy to agree. They reversed course and walked back the way they had come.

Actually, it wasn't much easier going down than it had been going up; their knees weren't toughened to it. They trudged on as quickly as possible, not wanting to have to spend another night on the slope. For one thing, the facilities at the castle at the top were surely better than those of the cave, and without nether monsters.

They came back to that cave, and now the ledge they wanted was above them. But if it was part of a double spiral, where was the lower loop of it? Grey saw no change in yesterday's mountainscape.

Then he looked beyond the mountain. "Uh-oh!"

Ivy looked at him. "What?"

"Look away from the mountain! What do you see?"

She looked. "Why, it's changed!" she said, surprised.

Indeed, the approach path from the original cave (now a picture) was gone. They were in a broad green plain, with thick grass and luxuriant trees. There were mountains in the distance—conventional ones, that had not been there before.

"This mountain is the same," he said. "But everything else is different!"

"I told you things could be strange in the gourd," she reminded him.

Grey strove to find a nonmagical explanation for this phenomenon. "Maybe the rain last night made the dormant vegetation of the plain grow."

"And the different mountains?" Ivy inquired snidely.

"I'm still working on them."

They resumed their trek. Just beyond the cave they turned a corner, and spied what they had missed the day before because of the distraction of the storm: a flight of steps rising to the higher ledge. The configuration of the mountain hadn't changed; they just hadn't been paying attention. That was a relief to Grey.

But the middle of this stairway was broken. Evidently a boulder or something had fallen here, and smashed out a section.

They had no choice: they had to scramble over the debris. Grey led the way, proceeding very carefully, finding secure handholds and footholds. The very jaggedness of it helped, because sharp edges were easier to grasp than smooth planes. He had to work his way up an almost vertical section, but got hold of the undamaged step above and managed to haul himself up. Then he lay on the step and reached down to help haul Ivy up. She was fairly athletic, which was a quality he liked, and made it up without too much trouble.

Then they dusted themselves off and moved up the remaining steps to the upper ledge.

Now the mystery unraveled. This ledge actually began here. It dead-ended below, and proceeded on up. It was as if it were the continuation of the ledge they had been on before, but had gotten sheered away and set lower. Perhaps this had happened long ago, and later someone had built the stairway to reach it, and still later the boulder had smashed the stairs. Grey wondered just how old this mountain was.

They walked up the new ledge, coming to the point above the cave they had spent the night in. Here there was a right angle in the ledge and in the rock below, almost like the prow of a ship.

Grey stopped abruptly. He gazed out across the plain again. Sure enough—it had changed some more. The grass and trees were different, and the distant mountains had come closer.

"This thing's a ship!" he exclaimed. "It's sailing through the valley!"

Ivy considered. "Yes, I suppose it is. I told you things are strange in the gourd."

That set him back. He was arguing the case for magic! There had to be some other explanation. Maybe the mists of the prior day had concealed most of the surrounding scenery, and it appeared to change as those mists cleared.

"Let's get on up to the top," he said gruffly.

They resumed their walk. Grey's legs were tired, and he knew Ivy felt the same. But the realization that they were back on track buoyed them both, and they made good progress.

Then the ledge became another bridge. This time it was no partial thing; it was a far-ranging span that narrowed alarmingly at the apex. Grey looked at it and quailed.

"Now all we need is a st—" Ivy began with disgust.

"Don't say it! It might come! The last thing we want is a— a you-know-what!" He refused to say the word "storm."

She smiled, a trifle grimly. "I think your unbelief is wavering, Grey! You are right; it is not smart to speak the names of those you don't want to hear. But even without that, how are we going to cross? I don't feel that steady on my feet."

She spoke for them both. "It gets so narrow—maybe we can sit astride it there, and sort of hump across."

"Hump across?"

"I've done it on schoolyard mounted logs," he explained. "You sort of put your hands down and lift your body and bump forward. You can move along pretty well when you get the hang of it. If you lose your balance, you just lock your legs around the log. You can't fall, really, if you keep your head." He sat down and demonstrated, awkwardly, on the flat surface.

"How clever!" Ivy exclaimed, delighted. "Let's go!"

Grey led the way again. This wasn't because he was brave, but because he just couldn't see making Ivy take a risk he wouldn't take himself. He pretended it was routine, but the truth was he was tight with fear. His hands were sweating, and his jaw was clenched; he hoped it didn't show.

He walked as far as he dared, because that was the most efficient way to travel. Then he got down on hands and knees. When the arch became too narrow for that, he put his legs down and straddled the stone. He put his hands behind and heaved, humping his body forward.

It worked. He kept doing it until the bridge peaked, descended, and widened. He tried not to look down, because that made him unpleasantly dizzy; there was nothing down there except cruel stone, far below.

When the stone became too wide he leaned forward until he lay on it, then lifted his legs, got to hands and knees, and moved on. It wasn't fun on the downslope, but it was a relief to be there.

At last he reached the solid mountain again, and turned. There was Ivy, not far behind him. She was not as nervous about falling as he, because of her belief in magic, but he remained nervous about her.

"That was fun," she exclaimed as she caught up to him.

But some of the green of her hair seemed to be on her face, and he knew she had felt almost as queasy as he. This climb was certainly a challenge.

They walked on up the path. The mountain was comparatively slender here, but high, and the ledge was smaller. They had to go single file. This time Ivy took the lead, because he wanted to be in position to catch her if she slipped and started to fall. The path was increasingly steep, without steps, and still lacked any kind of guardrail; he would have been happier crawling up it, but that would have been too slow. Night was closing in.

Then out of the gloomy sky came figures in the air. "Oopsy!" Ivy said, spying them. "Wyverns! Probably they forage here, picking off helpless climbers."

"Such as us?" Grey asked, trying to suppress dread. He knew what wyverns were: small winged, fire-breathing dragons. Of course he didn't believe in them—but certainly there was something ugly in the air, and that was apt to be just as bad for them as a fantasy creature.

"Yes. But don't worry; I'll use my talent to foil them."

"But your talent's Enhancement! Won't that just make them even more formidable?" Again, he was trying to make her see reason without actually expressing his disbelief in her magic. At some point they would have to have this out—but not way up here on this treacherously exposed path.

"Not necessarily. I'll show you."

The flying figures loomed close—and they did indeed look like dragons. But of course such things could be mocked up and even be made to fly. This was obviously a most intricately fashioned setting, so such threats were feasible. Certainly those creatures, whatever their true nature, could be dangerous. He didn't see how enhancing them could help foil them, assuming it could be done at all.

Ivy stood facing the dragons. She seemed to be concentrating. The dragons approached even faster than before, their beady eyes glinting, plumes of smoke trailing from their nostrils.

The lead dragon oriented and accelerated, flying directly

toward them. It jetted a column of fire. Grey started to scramble away, not wanting to get fried—but Ivy didn't move, and he couldn't leave her behind. So he forced himself to wait, hoping that she did know what she was doing.

The jet of fire missed. Then the dragon, looking surprised, missed also; it shot right past them, so close that they were buffeted by the hot breeze of its passing. What had happened?

The second dragon winged in toward them. It too missed with both fire and teeth, seeming as amazed as Grey was by this. Then the third one.

"What happened?" Grey asked.

"I told you. I enhanced them."

"But—"

"I made them faster. So they flew faster than usual, and whipped their heads around faster, and fired faster. So their aim was off. They can't score on us until they get adjusted to their new powers—and they won't have them when they're not attacking us."

Grey worked it out. He had driven a car once that was larger and more powerful than he was used to. Then he had come to a turn in the road, and almost careened off the road because his reflexes were wrong. He had made hasty adjustments, knowing that he could quickly wreck himself if he didn't. It could have been the same for the dragons. It would require precise timing and coordination of vectors to score with fire while on the wing, and if that timing was off, there would be no score. So what Ivy said made sense.

Assuming that she could really do what she claimed. But that was magic.

"Let's get on before they recover," Ivy said.

Good suggestion! They walked up the path while the dragons reoriented. When the dragons made their second strafing runs, they misjudged the range again and gave up in disgust. "See? I don't like to use my talent frivolously, but for self-defense it's all right," Ivy said.

Grey was just glad that the creatures had been programmed to miss. The threat had seemed real enough, and he could hardly wait to get off this mountain. He would try to reason with Ivy about the matter of the dragons at another time.

The path looped around the mountain again, but the diameter of the mountain was now so small that the circuit did not take much time. They walked up the last stretch to the castle itself, crossing one final bridge. The castle was, after all, full size, no longer looking like a dollhouse.

They paused at the great wooden door, and looked back. From this height they could see far across the landscape. It was definitely a riverscape; they were sailing (without sails) upriver toward distant lofty peaks that reflected red in the late sunlight.

Grey shook his head. He did not believe in magic, of course, but certainly this was a marvelous setting. Probably only this mountain was genuine; the rest would be formed from some kind of projection on a surrounding screen. As amusement parks went, this was the best he had encountered. It was too bad that it was too persuasive for some. Ivy would be a terrific girl if she only could rid herself of her belief in Xanth.

Ivy turned to him. "You've been great, Grey," she said, and quickly kissed him.

How he wished *he* could believe in Xanth!

5

RIVER

They had finally reached the door to the castle. Ivy was much relieved; she had been afraid that Grey would panic and fall when the wyverns attacked. She had even hesitated to explain in too much detail how she could nullify them, because she did not want him to have to come to terms with the concept of magic while they were dangerously exposed. Suppose he spooked and fell off the ledge? It was better to wait until things were more secure.

So now she merely kissed him and told him that he had been great. Indeed, he had been, considering that he did not believe in magic; it must have taken real courage to carry on in the face of that doubt. He should be a great guy, once he got over his confusion and saw Xanth for what it was.

She addressed the door: "Hey, door, don't you know me?"

The door didn't answer. Oops—she had forgotten that her father, King Dor, wasn't here. It was his talent to speak to the inanimate and to have it answer in the human language. He had resided so long in Castle Roogna that his magic had infused those parts of the castle that he used a lot. Thus she always talked to the castle door, and it normally opened for her because it recognized her. But this wasn't really Castle Roogna; this was an imitation one, a setting in the realm of bad dreams. So her father wasn't here, and his magic had not rubbed off.

"Uh, doors don't know people," Grey said delicately. "You have to turn the knob."

Ivy was getting tired of his patronizing attitude about magic. So she decided to make a small demonstration. She concentrated on the door, enhancing its affinity to her father. It was an emulation of the real front door of Castle Roogna, so there was a basis for this; if she made it even more like the real door, it would be able to respond in the manner of the original.

Then she spoke to it again. "Door, if you don't open this instant, I'll kick your shin panel!"

The door hastily swung open.

It was very satisfying to see Grey's gape.

Then he recovered. "Oh—it wasn't locked. Must have been blown open."

"By what wind?" Ivy inquired sweetly. The air was now quite still.

But Grey merely shrugged. The door might not be locked, but his mind was. It was most annoying.

They stepped in. The entrance hall was empty, of course. Ivy had seen many people and creatures she knew, scattered around the Enchanted Mountain, but rather than confuse things she had asked them to fade out. Since they were all ghosts, they had obliged. That way she had seen nothing that Grey hadn't seen, which made the climb easier. The same was true here in the castle, and it seemed better to leave it that way.

"It's empty!" Grey said, as if surprised.

"It isn't the real castle," she reminded him. "This is the dream realm, with settings for all the bad dreams. So there aren't any folk here except when they come to make up a dream concerning Castle Roogna, and then they aren't real folk, just the gourd actors."

He looked at her as if about to Say Something for Her Own Good, but managed to stifle it. "So where do we go from here?"

"Wherever this sailing mountain takes us," she replied. "We should keep watch, and when it passes some region I recognize, we can get off and I'll lead us home to the real Castle Roogna."

Again that Own Good expression crossed his face, but again it was displaced by Not Yet. "But if this is the—the realm of dreams, you won't be able to reach the real, uh, Xanth from here."

"Yes I will—when I see a section of the gourd I recognize. I've been through it before, you know. So if I see the sea of castor oil—" But she did not care to complete that thought; the notion of diving into that awful stuff made her sick.

"A sea of castor oil?" he asked blankly.

"Well, maybe it's just a lake of it. You know—the oil that leaks from castors, those little wheels that move furniture around. They feed it to children to make them feel bad."

"I remember," he said, making a face. "We get something similar from beans. That's the stuff of bad dreams, all right!"

"Wouldn't you know it—in Mundania it's the bad things that grow on trees!" she exclaimed.

"On plants, anyway," he agreed wryly. "We have many horrendous plants: nuclear, munitions, sewage—"

"So if I see that lake, I'll know where we are, and then I can go the same route I used as a child to return directly to Castle Roogna. There's a candy garden, and a bug house and other awful stuff."

"A candy garden is awful?"

"Because of the temptation. If you take even one lick of a lollypop, you're stuck in the dream realm forever, or worse. I think. I'm not quite sure, but I don't care to gamble. So we'll just have to stick to our own food until we get out of here."

"We finished our last bean sandwich," he reminded her. "Actually, if it had gotten any more battered and old, it would have tasted like castor-oil beans!"

She grimaced. "Well, let's get a good night's sleep, then hope that we can move on in the morning before we get too hungry."

He smiled. "We may be hungry, but there's not much temptation if there's no food."

Ivy was getting increasingly annoyed by his superior attitude. "You want temptation? I'll show you temptation!"

She led the way to the kitchen and flung open the door. There was a fine array of cakes and pastries laid out with glasses of delicious drink on the side. The heavenly smell was almost overwhelming.

"There *is* food here!" Grey exclaimed, amazed. He stepped in, admiring it. "But strange, too. What's this?"

"That's a patti cake," she explained. "I won't eat them unless I'm sitting down."

"Why?"

"Because," she explained patiently, "when you take a bite from such a cake, you get patted."

He paused, then resolutely continued his questioning. "What's so bad about that?"

"These are fresh cakes, so they give pretty fresh pats. So you have to protect any part of your body you don't want patted. It's worse with hot cross buns."

He pondered that, then smiled, then saw her frown and changed the subject. "What's this fizzing drink?"

"Boot rear. You had really better sit down for that."

Grey looked pained, and she realized that he had just bitten his tongue so as to stifle a laugh. He was using Mundane magic: pain to stop mirth.

"How about this one?" he asked, indicating a glass of brown fluid.

"Mocolate chilk."

"From mocolate choo-cows, no doubt."

"Exactly."

He sighed. "You're right. This is too tempting. I want to gobble it down despite your ludicrous puns."

"If you think it's ludicrous," she flared, "why don't you eat some, then?"

"Maybe I will!" he retorted. He picked up the glass of chilk and brought it to his mouth.

"No, don't!" she cried, flinging herself at him. She pushed the glass away before he could drink from it.

"Uh, okay," he said, disconcerted. "If you really feel that way."

"When are you going to get it through your Mundane head that this isn't Mundania?" she demanded. "Magic really does work here, and you can get into horrible trouble if you aren't careful!"

"I'm sorry," he said contritely, with his This-is-Not-the-Time-to-Disabuse-Her look. "Are there any other things to watch out for?"

"No, this should be safe as long as the setting isn't in use. But maybe we'd better check."

"Of course." He followed her out of the kitchen.

She led him through the castle. Everything seemed to be in order. It was dark and gloomy with the onset of night, as was appropriate for a bad dream setting. She was about to take him to one of the guest rooms where he could sleep— she would use her own room, of course—when she spied something odd.

"This isn't right," she said.

"It looks like just another door," Grey said. "What's wrong with it?"

"There isn't any such door in the real Castle Roogna."

"Oh, so it's not a perfect replica. Maybe it's a secret entrance for the spooks when they come to set up a bad dream."

"Yes, that's probably it," she agreed. "So we'd better stay away from it. There's no telling what's beyond it."

"What's the harm in looking?"

"The same as in eating the food here. We could be trapped in the setting."

He shrugged. "We seem to be trapped now, unless we want to go back down the mountain and out the picture cave and back into the real world."

"Mundania isn't the real world!" she protested.

"Let's just say it is my real world, and Xanth is yours."

So he still refused to believe. She hoped she would be able to convince him before he got into real trouble.

She showed him the guest room. "You sleep here," she told him shortly. "I'll be just down the hall, in my room. Don't do anything foolish."

"Foolish?"

"Like sneaking down to the kitchen in the night. It's better to go hungry until we get where we're going."

"Okay, no sneaking down to the kitchen," he agreed. "But is it all right if I dream a little?"

"Dream?"

"About you, maybe."

She paused. "Are you trying to pay me a compliment?"

He looked abashed. "Uh, I guess so."

"You think I'm crazy to believe in magic, but you still want to dream about me?"

"Look, I'm not being sarcastic!" he exclaimed. "I'm just not very good at impressing anyone I really like."

Ivy felt two-and-a-half emotions warring in her. "How would you like me if you learned I really was a princess of a magical realm?"

"I don't care what you are in what kind of realm! I just think you're a great girl. I wish—I don't know what I wish."

There it was again. He liked her only for herself, because he didn't believe any of the rest of it was true. What she had told him of her background was actually a liability by his perception, because he thought it meant she was making it up. She remained annoyed by his refusal to believe what she told him, yet flattered by his evident sincerity about the rest of it. She was seeing him in his worst light, she knew, because of his confusion—but she did like what she saw. Grey really was a decent person.

Well, when they got into Xanth proper, she would show him magic he could not deny, and then he would believe. When she saw how well he adapted to that, she would know how well she could afford to like him.

For there was one enormous barrier to any serious relationship between them: Grey was Mundane. That meant that he had no magic. When she had been trapped in Mundania, he had been a great comfort, and she had needed him to get back to Xanth. But now that they were on the verge of Xanth, the complexion of the matter was changing. She could bring him there and show him Xanth's wonders, but she well knew that any serious relationship was proscribed. The old rule that exiled anyone who lacked a magic talent had been thrown out by Grandpa Trent, so Grey could remain in Xanth, and indeed would probably have to because there might be no certain way back to his place in Mundania. But for a Princess and Sorceress to associate too closely with a no-talent man: no way.

That was one reason she had delayed using the magic mirror. She had been busy, of course, just climbing the mountain and getting Grey through. But she could have paused long enough to bring out the mirror and contact her folks. Indeed, they well might be watching her on the Tapestry. No, the Tapestry didn't reach into the dream realm, she remembered now. That increased her guilt. So she knew she would have to get through before too long, because Queen Irene would not brook too much foolishness on the way.

But if she had brought out the mirror on the mountain, and Grey had seen it operate and realized that its magic really did work, his whole philosophy might have been so severely shaken that he might have done something foolish. So she had waited until she could be alone.

Now she was alone. She brought out the mirror. "Mother," she murmured.

Queen Irene's face appeared in the mirror. "Well, it's about time, Ivy!" she said severely. "Have you any idea how we worried when you dropped off the Tapestry? Why didn't you call in before?"

Ivy smiled, seeing right through Irene's severity. "I was in Mundania, as you surely realized, Mother. I couldn't call; the mirror was dead there. But I came back as soon as I could."

"And where are you calling from? That *can't* be your own room behind you!"

"We're in the gourd, Mother. In a mock Castle Roogna. It

took us two days to climb the Enchanted Mountain, and only now could I—"

"*We?* Who are you with, Ivy?"

Ivy could see that her mother was not in an understanding mood. "A Mundane. He—"

"You spent two days and one night on that infernal mountain with a Mundane!" Irene snapped. "Have you any idea—!"

"I needed his help to get to the gourd access," Ivy explained. "Then he wanted to see Xanth, so I'm showing him. There really wasn't much other way I could repay him for his help."

Irene glanced closely at her. "Obviously not. Does he realize that he'll be a misfit in Xanth, and that there's little chance he will be able to return to his prior situation?"

"I tried to tell him, but he doesn't believe in magic."

"Doesn't believe in—!" Incredulity and outrage rippled across Irene's expressive face.

"Mundanes are like that," Ivy reminded her. "It's been a bit awkward here in the gourd, so I haven't pushed it. I'd like to get into Xanth proper first."

Irene sighed, somewhat grimly. "You should never have brought him this far. It's like pulling a live fish from water and not throwing it back. He's apt to be miserable."

"I know," Ivy said sadly.

"We shall arrange with the Night Stallion to move you out in the morning," Irene said. "Bring the Mundane out on the north turret then; we can't leave him in the gourd."

"I'll bring him," Ivy agreed. She felt so guilty, knowing how awkward it would be for Grey, stuck in a land where practically every person except himself could do magic. But it would have been worse leaving him in drear Mundania! From his description, Freshman English was just about as bad as the lake of castor oil. She really hadn't had a good choice to make, so she had gone with the lesser of evils—she hoped.

"Good night, dear," Irene said with motherly resignation.

"Good night, Mother," Ivy replied with daughterly guilt.

The mirror became blank, then showed her own face. It

was somewhat drawn. Embarrassed by her unwanted maturity, she forced a sunny smile, making herself look younger.

Then she put the mirror away, and got herself ready for the night. It took her some time to sleep, despite the seeming familiarity of her room.

She woke hungry as the morning sunlight beamed into her room. Her room was on the west side of the castle, but it didn't matter; this was the gourd, and it followed its own rules. Probably the ship/mountain had made a turn in the landscape/river, turning the castle around. She got up, washed, and concentrated on her dress, enhancing it into a fresher and cleaner state. It was Mundane clothing, but here it was subject to her magic.

She stepped out and walked down the hall to Grey's room. His door was closed, so she knocked. There was no answer.

She did not want to be late for the connection on the turret, so she knocked again, harder. "Grey! Grey! Are you up?" Still there was no response.

Worried, she opened the door. The room was empty. Grey was not a heavy sleeper, so he might have gotten up earlier and gone elsewhere in the castle. Not down to the kitchen, because he had promised not to, but—

"Oh, no!" she breathed. She hurried out and down the hall to the extra door. She had forgotten to make him promise not to go there, and if his curiosity had caused him to open it, they could be in real trouble.

The door was closed. Had he opened it and gone through, or had he left it alone?

She checked the rest of the castle, just to make sure. He was nowhere. So he must have used that extra door.

"Damn!" she said, using a villainous Mundane curse.

There was no help for it. She would have to go after him, and right away. She only hoped he hadn't gotten himself into more trouble than she could get him out of.

She packed her knapsack and put her hand to the knob. The door opened immediately.

As she expected, there was no sharp mountain drop beyond.

There was a lovely green landscape; a rocky slope, with bushes growing in clumps and trees in the distance. A faint path led from the door over the nearest ridge.

She stepped forward, so as to see beyond the portal that hid much of the view. Now she could see a wider section.

And there, sitting on a rock, was Grey. "Grey!" she called.

He looked up. "Ivy! Don't close the—"

Too late. The door slammed shut behind her—and suddenly it and the portal vanished, leaving her standing on the path. That path went on down the slope beyond the region where the door had been, and to a section of forest.

It was of course a magical portal, similar to the pictures into which they had stepped. Only those who had the right magic could use that door from this side. She had fallen into the trap exactly as Grey had.

Grey ran up to join her. "I was only going to look!" he exclaimed. "But I couldn't see much from the door, so I just took one step, and—"

"I know. It's a one-way door."

"A what?"

"Some doors, like some paths, are one-way. You can go forward on them, but not back. They don't exist in that direction."

"But that's nonsensical!" he protested.

"No, it's magical."

He looked down the path, evidently trying to see the vanished door. "One-way glass, maybe," he said. "You can see through it from one side but not the other. If only I could get my hand on it!"

He still refused to believe! And his foolishness had gotten them both stranded here on a magic route, so that they could not go to the turret on time and be transported directly to Xanth proper. "You idiot!" she cried, abruptly furious.

Grey hung his head. "Yeah, I sort of knew that," he agreed. "I shouldn't've come through. So I just sat and waited for you to find me. Only—"

"Only I was an idiot too," she said, her anger cooling as

quickly as it had developed. "Well, nothing for it except to follow this path."

"I thought maybe you would be able to—"

"My magic is Enhancement, not portal making. But it's not a complete disaster. This path must go somewhere." She realized that she could use the mirror to get back in contact with her mother, but she was with Grey again and preferred to wait. Maybe there would be some other way to reach Xanth, without having to make her error too obvious.

They followed the path up the slope and over the ridge. It went down across a shallow indentation, then over another ridge, then down into a small valley. There, masked by bushes and trees, wound a small river.

They came to the river, and stopped, startled. The water was bright red!

Grey squatted and dipped his finger into it. "Ouch, it's hot!" he exclaimed. "And thick, like—"

Ivy took his finger and sniffed it. "Blood," she concluded.

"Blood," he agreed. "A river of hot blood!"

"Yes."

"But how can such a thing be? I mean—"

"This is the realm of bad dreams," she reminded him. "Blood frightens most folk, especially when it splatters. This must be the source of the blood used in the most violent dreams."

"But that's—"

"Nonsensical? Magical?"

"Horrible," he said.

"There's no bridge, but the path continues beyond it," she said. "How should we cross it?"

Grey looked around. "Somehow I don't want to wade through it. There must be something we can use to make a bridge or raft. Maybe there's a boat; I mean, the regular users of this path must have a way to cross."

"They might jump," Ivy said. "Or have a fly-across spell; you never can tell."

Grey grimaced, still not believing in magic despite everything. "Well, since we can't jump that far and have no flying spell, we'll have to make do with Mundane efforts. Let me check along the bank."

They walked upstream. The forest became thicker, and there was a huge tree partway fallen across the river, but no boat or raft.

Grey eyed the tilting trunk. "Wind must have taken that down, but then it hung up in those trees on the other side. Looks about ready to fall the rest of the way."

"Yes," Ivy agreed, nervous about walking under it. If that huge trunk came down on them, it would drive them right into the ground.

"Maybe we can make it drop," he continued. "Then we could walk across on it, no trouble at all." He walked to the base and pushed with his hands.

The tree was so firm it was rocklike. Then Grey put up a foot and shoved. Ivy happened to glance at the top, across the river, and saw it wiggle. "You moved it!" she exclaimed.

"But it's still hung up. It's too well supported." He walked around the base. "Look, there's a branch, driven into the ground. That must be holding it up, while the top is hung up in the other trees. If I knocked out that bottom one, it would probably tear free and come right down."

"Right down on your head!" Ivy said, alarmed.

He looked up. "Um, yes. Maybe if I could pull on it with a rope, if I had a rope . . ." He looked around, but saw no rope. "Some vines, perhaps." But there were no vines. "On the other hand, if I got a pole and levered at the base . . ." But there was no pole, either.

"Maybe there's something better downstream," Ivy suggested. "We could walk down and see."

Grey nodded. They walked downstream, beyond the path that intersected it, but the land only cleared, offering nothing, and soon the river flowed into a much larger river, its blood diffusing in swirls through the clear water.

"We might swim around it," Grey said.

"No," Ivy said firmly. "See those colored fins?"

"Sharks! Feeding on the blood!"

"Loan sharks," she agreed. "They'll take an arm and a leg

if you let them, but I suppose they'll settle for just blood if there's nothing better."

"Loan sharks," he muttered, looking as if he had chewed on a lemon.

"We could follow the path in the other direction," Ivy said. "Down past where the castle was." But she was afraid that even if they managed to return to the castle, it would be too late for the rendezvous with her mother. Maybe it was time to use the mirror again, even if that made for a problem with Grey.

"Let's go back to the tilting tree," he said. "There has to be a way to bring it down."

She was glad to agree, because that would keep him occupied while she pondered what to do. She was getting increasingly hungry now; that alone would drive her to the mirror, if they didn't make progress soon. This setting was quite unfamiliar to her, and she didn't know what direction was best. The realm of dreams was odd to begin with, and she did not enjoy being lost in it.

They reached the tree. Grey scouted around. "You know, there's a pretty steep slope here," he remarked. "And only brush, this side. There were a lot of big rocks in the field we walked through."

"Yes," Ivy agreed, wondering what he was working up to.

"If we could roll one down here, to knock out that supporting branch—"

"Yes!" Ivy exclaimed, seeing it.

They hurried up the slope. Soon they were back in the field. There were several big rocks, ranging from knee-high to waist-high. "This one seems about right," Grey said, approaching the largest.

"But that's way too big to lift without magic!" she protested.

"And too big to move without a lever," he agreed. "But see how it's perched on the slope. I think it will work, with a little luck."

"Luck? I thought you didn't believe in magic!"

He smiled. "That kind, I do. Let me see what I can do."

He walked across the slope, and picked up a sharply pointed stone he had spied. Then he went back to the hung-up tree. "Yes, it's pretty good; certainly worth a try."

"Try what?" Ivy asked, baffled.

"Making a channel," he said. He squatted, and began digging beside the supporting branch.

"Don't do that!" Ivy protested. "You'll bring the tree down on your head!"

"No, this is only the end of the channel." He was already moving away, scraping the soft forest dirt into a cavity that was indeed lengthening into a channel.

"You mean—the rock? Down here?"

"Yes. It should roll in the direction of least resistance. It shouldn't take much of a channel to guide it. By the time it gets here, it should be rolling pretty fast."

"Why, that's brilliant!" Ivy exclaimed.

"No, only common sense," he said, pleased. "I'm not a brilliant guy; you know that."

Ivy thought about that as she searched for a sharp stone so that she could help. Grey didn't seem to think much of himself, and indeed he was generally unimpressive, but he didn't seem to fade much in the crunch. He just keep plugging away at whatever he was doing, and doing increasingly well. She liked that. She would never have thought of rolling a rock down a channel to make a tree fall across a river.

They dug and scraped, mounding dirt on either side of the channel, and evening out any bumps so that the rock could roll smoothly. When they reached the rock, they deepened the channel, undercutting the boulder.

The rock didn't move. It extended down into the ground. But Grey kept working at it, deepening the channel and maintaining its slope, so that when the rock did move, it would keep moving.

Ivy, fatigued and dirty, straightened up and stood back. "Maybe if we pushed, now," she said. She wondered whether she should offer to enhance his strength for this, but feared that he would take it the wrong way.

"Maybe," he agreed.

They got on the other side of the boulder, braced their backs against it, and pushed with their legs.

It moved. Surprised, they tumbled and scrambled out of the way.

The boulder crunched down into the channel, hesitated ponderously, then decided to move on. It rolled, slowly and raggedly, but determinedly.

They jumped to their feet and followed it down. Would it break out of the channel? It seemed to be trying to, as it rolled irregularly, but never quite made it. It gathered speed, and plunged into the bit of forest.

Just before the branch, the rock veered to one side, threatening to miss. But the edge of it clipped the branch, and the branch snapped with a loud crack. The tree shuddered, then slowly let itself down as the rock splashed into the river. Crunch! The top crushed into the ground on the opposite side and wedged into place.

"Oh, it worked, it worked!" Ivy cried, dancing with joy. Then she grabbed Grey, hugged him, and kissed him.

"Let's roll some more boulders!" he said dazedly.

She ran to fetch her knapsack. "Let's get across; we've used up half the day already."

Grey climbed onto the trunk and followed her. But in the middle, directly over the river, he paused, staring down. "I've been thinking," he said. "Where does all this blood come from?"

"I told you—it's just a prop from the bad dreams," Ivy said. "It doesn't have to come from anywhere. It's—" She stopped herself before saying "magic."

"But it goes somewhere," he pointed out. "It goes into the larger river. And if it doesn't come from anywhere, then we should have been able to walk upstream and get around it. It just seems too much like a regular river to me."

"Maybe there's a blood spring, farther up," Ivy said, losing patience. "Look, Grey, this place doesn't follow normal rules as either you or I know them, any more than dreams do. It's not worth worrying about."

"I was thinking," he continued doggedly, "that if it comes

from an—an animal, a big animal, that creature must really be hurting. I think we should go check."

Ivy opened her mouth to protest, but the insidious logic of it began to get to her. A big animal? What an awful thought!

"Very well," she said wearily. "Let's find out exactly where it comes from."

Grey completed his crossing and climbed down beside her. Then they trekked upstream. Ivy hoped that Grey's conjecture was wrong, but she couldn't discount it. Surely a big bucket of blood, self-restoring, would have done the job as well as this river! And why was the blood so hot? Temperature hardly mattered for bad dreams, just appearance. Also, why was it out here in nowhere, instead of more centrally located?

The river coursed interminably, forcing them to climb over ridges and through thickets. At one point there was a red waterfall of it, and they had to find a way up the precipitous slope before they could rejoin it. This was certainly farther than it needed to be for a dream prop!

Then they reached what might be the source: a hole in a bank. They piled stones and brush against the bank so as to make a ramp to the top, expecting to find a lake of blood beyond. But there was none; it was just a low hill. Ivy was relieved; there was no animal after all.

The hill moved. Ivy screamed and looked for something to grab onto, but all that offered was Grey.

They stood, frightened, as the center of the hill swelled upward. Then it paused, and slowly subsided. And swelled again. There was an odd wailing sound.

"This hill is breathing!" Grey exclaimed.

Now Ivy caught on. "This is a—a giant! With a hole in his side!"

"Impossible!" Grey said. But he looked doubtful.

They walked along the length of the hill. Soon they verified it: there was a monstrous head, its face turned to the side, breath howling in and out of its mouth. This really was a living, breathing giant!

"And he's tied down," Ivy said, pointing out cords that stretched across the outflung arms. "He can't help himself!"

"While he bleeds to death!" Grey said, appalled. He might not believe in magic, but he obviously accepted this giant. "We must help him!"

"Yes, we must," Ivy agreed. "But how? He's so big, and we have no tools or anything."

"Maybe we can ask him," Grey said.

"Ask him!" she exclaimed. "But he can't be conscious!"

"I think he is," Grey said. He approached the huge head. "Giant, can you hear me?"

The eyes blinked. The mouth pursed. "Hyesss!" the wind howled.

"How may we help you?"

The giant's mouth pursed again. This time the words were clearer. "Magic bandage in pocket."

Ivy looked. Sure enough, there on the chest was a bulge, and it was a pocket. She knew that a magic bandage would stop the flow of blood from the giant's wound, because that was the way magic worked. "It's here," she called to Grey.

The giant spoke again. "But first—name your reward."

Grey was taken aback. "I don't want any reward! Here you lie bleeding to death—I just want to help you!"

The giant was silent. Grey came across to join Ivy, and together they hauled the huge bandage out of the pocket. "What an irony!" Grey exclaimed. "The bandage right here, and he can't reach it himself!"

"Not irony," Ivy said. "Torture."

Grey's mouth opened and closed again. He nodded.

The bandage was as big as the mattress of a bed, but not as heavy. They pulled it across the giant's heaving chest and to his side. They let it fall to the ground beyond, then took turns dropping onto it, as it cushioned their landings nicely.

They dragged it to the spouting wound. Now Ivy saw that the blood jetted at high velocity from a relatively small hole no more than the size of a human head. The bandage was certainly big enough to cover it—if they could just get it on.

"I hate to think of the hydraulic force of that flow," Grey said. "Maybe that's the wrong term, but certainly it will blow away the bandage before we can get it placed."

"It is a magic bandage," Ivy reminded him. "I think we'll just have to try placing it, and see what happens."

"I don't want to depend on magic!" Grey said.

Ivy sighed inwardly. She could postpone this issue no longer. "I think you'll have to, this one time. You know we don't have a chance without it."

Grey looked at the wound, then at the bandage, then at the wound again. "I suppose the technology that can make a setting like this can make a way to deal with it," he said. "A force field or something, or maybe the hydrant gets turned off when the bandage comes near. So we'll just have to try it."

Ivy wasn't completely satisfied with that rationale, but at least it meant that Grey was ready to try the bandage. They brought it up close to the wound.

"Maybe if I shove it across from this side, and you go across and catch it from that side," Grey said uncertainly.

"Yes." Ivy ducked down and scooted forward. There was a clear spot of ground right next to the giant's side, below the jet, because the blood was shooting out so fast it didn't touch ground for some distance. She passed right under it, feeling its close heat, and straightened up on the other side. "Ready!" she cried over the roar of it.

Grey wrestled the bandage up so it leaned against the giant's side. He unfolded the cute little knife he carried and used it to slice away the wrapping, exposing the clean surface. When he had the bandage clear, he put away his knife, took careful hold, and nudged the bandage forward, edgewise.

It touched the rushing blood. Despite her confidence in its magic, Ivy almost expected the bandage to be caught and flung violently out to float in the red river below. But the edge of the bandage cut into the stream as if the blood were no more than a beam of light; there wasn't even any splash.

Grey gaped, but kept shoving. The bandage lurched across, cutting off more of the flow. Soon it was all the way across, and Ivy grabbed hold of it. She hauled it far enough to be centered across the wound, then pressed it onto the giant's skin by leaning against it. "Tamp it on!" she called to Grey—

and discovered that she didn't need to call at all, for the roar of the jet had stopped. She was right beside Grey, close enough to touch.

They pressed it tight all around the wound. Where the bandage touched skin, it adhered so firmly that there was no leakage at all. In the center, over the wound, it merely thrummed faintly with the pressure of the blood behind it. The job was done.

Ivy looked down the slope. The river of blood was still there, but dwindling because its source was gone. It would probably take days for all of it to clear, if it ever did; some of it might simply clot in place.

Grey shook his head. "There must have been a lot of pain there," he said. "Just sort of lying here while his life ebbed. I have a notion how he must feel."

Ivy thought of his life in Mundania. Indeed, he might have a notion.

"Now let's see if we can free him," Grey said. "It would take forever for me to saw through all those bonds with my penknife, but maybe he knows of a better way." He walked toward the ramp they had fashioned before.

"Maybe he'll be able to break free, when his strength recovers," Ivy said, following. "Now that he's not losing his blood—"

"I don't think so. Enchantments usually come in threes."

"What?" she asked, astonished.

"Threes. They set it up that way in fairy tales, so they probably do the same in fairy-tale settings. We have to play the game their way or it won't work."

"You believe in magic now?"

"No, just in the way promoters operate."

She was silent. There seemed to be no convincing him.

They came again to the head. "Giant, we have patched your wound," Grey said. "How may we free you from bondage?"

The huge mouth pursed. "Magic sword in scabbard."

"We'll try that," Grey said.

"Name your reward."

"I told you: no reward. I just don't like you being stuck

here like this." Grey headed down the giant's chest, looking for the scabbard.

Ivy ran after him. "For a man who doesn't believe in magic, you're doing very well!"

"Magic has nothing to do with it!" he exclaimed. "This giant has been treated rotten, and I don't like it. I don't care if it is just a setting, I can't just let it be."

He didn't believe, but he wanted to do what he thought was right. Ivy didn't know whether to be mad at him or proud of him.

The scabbard lay along the giant's right side, below the bandaged wound. It was huge—and so was the sword it sheathed. "I can't use that!" Grey exclaimed.

"I think you can," Ivy said. "You may not believe in magic, but it is obviously working. Put your hand on the hilt."

"This is crazy!" Grey protested. But he slid down, used his feet to unsnap the containing strap, and worked his way up to the hilt. The thickness of the thing was greater than the length of his body.

But he put his hand on it—and the sword reduced in size to fit his own proportions, the hilt fitting comfortably in his hand. He drew it out and held it aloft, amazed. "This—"

"Is a magic sword," Ivy said, somewhat smugly. "Now you can use it to cut his bonds."

"Uh, yes," he agreed, disgruntled. "I'd sure like to know how they managed this effect!"

He jumped the rest of the way down, then walked up along the giant's side. Wherever he saw a cord, he sliced carefully at it with the sword, and it parted. He walked entirely around the giant, cutting every bond, until he reached the left foot.

"Oops!" he exclaimed.

Ivy had been paralleling him on the top of the giant. She ran down the leg to see.

There was a giant metal manacle clamped about the ankle. A heavy chain led from it to a solid metal block beyond the feet. Even with every cord cut, the giant would be unable to walk away from this spot.

Grey continued on around the legs, cutting the remaining

cords. When he reached the monstrous scabbard, he reached up, shoved the tiny sword into it, and let go. Immediately the sword returned to its former size, filling the scabbard.

They returned to the giant's head. "I have cut the bonds," Grey announced. "But you have metal shackles on your feet. How can I get those off?"

Once more the mouth pursed. "Key on pedestal."

"Oh. I should have looked! I'll fetch it."

"Name your reward."

"Forget it, giant! I just want to get this job done." Grey headed back down to the giant's feet. Ivy followed, bemused again by Grey's attitude. He might at least have asked for that fabulous magic sword.

There was a key by the chains, longer than Grey's body. But he was catching on to the rules of this region. He put his hand on it, and abruptly it fit his hand.

He took it to one of the manacles. There was a huge key-hole there. He put the tiny key in and turned it. The manacle snapped open. The giant's leg was free.

He went to the other manacle and opened it similarly. Then he returned the key to its spot. When he let go, it became its original size.

"Okay, giant!" he called. "You're free now!"

"Moove awaay!" the giant called from the far-distant head.

They hurried back away from the legs. Then the giant stirred. The earth quaked as the limbs moved. The upper section lifted as the giant sat up. It was like a mountain being formed from a wrinkle in the terrain.

"Wheeere aare yoou?" the giant called.

"Down here!" Grey called back, waving.

The giant looked, and spotted them. The upper torso leaned down. "I asked you three times to name your reward for help-ing me," the giant said.

"And I told you three times no," Grey responded. "If you're okay now, we'll be on our way."

"But I want to know my benefactor," the giant said. "I beg of you, remain a bit and exchange stories, for the end of this is not yet."

"I don't like this," Ivy murmured. "He may want to eat us."

Grey stared at her. Then he shook himself. "No, I can't believe that would be in the script. But just to be sure, I'll ask." He cupped his hands about his mouth and called: "We are hungry, and we fear you are. Can we trust you?"

The giant laughed, and the booming of it echoed across the terrain. "I don't eat people! I understand they taste awful! I have a magic biscuit. I will share it with you in exchange for your company this hour."

"My friend fears we must not eat anything here," Grey called back.

"This is not dream food," the giant said. "I brought it with me from Xanth. It is safe to eat."

Grey looked at Ivy. "What do you say?"

Ivy's hunger pangs roiled up fiercely. If the giant turned out to be dangerous, she should be able to enhance him into clumsiness. "I say let's trust him. Maybe he knows the best way out of here."

"Okay," Grey called.

The giant extended his right arm. The huge hand came to rest on the ground before them.

Grey looked at her again. "Trust him?"

Ivy remembered that she was supposed to return from this quest safely. "Trust him," she said, and climbed onto the hand first. She hoped this was a good decision. She was a Sorceress, but her magic had its limits.

Grey joined her. Then the hand closed partway, forming a crude cage, and lifted. In a moment they were high above the trees, traveling swiftly toward the giant's face.

But the giant only set them on the flat top of a nearby mountain, where he could converse without having to lie down again or shout. He brought out a jagged fragment of biscuit that might have been broken from an outcropping of rock and set it beside them. Then he brought a piece of cheese as big as a house, and squeezed out a little grog from an enormous wineskin. "All from Xanth," he assured them. "Eat your fill!"

Indeed, he crammed a huge chunk of biscuit and cheese into his mouth and chewed with evident relish. Ivy could restrain herself no longer; she walked to the biscuit, used her foot to break off a piece, and scooped up some of the cheese. Both turned out to be excellent. They gobbled them down as if they hadn't eaten for a day or two—which was exactly the case.

"Now we talk!" the giant said, satisfied. "You tell me your tale, I'll tell you mine."

Ivy was content to let Grey tell their story, his way. She settled back against an escarpment of cracker and listened.

6

GIANT

Grey was feeling considerably better about this adventure, now that his stomach was full. The cracker and cheese made him dry, so he scooped up some of the puddled grog in his two hands and drank it. Whew! It was potent stuff!

Then he told the giant their story, condensed. How Ivy was a Princess of Xanth (why provoke her by saying otherwise in her presence?) who had been sent on a mission to find a lost Magician but had somehow landed in drear Mundania, as she put it. How he was an ordinary young man who happened to live in the next apartment, who had tried to help her find her way back. How they had climbed an odd mountain, stepped through a door to a new land, and discovered the river of blood. "So we came to help you, because it was the right thing to do," he concluded. "That's all there is to it."

The giant smiled. From this range it looked like a fissure in the face of a cliffside. "I think not." Then he told his story.

He was, it turned out, named Girard. He had been a young

(under a century old), carefree giant wandering the unexplored central regions of Xanth, when . . .

As Girard Giant talked, the grog made Grey relaxed and woozy. He found it easy to identify with the story, and seemed to live it himself, as if in a dream.

Girard had one bad character flaw, according to others: he was a do-gooder. When he spied an injured animal, he tried to help it. When he found a tree suffering in a drought, he tried to water it. And when he saw wrong, he tried to right it. Unfortunately, those on the receiving end did not always understand or appreciate his efforts.

For Girard was an invisible giant. There were a number of his tribe in Xanth; but they tended to be shy, and they didn't like to hurt things by treading on them, so they maintained distant profiles. They romped freely in their own ranges, but in recent years the human folk had been expanding and exploring more of Xanth, and this was reducing the giant habitat. They had to tread carefully indeed when human folk settled nearby, for humans could be extraordinarily inquisitive. Human folk also had magic talents, and that was a problem because some magic could harm the giants. So the giants retreated as the humans advanced, generally.

One day Girard spied a new human settlement, deep in the forest. He knew he should stay clear, but it happened to be one of his favorite forests, so he remained to see what was going on. It turned out that the beerbarrel trees of this region were especially potent, and the man who was tapping them was hauling the beer to a distant village. He kept the secret of the trees' location so that only he could tap them. Realizing that, Girard was satisfied, because it meant that no more humans would be coming here, and it would still be safe for giants as long as they watched out for this one homestead.

One evening there was trouble in the human house. It seemed the little boy had gotten into the cookie jar when he wasn't supposed to, and eaten them all, so that no one else could have any until the cookie bush in the family garden could grow more. He was sent to his room for the day as punishment.

But the boy, rebellious, sneaked out his window and ran away. Girard, watching invisibly, shook his head; he knew children were not supposed to do that. He watched the boy slink into the forest. Because night was coming, the forest was dangerous for small creatures; the spooks of the evening were always alert for helpless victims.

The little boy, naturally, soon repented his action. But it was too late: he had gotten himself lost. As night closed he gave up and curled up against a hoarse chestnut and went to sleep. It seemed that the heavy breathing of the wind through the leaves of the tree lulled him.

Predators closed from every side. Girard, looking down from above, could see them. The boy would shortly be a morsel; the only question was which predator would reach him first, and whether he would get in one good scream or none as he was chomped and swallowed.

So Girard, meddlesome as always, succumbed to his nuisance of a do-gooding instinct. He reached down and carefully picked up the sleeping boy before any predator could chomp him. He carried the boy back to his family's house and set him on the doormat. Then he used the tips of his fingers, and with the most delicate touch pried up the roof over the boy's bedroom. When he had the house open at that point, he lifted the boy again and set him on his bed in his room. Then he squeezed the house shut again, slowly, hardly making a sound. The boy was back where he belonged, and no one the wiser; when he woke in the morning he would think he had dreamed his running away, and with luck his folks might never know he had been gone.

Then Girard returned to the place where the boy had fallen asleep. He put his hand down by the hoarse chestnut tree and piled some dead leaves around the fingers, so that they might be mistaken for a sleeping form. The first predator to pounce on that would receive a surprise! Girard didn't plan to really hurt the creature, just shake it around a bit to discourage it from going after any more sleeping boys.

But the predators were smarter than he. They smelled the difference between Boy and Giant, and stayed clear. Girard realized this only later, after his little trap failed. At the time he didn't know, and while he waited in perfect silence he fell into boredom, and then into sleep himself. Thus his trap became a nap.

A night mare approached, bearing a bad dream intended for the bad human boy who had run away from home. She was Mare Crisium, Cris for short, and she was behind schedule and very rushed. The gourd was short-hoofed this night; several mares were getting their hooves trimmed, so their burden of dreams had to be carried by others. Thus Cris did not pause to verify the identity of the dreamer; the boy was supposed to be here and someone was here, so she kicked in the dream and galloped off for the next subject. She was later to get her tail severely tweaked for that error, but that was another story.

So it was that Girard dreamed the dream intended for the boy. It would have terrified the boy, but it had a rather different effect on the giant. The first part was routine: a brief rehearsal of the boy's flight from home. Then came the main entre:

A huge female figure loomed, garbed vaguely like the boy's mother. "Bad boy! Bad boy!" she screamed, her voice echoing like thunder. "When I catch you—!!"

The boy, of course, was supposed to cringe in fear and plead for mercy. He knew he deserved the punishment, and feared it horribly. But Girard gazed at the giantess—and saw there the woman of his dreams. The boy's dream, technically, but still a remarkably wonderful creature. He was smitten instantly with love for her.

The huge hand of the giantess reached down to catch the scruff of the boy's neck. Girard could not restrain himself; he took hold of that hand and kissed it with a resounding smack.

For a moment the giantess looked surprised. Then the dream censor cut in: TILT! TILT! ABORT! ABORT!

In a moment the dream dissipated, and Girard woke. He knew what had happened: he had reacted in a way the human

boy never would have, and that had tilted the dream the
wrong way and caused it to self-destruct. The night mares
were very possessive of their dreams; they wanted none of
them getting into the wrong hands. He had given an erroneous
signal and ruined it.

That lovely giantess was gone. Truly, it had become a bad
dream for him, because he would have given anything to have
seen more of her. Where did she live? How had she come to
participate in the dream? How could he find her?

From that moment his directionless life was over; he had
a quest. He had to find that giantess!

He asked everywhere, but none of the other giants knew
where she might be. None had even heard of her. "Must be
from some other tribe," one said. "After all, she was visible."

"She was in a dream; the rules are different there," Girard
pointed out.

"True. Maybe you should inquire in the realm of dreams."

That seemed like an excellent notion. The realm of dreams
was in the gourd, as everyone knew. Anyone could enter that
realm, merely by looking in the peephole of any hypnogourd.
The problem was that the person could not leave until some
other party interrupted the contact of eye and peephole. That
could become awkward.

Girard considered. He could ask another giant to stand by
and cut off his view into the gourd. But the problem was that
the outside giant could not know when the time was right;
Girard might be on the verge of discovering the giantess, only
to be cut off and never find her again. He really did not know
much about the gourd, so did not know what rules operated.
Maybe there was some way to break the contact from inside,
so that it would be under his own control. He decided that
since he would rather die than be without the giantess, he
might as well take the risk of dying in order to make the best
possible search for her.

He went to a private forest that had a glade where a hypnogourd plant grew. He lay down on his stomach between
the trees, wriggling to fit, and propped his chin next to the
gourd. He moved the gourd around until the peephole was

about to come into view. Then, chin still propped, he closed
his eyes and set the gourd firmly in place.

He opened his eyes. One eye found the peephole.

He was inside the gourd. He knew it was only his soul self,
not his physical body, but he felt the same, and would not
have known better had he not known better.

He was in a jungle. The trees were so big that they were
slightly taller even than himself, and that was certainly the
tipoff that this was not the real land of Xanth. They were
solid, too; as hard as rock maple, by the feel of their trunks,
or ironwood. It hadn't occurred to him that anything in the
dream realm could be that solid, but obviously it was.

Something tickled his bare toes. He looked down and saw
that giant vines were curling over them. They looked like
krakan weed tentacles, with big suckers. A sucker clamped
onto a toe with a slurping sound.

There was pain. It took a while to travel all the way from
his toe to his head, but it was authoritative when it arrived.
"Youch!" he bellowed.

In response, another sucker clamped on, with another slurp.
They were sucking his blood!

Girard didn't have to stand for that. He bent down and
pinched the first vine between his fingers, pulling it off his
toe. But it refused to let go. The sucker sucked so tightly that
it threatened to rip the skin off with it. After a moment, dou-
bled pain reached Girard's brain: it hurt to pull on that vine.

Meanwhile, more were rustling in, their suckers questing
for firm flesh. Soon his feet would be food for the vines, and
he would be unable to stop it because it hurt too much to pull
them off.

Girard reacted as giants do: he lifted his free foot and
stomped. The vines caught below it were squished flat. They
wriggled a moment, then expired.

He stomped again, this time right beside his caught foot.
"Take that, sucker!" he cried.

A few more stomps flattened all the vines around him. The

suckers, deprived of their stems, lost suction and fell away, to be stomped in turn. It served them right.

Girard walked on. He wondered whether the giantess—he thought of her as Gina, because that was the way she had looked in the dream—had come this way and been trapped and forced to work for the night mares in the bad dreams. If so, he was on the right track.

He came to a great halfway flat plain. Ahead of him a cloud formed, expanding rapidly. It was an ugly cloud, with mean curlicues at its edges and a droll gray face.

He recognized that cloud! It was Cumulo Fracto Nimbus, the worst freak of nature in Xanth. Fracto termed himself the King of Clouds, but he was just hot air, always up to mischief.

Fracto formed a mouth and blew out a blast of wind. Hot air? This was freezing! Girard stepped back, shivering. But Fracto followed, blasting him with sleet-laden gales. Snow swirled around him, turning his skin purple with cold. Soon he would be frozen by the ill wind!

Again, Girard reacted as a giant should. He inhaled hugely, then blew out a blast of his own. He blew that cloud topsy-turvy; Fracto's bulbous misty face turned upside down.

Fracto was so angry that lightning bolts shot out of his bottom. But they did no harm, because his nether side was aiming at the sky. A few incoming sunbeams were dislocated, to their great annoyance, but that was all.

Before Fracto could right himself, Girard blew again. This time the cloud was sent rolling across the sky with the sound of infuriated thunder. Girard kept blowing until the cloud was out of sight. So much for that nuisance!

He walked on. He hoped Gina had not been frozen by the cloud. Women were less blowhardy than men, so she might not have been able to blow Fracto away.

A new shape was coming across the plain. It loomed hugely. It was a sphinx—one of the few creatures structured on the scale of a giant. Usually sphinxes just sat in the sand and snoozed, but they could be ornery when aroused, and this one seemed aroused. Better to avoid it.

Girard turned away. But there coming up behind him was

a roc—one of the few other creatures able to compete with giants. The big bird looked mean.

More shapes were coming from other directions. This promised to get nasty! Girard lumbered into a run, taking such huge strides that the animals and birds were left behind. But not far behind; they pursued him relentlessly.

He came to a wall across the plain. If he stopped at it, the aggressive creatures would catch him, and he wasn't sure that would be very comfortable. So he ran right through it.

The wall cracked into jagged fragments and fell aside. Beyond it was a lovely pool with twenty lovesick mermaids. They screamed as Girard's foot landed in the water, splashing a third of it out.

Girard brought himself to a halt, standing in the pool. "What happened?" he asked, bewildered.

"You incredible oaf, you crashed through a setting divider!" a mermaid screamed. "We were just rehearsing for our scene, and you ruined it!"

"Your scene?" Girard asked stupidly.

"Our dream scene! We are scheduled to love a misogynist to death. He's supposed to fall in the pool, and we'll—but how can we do that when you've splashed out all our water?" She flexed her tail angrily.

"A setting divider?" he asked, equally stupidly.

"Do you think our space is limitless? We have to make good use of it! You're supposed to stay on your side of the divider in your own setting, and us in ours. But you crashed through! How will we ever get this scene in shape in time?"

He looked at her. She was tiny, in the human fashion, with her wet hair flung across her face and shoulders, but her shape was definitely there.

Then a black stallion appeared beside the pool. *What is the meaning of this?* the horse demanded speechlessly.

"This—this *giant* just barged in here and ruined our rehearsal!" the mermaid expostulated. "Look at our set, Night Stallion! We have a deadline—"

The horse's eyes flickered as if lighted from inside. Suddenly the broken wall was restored; in fact there seemed to be no wall at all, just the pool and a decorative garden beyond. The water was restored so that the pool was full.

"*Eeeek!*" a mermaid cried. "Here comes the misogynist! Get that giant out of here!"

Immediately the mermaids were assuming their places around the pool, brushing their wild wet tresses. The lead maid heaved herself up on a rock and inhaled, making her shape even more definite.

Then the setting disappeared, and Girard found himself on a featureless plain. He was disappointed; he had been curious to see how the mermaids would love the misogynist to death. Somehow it did not sound like a bad way to go. He wondered just what kind of creature a misogynist was.

It is a man who hates women, the stallion said, appearing before him. *Of course the real one is not here; the maids must address a stand-in while the dream is recorded. Then when the dream is carried to the real misogynist, it will be realistic enough to give him his most horrible fright.*

Oh. Now Girard understood. Still, he wondered about the details of it. Surely not more than one or two mermaids at a time could—

What brought you here? the stallion demanded.

Girard explained about the lovely giantess he had seen in the boy's dream. "I must meet her," he concluded. "I know she is the one woman for me!"

You fool! She is a mere figment!

"A what?"

An illusion. A construct for one use only. A piece of temporary scenery. She has no larger existence.

"But I *saw* her!"

You saw a dream figure, which dissipated with the dream. Beyond that she is little but a bad memory.

"But the mermaids are dream figures, and they are real, aren't they?" Girard asked.

The mermaids are regulars. They act in numerous settings. There are many calls for mermaids, even in bad dreams, but few for giantesses. The one you saw was what we term an ad hoc figment: an image generated for a single use only. Forget her; she is nothing.

"She's not nothing!" Girard protested. "I love her!"

You are an idiot. Go back where you came from, and don't bother us again.

Giants were not, as a class, smart, but they did not really like being called idiots. Girard began to heat up. "You mean I can't meet Gina?"

The stallion snorted derisively. *You even have a name for her? Go home, oaf!*

That did it. Girard got mad. He stood up straight, looked around, and saw only emptiness. But he knew that was mostly illusion. If he ran any distance, he would crash through another barrier. That would serve this arrogant horse right—and he might even be able to find Gina somewhere too, for he just knew she had to exist; after all, he had seen her!

He lumbered into a run, making the plain tremble. Sure enough, after only a few steps he crashed through a barrier. The featureless plain extended only a short distance before it became walls that were painted to resemble more featureless plain. It was a good illusion, but this was no dream; he could strike these walls and break them down.

Beyond the wall was a new setting: a house made of candy. It looked good enough to eat, and would make several mouthfuls for him, but he had been warned about this: eat nothing in the dream realm because it could lock him into it forever. He had his own supplies of crackers, cheese, and grog, and would eat those when he got hungry. So he ignored the house and lunged on.

Soon he broke through another barrier. The painted candy cane backdrop fell away, and he stepped into a nest of writhing tentacles. He slogged through them and broke through into a hillside teeming with goblins. They raised an outraged outcry at his intrusion, but he slogged on. He didn't care what the horse said about figments; Gina must be here somewhere, and he would batter down every partition until he found her!

He broke into an ocean setting. The stallion appeared,

standing on the water as if it were solid. *That does it, giant!
I'm putting you under restraint!*

"Go ram a bad dream under your tail!" Girard exclaimed
heatedly, for the exertion added to his anger was making him
very hot. He tramped on.

He crashed through another partition. This one contained
an ogre bearing a pointed stick. (Ogres weren't smart enough
to use spears.) "Then die, monster!" the ogre grunted, and
hurled the stick at him.

It struck Girard in the side. That stung, so he caught it
between his thumb and forefinger and yanked it out. It was
no more than a splinter, really, but it ripped a hole in his side,
and his blood poured out. He was about to reach for the magic
bandage in his front pocket.

Then, abruptly, he was flat on his back in a new setting,
and strings tied his body down. He was unable to sit up.

The stallion reappeared. *You have misbehaved, giant*, the
horse said. *You have wreaked havoc, and must suffer in consequence. You will remain bound until some innocent creature who knows nothing of your situation frees you. You must
offer that creature a reward three times, and if it accepts any
of those times, all will be nulled and he will be unable to free
you. Fare ill, oaf!*

With that the horse disappeared. Girard was left to his fate.

He lost track of how long he lay there, the blood pouring
from the wound made by the ogre. He soon gave up trying
to free himself; he could not. The bonds were magically
strong. So he slept most of the time, slowly weakening.

He realized, after a few days' thought, that he probably
could not bleed to death here, because this wasn't his real
body; what happened here was more apparent than real. But
he still did seem to be losing strength; why? A few more
day's thought developed an answer: his real body, out in
Xanth, was lying there without eating or drinking. That could
weaken him, in time. But still he could not escape. The bonds
held his dream body, and the peephole held his real body.

A nymph came by. "I'm sorry to see you in such distress,

giant," she said. "I would free you if I could, but I can't, because everyone knows how you barged in and bashed up several settings."

"I was looking for Gina," he explained.

"Gina? Oh, yes, the giantess who is a figment. I think if you just forgot about her, the Night Stallion might let you go."

"I can't forget her," Girard said.

"Gee, that's too bad. Well, I have to move on; I have a gig at the Castle Roogna set. I'm just one of the extras, but it's a major bad dream." The nymph departed. Nymphs were not noted for their depth or longevity of feeling.

Girard thought about Gina for the next few days. The horse said she didn't exist, but she had to because he had seen her. The more he thought about it, the more it seemed to him that a person had to exist if someone believed in that person, and he believed. So he could not afford to forget her, because then she might truly be gone.

A ghost floated up. "It must be bad, being mortal," he said. "I'd like to free you, but I have no substance. Besides, everyone knows how you bashed up those sets. Well, I have to go on to the Castle Roogna set; I'm playing a ghost who scared a bad child." He drifted on. Ghosts were not noted for great sympathy to mortal creatures.

Girard thought about the thing the ghost had said that echoed what the nymph had said. Everyone knew about what Girard had done. He was cursed to remain here until someone who knew nothing about his situation passed. How long would that take, when everyone knew about it?

Maybe it would be easier to forget about Gina. Then the horse might free him. But then Gina would not exist, and he couldn't abide that notion, so he gave it up.

A goblin wandered by. "Say, who're you, bug-brain?" the goblin inquired politely, after the fashion of his kind.

"Just a bound giant," Girard replied.

"Well, maybe I'd better free you, mud-foot," the goblin said. "I mean, your stupid blood's a menace to navigation.

How can we get to the Castle Roogna set when the blankety path is washed out by this stuff?"

"Name your reward," Girard said, remembering that he had to ask three times or it wouldn't work.

"A reward!" the goblin exclaimed. "Say, that's a nifty notion, hair-nose! How about a big bag of fool's gold?"

Now it happened that Girard had a small bag of fool's gold tied to his belt, along with his carving dagger. Perhaps the goblin had seen it, for goblins had extremely beady eyes. To the goblin it would seem like a big bag.

"Yes, you can have it if you free me," he said.

"Great!" The goblin tried to pull out one of the bonds, but couldn't budge it. He tried to bite through it, but his teeth did not dent it. He cursed at it, but though the nearby foliage wilted, the bond remained tight. "Sorry, can't break this bond, James," he said.

"That's Girard," the giant said.

"Girard! Hey, I know that name! Ain't you the one who—?"

"The same," Girard agreed sadly.

"But I'll take the gold anyway, because I did try," the goblin said.

But the greedy little creature was unable to liberate the bag of fool's gold either. At length, disgruntled, he stalked off. Goblins certainly were not noted for generosity or sensitivity.

Girard thought about the goblin for a few days. It seemed it was true that the acceptance of a reward made the rescue impossible. That was too bad. Who would be fool enough to go to the effort of freeing him without any thought of reward?

He wondered again whether he should forget Gina. But he found he just could not, even if he expired. If she couldn't exist, then he would cease to exist also. That seemed fair enough.

Then at last the young human couple came. Girard had so little hope left that he hardly bothered to awaken, and his voice was out of practice. But to his surprise the young man did not know of his situation and did not accept any reward, even though Girard diligently asked three times. What an amazing and worthwhile creature this was!

"So now at last I am free!" he exclaimed. "Because of you, Grey Mundane."

"That's Murphy," Grey said. "Grey Murphy of Mundania."

"Murphy! Hey, I know that name! Aren't you the one who cursed folk?"

"No," Ivy said. "It's just a coincidence."

"Well, I am glad you came, because now the horse's curse has been abated and I can resume my search for Gina."

"But if she's just a figment—" Ivy began.

"I've been thinking about that," Grey said. "If she is just a figment, why is the Night Stallion so eager to have Girard forget about her? I mean, who cares who believes in something that doesn't exist?"

Ivy looked at him as if suspecting an insult somewhere, but didn't speak. He realized too late that his question could be taken as a reference to her own belief in magic.

"The horse doesn't want me to believe in Gina," Girard said. "I don't know why."

"I think I do," Grey said, warming to his thought. "Here in the dream realm, things go by different rules. So some things that don't exist in the real world can exist here, because folk think they do. So maybe it is your belief in Gina that makes her real. Nobody else believes in her, but as long as you do, maybe she *is* real."

"Yes!" Girard agreed. "So maybe I can still find her!"

"So maybe you can," Grey agreed. "But maybe it would be better not to bash down any more sets while you're looking, or the stallion will tie you down again."

"But how else can I look?"

"Maybe we could talk to the stallion. There might be some kind of deal we could make. I mean, you want Gina and he wants you out of here."

"You want to negotiate with the Night Stallion?" Ivy asked, amazed. "How can you, when you don't believe in him?"

"I believe that there is some authority with whom we can deal," Grey said. "I don't care what his title is."

Ivy shrugged. "The Night Stallion isn't like other authorities. He's dangerous."

"What can he do—enchant me?" Grey asked. But there was a small core of doubt in him, because the giant seemed to have been enchanted. Of course that could all be part of the setting; still, Girard certainly seemed like a real person. "But how do we find him?"

"I can summon the Night Stallion for you," Ivy said.

"How? With a spell?"

"With my magic mirror," she said. She brought out a small hand mirror.

Grey shut his mouth. If she thought she could do something with that, let her try!

"Night Stallion," Ivy said to the mirror.

What concerns you, Princess? the mirror replied.

Grey jumped. Had the mirror really spoken? He had almost thought it had!

"My friend Grey wants to negotiate with you," she said.

In a moment, Princess.

Princess? Had he heard the mirror say that? Did that mean that he imagined that the mirror not only could talk but also accepted Ivy as a Princess of Xanth? They had told the giant their story, but Ivy had not identified herself to the mirror.

Then, a horse appeared. It was a great black stallion, standing like a glistening ebony statue. Its eyes flickered. *What is this? A man from Mundania?*

"Yes," Ivy said. "He just freed Girard Giant, and now he wants to make a deal."

The near eye oriented on Grey. *Deal?*

Grey plunged in. "You tied up the giant for a long time, hoping he would forget Gina Giantess so you could wipe her off your books. Well, it didn't work! He still loves her, and you can't get rid of her until you get rid of him. I think it's better to try another tack. Why not let him have her, and he'll take her out of here, and then you can forget them both?"

The sinister eye flickered again. *If you take the giant's part, you will share his fate.*

"Then I share his fate," Grey said stoutly, though his inner core of doubt was expanding. "What's right is right, and it isn't right to tie a man down and let him bleed a river of blood just because he's romantic!"

Again the eye flickered. A gray cloud surrounded Grey, and strange forces strove at him. Alarmed, he reminded himself that none of this was real; the setting might be impressive, but there was no such thing as magic, so it could not touch him. The stallion was trying to fake him out, and he refused to be faked.

Then things cleared, and the tableau was as it was before.

I can not deal with you, the stallion said, with seeming surprise.

"What I want is reasonable enough," Grey said reasonably. "Just give Girard what he came for, and we can all go."

He wants a figment!

"Look," Grey said. "I don't care what kind of a setup you have here or how it looks to the people who come in for tours. If you can make a setting as big as a whole mountain with a castle on top of it and fake flying dragons with fire and doors that disappear after being used, you should be able to make a giantess. That's all Girard wants: the lady he saw in your dream. It was your fault the dream hit the wrong person; if you put your night mares on a proper schedule they wouldn't be too rushed to check closely. Maybe instead of trying to punish Girard you should work with him to shape up your operation so such foul-ups don't happen next time." He saw Ivy trying to signal him to be quiet, but his dander was up and he was sick of authorities who pushed regular folk around. He had had more than enough of that in college! This horse was the mouthpiece of whoever ran this carnival, so he was telling him a thing or three.

It seems I must come to terms with you, though you know not what you are, the stallion said, annoyed. He turned to Girard. *The figment can exist only here, not in Xanth. Would you come here physically to be with her?*

"Sure!" Girard said.

Then so shall it be. The eyes flickered, and the ground shuddered.

A shape loomed from over the hill. Some huge creature was approaching.

It was the giantess. "Gina!" Girard boomed as her towering head came into sight. He lurched to his feet, and lumbered across to meet her.

"Girard!" she boomed back. "I was afraid you would forget me and I would cease to exist, for no one but you believed in me!"

"Never!" Girard cried passionately. They came together with a crash that shook the whole setting.

Satisfied? the Night Stallion inquired.

"You'll find work for him—for them both—here?" Grey asked. "No more tie downs?"

Work for them both, the stallion agreed.

"But Grey can't stay here!" Ivy protested.

The stallion turned to her. *Obviously not.*

"But you said he would share the giant's fate, if he took his part!"

The stallion paused, as if figuring something out. *And so shall it be. The two shall be linked by exchanging settings. Girard here, Grey there. Do you accept the exchange?*

"Exchange?" Grey asked.

His body for yours.

"Now wait—" Grey protested.

"He means he'll bring Girard's body into the gourd, and move ours out of it," Ivy explained. "It's a fair deal."

"Oh. Okay." That was a kind of sharing, he realized.

Once more the stallion's eyes flickered in the unmoving figure. Then the scene changed.

7

SHARING

I vy breathed a sigh of relief. They were in Xanth proper at
last! She wanted to hug the familiar acorn and birch bark
trees she saw around them, and kiss the familiar turf.

Grey stood beside her. He looked around. "Oh—another
setting," he said.

"It's not another setting," she said. "This is Xanth!"

"How can we tell?"

"I've lived in Xanth all my life! I know it when I see it,"
she said defensively.

He shrugged as if it didn't make much difference. "It does
seem to be where the giant was. See, there is the indentation
where he lay."

"And there is the gourd, right beyond the holes where his
elbows were propped," she agreed. "The Night Stallion
brought his body in and put ours out. Now if I can just figure
out where we are."

"I thought you said you know Xanth. Haven't you been
here before?"

"I know the general way of Xanth," she said. "The types

of trees, for example. But I stay mostly on the enchanted paths, and this must be way off those, because the giants don't use them. We'll just have to find our way to a path, and then walk down it to Castle Roogna."

"If this is a magic land, why don't you just enchant us there?"

"Are you making fun of me?" she demanded.

He raised his hands in the Mundane surrender signal. "I guess I don't know the rules."

"Well, it's because that isn't my kind of magic," she said, cooling. "My talent is Enhancement, not Transportation. I could make us walk there faster, but that's about all."

"I don't mind walking," he said. "It looks like a·nice place."

She was relieved that he hadn't thought to inquire about the magic mirror. Of course she could use it to contact her mother again, and she knew that she should do just that. It was right in her knapsack, along with the sign language book. But the episode with the giant had shown her more about Grey, and she wanted to work things out with him before turning up at the castle. The long walk should take several days, and that might be enough.

"But first we had better eat," she said.

"We had plenty of Girard's crackers and cheese."

"I'm not sure it's the same, in the gourd. I'm hungry again; aren't you?" That was one thing that was not in her knapsack: food.

He rubbed his stomach. "Yes, come to think of it. But—"

"There's a pie plant over there," she said, spying it. She walked over to it. It was young, with small pot pies in the budding stage, but she was able to enhance these into ripeness so she could pluck them. They were only warm, not hot, but that was the best this immature plant could do, even enhanced. She gave one to Grey and took another for herself.

"That's a nice trick," he remarked as he ate. Ivy didn't comment, because she knew it wasn't exactly a compliment. He thought she had found food provided by the Mundane management.

The thing about Grey was that he had acted forthrightly in the gourd even though he didn't believe in its magic. He had figured out a way to get the across the river, then had sought the source of all that blood and found the suffering giant. She would never have thought of that, because she took magic for granted. Then he had insisted on helping the giant, and had succeeded in freeing him. She liked that; it showed how Grey cared about people, even strange ones. Then he had faced down the Night Stallion, and that had to have taken sheer courage. Even if Grey didn't believe in magic, he knew that the stallion had power in that realm. Yet he had stood his ground and finally made his point.

"What did the horse mean when he said I would share the giant's fate?" Grey asked as he finished his pie.

"He meant that whatever he did to Girard, he would also do to you," she answered. "My little brother, Dolph, ran up against that when he helped Grace'l Ossian. But he didn't flinch, and in the end the stallion let him go, and her too. So when you didn't flinch either, he let you go."

"But he took the giant in! So I didn't share his fate. In the dream it seemed to make sense, about exchanging places, but now I'm not so sure."

"Maybe he interpreted it in another way."

Grey looked perplexed. "What other way?"

"Well, Girard got his girlfriend."

He looked at her, startled. "Are you my, uh—?"

Ivy felt herself blushing. "Yes."

"I—but I thought you were mad because I don't, uh, you know, believe."

"Not mad. Frustrated. But now we're in Xanth, I can show you how magic works, and it will be all right."

"Ivy, I don't care about magic! But I think you're, uh, great. You're just the sort of girl I always wanted, without really knowing it until I met you."

"I feel the same about you, even though you're Mundane."

"You mean you'd like me better, if I believed in magic?"

"Not exactly. You don't believe I am a princess, either."

"Well, I suppose you don't have to be magic to be a princess."

"I am both, and I want to convince you. But I like you because you don't believe in either."

Grey shook his head. "I don't understand."

Ivy decided that this was at last the time for candor on this subject. "Let's assume that I am what I say I am, even if you don't believe: a princess who can work magic. How would a man react, who believes?"

"Well, he'd figure you were a pretty good catch, I think. I mean, he could maybe marry you and be a king or something, and even if not, it could still be a pretty good life. And you're pretty, which doesn't exactly hurt."

"So you believe he would seek my hand for reasons other than my personality?"

"I didn't mean to say there was anything wrong with your personality! But yes, I think maybe he would."

"So how could I be sure that a man liked me for myself?"

"Well, you couldn't, really, if you didn't hide what you were. I mean, men don't always tell women the truth about things."

"Suppose he didn't believe what I was?"

He looked at her appraisingly. "Then, maybe, uh—"

"So when you tell me you like me, I can believe you—even if I am a princess."

He nodded. "I think I understand, now."

"And if you find out that I really am a princess?"

"I told you, I don't care about that! You can be anything you want to be, it doesn't matter to me. I just want to be with you, and have you want to be with me too."

"I am not sure I can believe you."

"I'm not lying!" he protested.

"I didn't say that. But I'm afraid your feelings will change when you learn more about me."

"I—"

"So I think it is time to convince you that Xanth is real, and magic, and all the rest. Before we get any deeper. Because there are complications about associating with a princess that you may not like."

"Well, of course if you are a princess, what would you want with me?" he asked, forcing a laugh. "I'm nothing, even at home, and less in any magic land."

"I have come to know you, and I like you for what you are," she said evenly. "I don't think you are nothing or less, I think you just aren't recognized as a worthwhile person."

"You wouldn't feel that way if you were really a princess."

Ivy felt a surge of anger, but controlled it. He really didn't know any better! "I would feel exactly as I do now. But if you were to—to marry me, you might find yourself in an embarrassing position."

"To mar—" He coughed, and started over. "Assuming that any princess would, uh, well, what would be embarrassing?"

"Xanth has no reigning queens, only kings."

"Oh." But obviously he didn't see.

"But that simply means that when a woman assumes the throne, she is known as the king. My mother was king for a while. Only a Magician or Sorceress can be king, you see."

"That lets me out!" he said, smiling. "I have no magic at all!"

"Yes. So if I were king, you would be queen."

He gazed at her, his mouth round. He swallowed. "Why does it seem that you're not joking?"

"So if you don't want to be Queen of Xanth, you shouldn't marry me," she concluded. "Because eventually, not soon I hope, I will be king."

He shook his head. "I—I realize this is all theoretical, Ivy. You're not saying you would—would marry me. You're just warning me of the rules of your land. So I'm keeping my head and just saying that if I were—you know, uh, married— I wouldn't really care what they called me. But you know, if you really were a princess, I sure wouldn't ask you—I mean, that just isn't my league!"

"But would you decline if I asked you?"

He whistled. "I wouldn't be able to! But—"

"You may change your mind," she repeated, "when the time comes."

He just looked at her, unable to comment.

Well, she had said what she had to say. She had given him fair warning. But that was probably the least of the hurdles ahead.

There seemed to be no path. Girard Giant had come here, but he had simply stepped over the trees; they couldn't follow his tracks. He had selected this to be private so his body wouldn't be disturbed, and private it was; there seemed to be no familiar animals either.

She could use the magic mirror to call home, of course. But she wanted to convince Grey about Xanth and magic first, and to give him time to think it through and come to his conclusions. If that made him hate her, they could settle it privately. If it didn't—well, she had to be honest with herself about her feelings. She liked him a lot, and the moment she let herself go, she could be in love with him. She condemned herself for being foolish, but he was a nice person, and she knew he wasn't chasing her for her position or power. That gave her a deep feeling of security that she had lacked before. She had discovered, in these last few days, that what she wanted in a man had nothing much to do with position, appearance, physical strength, or intelligence, but a lot to do with decency, conscience, and loyalty. She could trust Grey, and that made much of the rest irrelevant.

So she avoided use of the mirror, and would bring it out only in an emergency. They would pick their way south toward Castle Roogna—this did seem like the north central region of Xanth, though she wasn't sure why she thought that—and she would keep alert for things along the way that might help convince Grey of the truth.

"I guess I'd better make a path through this jungle," Grey said, stepping toward a patch of curse burrs.

"No!" Ivy cried, too late.

Grey brushed by the burrs, and several lodged in his trouser leg and dug their spikes through the material and into his flesh. "Youch!" He reached down to pull one off.

"Wait!" Ivy said, again too late.

Grey's fingers touched the burr. "Owmpth!" he snorted through his nose, evidently stifling a more coherent comment.

"Stay where you are," Ivy called. "Don't get any more on you. Those are curse burrs; the only way you can get them off is by cursing. One at a time; each curse has to be different and original."

"I wouldn't curse in front of a lady," he protested.

"And when you get them off, back out carefully. We'll find another route."

"I have a better way," he said grimly. He brought out his folding knife. "Any burr that clings to me is going to get sliced to pieces!"

"That won't work," Ivy said—yet again too late.

For Grey was already flourishing the little knife at the burrs—and all six of them hastily dropped off. Ivy stood openmouthed.

"That showed 'em," he said with satisfaction.

"You cursed them all off!" Ivy said. "With the same curse! That's not supposed to be possible."

"Of course it isn't," he agreed. "How could mere words affect sandspurs? You have to slice them off."

"Sandspurs?"

"That's what they're called where I came from. People do tend to curse when they try to get them off, I'll grant that, but there's no magic involved. Come on, I'll take off any that get on you. We can continue this way; it does seem to be the most open route."

Bemused, Ivy followed him. He would have to learn about curse burrs the hard way: when he tried to use the same curse against a new batch.

Sure enough, three burrs latched onto her skirt. "Can you get these off without cursing?" she inquired.

"Sure." He stepped close and extended his knife toward her skirt. "Turn loose of her, or I'll slice you!" he said with mock fierceness, and touched her skirt with the point of his knife.

The three burrs dropped off.

"Maybe these are a different variety," Ivy said doubtfully.

"Maybe they just know who's got their number," he retorted. Then he turned and faced ahead. "All right, you burrs, listen up: any of you who touch either of us will get hurt, so stay clear if you know what's good for you!" He smiled. "Now if curses work, that'll keep them clear."

Ivy shrugged. Grey stepped boldly forward, and she followed—and no curse burrs got on either of them.

How could this be? It was as if magic was stopping the burrs—yet Grey was Mundane, with no magic, not even any belief in it. It seemed more likely that his curses would fail to have effect than that his threat with the dinky knife would frighten all the burrs. Was it possible that they didn't know he was Mundane and thought his threat was backed by magic?

They passed beyond the curse burr patch and came to a stately tree with colored flowers. Grey walked toward it, evidently meaning to pick one.

"Careful," Ivy warned him. "That's a two-lips tree!"

"A tulip tree? No it isn't. I've seen them; their flowers are different."

"But you aren't where you came from. Here, a two-lips tree—" But Grey wasn't paying attention, so she let it go. He would find out.

Grey stepped close, reaching up for one of the larger flowers. It avoided him. He moved closer yet, stretching—and another flower nudged down and kissed him on the cheek with a significant smack.

He paused, startled. "I could have sworn that—"

"That's right," Ivy said smugly. "Those are kissing flowers."

"Impossible," he said. "Flowers can't kiss."

"Two-lips," she explained. "They like to kiss folk."

"I don't believe it." He stepped yet closer into the tree. "Let's see whether anything kisses me while I'm watching."

He waited, but nothing happened, to Ivy's surprise. Usually a two-lips tree would kiss anything that got within its range, making loud smacking sounds that carried across the forest. It was harmless, but embarrassing.

"Maybe it doesn't like the way you taste," she said.

"Maybe it's magical, so can't stand scrutiny," he retorted, stepping away from the quiescent tree.

"Just don't try that with a tangle tree," she said, disgruntled.

"I know what that is. But I'll have to see it grab something, before I believe it."

They went on. The vegetation thinned and the ground turned sandy. There was a feel of magic about it that bothered Ivy. There was something about this region, and it seemed to be associated with the sand. She didn't like mysteries in strange places; they could be dangerous.

"Wait," she said.

Grey paused. "Tired?"

"It's not that. I'm not sure I like this region."

"It seems nice enough to me. This sand is easy to walk on; we can make good progress before night."

"Not if we walk into a trap."

He shrugged. "I wouldn't want to do that. Where I live there can be quicksand—that's stuff that you can get caught in, so maybe you drown."

"Ours makes you speed up," Ivy said. "And slowsand makes you slow down, which can be awkward. But this seems to be something else. Let me see what I can do with it."

"Make a sand castle, maybe," he said, smiling.

Her talent was Enhancement, not Detection, but she decided to investigate in her fashion. As she stepped on the sand, she enhanced it, so that its qualities would become more obvious.

For a moment the sand just lay there. Then it rippled. Waves spread across it, as if it were water.

Ivy continued to concentrate, enhancing it further. She wanted to see whether it was dangerous.

The ripples became humps. Was this a dread sand dune, looking for subjects to turn into fossils? Her parents had encountered one of those once. Dunes liked to bury living creatures forever or until their flesh fell apart, leaving handsome bones. Ivy wasn't yet ready to part with her flesh.

Then a big central hump formed. It rose up and up, and

finally formed into a vague manlike form. It stood there, half as tall as Ivy, its hair formed of dry weeds and its eyes of mica pebbles. It had a nose made of a twisty root, and ears of tattered seashells.

"What are you?" Ivy demanded of it.

The sandman shifted shape, the sand humping as if driven by the wind, except that there was no wind. It assumed the shape of a four-footed animal with root horns and a viney tail.

"You haven't answered," Ivy said. The thing didn't seem dangerous, but she wasn't sure.

The sand changed again, becoming a small tree with a thick trunk and stubby branches that waved clumsily in the make-believe wind.

"Now look—" Ivy started.

"I wonder how the effect is achieved," Grey said, striding across to touch the sand formation. "I can't believe—"

Immediately the sand sifted down and became a featureless mound, its pebbles and shells and roots randomly distributed.

"Oh, you spoiled it!" Ivy exclaimed, annoyed. "I was about to find out whether it was dangerous."

Grey stirred the pile of sand with his toe. "It's not danger-ous; it's just sand. But it certainly looked like a sandman for a moment there! I knew it was illusion; I just wish I could have figured it out without destroying it."

"Well, I was about to do that," Ivy said crossly. But it did seem that the sandman was no danger; the feeling of strange-ness was gone.

Now the day was getting on. "We had better find a place to camp," Grey said. "There could be wild creatures in the night."

There could indeed! They had not encountered any bad ones so far, which was remarkable; maybe the curse burrs and sandman kept them out. But those things seemed to lack force, here, so she doubted it. She hoped there wasn't some truly formidable predator who used this region as its hunting ground, eliminating most of the other dangers. She would prefer to deal with a series of small menaces, rather than one

really big one, because she wasn't sure how effective her
enhancement talent would be against a truly formidable creature. Usually when she explored, she had Stanley Steamer
along, and he had taken care of personal defense.

She looked around, but there was no suitable camping
place. They would just have to go on, though her feet were
tired and her legs too; she wasn't used to this much contin-
uous walking.

"Maybe under that tree," Grey suggested, indicating a large
tree whose tentacles reached almost to the ground.

"That's a tangle tree!" Ivy shrieked, appalled.

"Yeah, I guess so. But we can't play this game forever.
I'm sure it's harmless when its bluff is called." He walked
boldly toward it, using one of the pleasant little paths that
approached it.

"No!" Ivy cried, dashing after him. "Nobody but an ogre
or a dragon messes with a tangler, and even they are careful.
Don't go near it!"

"I'm sure most creatures here feel as you do," Grey said,
proceeding without pause. "That means they will stay clear
of it, and we can spend a comfortable night under its shelter.
That seems ideal to me."

Ivy caught up to him and grabbed his arm. "You don't
understand! That tree will grab you and gobble you down the
moment you come within reach! I'm not sure I can protect
you from—"

But she lost her balance, and stumbled, and they both fell
right into the nest of the tentacles. Ivy felt sheer panic.

But the hanging tentacles remained quiescent. Not one
grabbed at them. The tree seemed to be asleep.

"Oh," Ivy said, relieved. "It must have feasted recently, so
it's not hungry. What luck!"

Grey shook his head. "You have an explanation for everything! Okay, it's not hungry. So let's camp here tonight. No
one else will realize that it's safe under here."

"True," she agreed faintly. She remained nervous about being this close to a tangler, but it certainly was true that a sated
tree was safe.

She located some milkweeds and a breadfruit tree; fortunately these were common all across Xanth, so they had bread and milk for dinner. There was also a pillow bush nearby, with extremely plush pillows; they made two beds of them under the tree. Obviously none of these plants had been harvested recently, because of the shortage of travelers.

Ivy lay for some time without sleeping, bothered by things. Where was the great menace that kept travelers away, and why were even the ordinary menaces so feeble at the moment? She had been making spot excuses for them, almost embarrassed because they were not manifesting adequately to convince Grey they were genuine. She had concluded that this tangle tree was sated, but she saw no recent pile of bones, and the tentacles did not look sleek and strong in the manner of a well-fed tree. This tree should be hungry, yet wasn't, and that made sleep nervous. Which reminded her: that sandman—probably it was related to the ones that came by night to put children to sleep, and perhaps it usually put travelers to sleep near this tangle tree, so the tree could snake out a tentacle and haul them in without resistance. Yet in the face of Grey's skepticism, the sandman had collapsed into inert sand.

There, maybe, was the crux of it: Grey thought that magic was mostly in her mind, that she saw it work because she believed it did. In Mundania she had been unable to demonstrate otherwise. But now they were in Xanth—and she still couldn't penetrate his unbelief. It seemed that he was constitutionally unable to accept magic, and that therefore the magic didn't work for him. That was a fundamentally unsettling notion. Suppose magic didn't work for anyone who didn't believe in it?

Now that was an interesting idea. Could that be why Mundanes didn't have magic talents? Because they didn't believe in them? But when they moved to Xanth, their children were exposed to magic from the outset and never learned *not* to believe, so had talents. If the Mundanes were just more openminded, they might turn out to have talents the moment they entered Xanth! After all, the centaurs had turned out to have talents, those who stopped thinking that talents were obscene.

No, that didn't hold up. Some Mundanes were open-minded, but none had ever had a magic talent. Some of their children were close-minded, but still had talents. Belief might be a factor, but not the major one. A person had to be delivered in Xanth to have magic.

So what was she going to do about Grey? It was foolish, she well knew, but she liked him. She liked him a lot. But the moment they reached Castle Roogna, any romantic relationship would be over. She was a princess, and while she didn't have to marry a prince, certainly her folks would not allow her to marry a Mundane! She had tried to explain that to Grey, but had gotten caught up in her own rebellion and discussed only the awkwardness of marriage between them, not the impossibility of achieving it.

What would happen if she insisted on marrying a Mundane? She would disappoint her parents terribly, and that hurt. They might have to take action, such as banishing her to Mundania, and that would hurt more. But if she went with Grey, would that make it worth it?

To live the rest of her life in drear Mundania without magic—that was an appalling prospect. Yet she could imagine doing it, almost, with him. Grey was completely ordinary, but there was something about him that appealed to her, and she knew his interest in her was genuine. Was that enough?

She shook her head in the darkness. She knew, objectively, that it was not enough. Love could be fun, but it didn't last if not soundly based, and for her to move to Mundania would be like a mermaid moving to land: possible, but problematical.

No, she could marry Grey only if he remained in Xanth with her—and that meant she had to have the approval of her parents. That meant in turn that she couldn't marry him. Yet her heart wished that she could.

She would simply have to get her heart under control. She knew that. But she also knew it was going to hurt.

Maybe when Grey finally learned that magic was real, he would suffer a revulsion against it and Xanth and her, and choose to go home to Mundania alone. That would solve her problem, as the decision would be out of her hands. But it still would hurt.

Ivy lay quietly on the pillows, her eyes closed, the tears nevertheless running down her cheeks.

She woke to the wan light of a shrouded morning. As her eyes adjusted she discovered Grey sitting beside her. "You okay?" he asked.

"Of course I am," she said, sitting up and shaking a stray leaf out of her hair. "Why do you ask?"

He shrugged. "I, uh, thought you were unhappy or something, maybe sick. I was worried."

She smiled. "I must look wretched! But that's because I'm not used to sleeping out. Let me find a brook to wash in, and I'll be better."

"Uh, sure. I'd have gone out and looked around, but I didn't want to leave you alone."

"I wouldn't want *you* going out alone," she retorted. "Not until you believe that the dangers are real."

They went out together, and did find a spring nearby. "Let me test it," Ivy said. "These things can be dangerous."

"Why? Are they poisoned?"

"Not exactly. Some are love springs."

"Oh, yes—they make the creatures who drink from them fall in love with each other. What a horror if we should drink from one of those!"

Ivy glanced at him sharply. Grey tried to hold his face straight, but couldn't, and had to laugh. She laughed too, more with relief than humor. "It's not as nice as that," she warned him. "Love may be a euphemism. When it happens, they breed immediately, being unable to restrain themselves, even if they are of two different species. It is believed that that's how the major crossbreeds got started—centaurs, merfolk, harpies, and so on. So you wouldn't want to drink from one by accident."

"Of course I wouldn't," he agreed, but he looked doubtful.

Ivy squatted by the spring and concentrated, enhancing it. If it was a love spring, the enhancement would cause it to

affect the plants growing around it, and they would start loving each other in whatever manner they could manage.

Nothing happened. "It's all right," she reported. "It's just
water."

"I'm sure it is," he agreed condescendingly. Again she had
to suppress her annoyance. *He didn't know any better.* This
was the other side of it: because of his ignorance, she could
trust his feeling for her, but it was also a constant source of
irritation. She wasn't used to such divergent feelings for the
same person.

They dipped out double handfuls of water to drink. Then
she washed her face and hands. The rest of her was feeling
a bit grubby, but she decided not to strip and wash. After all,
she would just have to climb back into the same dirty clothing. She had changed to her clean clothes the night in the
mock Castle Roogna, and then gotten those dirty trudging
along the river of blood and pushing the boulder. She would
probably have to throw away this Mundane outfit the moment
they reached Castle Roogna. She hoped Agenda, whose clothing it was, wouldn't mind.

That was funny, the way Grey had met such a series of
peculiar girls who used the room before Ivy was sent there
by the Heaven Cent. And the way Com-Pewter had been
there, with a bit of magic. Grey had told her that an odd
"program" from someone called Vaporware Limited had
changed the machine. She wondered whether Vaporware
lived in Xanth; that might explain a lot. Still, magic wasn't
supposed to work at all in Mundania, so a mystery remained.

"Com-Pewter," she said. "How did he do magic in Mundania?"

"My computer didn't do magic," Grey said. "It just had a
good translation program, so we could talk. I guess." He
didn't seem to be entirely satisfied either. "It sure was strange
what it did, though. It admitted at the end that it was setting
me up for you."

"Setting you up?"

"It had something to do with all those oddball females.

When I demanded a good one, it brought you. I don't know how, but I'm sure glad it did."

"No one brought me!" she protested. "The Heaven Cent sent me."

"Whatever. I think that program knew you were coming, somehow, and took the credit. But I don't care. My life was like dishwater until you came, and then it was like sunrise."

Ivy had learned about dishwater in Mundania, because the same dishes had to be used over and over again, which meant they had to be washed. "And I was a dishwater blonde," she said, remembering how the magic green had washed out of her hair.

"You were beautiful," he said.

She tried to think of some clever response, but her mind froze up. He was telling the truth. He had seen her unenhanced—drab really—yet had liked her. There could be no better compliment than that.

"We'd better eat," she said, changing the subject.

"I saw some—they looked like lollypops, growing out of the sand, back there," he said.

Ivy checked. "Sugar sand," she said. "Naturally sweet things grow in it. Here are some sugar doughnuts, and here's sugarcane." She picked some of each. "And a sugarplum tree over there. We'll get sick of sweets, but at least it's food."

They ate. "You're right," he said as he chewed on the candy-striped cane. "I am getting tired of sugar! I never thought I'd see the day!"

"How is it that you eat these magical plants, but still don't believe in magic?" she asked mischievously.

"Sugar doughnuts and sugarplums aren't magical," he protested. "Though I admit that in Mundania sugar sand and sugarcane have different definitions."

They moved on, bearing south. They came to a well-worn path. "Great!" he exclaimed. "Now we won't have to plow through brush!"

"This isn't one of the enchanted paths," she said. "Unknown paths are not to be trusted until their nature is understood. You never can tell where they might lead."

He peered at the tangled jungle across from the path. "Can't we risk it, this once? My legs are tired."

Ivy considered. Her legs were tired too. "Maybe if we're careful. If we hear anything, we should get right off it, though."

They walked down the path. It was indeed a nice one, well beaten down. It wound along the contour, passing a number of fine fruit and nut trees.

Then they turned a curve, and discovered three goblins blocking the path ahead.

"Oopsy," Ivy said. "Goblins are never good news. Run the other way!"

They turned and ran back around the curve—and discovered three more ugly goblins. They were trapped.

"They don't look very big," Grey said. "Maybe I could knock them down."

"There are always dozens more goblins near the first," Ivy said darkly. Sure enough, more goblins were already crowding in behind the three. They were squat little men, almost black, with big heads, hands, and feet, and huge grimaces.

"Maybe they're friendly," he suggested hopefully.

"Goblins are never friendly. I'll have to summon help." Ivy brought out her magic mirror. "Castle Roog—"

A goblin leaped forward and grabbed the mirror from her hand. "None of that, slut!"

Grey leaped for the goblin, but it was already too late; the mirror had disappeared amidst the throng. "Don't fight them!" Ivy screamed. "We'll have to talk our way out of this!"

Grey, seeing the throng, desisted; it was obvious to anyone that they could not hope to fight their way clear of such a number.

A goblin chief appeared, distinguished mainly by his greater ugliness. "You're going to *talk* your way out of this, wench?"

"I'm no wench!" Ivy protested. "I'm Princess Ivy!"

"And I'm the king of the dragons!" the goblin retorted. "Har, har, har!" All the goblins joined in the coarse laughter. "Well, I'm Grotesk Goblin, and we're the Goblinate of the

Golden Horde, and we don't care who you are!"

"Well, give me back my mirror, and I'll prove it!" she said.
"My father will recognize me."

"And will send hostile magic against us, if you are," the
goblin said. "We don't need any of that. Better if he just
doesn't know what happens to you." He turned his head to
the side. "Tell the Golden Gals to heat up the pot; we've got
two live ones for supper tonight."

Immediately a messenger goblin set off, running on his
stubby legs down the path. He really wasn't golden; it was
evidently just a name they had chosen.

This was getting desperate. Ivy knew she would not really
get boiled, because of her guarantee of a safe return, but as
usual she feared for Grey, who had no such assurance. How
could she get him free of this Golden Horde?

"And who're you—the king of the centaurs?" Grotesk demanded of Grey.

"Don't answer him!" Ivy warned. But once again she was
too late.

"I am Grey, from Mundania," Grey said.

"A Mundane!" the goblin exclaimed. "We've never cooked
a Mundane before. Do you believe in magic?"

"No."

"Well, now! Maybe we can have some sport with this one!"
The chief turned his head again. "What shall we do with the
Mundane?"

There was a horrible clamor of violent and obscene suggestions. Unsatisfied, Grotesk turned again to Grey. "You're
with the ha-ha princess here. What do you think of her?"

"Don't answer!" Ivy cried.

"Shut up, trollop," the chief said, swinging at her head.

Grey reached out and intercepted Grotesk's arm. "Leave
her alone!"

Immediately several goblins surged in and bore him back,
but the chief was not annoyed. "I think we have our answer,"
he said. "He likes her—and surely she likes him. There's the
key. Before we cook them, let's play with them. Take them
to the hate spring."

There was a roar of approval. Ivy and Grey were hustled on along the goblin path. Ivy was dismayed anew; she knew what mischief a hate spring would be.

They passed the goblin village. There was a bedraggled small centaur, haltered and tied to a stake. These goblins knew no limits. Nobody tied a centaur, lest it bring terrible retribution by centaur archers from Centaur Isle. Yet here was a young male, evidently bound magically, for no halter could hold such a creature otherwise.

They reached the spring a short distance beyond. It was dismal as springs went, shallow and muddy, with a tiny island in the center. The goblins hauled over a boat and put her in it. One got in front, and one in back, with paddles; both were extremely careful not to splash.

"You're afraid even to touch it?" Ivy asked. "Such water doesn't work unless you drink it."

"That's all you know, slattern," Grotesk called from land. "One touch of this anywhere on your body, and you hate the next creature you see to pieces, and will try to kill him any way you can. Go ahead, dip your finger; you already hate us, so it won't matter."

Ivy shivered, not dipping her finger; this was hideously potent stuff. No wonder the goblins had camped near it; they loved to hate.

They deposited her on the tiny isle, then paddled back, leaving her stranded there. Then they hauled away the boat and brought Grey up to the edge. "Very well, Mundane," Grotesk said. "You don't believe in magic? Then you don't think this hate spring will affect you. Go rescue her!"

"Don't touch that water!" Ivy called. "It will make you hate me!"

"Why couldn't I touch it and hate *you?*" Grey asked the chief. "Then I wouldn't hate her."

"Go ahead!" the goblin agreed as the horde laughed. "One touch, one hate; we don't care how much you hate us as we cook you. Maybe you'll even utter some nice Mundane curses to entertain us. But you can't reach your girlfriend without crossing that spring, and when you see her or touch her you'll hate her. So you might as well get on with it."

"What good is it to go to her, if you're going to cook us anyway?" Grey asked. "I might as well just stay here and not cooperate with you at all."

There was a groan from the throng. They didn't like that threat because it ruined their sport.

"Very well, Mundane—if you cross to her, I'll let you go. We'll only eat her."

"Don't deal with him!" Ivy cried. "Goblins can't be trusted!"

"No, I want to rescue her," Grey said, in that infuriatingly reasonable way he had. "You have to let us both go, or I won't cooperate."

Grotesk pondered a moment. Then his eyes lighted cunningly. "Suppose I let you decide her fate, when you get there? You go free and you take her with you if you want."

"Yes, that seems fair," Grey agreed.

"Don't do it!" Ivy screamed. "He'll break his word the moment you're across! And you'll hate me!"

"I don't think so," Grey said. He stepped toward the pool.

"No!" Ivy cried despairingly. "No, no, no!" It was crazy, if Grey was going to die anyway, but she didn't want him to die hating her.

Grey waded into the water. A jubilant cheer rose from the Golden Horde. His eyes were fixed on Ivy as he proceeded, the water rising gradually to his waist as he crossed.

Ivy stood, transfixed by horror. A man who hated her was coming for her, and she could not get away without touching the water herself. She discovered that there was one thing worse than having him hate her: for her to hate him back. She had to try to salvage her own emotion, so as to remember him with pleasure instead of displeasure.

He strode out of the water, his trousers clinging to his legs. He came to stand before her, his eyes still fixed on hers. Ivy knew her tears were flowing. She had seen the need to break up their association—but not this way, oh not with hatred!

"I want you to know, Grey," she said falteringly, "that, that whatever you feel for me now, I still think you're wonderful. Do you hate me very much?"

"Hate you?" he said, bewildered. "Ivy, I *love* you!"

She stared at him. "You—you're not cruelly teasing me?"

For answer he swept her into his arms and kissed her, hard. Suddenly she could not doubt: this was the passion of love.

Then she realized that the cruelty was that of the goblins. This wasn't a hate spring at all, it was just a muddy pond! The Golden Horde was trying to make complete fools of them both!

And that meant that she was not stranded here. She could cross the pond just as Grey had. She could escape—and take Grey with her, protecting him with her security.

"Oh, Grey," she said. "I'm so glad! Hold my hand tight; we're getting out of here!"

"Of course," he agreed.

But it wasn't enough. Her emotion was overflowing and demanded a more significant expression.

"Grey, will you marry me?" she asked.

He paused, amazed. Then he recovered. "Yes, certainly, Ivy. But—"

She cut off his protest with another kiss.

8
GAP

Then he released her. Even though the water wasn't poisonous, those goblins were mean characters, and the two of them still had a problem about winning free. He was not at all sure the goblin chief would honor his promise to release them, but he hoped to shame the little man into it.

But it was hard to concentrate on such things in the face of what had just happened. Ivy had asked him to marry her—and he had agreed. What an incongruous occasion for such an engagement.

"We're not out of this yet," Ivy said. "I've got to get my mirror back. Then I can call for help. If you can think of a way to get it for me—"

"Maybe I can," he said, his mind spinning. It was as if what had just happened between them had revved up his brain so that he was thinking with uncommon clarity and power. "The hate water isn't real, but it occurs to me that most of the goblins may believe it is. The chief would know the truth, but keep the unruly minions cowed by threats to use the water on them. That means we can bluff them."

"But in a moment they will see that you don't hate me!" Ivy said worriedly. "Then they'll all know."

"I don't think so. If I claim to have powerful magic that makes me immune——"

"But Grotesk will know that's not true!"

"But he won't dare say so, because then his hold on the others will be weakened. He will have to support me, though he hates it. So I can force him to honor his deal, because he'd rather let us go than lose his position and maybe get thrown in the pot himself by the angry dupes."

Ivy's face clouded, then brightened as she understood. "Grey, that's brilliant!" she exclaimed.

"Something about you that brings out the best in me," he said wryly. Indeed, that seemed to be true. He had never been in love before; this episode had brought it out, and he seemed almost to be floating. Suddenly he had confidence in himself such as he had never had before. "While we're at it, we'd better rescue that poor centaur, too; it will be bad if they take out their wrath on him."

"You care so much about others who are in trouble, like Girard Giant," Ivy said. "I think that's why I love you."

He hadn't thought of it that way. He had just done what he felt ought to be done, without thought about whether it impressed her. In fact, she had seemed irritated when he insisted on seeking the source of the river of blood. Maybe that was what had been wrong with his life before: he had been trying to impress people, and had had inadequate resources, instead of just focusing on what was right. But now, with Ivy, he didn't care about any of that; he just wanted to make her happy.

Then he thought of something else. "But can I justify telling them something I know is not true? I mean——"

"You're playing their game," Ivy said quickly. "They told you this was a hate spring. So you agree, but tell them your magic counters it. You're a liar only if they are."

He wasn't quite sure of that logic. Still, this whole realm was a setting, a phenomenal setting, and it was easiest to go along with its rules. That's why he referred to goblins instead of dwarves or simulacra, and to the centaur instead of trying to figure out how the thing was animated. "Okay, for now, until I reason it out better. Take my hand; my supposed magic must seem to extend to you while you are in contact with me, so you can brave the bad water."

She took his hand. Hand in hand they waded into the water. "See, goblins!" he cried. "My magic counters your hate water! I can wade in it without hating anyone—even you!"

The goblins watched, dismayed. They looked to their chief, but Grey preempted Grotesk's response. "You know that's true, don't you, chief!" he cried, playing up to the lie. "You know that if this water touches others, they will be affected by it." He extended his free hand and made as if to scoop some water. "If I splash them—"

"Don't do that!" the goblin chief exclaimed with evident alarm.

Grey put on his cruelest smile, hoping it worked. He had guessed right: Grotesk had to support him in this ruse! "Yes, you know what will happen! So don't tempt me, sour-snoot!"

The chief didn't tempt him. The goblin had to maintain the illusion of the water's power. "You said you were Mundane!"

"Well, maybe I exaggerated," Grey said. Mundanes, of course, were not supposed to have magic. But Grotesk could not point that out, without giving away his own secret.

They waded up to the edge, but did not step out of the water. "Now before we go, I want you to return the lady's property," Grey said. "Bring her mirror."

"Har, har, har!" a goblin in the rear laughed. "Fat chance!"

Grey leaned down so that his hand was within reach of the water. "If the goblin who spoke cares to step forward, I have something for him," he said evenly. The truth was he was quite nervous; how far could he push this bluff before the goblins called it?

There was a silence. Grey looked around as if perplexed. "What, is no one in the Golden Horde thirsty?" he inquired. "Well, perhaps if I proffer a free sample—" He swished his hand through the water.

"Bring the mirror!" Grotesk shouted.

There was a stir, and soon a goblin brought the mirror. "Don't splash!" he pleaded.

"I won't splash if I get what I want," Grey said. "Ivy, take the mirror, but don't let go of my hand. I can't protect you if you aren't in contact."

"Yes," Ivy said, doing a marvelous job of looking very nervous about the water; she clung tightly to his hand. She reached forward; the goblin stood at the bank and extended the mirror, and she took it while the chief glowered.

"Now we shall need transportation away from here," Grey said. "Bring the centaur."

But Grotesk had just figured out a cunning counterploy. "Back away from the water!" he cried. "Get out of splashing range!"

Uh-oh. That would allow the chief to keep his secret, and grab them when they left the pool. "Ivy, do you have a cup?"

Ivy reached over her shoulder, set the mirror in her backpack, and pulled out a cup.

"Dip it full, and throw water at anyone who looks troublesome," Grey said.

She dipped it. Then they stepped out of the water, still holding hands. The goblins retreated. Grey saw that a number of them held stones or clubs, but no one acted because the chief hadn't told them to. Grotesk couldn't afford to act until that cup of water was gone—and he couldn't afford to have them throw it on any goblins and demonstrate its worthlessness.

They walked across to the centaur. "Can you carry both of us, if we free you?" Grey inquired.

"I think so," the creature replied. "I've been a beast of burden for these monsters; I'm miserable but strong. But this is a magic halter; only the chief can untie it."

"The chief, eh?" Grey glanced across at Grotesk and realized that this was another bluff. "Well, I have a special talent with knots, too, so—"

"No, Grey," Ivy murmured. "No one in Xanth has two magic talents."

Grey was sure the halter wasn't magic; it was just so constructed that the centaur's own hands could not reach the key clasps to undo it. But he had to play by the rules. "Well, maybe my magic knife will cut it," he said loudly.

He brought out his knife and sliced at the tough material of the halter. Fortunately, he kept his knife sharp; the strands parted. Some fevered sawing severed the section under the centaur's arm. "Now it is broken; you can lift it free," he said.

The centaur did just that. In a moment the halter was off. "That's some knife!" he exclaimed. "I got a sharp-edged stone once and managed to saw at it without being observed, but the magic was too strong, and I got nowhere."

"Now we shall ride you out of here," Grey said. "The water will not affect you as long as you are in contact with me, so don't be concerned if it splashes out of the cup." That was literally true: the water would not affect the centaur while in contact—or at any other time. "She will fling it at any goblin who comes too close. Are you ready?"

The centaur glanced nervously at the cup. "Yes," he said uncertainly.

It was tricky mounting without letting go of Ivy's hand, and for the sake of appearances he had to keep holding it. But the centaur reached back and helped her up, and then Grey got up behind her.

"Start walking," Grey said. "Slowly, so as not to make them do anything foolish, until we get away from this camp."

"Gotcha," the centaur said. He stepped carefully forward.

"I'm sure you can run very fast when you need to," Ivy remarked.

But goblins closed in across the path, lead by a subchief. "I think it's a fake!" the subchief cried. "That water's lost its hate!"

Ivy flung the water at the subchief. The goblin tried to leap back, but the water caught him and also splashed across several others near him.

The first thing the wetted goblins saw was the ugly faces of their companions. For an instant they stared. Then they exploded into violence. The subchief swung his club at the one he faced, and two others fell to pummeling each other.

"Let's get out of here!" Grey said.

"You can do it!" Ivy cried to the centaur. "You're super-strong and fast!"

The centaur needed no urging. He leaped over the nearest goblins and shot off down the path. The goblin fight was spreading, and none of the nearest ones were chasing the centaur. But the more distant ones raised a cry of alarm. "Get them! They're escaping!"

But it was too late. Even doubly loaded, the centaur could run faster than the stubby-legged goblins, especially on the well-beaten path. A few stones flew, but missed. They had made it to freedom.

Well away from the goblin camp, they left the path. "We had better find a river and wash off the hate water on your legs," the centaur said. "Otherwise it will affect the two of us the moment you stop touching us."

"Not to worry," Grey said. "It's not magic water; that was Grotesk's bluff."

"But it *is*," the centaur insisted. "It made those goblins fight the moment it touched them!"

"That was psychological. They believed it would affect them that way, so it did."

"Well, I believe in it!" the centaur said. "I saw it work more than once, when the chief wanted to discipline someone. I want it all off me before you get off me."

Grey shrugged. It made sense for a magical creature to believe in magic. "Do you know where a suitable river is?"

"Yes, there's a stream not far from here. It flows into the Gap."

"The Gap!" Ivy exclaimed. "We're going there!"

"But it's dangerous!" the centaur protested. "The Gap Dragon runs there!"

"We'd better introduce ourselves," Ivy said. "I'm Princess Ivy of Castle Roogna."

"Really?" the centaur asked, amazed. "I have heard of you. You enhance folk."

"Yes. I helped you run faster and stronger."

"You did indeed! I have never done so well before, even without a double load. I thought I was just scared! I am called Donkey."

"What?" Grey asked.

"Because I'm small and gray, and have big ears," he explained. "The others always teased me, so I preferred to go out on my own. But then the goblins caught me, and I had no friends to realize I was missing. Thank you so much for rescuing me!"

"I'm Grey," Grey said. "Not the color, just the name. I'm from Mundania."

"But then how can you do magic?"

"I can't. It was all a bluff. That's why I knew the water wouldn't hurt you."

Donkey considered. "All the same, I'd prefer to wash it all off. Just to be quite sure. Centaurs don't like to take avoidable chances."

So they went to the stream. Donkey walked carefully to the center, then slowly settled down. "Wash it all off before we separate," the centaur said. "We wouldn't want to hate each other."

Ivy giggled. "I never took a bath with my clothes on before!"

"Me neither," Grey agreed.

They splashed water on themselves, remaining in contact with Donkey, letting the current carry away the bad medicine.

There was a stir in the water downstream. "See, the fish are fighting," Donkey said. "It's still potent!"

"Coincidence," Grey said. But he wondered. There had been a number of funny events recently, and not all were easy to accept.

For one thing, the way those goblins had fought—when the subchief had expressed his disbelief in the power of the water. Why, then, had it affected him? Had his disbelief been a bluff? Or had he decided to support the supposed power of the water, the way Grotesk did? Or had he wanted the captives to escape? None of that seemed to make much sense.

And the centaur: now that they were relaxing, Grey was studying the creature. He found no artificial connection between the man and horse aspects. Donkey seemed to be exactly what he claimed to be: a living centaur. The river was not shorting out his circuits. His body was warm. Part of him was definitely human and part definitely animal. How could this be, without magic?

"We'd better get undressed so we can rinse out our clothing thoroughly, then hang it up to dry," Ivy said. "It is overdue for a washing anyway."

"But—" Grey protested.

"It's all right," she said. "We're betrothed."

"But—"

"And centaurs never wear any clothing anyway," she continued. "They don't have any concerns about people." She unbuttoned her blouse and drew it off.

Grey didn't argue further. She was right: they did have to get washed and hang up their clothing to dry. They were engaged to be married. It had happened so suddenly that he still could hardly believe it, but he was not going to deny it. He didn't care what kind of setting this was or whether magic was real, it was wonderful being with her.

Soon they were bathing separately, Ivy and Donkey at last satisfied that the hate water had been washed clear by the pure stream water. The day was late, now, but they hung up their clothing to catch the declining rays of sunshine. Then he and Ivy sat on a clean patch of grass and let the sun dry them, too. Donkey didn't need to sit; he stood in a separate sunbeam, after shaking his body violently.

Grey tried not to look at Ivy's bare body, but didn't want to be too obvious about not looking, lest she think she was ugly. She wasn't; in fact she was his very model of a teenaged girl.

"Are you sorry?" she inquired.

"Huh?"

"About being betrothed to me?"

"Oh no!" he exclaimed. "I—it's more than I ever hoped for! I—when you—when I woke before you under the tangle tree and saw you sleeping, I just had to keep looking at you, because as wonderful as all this crazy land may be, you are the craziest and most wonderful thing that ever happened to me, and I wish it would never end. I mean—I don't know what I mean, but—"

"You know there is trouble ahead," she reminded him. "I was resolved to let you go, no matter how much I liked you, because I knew we couldn't marry. But when you came for me through that water and didn't hate me, suddenly I didn't care anymore what my folks think. My little brother's got two betrotheds; I'm entitled to one, I think. But you have to be willing."

"I'm willing! I just never thought that you'd—I mean that you were serious—I mean—"

"You don't know what you mean," she repeated for him. "Are you beginning to believe in magic, a little?"

He looked at the centaur, and still could not explain him away. "If loving you is believing in magic, then I believe," he said.

She smiled. "I think I have never had a better compliment!"

"I am amazed that you profess to disbelieve in magic," Donkey said. "We centaurs try to maintain a certain diffidence about it, but there is absolutely no doubt of its validity. Haven't you felt Ivy's Enhancement yourself?"

Grey considered. "I suppose I have, but—"

"You are too full of buts," Ivy said. "Shut up, or I'll kiss you."

"But—"

She leaned over and kissed him.

Grey shut up.

In the morning they discussed the matter, and decided to travel together down the river to the Gap Chasm. Donkey knew the way, and the location of the best trees along it, while Ivy knew the Gap Dragon, so that they could enter the chasm safely. None of them cared to remain in the vicinity of the Goblinate of the Golden Horde, for the goblins were surely out looking for them and would not treat them kindly. They agreed that it was best to get on the other side of the Gap with reasonable dispatch.

Grey had read of the Gap and the Gap-Dragon, but reserved his belief in such things until he actually saw them. A trench across the state of Florida a mile or so deep? As he understood it, there wasn't any part of that state anywhere near that elevation above sea level, so such a chasm would be impossible even if it were possible. With a great whomping, steaming, ferocious dragon running along the bottom? More likely it was a railroad cut with an old-fashioned steam engine chugging along on its track.

Some chocolate milkweed pods grew along the river, and some mushrooms, which turned out to be little rooms full of mush. Some were cornmeal mush, and some were oat mush or wheat mush. They didn't taste like much, but the chocolate milk provided a bit of flavor. At least they were filling.

"How do you like it?" Ivy asked.

He could tell by the sparkle in her eyes that she was up to some mischief, so he answered cautiously. "Mushy stuff was never my favorite."

"That's what my little brother always said—until he met Nada."

"Nada?"

"Nada Naga, his betrothed—I told you. But she cured him in a hurry, and now he loves mush."

"I could use that cure myself," he muttered, still not seeing her point. "How did she—?"

"I thought you'd never ask!" She stepped to him, wrapped her arms around him, and kissed him so emphatically that his head seemed to float.

"But—" he said when she gave him a chance to breathe.

"Mushy stuff," she explained.

Oh. Grey felt completely stupid; he had walked right into that one. Yet somehow he wasn't bothered; it was about as nice an experience as he could imagine.

"Did I embarrass you?" she asked.

"Uh, no, of course not!" he protested immediately.

She glanced at Donkey. "I'm not sure. What do you think?"

"He's flushing and perhaps stammering," the centaur said. "I believe it is likely that you did embarrass him, though he is attempting to deny it."

"That's what I thought." Ivy faced Grey again. "The brassies know how to handle that."

"The brassies?" Grey tried to remember what the brass folk had done in the books he had read.

"They apologize," she said. "Do you know how they apologize?"

"Uh, no, I—"

She hauled him in again and kissed him with even more authority than before. This time his head seemed not only to rise, but also to swell to the size of a helium weather balloon and float across the landscape, buffeted by stray playful breezes.

From somewhere far away her voice came: "Do you accept my apology?"

He tried to get back to earth. "Uh—"

Then Donkey's voice: "Evidently the apology was not sufficient. He seems frozen in place."

Ivy's voice, again: "True. I will simply have to make a better apology."

Then she kissed him a third time. His head heated and expanded so rapidly it exploded, and bright fragments of the balloon fluttered down into the forest below to decorate the trees with seeming flowers. Bees buzzed up to attend to those flowers, and came away with buckets of nectar. Oh, the sweetness of that kiss!

"Do you accept my apology?" Ivy asked again.

Grey strove valiantly to get his head back together. "Uh, yes, sure!" he gasped, finally catching on. He wasn't sure he could survive the next kiss.

"Alert!" Donkey said. "I hear goblins!"

Suddenly Grey was back in focus. "Let's get out of here!"

"We'd better do it as we did before," Ivy said briskly. "I'll enhance you, Donkey, and we'll ride you. That way we'll leave them behind again."

"Certainly," the centaur agreed.

Ivy scrambled into her pack, and they both scrambled onto the centaur's back, and the centaur took off with a terrific leap just as a goblin burst into view.

"Tallyho!" the goblin cried, and blew on a horn he carried, alerting the others. The sound was amazingly loud and vulgar.

"I hate those stink horns," Ivy said as they raced through the light foliage beside the stream.

The centaur was proceeding vigorously, psychologically buoyed by Ivy's supposed Enhancement. But the stream was extremely winding and clogged with rocks and brush, so full speed was impossible. The goblins were running along the ground on either side, evidently small enough to duck under the worst of the obstructions, so were not falling behind fast enough. "We've out to get well ahead before we reach the Gap," Ivy said.

"Why, if you know the Gap Dragon?" Grey asked.

"Well, for one thing Stanley isn't likely to be right there when we arrive. For another—"

"Oops, we're here!" Donkey said, skidding to a halt as the landscape opened out ahead of them.

"Rats!" Ivy swore. "The gobs are too close!"

"I'll run along the edge," the centaur said, turning abruptly. "I believe there's a passable descent not far to the east."

Now Grey got his first clear look at the Gap. Suddenly he felt dizzy. It was a sheer drop-off hundreds, no thousands of feet down to a bottom shrouded in fog. The morning sunbeams cut sharply across the cliffs of it, looking like sparkling ramps to the depths. The stream plunged over the edge and plummeted so far that there was no sound of its landing. No wonder they needed time to find a safe way into it.

"Somehow I don't think we're in Florida any more, Toto," he murmured, awed. How could he explain *this* in terms of the close-to-sea-level terrain they had ridden through on the way to No Name Key?

"What?" Ivy asked over the wind of their motio that terrifying descent. Her greenish hair was flu in his face.

"The ramparts of my disbelief have just taken a hit," he explained.

"It's about time!"

The goblins burst into view again, trying to cut them off. But Donkey made a phenomenal leap and sailed over their heads, and landed running. Again they were left behind. But they did not give up; they charged along the brink of the great chasm, waving their clubs and throwing their rocks, which were missing by a less-than-comfortable margin.

"There it is!" Donkey cried, drawing up before a narrow side crack that extended from the major Gap.

Grey looked. There was a little path that crept down from the crack and found some rubble at the edge of the main chasm. It did seem to wind on down, but they would have to go single file, and slowly. The goblins would be upon them long before they could complete any part of that tortuous descent.

"There's a great multiflavor pie tree," Ivy said. "I'll enhance it, and hold them off with pies while you two get down."

"*I'll* hold them off," Grey said.

"But you don't believe in the magic!" she protested. "Those are crabapple pies, pepperpot pies—they can be really effective, if I—"

"I believe in you," Grey said firmly. "And I'm beginning to wonder about magic. Now just get out of here. If I can't make a stand to defend the woman I love, what good am I?"

She looked ready to argue, but the centaur spoke. "He's right. He can do it. You go down first."

Ivy made her decision. "No, you go first, Donkey. I'll follow right after I've enhanced that tree."

Without further word the centaur started down the path. Sand and pebbles skidded out under his hooves and slid down the cliffside, but the path held.

Ivy ran to the tree and flung her arms about its trunk. Grey rubbed his eyes; he could have sworn the pies were growing, becoming larger and better defined in seconds.

Ivy stepped clear. "Follow as soon as you can," she

said. "I'll fetch Stanley, so if you're in doubt, just keep throwing pies at them." She kissed him fleetingly. "I'm enhancing your strength, aim, and endurance. Believe in me!" Then she was gone, into the crack.

Believe in her? When she put it that way, he had to.

The goblins were already appearing. Grey looked at the tree. Now his eyes seemed much more finely attuned; he recognized every variety of pie. He grabbed a pepperpot pie whose peppers looked huge.

The first goblin charged up, waving his club. "I'll destroy ya, creep!" the goblin yelled.

Grey calmly threw the pie in his face. The peppers puffed into powder. The goblin broke into a spasm of sneezing. He sneezed so hard that his little body flew backwards into the goblin behind him, and a cloud of pepper surrounded them both. Soon several goblins were sneezing—and several sneezed themselves right off the brink of the precipice.

Well, now! This seemed to work well enough. The goblins seemed to have used up all their stones, and there were none nearby for them to pick up. That meant that they were confined to their clubs, which meant they had to get close to be effective. Which meant in turn that he could score on a goblin with a pie before a goblin could score with a club. There were about thirty goblins, but the approach was narrow, so that only one could come at him at a time.

He felt like Horatius at the bridge: the bold Roman gate-keeper who had held off the attacking Etruscan army while the Romans chopped down the bridge that was the only access to the city. One man could indeed hold off an army—if the army had to send just one man against him at a time, and he was able to slay that man. But he had to be good.

Ivy's Enhancement really seemed to have taken, because he felt phenomenally good. His aim with the first pie had been perfect, and he felt strength to heave them much farther if he needed to. He felt like a superman. Maybe it was the power of love. Goblins, beware!

The goblins completed their sneezing; the cloud of p~ had finally dissipated. That one pie seemed to have ~

about three of them. Maybe it wasn't magic, but it had worked well enough.

A goblin charged him, club lifted. Grey quickly plucked a crabapple pie, chose his moment, and hurled it with uncanny accuracy at the little brute. It smote the nasty little man right in the face, and the apple fell away—except for a crab pincer that had fastened on the goblin's ugly nose.

"*Youff!*" the goblin cried, spinning around and banging into the one behind him.

"You sure are crabby!" the other retorted.

"I'll crab *you*," the first exclaimed. He ripped the pincer off his nose and thrust it at the other's eye. The pincer snapped at the eyeball.

"Oh, yeah?" the second exclaimed, swinging at the first with his club.

There was a melee, in the course of which three more goblins fell off the edge.

Another goblin charged Grey. Grey plucked a popcorn pie and hurled it, again with stunning accuracy. He was amazed at himself; he had never been a hurler like this! If it wasn't Ivy's Enhancement, what else could account for it?

The pie struck the goblin on the chest, and the popcorn popped like a series of tiny firecrackers. Bits of puffed corn flew into his face and beyond him into the faces of the ones following. Yet another spot quarrel broke out, as one goblin blamed his neighbor for the corn and swung his club. Two more goblins fell off the ledge.

Grey discovered that he liked this type of combat. It was mainly the goblins' own orneriness that got them boosted into the chasm. If they just quit coming, no more would be hurt. He had plenty of pies remaining.

Another goblin charged. Grey picked a pecan pie. Once more his aim and force were uncanny; he scored on the goblin's big head before the creature got at all close. The pie crust clanged like a can, and its contents soaked the goblin with yellow juice. "Oooo, ugh!" the goblin cried, outraged. "You peed on me!"

So that was the magic of the pecan! He had assumed it

was a nut pie. Well, he had been wrong. He was glad he hadn't tried to eat it.

Other goblins charged in turn. He picked other pies and shoved them in their faces, long distance. He should have been tired by this time, but he wasn't; his strength was maintaining just as had that of the centaur. He hurled a shoe-fly pie, and its shoe kicked the rear of a goblin and booted the goblin over the edge. He threw a papaya pie, and it sang "I'm papaya the sailor man!" and whistled as it slugged the goblin.

At last he was down to two pies, having used all the rest. Three goblins remained. He knew he couldn't afford to let even one remain above while he descended the path, because that one could scuff the sand and perhaps start a little avalanche that would destroy his route. How could he be sure of taking out three with only two pies?

Well, he would just have to go hand to hand with the last one. He glanced at the pies: one was custard, the other pineapple. Neither looked promising, but they would have to do.

He picked the custard. "Custard's last stand!" he cried as he heaved it at the charging goblin.

The custard struck squarely on the ugly face. The gloppy stuff wrapped itself around the bulbous head and clung tenaciously. The goblin pawed at it, trying to get his eyes clear, but before he succeeded he stepped off the cliff and was gone. Only the fading sound of his cussing remained. Well, it *was* a cuss-tard pie.

The last two goblins consisted of the subchief, who had tried to stop them before, and one henchman. "Charge him together, and one of us will get him!" he said.

"But there's no room!"

"Yes, there is, if we charge slowly and carefully and keep in step." And indeed there was, this way, for the narrow ledge had been widened by the tramp of the prior goblins' big feet. The two approached carefully.

Grey was worried. The enemy had finally gotten smart. He had only the one pie left, and while he could score on one goblin, the other would be able to charge him from close range and perhaps sweep him off the ledge in the manner of a football blocker. These goblins didn't seem to care what losses they took, as long as they got him.

Well, he would just have to use what he had. He picked the pineapple pie and hefted it. He would throw it at the subchief, who was surely the more cunning and motivated of the two. Then he would handle the other in whatever way he could.

"Watch out—that's a pineapple!" the subchief cried.

Both goblins halted. Then they started backing away.

Grey was surprised. Was this a ruse? Were they pretending fear, so that he would relax and then they would turn on him and catch him off guard? He resolved not to be drawn out of position.

The two goblins retreated all the way back out of sight. This was curious indeed! What were they up to? He didn't dare try to follow them—but if he started down the path, they could return at any moment and wreak mischief on his head.

Maybe he could fake them out. He got down on the path, then squatted, so that he could duck down into the small crevice. They would think he had started down when he hadn't; then when they came, he could smite one of them with the pie.

He waited. Sure enough, soon he heard them returning. He waited until they sounded close enough, then stood up, pie ready.

The two goblins were there—but so was another creature. It looked like a male sheep with horrendously broad and curled horns.

The subchief spied him. "So it was a trick, Mundane! You can't fool a cunning goblin. And your pie can't stop this battering ram!"

The sheep charged, head down. A battering ram! That certainly could knock him off the edge.

Grey, poised with the pie, decided to ditch it. Maybe the ram would hurtle right past him if he ducked at the last moment.

He hurled the pie over the head of the ram, at the two waiting goblins. It struck the subchief—and detonated. Juice

and pineapple bits exploded outward, and both goblins were
blown off the edge.

So that was the pun in pineapple. It was made of grenades.
He should have guessed. No wonder the goblins had been so
wary of it.

But his distraction caused him to wait too long. The battering ram was almost upon him, unstoppable, and he had no
time to dodge it.

"No!" he cried. "It can't end like this!"

The ram set his hooves and skidded to a stop just as he
reached Grey. He was so close that his nose nudged Grey's
nose.

"Why, you're just an ordinary sheep," Grey said, petting
the animal. "You don't mean me any harm, now that the
goblins are gone. Why don't you go off and graze?"

The ram nodded almost as if he understood, and com-
menced browsing on the adjacent foliage. No battering ram
at all.

Now at last it was safe to start down the path. Grey proceeded.

It turned out to be a tricky descent, but manageable. He
saw the centaur's hoofprints, and now and then Ivy's, so
would have known he was on the right trail, had there been
any doubt. The face of the cliff was awesome, but the path
was secure, and he did not feel the fright of heights he might
have.

He wondered about that. He felt better, and had done better
than he ever would have expected. He had been cool and
poised throughout, and handled the goblins almost perfectly.
Ivy had said she would enhance him, and he did seem enhanced—but could his love for her account for it? And those
pies—they had acted in ways real pies never would have.
Science would be strained to account for those effects, but
magic had no problem. As for that centaur—how could anything but magic account for him? There was such a thing as
gene splicing, but it didn't work that way; a man could not
be grafted onto a horse. Not in this century.

And of course there was the Gap Chasm he was now climbing down into. He could not doubt its reality! But how could he have come to it in the real world? If this were a mere amusement park setting, how could there be anything of this sheer scale?

Was he coming to believe in magic after all? Maybe he was, because Ivy did, and he did love her. If she loved him enough to marry him, he should love her enough to share her belief. Maybe that didn't make much objective sense, but it made a lot of emotional sense.

At last he made it down to the base of the chasm, as afternoon was setting in. Where had Ivy and Donkey gone? He knew the answer: Ivy had mounted Donkey, enhanced him, and he had galloped off indefatigably to locate the Gap Dragon. It might be a while before they found that creature.

He looked around. The bottom of the chasm was like a long, narrow valley, with green grass and a river crossing it, from the stream they had followed above. He walked to it and threw himself down for a drink. Beside it grew some lady slipper plants, with an assortment of delicate feminine slippers. Farther along was a potato chip bush. Good—he was hungry, too. He sat down beside it and started picking and eating the chips.

Magic? If this was magical, yes, he believed in magic.

Now at last he was tired. Whatever reserve of strength he had drawn on was gone, and he needed to rest. He leaned against a stone and relaxed.

His eye traced the short course of the river across the valley cleft. It did not turn to run along the valley, but continued on up the far cliff in a reverse waterfall, finally disappearing over the top. That was nice; no sense in flooding the Gap, in case there was no decent exit for the water.

His eyes closed. He hoped Ivy and Donkey returned soon. Certainly it was pointless to go looking for them; he had to wait right here where they could find him.

Up the cliff? Suddenly he blinked awake, looking again across the valley. Then he lurched to his feet and followed the river across.

There was no doubt: the water made a right-angle turn and

sailed upwards in a geyser. It did not fall back to earth as a real geyser would; rather it seemed to slow as it neared the top, and to curve, finding the brink and going beyond it.

Grey shook his head. Now it was clear: he had *better* believe in magic! Otherwise he would believe he was crazy.

He returned to the rock near the potato chip bush and settled down again. In a moment he was deep in a snooze.

He woke to the sound of a series of thuds that shook the ground. *Whomp, whomp, WHOMP!* He jumped up, alarmed; he didn't like the sound of that.

Something was definitely coming in the dusk. He saw steam blowing upward in gusts. That must be the Gap Dragon—but where was Ivy?

Then Donkey galloped up. "Here he is!" the centaur cried, spying Grey.

Immediately the dragon veered. It had a horrendous big head from which the steam puffed regularly, and a long supple torso—and there, riding the top of one arcing coil, was Ivy!

The dragon slowed as it came up. Ivy dismounted and ran across to Grey. "You made it!" she cried as she tackled him in a breath-knocking hug. "I was so worried!"

"Uh, nothing to it," Grey said. "I mean, after you enhanced those pies for me, and enhanced me too, so I could handle all those goblins—"

She looked at him, her face shining. "You mean you believe?"

"I guess I do, now. I mean, after what I've seen—"

She kissed him passionately. "Oh, wonderful!" she exclaimed between kisses. "Now it's perfect!"

Then she introduced him to the dragon: "This is Stanley Steamer, the Gap Dragon," she said, hugging the dragon's horrendous head. The steam stopped for a moment; the dragon was evidently holding his breath so as not to burn her. "And Stanley, this is Grey Murphy, my betrothed." The dragon acknowledged with a twin jet of steam through his nostrils; it seemed that any friend of Ivy's was a friend of his. This was just as well, because he had a huge mouthful of teeth, and great claws on every one of his six feet. This was certainly no creature to run afoul of.

Then they settled down for the night, because the darkness was closing. The top of the chasm walls remained bright, but the shadow started below. The dragon curled around them, and the three piled pillows Ivy found and lay in the center. It was very nice.

"Yes, the river does flow uphill, here," Ivy explained in the morning. "It's the only way it can get out of the Gap. There's another, larger river further east that goes the opposite way. We could ride one of them up, but that really isn't safe. So we'll just have to take the tedious footpath up, near the invisible bridge."

"Invisible bridge?"

She smiled. "I'll show it to you, when we get there. In fact, we'll cross the Gap on it, because the path up is really better on the north side. Then we'll be on the enchanted path, and on our way to Castle Roogna." But then she sobered abruptly, looking pensive.

"Is something wrong?" Grey asked.

"Nothing that hasn't been wrong from the outset," she said enigmatically. "Don't concern yourself about it." Then she smiled and kissed him, and his attempted concern was dissipated before he could express it.

It did not take long to get to their Gap exit, for Grey rode Donkey and Ivy rode the dragon. "See—here it is!" Ivy said, pointing upward. "The bridge!"

Grey looked. There was nothing there. But of course it was supposed to be invisible, so that made sense—he hoped.

They dismounted. Ivy hugged the dragon farewell. It was evident that there was a deep and abiding friendship between this damsel and this dragon. Grey almost felt jealous of it. He had come so recently on the scene, while they had been friends, Ivy said, since she was three: fourteen years!

Then they climbed the path up the side. It was a better path than the other, and it was possible for them to walk side by side in sections of it. Still, it was a long, wearing climb. This must be a lot like the Grand Canyon.

"Tired?" Ivy asked, and he had to admit he was.

"Not anymore," she said, squeezing his arm. And, indeed, he felt new strength. Her Enhancement really did work! It was easy to appreciate it, now that he believed.

They reached the top, and Ivy led the way to the bridge. Suddenly she stepped into the air above the chasm. Grey cried out in alarm, then saw she was standing, not falling. There really was a bridge there.

Grey and Donkey followed her. The bridge had handrails and was quite secure. When he shut his eyes, Grey was quite satisfied with its solidity. Only when he opened his eyes and looked down, down, way far down, did he get dizzy. So he focused on Ivy, no uncomfortable task, and walked on across without looking down again.

At the far side Ivy turned back to wave to Stanley, far below. The dragon responded with a great puff of steam. Then it was time to follow the magic path to Castle Roogna.

9

ULTIMATUM

They walked along the familiar enchanted path. Within a day they would reach Castle Roogna, especially if she enhanced Donkey again so he could carry them swiftly. But Ivy intended to spend one more night on the road, because she was afraid of what would happen when they arrived.

She saw that Grey and Donkey were tiring, and that was natural. She had enhanced them before so that Donkey could carry them rapidly and Grey could fight off the goblins, but that had to be followed by a period of rest, and they hadn't had enough.

"There's a nice coven-tree near here," she said brightly. "Let's camp for the night."

The two were happy to agree. Perhaps they had their own doubts about the encounter at Castle Roogna.

The coven-tree was off the enchanted path, but was itself enchanted to be safe for travelers, and it served as a way station. Indeed, it served as a place of exile for those out of favor with Queen Irene; they had to remain there until she suffered a change of heart, which might not occur swiftly. Ivy had spent more than one night here when she pushed her luck too far, and Dolph had often been sent here for trying to peek into Nada's room at night. He would change into something small, like a spider, and try to crawl through a crack, hoping to catch her in panties. The truth was that he had seen her without her clothing often enough before she ever came to Castle Roogna, but now she was a Guest of the Estate, and he was Underage, so the sight of her panties was forbidden. Ivy thought the whole business was funny, but her mother took it more seriously.

The tree was enormous, with a huge spreading top that was watertight, and large curling branches that made excellent supports for pillows. The temperature within its environment was fairly constant; it cooled some at night and warmed some by day, but not as much as the outside forest did. There were numerous fruit and nut trees nearby, and edible plants such as sugar beets and honey suckles. It was an excellent place to camp, when a person wasn't sent here as punishment.

They foraged for supper, then harvested some pillows and went to niches in the separate branches. No branch was large enough for two people to use together, unfortunately, but they were very comfortable for single occupancies. By unvoiced common consent they did not talk about the morrow; it would come too soon.

So it was, on that soon morrow, they arrived in nervously good order at Castle Roogna. Grey and Donkey were rested and clean, and Ivy had brushed out her hair with a bottlebrush from a bush as well as she could. Now what was to happen would happen.

They were expected, of course. Ivy knew that her little brother would have been tracking her via the Tapestry, once she entered Xanth proper. It might have taken him a while to locate her, because she had been out of Xanth for so long, and he would not have known exactly where to look, but probably within a day or so he had found her. Had they not succeeded in getting clear of the goblins on their own, help would have come.

Why hadn't her parents sent out a party to fetch her in sooner? Ivy knew why: because they had seen her with Grey and wanted to study the situation. She had been aware that someone was probably watching when she teased Grey and kissed him so ardently; she wanted them to have no doubt about the nature of her relationship with Grey.

This was in fact her first truly major act of defiance of her parents: taking up with a Mundane. It was bound to send shock waves of scandal reverberating throughout Castle Roogna and the length and breadth of Xanth. Of all the mischief she might have gotten into, this was just about the most treacherous. The Princess and the Mundane! This was going to be no fun session coming up.

Dolph came out to meet them at the bridge over the moat. He was excruciatingly neatly dressed, and his hair was freshly combed: a thing seldom seen. "I am glad to discover you safe, Ivy," he said formally.

"Thank you, Dolph," she said as formally. She turned to her companions. "This is Donkey Centaur, who helped me escape a problem with goblins. And this is Grey, my betrothed."

"I am so happy to meet you both," Dolph said, extending his hand to each in turn. Then he leaned close to Ivy. "Whew! You really did it this time, dummy!" he said confidentially. "Mom's fuming! If you thought I was in hot water when I came home with Nada and Electra, wait till you feel yours!"

"Tough tickle, squirt," she replied in the same low tone. "You better back me up, if you know what's good for you!"

He pretended to consider. "Weeeell . . ."

"I'll tell Mom about that time you—"

"I know what's good for me!" he agreed hastily.

Then they both laughed. Ivy knew that her little brother was thrilled to see her with boy-trouble, after his three years of girl-trouble. There was never any doubt about his support.

Then Nada and Electra came out, as befitted juvenile protocol. Both were nicely dressed and mannered, for this occasion. This was normal for Nada, but not for Electra.

"This is Nada, Princess of the Naga," Ivy said, and saw both Grey and Donkey take stock as Nada smiled, for she had become beautiful recently. "And Electra." Electra was merely cute, to her perpetual annoyance. "My brother's betrothees."

"Which one?" Donkey asked, evidently having missed this nuance of the situation before.

"Both," Ivy explained. "He hasn't chosen between them yet." That was an oversimplification, but it would do for now.

They walked on into the castle. "They're in the throne room," Dolph said unnecessarily. "You better have your lines rehearsed before they throw you in the dungeon!"

Ivy did not dignify that remark with a response. She rehearsed her lines, mentally.

They trekked to the throne room. King Dor and Queen Irene were there, gravely awaiting them. Their faces were contrivedly neutral.

Ivy gulped. "Let me do the talking," she whispered to Grey.

"Fat chance!" the tile she stood on retorted. Grey looked startled.

"My father's talent," Ivy explained quickly. "Talking to the inanimate—and having it talk back. And does it ever talk back! Some of his magic collects where he goes often, like this doorway."

"Any idiot knows that!" the tile sneered.

"Shut up, you deadwood, or I'll stomp you!" Ivy whispered fiercely.

"Yeah? I'd like to see you try, pudding-brain!"

Ivy lifted a foot threateningly.

"With a *lady slipper?*" the tile demanded. "Get on with you, or I'll blab what color your panties are!"

"Don't you dare!" Ivy snapped furiously.

"I'll stomp it," Grey offered. "I'm wearing thick hard-soled Mundane shoes."

The tile was abruptly silent.

"I think you have a way with these things," Ivy said, smiling. Then she squared her shoulders, set her little chin, and marched on into the throne room. Grey followed, and Donkey.

Silently they took their places before the two thrones. Ivy's parents surveyed them for what seemed like half an eternity. Her father was not a large man—in fact he was about Grey's size—but was horrendously regal in his crown and royal robe. Her mother was stunning with her green hair and green gown. Ivy had always been secretly jealous of Irene's generous proportions; Ivy herself was relatively modestly endowed. But her mother's eyes were narrowed: a sure sign of mischief.

At last King Dor spoke. "Welcome home, daughter. Please introduce your companions."

Ivy turned and indicated the centaur. "This is Donkey Centaur, whom we rescued from the Goblinate of the Golden Horde, and who in turn protected us from recapture by carrying us clear of that region. I hope he will be welcome at Castle Roogna."

King Dor focused on Donkey. "Are you of good character, Donkey?"

"Of course, Your Majesty."

"Then you are welcome here. You may use the orchard freely, and one of the castle staff will show you the premises. I shall assign—"

Queen Irene nudged him. He glanced where she indicated. "Perhaps Electra will volunteer for that task." For Electra was bouncing on her toes, back near the door, her hand raised eagerly. Of course she wanted to exchange rides for information. The girl was fifteen, but looked as young as Dolph and retained her childish ways. She could be a lot of fun; Donkey would like her.

Ivy swallowed. "And this is Grey of Mundania, my betrothed."

There was a distinctly awkward silence. Then Dor's throne spoke. "Oooo, what a scandal! No princess ever—"

Irene kicked it with the side of her foot, and it shut up. But there was a low snickering from other artifacts in the room. The inanimate was enjoying this situation.

"We shall discuss that matter at another time," Irene said.

"Grey, it may be that my daughter has not made her situation clear to you. Do you understand the problem we have with Mundanes?"

"Of course he does!" Ivy said quickly. "I told—" Irene flashed a look at her which had the same effect as the kick at the throne, for much the same reason. Ivy had to stand aside.

"Your Majesty, Ivy told me that she was a Princess of Xanth, a land where magic works," Grey said carefully.

"Did you believe her?" Irene put in.

Grey spread his hands, in the Mundane way he had. "I believed she believed."

"And you did not?"

"Magic doesn't work in Mundania, Your Majesty."

"You are evading the issue, young man," Irene snapped.

Grey jumped guiltily. "I, uh, did not believe her."

Dor tapped his fingers on the armrest of his throne. "Do you believe her now?"

"Yes, Your Majesty."

"So now you want to marry her?" Irene demanded.

"Uh, yes."

Ivy gritted her teeth. How awful that made him look!

"Why?"

Grey was surprised. "Because I love her," he said. "In spite of her being a princess."

Irene seemed ready to burst. Ivy quailed. "In *spite* of?" Irene inquired.

"Well, she told me how complicated it would be, and really I'd rather, uh, have her all to myself, but she is what she is and I guess I'll have to live with it."

Both King and Queen stared at him. Ivy closed her eyes. This was going even worse than she had feared.

"So you consider it a liability to be a princess—or a queen," Irene said with deceptive calmness. The decorative exotic plants set around the throne room writhed, sensitive to the building storm.

"Yes, Your Majesty. I'm sorry if I have offended you, but

that's the way I see it. I mean, it's such a big responsibility, in such a weird land."

Irene shot a look at Ivy. "Did he ask you to marry him before or after he believed you were a princess?"

Ivy laughed, embarrassed. "Neither, Mother. I asked him. Before he believed."

Irene exchanged a glance with her husband. She shook her head as if bewildered. Then she focused again on Grey.

"There is a great deal more to be decided on this matter, and we have not yet come to a decision. But I think it is safe to say that we like you, Grey of Mundania."

Ivy's mouth dropped open. "Uh, thanks," Grey said.

King Dor stood. "This audience is at an end."

Grey was given a bed in Dolph's room, though there were chambers free. Ivy didn't protest; she had been afraid Grey would not be allowed to stay in Castle Roogna. Probably this was her parent's way of chaperoning one boy or the other, or both. At any rate, she did not get to see Grey for a while, but knew he was in good hands.

She went to her room, eager to get properly cleaned up and changed. She knew that her Mundane clothing was a poor outfit for a princess, even when clean, and this was not.

She had hardly entered, when there was a knock. "It's your father," the door said.

"Let him in," she said, smiling. It was nice to be back where the parts of the building talked.

The door opened and King Dor entered. Ivy ran to him and flung herself into his arms. In the formal encounter in the throne room she had had to be proper and princessly, and this was back to normal. "Oh, Daddy, I missed you!"

"I think not as much as we missed you," he replied, hugging her tightly. "When we were unable to trace you, we realized that you were either in the gourd or in Mundania. When you didn't call in, we knew it wasn't the gourd. That meant trouble, but there was no way to locate you, let alone reach you. Your mother was having conniptions."

Ivy had to smile at that. Conniptions were nasty little things that floated in to pester anyone who was severely upset. They were harmless but messy, and Queen Irene would have been acutely embarrassed to have them there.

"I was in Mundania, all right," she agreed. "I think Murphy's Curse interfered with the Heaven Cent again, and garbled where it sent me. So I went where a Mundane named Murphy needed a girl, instead of where Good Magician Humfrey was."

"Murphy? You said his name is Grey."

"Grey Murphy. Mundanes use two names. He helped me return to Xanth, and then I brought him in. I knew I shouldn't, but I liked him."

"He's a nice boy. But you know you can't marry him."

"Where is it written that a Xanthian can't marry a Mundane?" she flared.

"Oh, a Xanth-Mundania union is possible. But the rules for princesses are more stringent. There would be turmoil in the kingdom if you became king and were married to a Mundane."

Ivy sighed. "I know. But maybe Dolph can be king instead. Or maybe some other Magician will turn up."

"If that happens, you will still be needed as a reserve. We have too few Magicians and Sorceresses; we must conserve every one. So you must maintain your eligibility. This is part of your responsibility as Princess and a Sorceress. You know that."

Ivy sighed. She did know it. She had been carried away by her emotion of the moment, and pretended that the somber realities of her position did not exist, but they did.

"But I can't tell Grey no, after I asked him!"

"You may not need to, once he understands the complete picture."

"Because he will break it off himself," she said.

"Yes. He seems to be a man of integrity and conscience."

"Yes he is!" she flared. "That's why I love him!"

"I understand how you feel. But you know it isn't enough."

Ivy nodded soberly. She knew.

King Dor left. But Ivy hardly had time to get cleaned and

changed before her mother showed up. Again there was the embrace. Then they sat down on the bed for serious woman talk.

"How did it happen?" Irene asked.

"You know how, Mother! First I saw he was decent; then I saw that he liked me only for myself. You know how rare that is, here in Xanth!"

"I know, dear. I marked your father for marriage when I was a child, because of his position. If he hadn't been slated to be king some day, neither I nor your Grandma Iris would have given him a second thought. Then it was a challenge to land him, of course, but that was excellent sport."

"I guess it worked out," Ivy said. "But I sort of wanted to marry for love."

"Oh, there was love. I have always loved your father, and he loved me, though we sometimes had strange ways of showing it. But it was his position that enabled it."

"But for me there was no Magician, and anyone else— well, I just wanted romance, and that's what I found."

"I do understand, dear. But you know it cannot be."

"There has to be a way!" Ivy said, not really believing it. "Somehow, some way!"

Her mother merely smiled sadly, and left.

Ivy tried to rest, but could not, so she went to Nada's room. Nada greeted her with a fierce girlish hug. Then they talked.

"It is an irony," Nada remarked. "I don't love your brother, but will marry him. You do love Grey, but can't marry him. If only we could exchange emotions!"

"That wouldn't work," Ivy pointed out. "Grey and Electra would be left over."

"And Grey's not a prince," Nada agreed. For Electra had to marry a prince or die.

"Why do we get into such picklements?" Ivy asked rhetorically.

"It may be the nature of princesses."

Ivy had to laugh. Nada was just about the best thing that had happened to her in recent years, because she was indeed a princess, and Ivy's age, with a perfect understanding of all her concerns.

"How did it happen?" Nada inquired after a moment.

"I was stuck there in Mundania, and it was so drear, and Grey was so nice. I sort of encouraged him, because I wanted his help, but the more I got to know him the better I liked him. Then when he helped me return to Xanth, and he didn't believe in magic or that I was a princess but still liked me, I just kept liking him more. I knew it was foolish, but I didn't want to give him up. One thing led to another." She shrugged. "I guess it sort of sneaked up on me. Not very romantic, after all."

"It will do," Nada said with a sigh. "My betrothal was not romantic at all." For it had been a political liaison.

"But I do love him," Ivy said. "And I know my folks won't let me marry him. Oh, Nada, what am I to do?"

"Elope?" Nada asked.

Ivy stared at her. "Do you think it's possible?"

"Possible, yes. The question is whether it's desirable."

"It would mean alienating my folks. I would never get to be king."

"But if you don't—"

"I will lose Grey." Ivy considered the alternatives. "Oh, Nada, I can't give up either my folks or Grey!"

Nada just looked at her, understanding.

In the evening she met Grey for the formal meal. He was with Dolph, of course, so she couldn't kiss him. They were on palace rules. She took his arm, and Dolph hooked up with Nada. Electra seemed satisfied to walk with Donkey.

"Your brother is most talented," Grey said as they walked to the dining room. "He has been showing me his forms, and we have talked."

Ivy made a wry face. "I hope it wasn't too boring."

"No, it was very interesting. He says there is only one thing to do."

"Don't say it!" Ivy warned. How like her brother, to blab about the elopement!

Grey shrugged. "Yes, I told him it was foolish. But he says tomorrow we must all go to your room and verify it with the Tapestry."

"Verify?" This sounded odd. Was her brother already planning an escape route for her?

"He says Donkey and Electra are hot on it, too. They actually believe it will work."

"They aren't princesses," Ivy remarked dryly.

He glanced at her curiously. "What does that have to do with it?"

They were in public, so she couldn't answer. Fortunately they were just arriving at the dining room, so she didn't have to. "I'll explain later," she said.

But in the evening Nada come to see her. "Oh, Ivy, Electra told me! They could be right!"

"About eloping? You know that's complicated!"

"No, about finding a talent for Grey!"

"Finding a—you mean that's what Grey was talking about?"

"Yes! Dolph thought of it, and he told Electra, and she told Donkey. Of course a notion doesn't have to make any sense to thrill Dolph or Electra, but Donkey's a centaur! If he thinks it's possible, we'd better take notice. If Grey had a talent, your folks wouldn't be able to oppose your marriage, because he'd be just as good as anybody else."

Ivy quelled her hope, knowing it would only hurt her worse if it flew and crashed. "Grey's a Mundane! They have no magic."

"Donkey says that all assumptions have to be periodically questioned. For centuries it was thought that centaurs had no talents, but when they questioned it, they discovered that they did have magic, if they just accepted it. The centaurs of Centaur Isle still refuse to believe it, but they are mistaken. So maybe that is also the case with Mundanes."

"I don't think so," Ivy said. "Many Mundanes entered Xanth when Grandpa Trent assumed the throne, and he checked thoroughly but couldn't find a single magic talent in any of them. Their children have talents, but not the original generation. Later he even had me enhance some of them to see if that would make their talents manifest, but it didn't. Mundanes just don't have magic."

"Well, it won't hurt to check," Nada said. Ivy didn't argue. But she knew it was a hopeless quest.

In the morning, after breakfast, they all piled into Ivy's room to view the Tapestry: Grey, Dolph, Donkey, Nada, and Electra. "See, there are some dis, dis—" Dolph started.

"Discontinuities," Donkey supplied.

"In the record," Dolph continued, excited. "We can't follow you into the gourd, because the Tapestry doesn't register dreams. But we can trace your whole trip in Xanth, if that's okay with you."

"Why not?" Ivy said. "But I really don't see what it will prove." She suspected that her little brother wanted to peek at any mushy stuff she might have had with Grey.

"So let's go back to the beginning," Dolph said. "When you switched places with the giant."

The Tapestry obligingly showed the picture of Girard Giant, lying with his chin propped on a fist, staring into the tiny gourd. Then he was gone, and Ivy and Grey stood where his head had been.

They watched as the two of them made their way out of the clearing. They saw Grey blunder into the curse burrs— and then get rid of them.

"Wasn't that magic?" Dolph demanded. "He nulled them all! Nobody ever did that before!"

"No such luck," Grey said. "I merely threatened them with my penknife. If there's any magic, it's in the knife."

The picture on the Tapestry froze, becoming mere colored thread. "A magic knife?" Dolph asked. "We should look at that."

"How would a Mundane knife be magic?" Donkey asked.

Grey brought it out. "I pretended it was magic, but that was a bluff. I didn't believe in magic. See, it is just an ordinary penknife." He unfolded the little blade.

"We can test it," Dolph said. "Ivy, enhance it."

Ivy took the knife and concentrated on it. Nothing happened. "I think it's dead," she said. "It's not responding at all."

"Let me try it," Donkey said. "I have tough hooves, so have had to use a magic blade to trim them. They've gotten overgrown since I've been on my own. If this can cut them, it may be magic."

The centaur held the knife carefully and bent down to reach his right forehoof, which he set on one of Ivy's chairs. He carved at the edge of the hoof, which was indeed somewhat ragged.

The knife slid across the hoof without cutting in. Donkey tried again, with greater pressure. This time the blade dug in, but wouldn't cut; it was lodged in its niche. "No magic I can fathom," Donkey said.

"Maybe it's not the blade, it's Grey," Dolph said eagerly. "That's what we're trying to prove, you know. See if Grey can cut your hoof."

"Let a nonspecialist cut my hoof?" Donkey asked, appalled.

"Just to see if he has magic, Don," Electra said cajolingly.

The centaur yielded. It was evident that the two had become very close, in the past day. Ivy realized that after three years playing second to Nada, Electra was delighted to have a new friend. This did not affect her betrothal to Dolph, of course; she loved him and would die if she did not marry him. But in other respects she was an ordinary girl, with ordinary feelings. Ivy was not as close to her as she was to Nada, but it was true that Electra brightened Castle Roogna and was a lot of fun.

Grey took the knife. "You want me to cut a sliver off your hoof?" he asked uncertainly. "My knife is sharp; it should be able to do that."

"My hoof is magically hard," Donkey said. "That's not my talent; my talent is to change the color of my hooves." He demonstrated, and the brown became green, then red.

"Oooo!" Ivy and Nada said together, delighted.

"But then how—?" Dolph asked.

"All centaurs have magically hard hooves," Donkey explained. "It's part of being centaur, like having perfect aim with the bow and superior intellectual abilities. It doesn't count as a talent."

"Well, it seems to me that a sharp knife should cut a hoof," Grey said. "Magic or not. That's the way of knives and hooves." He put the knife to the hoof and carefully carved.

A curl of hoof appeared.

"There!" Dolph exclaimed. "He did it! He's magic!"

"No I'm not," Grey said resolutely. "I just know what's what. I knew this knife would cut that hoof."

"But that knife wouldn't cut for me!" Donkey protested.

"Because you thought it wouldn't," Grey said. "It was psychological. You could cut it if you really tried."

Donkey turned grim. Grey had insulted him. But Electra jumped in. She caught the centaur's arm, getting his attention, and drew herself close to his ear. "He's Mundane!" she reminded him. "They don't know about manners."

Grey looked up. "Now wait—"

Nada interceded, approaching Grey in much the same manner. "She means that different things bother different people. Some of us don't like to be called reptilian; others don't like to have their integrity questioned."

"Reptilian?" Grey asked, distracted. Indeed, Nada hardly looked the part; she was wearing the kind of dress that would have sagged on Ivy, showing contours that tended to make men stop in their tracks and ponder nature.

Ivy felt a tinge of possessiveness and jealousy. Then she had another thought, and suppressed it. If Grey could be distracted by someone like Nada, perhaps it was best that it happen. It might be better than the present problem.

Donkey stepped back in. "I am sure I misunderstood. I apologize for mistaking your meaning."

Grey looked at Ivy, alarmed. Ivy remembered the joke she had played on him, using the brassie mode of apology. She burst out laughing.

The others looked puzzled. Then Nada caught on. "Brassies . . ." she said. Then, with mischief: "Did I embarrass you, Grey?"

"No you didn't!" Ivy cried.

After that, they all were laughing. Obviously Grey didn't want to be hugged and kissed by the centaur, and Ivy didn't want Nada doing it to him either.

"What I meant," Grey said determinedly when they settled down again, "was not any questioning of your integrity, Donkey, but that we all are affected by what we believe. I could not believe in magic for the longest time, because it doesn't exist in Mundania. You can not believe in the sharpness of my knife, because maybe you don't have experience with Mundane steel. But now that you have seen it work, you could do the same yourself."

"Let me try it again," Donkey said, a trifle tightly. He took the knife and carved exactly the way Grey had, holding the blade more firmly to the hoof.

A similar curl of hoof appeared.

"You see?" Grey said. "No magic, just sharpness and confidence. You now believe in my knife the way I believe in magic: tentatively."

"I take your point," Donkey said, relaxing. "May I borrow this knife? This is an opportunity I should not let pass by to get my hooves in shape."

"Certainly," Grey said. "But we may have to find a sharpening stone if it gets dull."

"There's one in the dungeon!" Electra said eagerly.

Dolph frowned. "Do you know what you've done, Grey? You've just cherry-bombed my proof that you had magic!"

Grey shrugged. "That's because I don't have magic. We all know that."

"No we don't!" Dolph insisted. "Let's get on with the viewing."

The Tapestry resumed its animation. Ivy noted that with a certain annoyance; her little brother was getting entirely too good at controlling it. He had to have been watching it a great deal during her absence.

"So your knife is sharp," Dolph said. "But look how those curse burrs fall! They don't care about sharpness; they stick you no matter what. So—"

"Well, I cowed them," Grey said. "They knew I had the knife and was ready to use it, so they gave up. That wasn't magic, that was intimidation."

"What?" Dolph asked.

"He scared them," Donkey said, translating as he carved his hoof.

"Oh." Disgruntled, Dolph returned to the Tapestry.

They watched the episode of the two-lips tree. One flower kissed Grey, but the others did not. "How about that?" Dolph asked. "He turned them off!"

Grey smiled ruefully. "Sure. After the first one got a taste of me, the others wanted nothing to do with me. That's not magic, that's B.O."

"That's what?"

"He stunk," Donkey said, translating again.

Ivy and Nada managed to keep straight faces, but a titter squeezed out through Electra's hands, clapped over her mouth.

Dolph, oddly, did not find it funny. He returned grimly to the Tapestry.

The figures in the scene proceeded to the sandy region. The sandman rose up, assumed the forms of a small ogre, a holy cow, and a nonenti-tree, then collapsed back into a mound when Grey touched it.

"See? See?" Dolph cried. "He destroyed it! That's magic!"

"It was an illusion," Grey said. "When I touched it, it stopped, as illusions do, no credit to me."

"No credit to you," Dolph agreed, displeased.

The Tapestry figures went to the tangle tree. "It was sated," Ivy said before Dolph could make a case about its quiescence.

"Well, I can check that," Dolph said resolutely. The picture focused on the tree, running backwards. The day brightened and dimmed, and brightened again, and dimmed again. "See— no captures," Dolph said. "That tree hadn't eaten in days! So—"

"It could have been dormant—or sick," Ivy said. "Or maybe the magic didn't work very well around Grey, because he was fresh from Mundania. No proof of magic."

Donkey nodded. "It does seem possible. Natives of Xanth relate well to magic, having experienced it all their lives, but Mundanes may have a depressive effect. That won't remain, now that Grey accepts magic."

Dolph buzzed the scene forward until the two of them were captured by the goblins. "There's Donkey!" Electra exclaimed.

They watched as Ivy was put on the isle, and then as Grey waded through the pool to reach her.

"Isn't that romantic!" Nada breathed as the two embraced on the isle.

"That's when we became betrothed," Ivy said, thrilled again by the sight. "It was no hate spring after all, but I was so relieved—"

"No hate spring?" Dolph asked. "Let me check."

"Oh, don't waste more time," Ivy said. But the scene was already revving back. He was really making that old Tapestry jump! The days and nights flickered by—and abruptly stopped at a variant of the scene.

"What's that?" Ivy asked.

"Earlier captives," Dolph said. "I made it do a Seek on that subject. This must be before Donkey was captured."

"It is," the centaur agreed.

The scene was of the goblins of the Golden Horde, dragging two captives to the spring. They were elves, male and female. They were brought before the chief. The Tapestry did not make sound, so the words were lost, but it looked as if the elves were a couple who had been traveling together. They were young, and the man was handsome and the maid was pretty, and they stayed close together. Lovers or newly married, going from one elf elm to another, perhaps to visit kin. They would have run afoul of the goblin trails and gotten trapped.

The goblins did the same thing they had done with Ivy and Grey: they boated the girl to the isle and left her there, then turned him loose at the edge. The man was in obvious distress, as was the girl: should he try to cross to her or leave her? The goblins were gloating, and their big cook pot was boiling.

The elf decided to call the bluff. He waded into the water, crossed—and threw the girl into it. She charged out and attacked him, while the goblins applauded.

They watched in horror as the two elves fought. There was no doubt: they now hated each other. Soon the man held the girl under until she drowned, then charged out of the pool to attack the goblins. They hurled spears at him, bringing him down, and dumped his body into the pot. They used a line with a hook on it to catch her floating body and haul it out, then dumped clean water over it to clear the hate water, and dumped it into another boiling pot.

The picture faded into a neutral plaid pattern. The six young folk stared at each other, their eyes and mouths round with horror. There seemed to be no doubt about it: the spring was hate.

Grey worked his mouth. "I, uh, it didn't do that to us. So maybe it worked on the elves because they believed it would."

"In that case it would have worked on Ivy," Donkey pointed out.

"No, it didn't work on me because I didn't believe in it, and then she didn't believe in it."

But the others were uncertain. "I think it's real—and you had magic to null it," Dolph said.

They discussed it, and found themselves in doubt and divided. Had Grey used magic to null the hate spring, or had something else depleted its power? They could not decide.

In due course the parents were ready to give their verdict. Grey and Ivy stood before them in the throne room, and King Dor said what he had obviously been coached to say:

"We can not sanction a marriage between a Princess of Xanth who is a Sorceress, and a common man who has no magic. We do not seek to dictate our daughter's choice of a man to marry, and have no personal objection to the one she has chosen, who strikes us as a fine young man. But in the interest of Xanth we must insist that she marry either a Prince or a man with a significant magic talent. We therefore deliver this ultimatum: demonstrate that this man, Grey of Mundania, is either a recognized Prince or has a magic talent. Until one of these conditions is met, this marriage will not have our sanction."

Ivy looked at her father, then at Grey. She could neither defy her parents nor give up her love. She stood there, and her throat was too choked for her to speak, and the tears overflowed her eyes and coursed down her cheeks.

Grey spoke. "I have come to understand a little about your magic land," he said. Ivy knew with a sick certainty that he was going to do the decent thing. "I think I could learn to love it, as I love your daughter. I accept your ultimatum as fair. Ivy is not a woman, she is a Princess, and she must do what is best for Xanth. I am neither a Prince nor a Sorcerer, and can never be either. Therefore I—"

"Wait!" Dolph cried from behind.

Queen Irene's eyes snapped to him. "This is not your decision," she said tightly. "You have your own decision to make."

"But it is my business!" Dolph said rebelliously. "Because Ivy's my sister and I love her and I think you're wrong about Grey! I think he has magic, I don't care where he's from. I want to find that magic!"

Irene glanced at Dor, who shrugged. "Allow me to point out, son," she said with a certain parental emphasis that boded ill for his future freedom, "that there is no time limit on this ultimatum. Grey has as long as he needs to find magic; it is merely that he may not have our approval to marry Ivy until he does, any more than you may marry before you clarify your own situation."

"Yes! So Grey should not break the Betrothal until we get this straight! I think he has a talent, and I know how he can find it!"

"If you are referring to the episode of the hate spring," Irene said evenly, "the evidence is inconclusive. We have no way of judging the potency of that spring at the time they were there. It may have variable potency, depending on the season or other factors."

"No! I mean he has to have magic, because of the Heaven Cent!"

Now everyone was interested, even Ivy herself. What wild notion had her little brother come up with this time?

"The Heaven Cent appears to have been fouled by Murphy's curse," Irene said. "We have noted the alignment of the names; it is indeed the kind of thing that can happen when magic goes wrong. The cent will have to be recharged before the search for the Good Magician is resumed."

"I don't think it fouled up," Dolph said. "I think the cent worked. It sent Ivy to the place she was most needed: Mundania, where Grey needed her. We thought the Good Magician needed her most, because of his message to me, but maybe that wasn't so. Or maybe Grey is supposed to help find the Good Magician. So he must have the magic we need to do that!"

Ivy gazed at him, astonished. Dolph's crazy notion might just be right! She saw that the others were just as surprised.

"So we should take him to Parnassus to ask the Muse of History what talent is listed for him," Dolph concluded triumphantly.

Again Irene exchanged a glance with Dor. Again he shrugged.

"Grey may go to Parnassus to inquire," Irene said after a moment. "Certainly we bear him no malice, and stand ready to facilitate any effort he wishes to make on his behalf. We shall arrange suitable transportation for him. But you, Prince Dolph, will remain here. You have not yet resolved your own dilemma."

"Awwww—"

Irene's hair seemed to turn a darker shade of green. "Ooo, you've done it now, you impertinent boy!" one of the thrones said. "You'll never—" Irene's kick cut it off.

But Ivy was looking at Grey for the first time with genuine hope. She would go with him, of course. Maybe the Muse really did have a talent listed for him! After all, if the Heaven Cent had not fouled up and this was part of the good Magician's plan, Grey might indeed . . .

She was not even aware of the termination of the audience. She was too busy hugging Grey, wild with hope.

10

PARNASSUS

G rey was torn. He loved Ivy and wanted to stay in this magic land, but knew he didn't qualify. The decent thing to do was to call it off with Ivy and return to drear Mundania and the horror of Freshman English. He knew he didn't have any magic. But now, with Ivy holding him and Dolph so excited about proving he *did* have magic, he found it all too easy to go along. At least it would mean some more time with her.

What was this Parnassus? There had been some kind of assignment relating to that in school, but he had just skimmed over it without comprehension, as usual. Something Greek, a mountain in Greece, where people went to see the oracle. That was all he could dredge up.

Ivy set about organizing it. Dolph could not go, but his two fiancées would: the cute child Electra and the lovely Nada. That promised to be an interesting trip: Grey and the three girls.

Next day they started off. It was a good thing he now believed in magic, because he would have been in trouble otherwise. Ivy had somehow called in two winged centaurs and a horse with the head and wings of a giant bird, and these were to be their steeds for the trip.

"But there are four of us," Grey said. "I don't think it's smart to ride double—not if we're flying."

"We won't ride double, exactly," Ivy said. "Nada will be with me."

"But Nada weighs as much as you do!" he protested. Indeed, Nada weighed more, and in all the right places.

Ivy just smiled. "Let me introduce you," she said, leading the way to the new arrivals.

The first was the handsome centaur male, like a muscular man from the waist up, and like a horse below and behind, with huge wings. This was Cheiron. The second was Cheiron's mate, Chex, whose long brown hair merged into her mane, and at whose ample bare breasts Grey tried not to stare. The third was Xap, a golden yellow hippogryph, Chex's sire, who spoke only in squawks that the others seemed to understand.

Grey was to ride Cheiron. Ivy rode Xap, and Electra rode Chex. Nada approached with Ivy—and abruptly became a small snake. Ivy put the snake in a pocket and mounted. So that was the secret! He had forgotten that Nada was a naga, a human-serpent crossbreed, able to assume either form. She had seemed so emphatically human! She had made herself small so that her weight did not become a burden, knowing that her friend Ivy would not let her fall.

Grey looked at Cheiron. "Uh, I've ridden a centaur before, but not a winged one. Your wings, uh—"

"Sit behind them," Cheiron said. "And hold on tightly. My magic enables me to fly not by powerful wingstrokes, but by lightness of body, and you will be lightened too. You could bounce off if not prepared."

"Uh, yes." He walked to the side, but Cheiron stood taller than Donkey, and there were no stirrups. How could he get on?

Chex came up. "I will help you." She reached down, put her hands under Grey's arms, and lifted him up. He flailed, surprised, and felt his back brush something soft. Then he was over Cheiron's back and settling into place.

He leaned forward and got a double handful of mane as the great wings spread. Suddenly he felt light-headed and light bodied; indeed it seemed he might bounce off!

Cheiron leaped and pumped his wings, and they were airborne. Grey felt as if he were floating. There was definitely magic operating, but it was good magic.

He looked to the side. There was Xap, flying strongly with Ivy, his bird's beak seeming to cut right through the air. Behind him Chex was lifting too, with Electra gleefully aboard. With each stroke of the centaur's wings, her breasts flexed. Now Grey knew what he had brushed as he was lifted.

Electra saw him looking, and waved. He took the risk of releasing one handful of mane in order to wave back. How could he be afraid when the child wasn't?

"It's hard to believe that she's two years older than Chex," Cheiron remarked, turning his head briefly so that his words were not lost in the wind.

"What?" Grey asked, confused.

"Ivy and Nada are seventeen. Electra is fifteen. Chex is thirteen. But our foal Che is now a year old, being tended by his granddam Chem. It can be awkward to judge by appearances."

Grey looked again at the pair. Electra remained a child, and Chex a very mature figure of both horse and woman. "No offense, but I find that difficult to believe," Grey said. But now he was remembering something Ivy had said about that; it had faded from his memory because it was part of the magic he had not then accepted.

"I thought you would; that is why I mentioned it. Chem was part of the party that went to find Ivy when she was lost as a child of three. It was on that journey that Chem met Xap. There was no male centaur she found suitable, and Xap as you can see is a fine figure of a creature. So she bred with him, and in the following year Chex was birthed."

"I, uh, am surprised that you discuss it so openly," Grey said, somewhat at a loss.

"We centaurs are more advanced, and therefore more discriminating about proprieties than are human folk," Cheiron explained. "We treat natural functions as what they are: natural. We reserve our foibles for what counts: intellectual application."

"Uh, sure. But Chex—I thought centaurs aged at the same rate as human beings." Now he realized what his problem was: the same as the one with buxom Nada. Nada looked and acted too human to be credible as a serpent until she actually changed, and Chex looked and acted too mature to be credible as an adolescent. He was coming to accept magic, intellectually, but there were aspects of it that his deeper belief still resisted.

"Ordinarily they do. But animals age faster. Since Xap is an animal, Chex was blessed with the natural consequences of the crossbreeding: wings and faster maturity. She grew at a rate between that of her two parents, and reached sexual maturity at age six, rather than age three or age twelve. Her dam, aware of this, tutored her intensively so that her intellect kept pace. Thus it was that she was a fit mate for me at age ten, though I was more than twice her chronological age. For that I am duly grateful, for winged centaurs are rare."

"Uh, how rare are they?"

"We two, and our foal, are the only ones in Xanth."

Grey had to laugh. "That is rare!" He looked once more at Chex. "She looks so, so human, uh, in front, it's still hard to believe she can be so young."

"You will find her young in no respect other than chronological," Cheiron assured him. "It may be more convenient for you to think of her as my age, ignoring the chronology."

"Uh, yes, that seems best." So he really wouldn't have to make the adjustment that was giving him trouble.

They flew southeast, down toward what on the Florida map would have been Lake Okeechobee. From this height he really would not have known this was Xanth instead of Florida; the trees and fields and lakes seemed similar.

Then he spied a cloud ahead. It did not resemble any

Mundane cloud. It had a puffy,, angry face. "I've seen that cloud before!" Grey exclaimed.

"That is Fracto, the worst of clouds," Cheiron said. "Wherever there is mischief to be done in the air, there he is to be found. Apparently he tunes in magically. We shall have to take evasive action before he gets up a charge."

"But he was—was in the gourd!" Grey said. "I thought there was no contact between there and here. I mean, that's the realm of bad dreams, isn't it?"

"Correct. That would have been the dream Fracto; this is the real one. Their natures are identical."

The trio angled down toward land. The cloud tried to extend himself below to intercept them, but was not fast enough. Fracto could not catch them in the air, and would have to settle for raining on them.

But the three flying figures did not actually land. They brushed by the treetops as if searching for a suitable region— and kept on going. Before the cloud realized it, they were beyond, and lifting once more into the sky. Fracto tried to turn about and go after them, but there was a fairly stiff wind that prevented him. He turned a deep mottled gray and skulked off, seeking other mischief.

"Serves you right, soggy-bottom!" Electra called back nastily.

"She has been associating with Grudy Golem," Cheiron said. "That is one of his old insults."

Maybe so. But Grey was satisfied with it. He didn't like Fracto.

By evening they were approaching a feature of the landscape that definitely was not part of the Mundane peninsula: a mountain. At its jagged peak grew a monstrous tree, and on the tree perched a mind-bogglingly monstrous bird.

"Mount Parnassus," Cheiron said unnecessarily. "We may not fly all the way to it, because the Simurgh does not appreciate clutter in her airspace. We shall set you down at the base of the mountain, and wait there for your return."

They glided to a camping site Xap knew about close to Parnassus. Ivy brought out the little snake and set it on the ground, and suddenly Nada was there again, just as lovely as before. She was nude, but Ivy had her clothes ready, and in a moment all was in order. There were blanket and pillow bushes nearby, and a beerbarrel tree that was filled with boot rear. "Oh, I love it!" Electra exclaimed.

Grey remembered Ivy's warning, in the mock Castle Roogna atop the dream mountain. Did the stuff really work? He could not resist trying some and finding out for himself. So while the others settled for water from the nearby stream, he and Electra drew foaming cups of boot rear from a spigot set in the bulging trunk.

"Bottom's up!" Electra said, and took a swig. Then she jumped into the air. "What a boot!"

Grey just didn't believe it. He sipped his own drink, while Electra waited expectantly.

Nothing happened.

"Maybe you didn't drink enough," she said, disappointed.

Grey tilted the cup and swallowed a big mouthful. There was no effect. It seemed just like root beer.

"Let me taste yours," Electra said suspiciously.

Grey gave her his cup. She sipped, then drank, and did not jump. "It's a dud!" she said. "Yours must have gone flat! Mine gave me a good boot!"

Grey tried hers, but with no effect, and after that it didn't work for her either. "The whole tree's gone flat!" she said. "I must have gotten the only sip that was fresh enough." But she remained perplexed.

They returned to the camp, where the others had gathered a nice collection of fruits, nuts, and bolts. They had even found a gravy train and a hot potato collection, so had potatoes and gravy.

The more he experienced of Xanth, the better Grey liked it. Its ways really were better than those of Mundania, once he got used to them, even if some, like the boot rear, were overrated.

They slept individually, with the three four-footed creatures spaced around the outside of the camp, sleeping on their feet. Grey had a suspicion that Xap the hippogryph would be aware of any danger, and would deal with it swiftly. That beak looked wicked.

In the morning, after breakfasting on eggs from an eggplant, fried on a hotseat, along with green and orange juice from nearby greens and oranges, they set out afoot for the heights of Mount Parnassus. They had to cross a stream at its base; rather than risk wading through it, they located a narrow place and jumped across.

"Now we'll be all right if we can avoid the Python and the Maenads," Ivy said.

Grey could guess why a python might be awkward, but the other wasn't clear. "What—?"

"Wild Women," she clarified.

That sounded intriguing, but he knew better than to say so. "Suppose one of them comes upon us?"

"That depends. Electra can shock the first one, but then she has to recharge for a day. Nada could become a big serpent and bite one, but she would be no match for the Python. I can do a certain amount by judicious Enhancement. I could also use the magic mirror to call home, if there was time. But of course my snoopy little brother will be watching us on the Tapestry, and he'll alert someone if there's trouble. Xap has been here, and could run in to carry a couple of us away. But he really doesn't like being limited to the ground. It will probably be best if we get through without running into any of those creatures. Since Clio will know we're coming and why, that should be possible. She wouldn't wish any harm to us."

"Clio?"

"The Muse of History. Weren't you listening when we planned this trip?"

"Uh, I hadn't caught her name."

Ivy smiled. "I was teasing, Grey. I don't expect you to know everything about Xanth yet. Not today."

"But just wait till tomorrow!" Electra put in, laughing.

There was a clear path up the mountain. Electra led the way, full of juvenile energy. Ivy was next, and then Grey with Nada bringing up the rear. They all had walking sticks they had found at the campsite, and these were a great help, because they walked briskly on their own, hauling the living folk along.

They came to a fork in the path. Electra halted. "I can't tell which one is right," she said.

"Let me check," Nada said. She became a long black snake and slithered up past them. She paused at the fork, putting her head to one side and then the other, her tongue flickering in and out. Then she became human again. "The right one. The left one smells of Maenad, fairly fresh. Let's move on quickly."

Grey would have liked to loiter, so as to catch a glimpse of one of the Wild Women. Did they wear clothing? But the others were evidently alarmed, so he moved along with them.

The path became steep. Even Electra was breathing hard. Nada gave her walking stick to Grey and assumed her natural form: a serpent with her human head, unchanged except that the hair was shorter. Obviously she didn't want her hair to drag on the ground. Just as he had tried without perfect success not to stare at Chex's bare bosom, and not to stare at Nada's barely clothed contours in the human state, he now tried not to stare at her incongruous juxtaposition of human and reptilian parts. It was a good thing he now believed in magic.

He offered the extra walking stick to Ivy, but she declined. "I have enhanced my own endurance," she explained. Indeed, she looked relatively cool and rested. Electra was satisfied with her single stick, scrambling athletically over rocks and roots, evidently regarding the climb as a challenge. So he took a stick in each hand, and was propelled along by them. It was as if he had a second set of legs.

The slope of the mountain became almost sheer, but the path cut its ledge cleverly through it, and led them without mishap to the home of the Muses. This was an ornate building set into the steep slope, girt by stone columns and arches and guarded by carved stone creatures. Grey had learned enough of Xanth to realize that those statues just might come alive and attack, if intruders misbehaved.

A woman sat in a court in front of the building. She had a shelf of books beside her desk, and was writing with the point of a bright feather on the middle section of a scroll that rolled up above and below.

Ivy stepped forward. "Clio, I presume? May we speak with you?"

The woman looked up. She was in white, and her curly hair was verging on the same color at the fringes, but there was an ageless look of preservation about her. There was no telling how long she had lived or how much longer she would live, but a fair guess might be centuries, either way. "I am. And you would be Ivy. I was aware of your impending visit; I had just not realized that this would be the day."

"This is Grey, my betrothed from Mundania," Ivy said, indicating Grey. "And Nada, Princess of the Naga, and Electra, from maybe nine hundred years ago, both betrothed to my little brother."

Clio smiled. "Ah yes, I remember. That's in—which volume is it? There are so many, I sometimes lose track."

Ivy stepped closer. "Are these the volumes? Maybe I'll see the title." She peered at the shelf of books. "*Isle of View, Question Quest, The Color of Her*—" She was overcome by a rogue giggle.

"No, dear, those are future volumes," Clio said. "I have written them, but they haven't yet happened, in your terms. Look farther to the left."

Ivy looked to the left. "*Man From Mundania*—hey, does that have anything to do with—?"

"Of course, dear," Clio replied. "And a fine volume it is, if I do say so myself. But that is not where—"

"Oh, yes." Ivy looked again. "*Heaven Cent, Vale of the Vole, Golem in the*—"

"That's it!" Clio exclaimed. "Now I remember! *Heaven Cent*, when Prince Dolph went in search of the Good Magician Humfrey and got betrothed to two excellent young women." She smiled at the two girls. "It is so nice to meet you at last! I've written so much about you!"

Grey, meanwhile, was amazed. Several future volumes of

Xanth history had already been written? And what was the title that had so titillated Ivy? He sidled closer, so that he could read the words on the spines of the volumes.

"You mean you already know how it turns out with us?" Electra asked Clio. "Which one of us married Dolph?"

"Of course I know!" Clio said. "It is my business to know. That is certainly an interesting episode, and I envy the two of you the experience of its resolution."

Grey got his eyes lined up on the titles. It was awkward, because he was still a bit too far away, and the angle was bad, but he was just able to piece out the words. *Geis of the Gargoyle, Harpy Thyme*—but these weren't the ones Ivy had seen.

"Do you think you could—I mean—" Electra said.

"Naturally not, dear," Clio said in her kindly fashion. "If I told you the resolution, it would spoil it for you, and you wouldn't like that, now would you?"

Grey realized that he was too far to the right. He was reading titles even farther in the future! But he was heading leftward, and should soon intersect the ones Ivy had called out. *Demons Don't Dream, The Color of Her*—ah, there it was at last! "Panties!" he exclaimed aloud, laughing.

There was a sudden silence as all the others looked at him. He felt himself flushing. "Uh, I was just—"

"You really should not be peeking at future titles," Clio said firmly. "Suppose the news got out? There could be chaos!"

"I'm, uh, sorry," Grey said, abashed. "I won't tell, if that helps."

She gazed at him for an uncomfortably long moment. "There is considerable irony in that statement, do you realize that?"

Grey spread his hands. "I, uh, no, not exactly."

Clio sighed. "My fault, perhaps; I should not have been careless with the volumes." She touched the top of the bookshelf, and the air before the tomes fuzzed and turned opaque. The open shelf had become a closed shelf, a wooden panel hiding the books. "Now, Ivy, why is it that you came? I seem to have lost the thread again."

Ivy seemed for a moment to have lost the thread herself, but she recovered it promptly. "I want to marry Grey, but I can't unless we find a magic talent for him, and we think there's just a chance he might somehow have one, and surely you know—"

"My dear, my dear!" Clio said. "I can no more tell you in advance about Grey's talent than I can tell Nada and Electra how their triangle with Dolph will turn out! It would not be ethical, quite apart from the complications of paradox."

"Oh, Clio!" Ivy said, looking woebegone. "It's so important to me! I love him, and if—"

Clio raised both hands in a stop gesture. "I understand, Ivy, believe me I do! But this is a matter of professional ethics. I can not compromise in this matter, no matter how much I may wish to. This is a situation you must see through in your own fashion."

Ivy was crying now. Grey was deeply touched to see her break down so quickly on this issue, though he understood the Muse's position. He stepped to her and enfolded her. "She's right, Ivy! We have already seen too much. We have no right to put her in this position."

"You are a fine young man," Clio said. "Perhaps I can say this much: it will not be long, now."

"Thank you," Grey said, uncertain what she meant. He guided Ivy back the way they had come. Nada and Electra followed, pausing only to thank the Muse individually for her attention. Soon they were on their way back down the mountain.

The descent was hardly less arduous than the ascent. Ivy's tears in due course condensed to sniffles, and then to mere depression. She had evidently put more hope in this than she had let on. Grey's mood was hardly better. To have come so close to an answer, only to have that hope dashed—

"Are we far enough away?" Electra asked.

Ivy stared at her dully. "For what?" Grey asked.

"To talk."

"Maybe we should get the rest of the way down, before we relax," Grey said, not certain what she had in mind.

She looked disappointed. "I suppose so. But I'm about ready to burst!"

Grey looked around. "Oh. Well, there're bushes around. We could wait while you—"

She laughed. "Not physically, dope! Mentally! With my news!"

"Tell us your news when we're clear of Parnassus," Nada said. She was in her girl-headed-serpent form, sliding fairly readily down the slope.

They resumed their motion. In due course they reached the fork in the path. But they had hardly gone beyond it before there was a clamor from below.

Ivy came to life. "The Maenads!" she exclaimed. "They're below us!"

"And the Python," Nada said, changing briefly to full snake form, then back. "I smell them both, now. They must have crossed the path and smelled our scent."

"We must run!" Ivy said, flustered.

"We're too tired," Nada pointed out. "Even fresh, we could not go faster than those monsters."

"Maybe if we split up," Grey suggested. "That might confuse them, and they might go the wrong way—"

"*Which* wrong way?" Ivy asked. "If some of us are each way—"

"I'll decoy them!" Gray said. "You three go back up the path where your scent already is, and I'll run down the other and make a noise to attract them."

"But you don't know the first thing about this mountain!" Ivy protested.

"It's my responsibility," he replied. "I—"

The noise below grew abruptly louder. The Maenads were rounding a curve and would soon be upon them.

"Go!" Grey cried, pointing to the path they had just come down. He himself ran down the other.

Ivy and Electra turned and started up. Nada was on the

other side of him; she assumed woman form and started to step across just as he began running. They collided.

At another time he might have found this event interesting, for Nada was contoured somewhat like soft pillows. But in this rush he was afraid he had hurt her. "Nada! Are you—"

He broke off, for she had disappeared. Realizing that she had changed form to avoid falling to the ground, he ran on. She would join the others, in one form or another, and they would hide. All he had to do was decoy the monsters.

He slowed, and glanced back. There was a Wild Woman! She was indeed naked, with flaring tresses and a figure suggestive of an hourglass. She was gazing up the path the others had taken.

"Over here, nymph!" Grey called, waving his arms.

Her head turned, rotating on her shoulders as if mounted on ball bearings. Now he saw her eyes. They were insanely wild. He had not taken these Wild Women seriously, but those eyes sent a chill through him. This was no sweet young thing; this was a rabid tigress!

The Maenad launched herself in his direction, uttering a harsh shriek of hunger. Her legs were beautiful, her breasts were beautiful, her face was beautiful, but that shriek was spine-tingling. She opened her mouth, and he saw her pointed teeth, and saw her tongue flick out the way Nada's had when she was in serpent form. There seemed to be candle flames inside her eyeballs. "YUM!" she screamed, reaching for him with hands whose nails were like blood-dipped talons.

Grey spun about and resumed his running. But the Wild Woman was fast; she kept pace. He couldn't draw far enough ahead of her to get off the path and hide; he had to keep going. He heard the screams of the other Maenads farther behind. They sounded just as bloodthirsty.

The path twisted as if trying to make him stumble, but he ran with the surefootedness of desperation and kept up speed. He began to leave the Maenad behind. But now his breath was puffing, and he was tiring rapidly; he had not been fresh when he started. He could have used a dose of Ivy's Enhancement!

He had had the bright idea to be the decoy. It had been the gallant thing to do. But now he was in trouble. How was he going to get out of this?

Something touched his chest at his breast pocket. He reached up, thinking it was a snag of a branch—and felt a tiny snake. Its head was poking out of the pocket.

For an instant he felt shock. Then his fevered mind put two and two together. "Nada!" he gasped.

Indeed it was she. Instead of falling to the ground, where she might have been trodden on, she had evidently clung to his shirt and slipped into his pocket. In his preoccupation with the Maenads, he had not noticed.

"Sorry I got you into this!" he puffed. "I don't know where I'm going, but I don't dare stop!"

The snake did not reply, which was perhaps just as well. At least she understood that it had been an accident.

Despite his tiring, he was leaving the leading Maenad farther behind. Was she also tiring or merely hanging back to allow the others of her ilk to catch up? He might have turned and dealt with one, though he did not like the idea of striking a lovely bare woman. But he knew he would have no chance against the pack of them.

But if he got far enough ahead, he could dodge off the path and hide. They would charge on past, and then he would return to the path and run the other way. He hoped. If he went off the path and they winded him, he would be in deep mud for sure!

He rounded a bend. Suddenly he was charging toward a pretty spring. Another hate spring? The others had concluded from the evidence of the Tapestry that that one had been valid, but had somehow lost its potency by the time he and Ivy reached it. Certainly it had not worked on them! But there was no guarantee that this one would be similarly powerless. In fact it might be a love spring. It glimmered with a pale reddish hue, as if potent with some kind of magic. Suppose he splashed through it, then saw a Maenad?

These thoughts flitted through his pulsing brain as he ran toward it. By the time they had run their course, he was almost at it. He veered to avoid it, but stumbled; only by frantic windmilling did he stop himself from pitching head-first into the water.

Nada fell from his pocket and splashed into the spring. Appalled, he watched the little snake thrashing. Should he reach in and pull her out? Then he would be affected too!

She changed to her human form. She shook the water from her eyes and looked directly at him. "Hey, hi, handsome!" she exclaimed.

Well, it wasn't a hate spring. "Nada, get out of there! The Wild Women are coming!"

She hiccuped. "No! You come in! It's nice!"

Was it a love spring? He didn't dare touch it! "Get out!" he repeated. "If they catch you they'll tear you apart!"

But she demurred. She sat in the shallow water, her breasts lifting clear and dripping. Even in this danger, he was struck by her sex appeal. She might be half serpent, but she was all woman. "Come in! You'll like it!" she invited. She hiccuped again. "This wine's wonderful!"

"You're intoxicated!" he exclaimed, catching on.

"No, I'm drunk!" she corrected him. "This must be the Maenad's wine spring. Pretty soon I'll be raving wild just like them! What fun!"

Now the Maenads came into sight. They spied Nada in the wine spring, and screamed with outrage.

There was no help for it. He had to haul her out of there before the Wild Women got their claws on her. He would just have to resist the intoxicating effect of the water.

Grey waded in. The water was bathwater warm, and felt somehow soft against his legs as it soaked his trousers. He reached down to take hold of Nada.

"Oooo, goody!" she exclaimed, reaching up to embrace him.

"None of that!" he rapped. "Come on out! We have to run!" But she was slippery with the wine-water, and his hands merely slid over her marvelous flesh, stroking regions they should not.

"Oooo, fun!" she said, wrapping her arms around his neck

and hauling his face in for a wet and sloppy kiss. He turned his face aside, but that was the least of his problems.

He couldn't get her out. She was too slippery and too affectionate. Meanwhile the Wild Women were charging in; already it was too late to escape them. He would have to try to fight them.

"Change into your snake form!" he told Nada. "Get back in my pocket! I'll need both hands free to shove them away; I can't hold on to you."

"Serpent form?" she asked, still trying to kiss him.

The Maenads came to the pool and circled it. Their eyes glowed and their teeth glistened and their claws quivered expectantly. Grey knew the two of them were done for. In a moment the Wild Women would plunge in from all sides and tear them apart.

Then he had another desperate notion. "Make it a big snake! Your biggest and fiercest ever!"

"Big?"

"Huge, gigantic, fierce!" he cried. "To fight the Wild Women!"

Finally she caught on. "Nasty women!"

"Terrible women! Do it!"

Nada changed. Suddenly he had his arms around a python that must have weighed twice as much as he did. It was Nada, but horrendous.

She hissed at the Wild Women. They stared, for the moment startled from their madness. Then their blood lust returned in force, and they charged into the pool.

And paused. A look of dismay spread across their several faces. "Where's wine?" one asked, her words barely distinguishable.

Several of them scooped up handfuls of the water, tasting it. Their dismay intensified. "Wine gone!" one exclaimed in sheerest horror.

"Get out of here, Nada!" Grey said.

Nada undulated to the edge of the pool and out. The Maenads, distracted, seemed hardly to notice. They were busy sampling their pool, verifying that its magic was gone.

Grey waded out, struck by the similarity of this scene to that of the goblins with their hate spring. Something strange had happened again, but he couldn't pause to analyze it. He hurried after Nada.

She headed for the deepest forest, moving well despite her intoxication. Of course it was impossible for her to stagger or fall, in this form. He plowed into the foliage, fighting through the branches and leaves. At any moment the Maenads might recover from their shock and resume the pursuit!

Nada drew up beside a huge chestnut tree. She stopped under a large chest of nuts, and resumed human form. "Now kish me," she invited, extending her arms to him again.

Grey straight-armed her, gently. "You can't be drunk," he said. "That water has lost its potency."

Her eyes widened. "Suddenly I'm sober!" she said. "How did you do that?"

"I didn't do it!" he protested. "You must have just thought it was wine, so—"

"Grey, look at me," she said sharply.

He looked into her face. Her eyes were completely clear, her mouth firm. "I am not drunk now, but believe me, I was a moment ago. I had lost all perspective. All I thought of was being with a handsome man. I had conveniently forgotten that you and I are betrothed to others. I would never do that, sober. That water intoxicated me instantly, and that was no illusion. It didn't stop until just now. You did it, Grey!"

"But I couldn't have! It would take magic, and I have no magic. You know that."

She cocked her head. "Electra—what was she about to say to us, there on the path, that was so urgent? She may look like a child, but she's got a good mind."

"She was full of some news she had, but—"

"I think I know. This experience jogged my memory. Grey, when Ivy asked the Muse about your talent, she said that it would not be ethical to tell us about it in advance. Wasn't that it?"

"Yes, something like that. But what relevance—"

"Think about it. How could she tell us about a nonexistent thing?"

Grey froze. "But that must mean—"

"That you do have a talent," she finished. "She slipped, Grey, and Electra was the only one to catch it. That's what she was so bursting to tell us! *You do have magic!*"

Grey was stunned. "Oh, Nada, I could kiss you!"

"No you don't!" she said firmly. "Not when I'm sober."

"Uh, I meant that as a figure of—"

She smiled. "I know. Just never forget that I am Ivy's friend—a good one."

"I never did."

"You never did," she agreed ruefully. "*I* did, when drunk. But this has given us the key. What could your talent be?"

"Sobering drunk women!" he quipped, laughing, still not quite believing.

"More than that, I think. You denatured their whole pool!"

"But if that really is a magic spring, I could no more nullify it all than I could—"

"Nullify the goblins' hate spring," she concluded.

Grey thought about it. "Nullifying magic springs? That couldn't be, because it did make you drunk."

"Before you got into it. It didn't make *you* drunk. Once you applied your will to it—and just now to me—you countered it, instantly. Magically."

He nodded. "When I set my will to it. But is it possible that something else changed those springs? Maybe Ivy denhanced that hate spring; I mean, if she can enhance, maybe—"

"Ivy wasn't here for the wine spring," she reminded him. "And don't accuse me of doing it! I have no talent; my magic is in my nature, changing between my component species. Maybe some day the nada will develop talents, as the centaurs did. No, you did it, Grey. Your talent must be making magic springs harmless."

"But I'm Mundane! How could I have a talent?"

She shook her head. "I don't know, Grey. But considering

what the Muse said and what happened here, I'm pretty sure you do. And that means—"

"I can marry Ivy!" he exclaimed jubilantly.

"Yes. If Queen Irene thought this was a good way of denying you without actually saying no, she made a mistake, because now she can't say no!"

"All we have to do is escape the Wild Women and get together with Ivy and Electra, and everything's okay," he said, a trifle ruefully. He knew they weren't safe yet.

Indeed, a Maenad was coming toward them. The Wild Women knew where they were but had been too dazed by the loss of their wine to organize.

"I can change form and slide through the thicket," Nada said. "But I wouldn't leave you here alone."

"That one coming here doesn't look wild anymore," he said. "Maybe they're tame when not drunk."

"Tame Maenads could cost you your marriage, too," she said, squinting at the woman's perfect proportions.

"Maybe I can climb a tree, and you can go for help."

"Wild Women can climb."

"Let's just see what she wants. Maybe it's not an ultimatum," he said without much confidence.

The Maenad came close. "Magician!" she called. Her speech was clear, now that she was sober.

Grey was too surprised to speak, but Nada took over. "What do you want with the Magician?"

"I'm no—" Grey started, but she elbowed him in the belly.

"We did not know your nature when we pursued you," the Maenad said. "We apologize, and beg you to restore our wine spring. We will do anything you desire."

"The Magician has all he desires," Nada said, her elbow poised to jab him again if he protested. Grey kept his mouth shut.

The Wild Woman looked at Nada's bare form appraisingly. "Indeed we can see that, serpent-woman. But if there is anything else he desires—food, an honor guard, servants—"

Nada considered. "The Magician was only visiting Parnassus. He has no need of your services. I will try to prevail on him to restore your wine spring, but I can not guarantee success. The best I can promise is that if you do not annoy him further, he will not do anything worse to you. If he is so inclined, he may see to your pool."

The woman fell to her knees. "Oh, thank you, thank you! We are but shadows without our wine! We would be unable to fight the Python."

Nada nodded. "The Python. Is he near?"

"He was following us up the path before we caught your scent. He must have taken the other fork, for there was the scent of live girls there."

Both Grey and Nada jumped. The dread Python—going after Ivy and Electra?

"We must be on our way," Nada said. She turned her face to Grey. "Magician, if you will at least consider their wine spring—"

Grey was uneasy about this deception, but realized that she was trying to get them out of this without having to fight. "Very well, serpent-girl," he said gruffly.

They drew themselves out of the tangled brush and followed the unwild woman back to the spring. "Understand, if the Magician restores your wine, and you then get drunk and wild and become troublesome to him, I can not be responsible for his temper," Nada warned them.

"We will stay far away from him!" the women promised in chorus.

Grey stepped up to the spring. If he really had denatured it, then he should be able to restore it. If he had not been the one responsible for what had happened, then he hoped that whatever was responsible would play along.

How should he go about this? Well, if it had been his will that did it to this pool and the hate spring, maybe his will could restore it. So he concentrated on the water, which was now quite clear. He willed for it to be restored, and for the pale rose color to return, since that was evidently the signal of its potency. *Be wine again!*

Was there a flicker of something? He squatted and touched the water with one finger, willing the color to intensify.

Immediately the water turned a rich red.

Alarmed, he straightened up and stepped back. What had he done? That was too much color!

A Maenad scooped up a palmful of water and sipped it. Her eyes went round. "Blood!" she exclaimed.

Oops! Grey looked at Nada with dismay.

"Blood?" another Wild Woman asked. Then several more scooped up sips. "Blood!" they agreed. "Blood flavored wine!"

Grey edged back. If they could get a running start—

"Oh thank you, Magician!" the Maenad spokesnymph exclaimed. "This is so much better than before! Now we can satisfy both our thirsts at once!"

"Quite all right," he said benignly. Then Nada took his arm, and they walked back down the path.

The Maenads, jubilant, clustered around the pool, guzzling the water as if there were no tomorrow. They paid no further attention to the two visitors.

Grey was almost floating, not because of their escape but because of this vindication of his magic. He had tried to turn the pool pink, and when that was slow he had tried for full red—and with his touch it had gone all the way! No one else could have known what he was thinking, so it had to have been his own effort. His own magic. He did have magic!

But the riddle remained: how could he have a magic talent when he was Mundane? Everyone agreed that no Mundane had magic. Could everyone be wrong?

"We had better get back to Ivy and Electra," Nada said. "I don't like the sound of that Python going after them!"

The Python! Grey was tired, but that abruptly passed. "I'll run! You get small and get into my pocket! We've got to get there as fast as we can!"

"Right you are, Magician!" she agreed with a wan smile. She held his hand, leaned over his arm (oh, that body!), and became a snake spread across his hand and forearm. He lifted her to the breast pocket. Then he began to run.

He had no idea what he would do if he encountered the Python. He just knew he had to get there before Ivy did.

Then, abruptly, he stopped. How could he be sure of finding Ivy and Electra quickly? He had only a vague notion of the layout of this mountain and its bypaths, and Nada had no better knowledge. They could blunder about for hours while the Python caught and gobbled the girls.

Nada's snake head poked out of his pocket, questioningly. "We need a guide," he said. "Someone who knows every wrinkle of this mountain, so we can go directly to the most likely place, and get around the Python if we have to."

The snake head nodded, but without full conviction. He knew why: where could they get such a guide on such short notice?

The answer was obvious: one of the Maenads.

Grey turned about and marched back to the blood-wine spring. "Ahem."

The clustered Maenads jumped. "Oh, Magician, don't change your mind!" the spokesnymph cried. "We have done nothing more to annoy you!"

"I want a guide," Grey said. "Someone who knows this mountain perfectly."

"We all know it, Magician! If this is your demand, we must accede. Choose one of us to serve." And the Maenads lined up, setting their jaws, each obviously hoping he would not choose her.

This was no good! He needed a willing one, who would do her honest best. "Ah, er, a volunteer. Someone who wants to do it, to help me find my friends."

They burst into cruel laughter. "Magician, none of us want to help anyone! We are wild, bloodthirsty women! We are tame only for the brief time it takes to lure an unwary man close enough for the pounce, when he takes us for succubi." There was more laughter; they found such an error hilarious.

This wasn't getting anywhere. If he pushed his luck, they might forget their fear of him, and that could be awkward. But he still needed that guide.

"Well, er, maybe if one of you can pretend to be tame for this one task, in return for an, er, reward." He didn't know what reward he could sincerely offer, but was sure that none of them would do it unless either threatened or rewarded generously.

"Help someone for *hours?*" the spokesnymph demanded. "Impossible!"

But one Maenad came forward. "I—I might."

The spokesnymph shot her a withering glance. "That's right, Mae! You're always the last to rip out a gobbet of flesh. It's almost as if you don't really like hurting folk!"

"That's a lie!" Mae cried fiercely. But her attitude suggested that it wasn't. It seemed there were misfits even among the Wild Women.

"Very well," Grey said briskly. "Come along, Mae. Can you smell the trail of a normal woman?"

"Yes, very well," Mae agreed.

"Then sniff out the trail of the two young women who were with us before. We want to reach them before the Python does."

"They took the other fork," Mae said. She set off at a run, her bare bottom twinkling.

Grey watched for a moment. Then the snake wriggled in his pocket, reminding him that he was not here to watch twinkling bottoms. Embarrassed, he lurched into his own run, following Mae.

11

PYTHON

Ivy hated to see Grey go, but the Maenads were coming and there was no time to argue. She saw him collide with Nada, and Nada changed into her snake form and disappeared, apparently hanging onto him. Well, at least he would have competent help. She dreaded what would happen to him alone.

Electra was already running up the path, her walking stick jumping. Ivy enhanced her own stick, and it practically propelled her along the same route. If only their party hadn't gotten divided, maybe they all could have hidden.

It worked: the Wild Women went charging up the other fork, attracted by Grey's foolish yelling. But now what was he going to do? He didn't have the first notion about survival in Xanth.

She remembered the magic mirror. But she had assumed that she would be in the middle of whatever trouble occurred. If she used it, she would have to explain that the one in trouble was somewhere else, and by the time help got there, it might well be too late. Oh, what an awful pass this was!

"Nada will help him!" Electra said, divining Ivy's concern. "She can become a pretty big serpent and hold them off. And Grey—there's something about him."

"I had noticed," Ivy said, smiling briefly. Electra was right: Grey had gotten through some phenomenal scrapes, such as with the goblins, despite his ignorance of magic.

"And he has a talent!"

Ivy paused. "What?"

"The Muse—she said she couldn't tell us about his talent, but it wouldn't be long before we knew. That means he does have one!"

Ivy was amazed. "Why—so she did! But what could it be?"

"Maybe something he needs right now, 'cause she didn't say he was going to be in real trouble. Maybe he can make Wild Women fall in love with him—"

"That's very reassuring," Ivy said sourly.

Electra was embarrassed. "I mean, maybe, that is, he would not love them—who would love a Maenad?—but if they—well, maybe something else, like turning into a dragon."

"Maybe." Ivy felt light-headed, thinking about the prospect of a talent for Grey. That meant they could marry!

They stopped climbing, as it was obvious that the Maenads were not coming this way. Grey's ploy had worked, but now it was hard to know what to do. If they went back too soon they might run into the Maenads, but if they waited too long and Grey needed help—oh, this was awful!

Then their problem was solved, in a worse way. They heard a quiet rustling down the trail. Something was coming up, and it didn't sound like Grey.

In a moment the huge head of a monstrous serpent rounded a turn. It was the Phython!

"Run!" Ivy cried.

But the great baleful eyes of the creature caught them both before they could act. They stood transfixed, unable to move or even to speak.

The head was so big that the jaws could take in either one of them without difficulty. The sinuous body was obviously able to digest them. They were this serpent's prey!

"Aaaah, young women!" the Python hissed, seeming to speak. "My favorite repast! But first you must worship me. Bow down before me, grovel low, humble yourselves before the horrendous maleness I am!"

This was awful! But somehow the infinite menace of the Python was mitigated by an almost infinite appeal. She was terrified, yet a part of her also desired to be consumed by this monster. Thus it was not merely the magic mesmerism of the reptilian gaze that held her; it was the weakening of her will to resist. What a horror, to know what was to happen yet not want to fight it!

"Down!" the Python hissed. "Bow down, tasty morsels! I require my homage before I feed!"

Dutifully they got down, still held by that sinister gaze. But Electra was a little ahead of Ivy, and her body momentarily interfered with Ivy's line of sight to the eye of the Python.

Suddenly she was free of the awful compulsion. Now she was revolted. How could she ever have desired any part of that disgusting reptile?

But Electra was still under the spell. Ivy scrambled forward, shielding her eyes against the gaze, and threw her body down before the girl's face, interrupting her line of sight too. The Python was like a hypnogourd, completely captivating those who met his gaze but losing power the moment the contact was broken.

But it was too late. The gigantic jaws were hinging open, and in a moment one or both of them would be snapped up. The Python did not need to mesmerize them the whole time, only long enough for him to get within striking range. He was within it now.

"Shock him!" Ivy whispered, putting her hand on Electra's arm. "I'll enhance you!"

The head plunged down, the daggerlike teeth leading. Both girls rolled to the side, and the jaws snapped closed just beside them. "Now!" Ivy cried, hanging onto Electra's arm.

Electra flung her free arm across and smote the Python on the side of his massive snout. The blow itself was laughable; she might as well have struck the trunk of a tree. But it was charged with all the electric power of her magic talent—enhanced by Ivy's own talent.

There was a jolt so strong that even its backlash stunned Ivy for a moment. The Python stiffened, then collapsed, his head drooping to the path beside them, his latter coils writhing without direction. Electra's shock had knocked him out.

Ivy sat up, her senses reeling. She discovered she didn't really like such close calls. "Come on,'Lectra—we've got to get away before he recovers."

Indeed, the head was showing signs of animation. The monster was so big and tough that even that terrible shock was enough to set him back only briefly. Ivy thought fleetingly of trying to bash the Python with a stone, but realized that her strength, even if she enhanced it, would barely be enough to dent the giant skull. It was safer to flee.

They got up, wobbly on their feet. The path below was blocked by the thrashing length of the reptile; they would have to go back up. But soon he would follow them, and this time they would not be able to shock it, for Electra was depleted. She was no Sorceress; she could not exercise her talent twice in one day. Ivy herself had no limit, but what point would there be in enhancing the Python? That would only make him worse!

"We can't outrun him!" Electra gasped. "We'll never make it to the top!"

Ivy had to agree. "We must find a safe way off the path, where he can't follow or at least will be too slow to catch us." She did not voice her private doubts about their ability to find any such way.

They stumbled on, holding hands so that Ivy could enhance Electra's stamina. And there, beside a nettlebush, was a contorted little path departing from the main one. They had not noticed it before.

"But the nettle!" Electra protested. "It will hurt us!"

"Let me at it," Ivy said. She stood before the bush, thinking how pretty it was, and how decorative its spines were, more bluff than substance, and how such bushes never did really sting nice girls, only mean serpents. The bush became prettier, its sharp edges softening. She touched a leaf, cautiously, and it did not sting her.

She brushed by the bush, and Electra followed, trusting Ivy's talent. The nettle did not sting her either.

Then Ivy addressed the bush again, silently. Now she concentrated exclusively on its detestation of all things reptilian, especially monstrous Pythons. It would sting any such creature viciously.

They walked on down the path, no longer feeling the urgency of panic, but not delaying either. They needed to get somewhere safe before the Python found a way to get past the bush.

The path was evidently little used, but Ivy sensed some enchantment on it. She enhanced this, and the path became clearer, with some protective magic. Someone must have used it regularly, once, to visit the Muses.

"Who else lives on Parnassus?" Ivy asked. It was something she knew she ordinarily could remember, but in her present state she couldn't recall all the details.

Electra considered. "Gee, I don't really know. There's the Simurgh on the Tree of Seeds at the top, and the Python and the Wild Women."

"And the Tree of Immortality on the other peak," Ivy added. "But this path's going down, so it must be to somewhere else. I just want to be sure it's better than what we're hiding from."

"*Anything's* better than that horrible monster!" Electra exclaimed. "I mean, I suppose it's pretty bad getting eaten, but that awful gaze—somehow I knew that what the Python planned was worse than eating."

Ivy shuddered reminiscently. "I hate to say it, but if that thing fights with the Maenads, I favor the Wild Women. But this path—there's something about it I don't understand. I wonder if we should follow it any farther."

"Well, if the Python doesn't follow—"

There was a crash above, as of a bush getting ripped out of the ground, nettles and all.

Wordlessly, they resumed their flight down the path.

Abruptly it debouched in a valley hollowed from the side of the mountain. Huge stone ruins stood there, the remains of some vast ancient temple. Rounded columns reached toward the sky, the roof they once supported gone. Sunlight angled across the stones, making the scene totally bright and stark.

"What is this?" Electra asked, stepping onto the stone platform that must once have been a beautiful floor.

Before Ivy could answer, a robed, bearded old man appeared from behind a ruined wall. "Pythia!" he exclaimed. "Just in time!"

"What?" Electra asked.

"You are the new priestesses. It was foretold you would come, but we were afraid it would be too late. Come this way!"

"But we aren't priestesses!" Ivy protested. "We are merely innocent maidens who—"

"Of course. We shall have to clean you up, and you can serve immediately."

"We're tired and hungry," Electra said. "We have no intention of—"

"We have excellent food and drink for you."

Ivy exchanged half a glance with Electra. They were both hungry. They decided to hold their protest until after they had eaten.

Part of the ancient temple remained roofed. Here there were several chambers, and there really was good food. The girls feasted gluttonously on hayberry longcake and ice chocolate drinks. A quiet old woman brought a basin of water and sponges and cleaned them off while they were eating, then presented them with rather pretty white robes to don in place of their soiled and torn clothing.

Without even quite paying attention, they found themselves garbed like, well, priestesses, with pretty diadems on their heads and sylphlike gowns. Ivy was surprised to see how pretty Electra looked. "You're growing up, 'Lectra!" Ivy remarked appreciatively.

Electra grimaced. "I'm in no hurry. All too soon after I

come of age, so will Dolph, and then he'll have to choose, and then—"

Ivy knew why she didn't finish. They both knew that Dolph would choose Nada to marry, and then Electra would die. She was safe only as long as she remained betrothed to Prince Dolph; when that ended, her nine hundred or so years would catch up with her, and she would shrivel into extinction. Unless they found some way around the dilemma.

"Hark, the Client is arriving," the original old man announced. "We had better use the older one first. Do either of you have any idea how this is done?"

"No!" Ivy and Electra said together, resuming their nervousness about the proceedings.

"Excellent! Have either of you ever had relations with a man?"

"We are both betrothed," Ivy said a bit stiffly. "What—"

The man was taken aback. "But you are so young! We require virgins. Why didn't you tell us this before?"

"You didn't ask, dodo!" Electra said with her usual asperity. "Anyway, who said we're not—"

Ivy tried to caution her, but was too late, as was usually the case when dealing with Electra.

"Ah, so you *haven't* been with a man!" he exclaimed.

"What difference does it make?" Ivy demanded. She had heard of virgin sacrifices and didn't like the sound of this at all.

"Only truly innocent young girls can serve as Pythia," he explained. "That way we can be sure their words are uncorrupted."

"Uncorrupted?" Ivy still didn't like this, and now Electra was catching on, and keeping silent.

"The Pythia must sit on the tripod and speak in tongues for the Client. This is the manner of our oracles."

Oracles! Now Ivy remembered something. "They make predictions!" she said.

"Certainly. The very best predictions. That is why Clients come here."

So they weren't to be sacrificed or ravished. Still, there was too much in doubt. "What happened to the Pythia you had before?"

"After too many years they grow up and get married," the man said. "Then they lose their innocence and are useless for this work. We have been looking for replacements for some time. You two should do very well, and it is an easy life between predictions. You have no other work to do, and will be well fed and clothed, and of course never molested. All you have to do is answer the questions of the Clients."

"Suppose we don't know the answers?"

"That is why you sit above the magic cleft. The answers are always provided. You will have no difficulty."

"Suppose we'd rather go home?"

He looked blank. "No girl wants to go home after qualifying for this elite position!"

Ivy exchanged the other half of her earlier glance with Electra. It didn't seem wise to make too much of an issue at the moment. For one thing, they didn't know where the Python was. Once they understood the situation better, they could see about getting away.

So Ivy went out to the tripod, and Electra stood on the sideline. The Client was there: a centaur from Centaur Isle, handsome and haughty. She could tell his origin by his quiver of arrows: the Isle centaurs had the very best equipment, and their arrows were feathered with a design that was reserved for them alone. Indeed, non-Isle centaurs could not use those arrows; their heft and balance and flying properties differed in subtle ways, so that only true Islers could fire them accurately.

The tripod was perched over a deep dark crevice in the stone. That made Ivy nervous; she could not fathom its depth, and heard a faint hissing far down. There was also a warm updraft issuing from it with a peculiar odor. It made the hair on the back of her neck tingle.

But this was the place, and this was the job—until she could get out of the center of attention and see about getting herself and Electra away from here. She had not told these oracle folk that she was a princess, fearing that would only make them more eager to keep her. She just wanted to get along, for now.

She took her seat on the tripod. Now the updraft caught her filmy white robe, lifting it, exposing her legs. She tried to hold the cloth down, but this was futile; there was too much air. Fortunately the skirt was not full circle; it rose until it formed a bell shape, and stopped there.

She remembered the mouthy tile at Castle Roogna that had threatened to tell the color of her panties until Grey shut it up with his hard-heeled Mundane shoe. Was there something down in this crevice, gazing up? She had not much liked this business to begin with; now she was coming to hate it. Her panties were her own business!

The centaur approached. "Ask your question," the old man said.

"O Pythia, I am Centurion Centaur. What is the state of my magic?"

Oops! Ivy knew that was an exceedingly awkward question. The centaurs of Centaur Isle did not believe in magic talents for themselves; they regarded a talent as fit only for the lower classes, such as human beings. The mainland centaurs were more liberal and accepted their talents, but this was not yet the case with the Islers. What could she say? The chances were that this centaur did have a talent but would prefer to die rather than acknowledge it, and if it became known he would be exiled from the Isle. So he had nothing to gain by the truth. Should she lie and say he had none, thus satisfying him and securing his future with his kind? But even though this oracle business was none of her desire, how could she bring herself to lie? Thus neither the truth nor the lie was acceptable.

She sat frozen, unable to speak. No wonder the proprietors preferred completely innocent girls. No one who was aware of the trap of this office would accept the job. Even if she took the expedient course and lied, suppose later his talent manifested and her oracle was thus proven wrong? That would discredit the whole business, and somehow she knew that was no good outcome either.

Then the air wafting from below turned hot, and increased its motion. It pushed on her flaring skirt so hard she was half afraid she would be lifted into the air. Her legs were stinging. The fumes became choking; she coughed and tried to hold her breath but could not. She inhaled, and the foul stuff flooded her lungs.

Her chest burned, and her head became light. She felt dizzy. Indeed she seemed to be floating now, though she hadn't moved. The stone beneath her seemed to turn translucent, so that she could see through it, down to dim shapes of goblins and demons far below, going about their noxious business. The air around her seemed to be going the opposite way, turning thick, opaque, as if a monstrous fog were solidifying around her.

"Let me out of here!" she screamed. But only gibberish came out of her mouth, as if she were speaking Mundanian.

Then hands were pulling her off the stool. She flailed, trying to fight them off, but they wrestled her away from the crevice and its blasting fumes.

"What did she say?" the Centurion demanded.

"She spoke in tongues," the old man explained. "We must interpret it for you. A moment while we consult."

"Be quick about it," the centaur said with the natural arrogance of his kind. "The matter is important."

The old man stepped aside to talk privately with the two old women who operated the premises. They talked for some time, waving their arms animatedly.

Meanwhile Ivy was coming out of her delirium. The fog was lifting and the ground was turning solid again. "Are you all right?" Electra asked anxiously. "You looked awful on that tripod!"

"The fumes choked me!" Ivy explained. "I tried to call for help, but it came out gibberish."

"You mean *that's* what you cried out? It wasn't a prophecy?"

"It certainly wasn't! I had no idea what to say."

"But they are—"

"I know. I think it's all a big—"

She broke off, spying something awful. The Python was sliding onto the stone floor!

Electra saw him too. "He caught up!" she exclaimed. "He found us! Don't look at his eyes!"

They retreated from the monster reptile. They ran toward the proprietors. "The Python! The Python!" Ivy cried to them.

The old man looked up. "Of course. He is your guardian, Pythia. He protects the premises from molestation."

"But he's going to eat us!"

"Nonsense. He eats only intruders, not priestesses." The man returned to his animated consultation.

Meanwhile the Python was still coming after them. "He doesn't know we became priestesses!" Electra said. "He knows we came from the mountain path!"

"Maybe the centaur—" Ivy said.

They ran to the waiting centaur. "That serpent is after us!" Ivy told him.

"But I haven't had my answer yet," Centurion said, annoyed.

"And you may not get it, if I get eaten!" Ivy retorted.

"Here, here, this won't do!" he said. Suddenly his bow was off his shoulder and in his hands, an arrow nocked. "Withdraw, Monster, or it will be the worse for you!"

But the Python merely elevated his snoot and came on.

The bow twanged. An arrow appeared in the reptile's nose. "That was a warning shot," Centurion said. "I have ninety-nine more arrows. The next one will be in the eye. Back off, Monster."

Ivy had always known that centaurs were brave and skilled warriors, but she was amazed even so. This one had no awe at all of the Python, and it was evident that he could fire an arrow exactly where he wanted.

But now the proprietors realized what was happening. "Don't shoot at the Python!" the old man cried. "He's our guardian!"

"He will be a blind one if he slithers one more slither forward!" Centurion retorted.

Meanwhile the Python, evidently stung by the barb, paused.

He oriented an eye to fix on the centaur—but discovered the flinty point of the next arrow aimed directly at the pupil. If the Python had not been aware of the proficiency of centaurs before, he had had a recent reminder. He hesitated again.

Two more people burst out of the jungle where the path exited. A nondescript young man and a luscious nude young woman. "Grey! Nada!" Ivy exclaimed, thrilled.

The Python coiled around to meet this new challenge. Certainly it was a better prospect than the nervy centaur.

"Don't look at his eyes!" Electra screamed to Grey.

Meanwhile Ivy got a clearer look at the girl behind Grey. That wasn't Nada—that was a Maenad! What had happened?

Grey, true to his sometimes infuriating nature, ignored the warning. He stared the Python right in the eye.

Ivy froze, appalled. So did everyone else, for their own assorted reasons. So did Grey—and the Python. The two were locked into that deadly gaze.

Then the Python moved. His head sank slowly to the ground. His coils thrashed aimlessly.

Ivy felt her mouth hanging open. She looked around and saw that the jaws of the proprietors were similarly slack.

Grey walked forward. "Are you all right, Ivy? We were afraid maybe the Python—"

"You—you stared him down!" Ivy exclaimed.

"Of course he did, dummy!" the Maenad said. "He's a Magician!"

"Well, not exactly that," Grey said, abashed.

Electra hurried up. "Where's Nada?"

There was a motion at Grey's breast pocket. A snake's head poked out. Grey put up his hand, and the snake slid up into it and around his arm. Then Nada manifested in her human form, her feet landing neatly on the stone as her arm was steadied. She was naked, of course, because she was unable to transform her clothing when she changed form. "But something very like it, I think," she said. "Do you know, Ivy, he nulled their wine spring, then restored it more potent than before?"

"He has a talent! He has a talent!" Electra exclaimed, jumping up and down. "I knew it! I knew it!"

"What is this Maenad doing here?" Ivy demanded, focusing on the lesser matter because she wasn't quite prepared to tackle the greater one.

"Well, this is, uh, Mae," Grey said. "She—I—we—"

"Oh?" Ivy inquired, looking more closely at the creature. Mae Maenad was just as nakedly wild and voluptuous as before, surely quite intriguing for those who liked that type.

"The Magician needed a guide," Mae explained. "So I showed him the off-trail the Python uses and sniffed your scent thereon, so he could find you."

"It's a good trail for serpents," Nada put in. "But there was an uprooted nettle bush there that really had it in for serpents, and I had to return to his pocket. Then the nettle couldn't touch me."

"But how did he tame you?" Electra asked. "Everyone knows that Maenads can't be—"

"Well, I don't really like blood," Mae confessed, abashed. "When he made our spring blood—"

"Now I have to reward Mae for her help," Grey said. "But I'm not sure, uh, how."

Ivy realized that she had better figure out a suitable reward soon, because she didn't trust whatever the Maenad might think of. That Wild Woman was entirely too well formed.

"What happened to our guardian?" a proprietor demanded.

"Nothing bad," Grey said. "I just, uh, nulled him so he wouldn't hurt anyone. Here, I'll revive him for you." He walked across to the Python and touched the huge head.

The thrashing stopped. The head lifted. The eyes blinked. "Go about your business," Grey said. "We are visitors here, not intruders. Here, I'll pull out that arrow for you." He put his hand on the shaft.

"You can't dislodge that arrow," Centurion said. "It has a magic point. Only a centaur can—"

He broke off as the arrow came loose. The point was red with blood but intact.

The Python quivered as if recovering from a fundamental shock, then slithered away across the stone.

"I guess it did hurt," Grey said. "Here is your arrow back, centaur."

"Thank you, Magician," the centaur said, looking much the way the Python had. He accepted the arrow.

The old man approached. "What is your business here, Magician? We have no prior knowledge of you."

"Well, I, uh, just came to rescue Princess Ivy and Electra. It was nice of you to take care of them."

"*Nice?*" Ivy and Electra demanded together.

"*Princess?*" the proprietor demanded at the same time.

"Uh, yes," Grey said innocently. "This is Princess Ivy of Castle Roogna, and this is Princess Nada of the Naga. Didn't you know?"

The old man looked somewhat out of sorts. "We did not inquire," he said gruffly.

"Well, they'll be leaving now," Grey said. "Thank you again."

"Wait—what about my oracle?" Centurion asked.

"We have interpreted the message," the old man said quickly. "It is: 'no Centaur has less magic than you.' "

"Oh." The centaur nodded, quite satisfied. "Yes. Quite. Thank you. I shall be on my way." He suited action to word, in the fashion of his kind.

"But we need our Pythia!" another proprietor cried. "If you take these two away, Magician, what will we do?"

Ivy stepped in. "Mae, how would you like to have the Magician arrange for you a new situation with a hard stone room, a dismal white gown, no raw meat at all to eat, and regular sessions with fumes that really drive you wild?"

Mae's face seemed to catch fire. "What a wonderful thing!"

Ivy turned to the old man. "Here is your next priestess, proprietor. You know she's a virgin; these Wild Women don't love men, they eat them. Put her on the tripod and she'll babble an incomprehensible streak you can interpret to your heart's delight."

"But she's a Maenad!" he protested.

"But a tame one! The Magician tamed her." She turned back to Mae. "He did, didn't he? You won't try to tear people apart anymore?"

Mae was a Wild Woman but not stupid. "He tamed me! He tamed me!" she ' exclaimed. "No more Miss Nasty Nymph!"

"But the Maenads are incorrigible!" the old man said. "That's why we have the Python! To hold them off!"

Nada stepped in, in the perceptive way she had. "This one is different. She no longer fights with serpents or tears men apart. See." She assumed her snake form, the large version. Mae, understanding, reached down to pet the snake's head, though she did look a bit nervous about it. Then Nada resumed human form. "Now kiss the Magician without biting him," she said.

This really set the Wild Woman back. "Do I have to?"

"Does she have to?" Ivy echoed, disturbed for a different reason.

"Well, I suppose she might kiss the proprietor . . ."

The old man stumbled back, terrified.

"Point made," Ivy agreed with resignation. "Kiss her, Grey, but don't enjoy it too much."

Grey did not look quite as upset about the prospect as she might have wished. He turned to face Mae, and she stepped into his embrace. They clinched and kissed, holding it a good long time.

"See?" Nada said to the proprietors. "She is perfectly tame—affectionate, even. One might even call her lovable."

"Let's not go that far," Ivy muttered.

The proprietors were daunted by this display. "Perhaps she will do," the old man said.

"But let's stop that kiss before she gets un-innocent notions," an old woman added.

Ivy agreed completely. To her relief, they finally completed the kiss.

Mae looked dazed, and the candle flames in her eyes were flickering. "Maybe I have misjudged men," she said. "They—"

"They aren't all like that!" Ivy said. "This one's a Magician, remember. Ordinary ones won't be worth your while. You don't have to eat them, just ignore them."

"Yes, of course," Mae agreed. But she did not look entirely convinced.

"Come with us," one of the old women said. "We must clean you and garb you."

"Clean me?" Mae asked, alarmed.

"They just sponge you off," Ivy explained quickly. "It doesn't hurt. They just want you to look pretty for the Clients."

"Look pretty . . ." Mae repeated, glancing sidelong at Grey. "Yes, maybe that is best."

"Let's get out of here!" Ivy said briskly.

Nada held her back. "One more thing." She turned to the old man. "Is there a path around the base of the mountain we can use to return to our starting place?"

"Certainly; all the Clients use it. Right that way." He pointed.

"Thank you," Nada said, flashing him a smile. She was better at that than Ivy was.

Electra led the way, skipping toward the indicated path. Ivy took very firm hold of Grey's hand and led him away from the ruins. Nada followed, the suggestion of a smile on her face. She reverted to naga form, as it really was best for windy paths.

Grey had not spoken a word since the kiss. Ivy turned on him the moment they were out of sight and earshot of the ruins. "Well, why so smug, Grey? Did she make that much of an impression on you?" She was angry for what she knew was no good reason.

Grey opened his mouth. Redness welled out. He turned to the side and spat blood. "I, uh, couldn't say anything, because if the blood showed they wouldn't believe she was tame."

Ivy stared. "She *did* bite you!"

He found a handkerchief and dabbed at his lip. "Yes. I think it was involuntary, like a sneeze. She just couldn't get that close to a man without attacking, at least a little. I couldn't break the kiss until she let go. So I sort of concentrated and nulled her magic nature until she had to stop."

"So that was what made her so respectful!" Ivy exclaimed. "She felt your power!"

"I guess so. I think she was sorry about it anyway. But she's been a Wild Woman all her life, and it must be hard to change right away, even if she really doesn't like blood."

So the Maenad had not quite lost her taste for violence. Somehow Ivy felt better. "You poor dear," she said, abruptly full of sympathy. "Let me enhance your healing." Since the wound was in his mouth, she touched his lips—with her own. She enhanced the kiss, making him recover rapidly.

Soon they resumed their walk along the path, holding hands again, but with better rapport than before.

Chex was glad to see them. "We heard some commotion, but did not want to intrude," she said. "Did the Muse answer your question?"

"Not exactly," Ivy said. "But we did learn that Grey does have a talent. It seems he nullifies magic, when he wants to. That explains a number of little mysteries."

"I should think so," Chex agreed. "But are you sure? I saw no evidence of magic on his part before."

"Let's test it!" Electra exclaimed with her usual exuberance. "Let him try to stop you from flying!"

"But I don't want to do that!" Grey objected.

"Not permanently," Ivy reminded him. "Just enough to demonstrate your power." She didn't add that she herself needed reassurance about it. He had subdued the Python, but that might have been because the big reptile couldn't hypnotize Mundanes or maybe had trouble with men. He thought he had nulled the Maenad, but it might have been because continued close contact with him stirred certain natural, hitherto suppressed romantic urges in her. Could she, after all, be so emphatically a woman in every physical respect without having at least a little womanly passion? The glow in her eyes had been something, after she kissed Grey. But Ivy did

not want to discuss such things openly. It would be embarrassing if she were mistaken.

"It does seem like a good test," Chex agreed. "Here, Grey,
get on my back. If you can prevent me from taking off, I will
know you have magic power to counter mine."

Grey climbed on in the awkward way he had. Ivy marveled
that she found his clumsiness endearing, but she did. Grey
was nobody's idea of a dashing hero, just a decent man.

Chex spread her wings, braced herself for a leap, and
flicked her tail twice. The first time the tip touched Grey, the
second time it touched her own body. That of course was her
magic: the flick of her tail made whatever it touched become
light, so that her wings had much less weight to lift. That was
why she was able to fly without having wings ten times as
large as they were.

Chex leaped—and stumbled. She came down solidly on all
four hooves, a look of surprise on her face. "I can't get light!"
she exclaimed.

"I nulled your tail," Grey explained. "Do you want me to
reverse it?"

"No. Let me try again." She flicked her tail several more
times, but with no better effect. "Indeed, there is no effect,"
she confessed. "Very well, reverse it."

Nothing showed. Chex flicked her tail again—and suddenly floated into the air, her wings only partially spread. "Oh
my goodness!" she exclaimed, frantically pumping her wings
to get her balance.

Grey hung onto her mane as they wobbled in the air. "Rebound!" he said. "All those prior flicks must be taking effect
now, making you too light."

"Can you null me just slightly?" Chex asked, evidently
fighting to prevent herself from sailing way up out of control.

"I'll try." Then she stabilized and came slowly to earth.

"He has magic," Chex announced as Grey dismounted. Her
mane was in disarray, and she looked flustered.

"Rebound," Nada said. "That must be why the Maenads'
wine spring got even stronger than before when you canceled
the null. That's some magic!"

"That's like *my* magic," Ivy said. "I simply enhance, but you can enhance by rebound!" She was impressed by the demonstration; she trusted Chex's judgment. "But I wonder how general this talent is."

"See if it works on me," Nada said. "Stop me from changing form." She went to Grey and held out her arm.

He took it. They stood there, doing nothing.

"Well, go on, try to change," Electra said.

"I *am* trying!" Nada replied.

"Oh." Electra smiled. "Well, then, let her do it, Grey."

Suddenly Nada turned into a serpent with a human head at each end. "*Eeeek!* What happened?" she cried in chorus.

"Rebound!" Ivy said, amazed. "Quick, Grey, null her down a little!"

The heads disappeared. For a moment the serpent had no head. Then Nada's regular form appeared: the body of the serpent, with just one human head. "That was horrible!" she said. "I never had trouble with my natural form like that before!"

Cheiron nodded. "Undisciplined magic is dangerous. We should cease these experiments until a safer program of testing can be established."

"Yes," Grey agreed immediately. "I don't want to mess anyone up. I'm not used to having a talent at all."

But Ivy could not be satisfied yet. "They were calling you Magician."

"I never claimed to be that!" he protested. "The Maenads assumed—"

"I am a Sorceress," Ivy continued evenly. "That is the same as a Magician, only female, the terminology a vestige of what my mother calls Xanth's sexist heritage. Nothing short of Magician-level magic could null my talent. So let's find out if—"

"I advise against this," Cheiron said. Chex nodded agreement, and Xap squawked.

"No, I really want to know," Ivy said. She had always managed to get her own way, ultimately, and she intended to have it now. "I want to know if Grey is Magician level. Try to null me, Grey."

"I, uh, really don't think—" he began. Then, seeing her set face, he yielded. "But I'm not sure exactly how, uh, it would work."

"I'll try to enhance something, and you try to prevent me." She looked around. Her eye fell on a glowworm just poking its head up as the evening approached. "I'll enhance that glowworm."

She picked up the worm. It wriggled in her hand, glowing faintly. Grey put his hand on her other arm. "Very well—I'm nulling you," he said.

Ivy felt nothing. She concentrated on the worm, willing it to brighten.

It flickered, but did not increase its light. She concentrated harder, but it remained dim. She put forth all her effort. Then the glow brightened slightly. Grey had definitely crimped her style!

"Now unnull," she said.

The glowworm flashed like a lightning bug, so brightly that the entire region became noon-lit. Then it exploded, burning her hand.

They stared. The glowworm was gone; only ashes remained.

"We killed it!" Grey said, appalled.

Ivy looked at her smarting hand. "Oh, I wish I hadn't done that!"

"Precisely," Cheiron said, in a fools-heed-warnings-not tone. "Now we know that Grey truly is Magician caliber. No more experiments."

"No more experiments," Grey agreed, staring at the ash.

"No more experiments," Ivy agreed. Then she started to cry. That poor glowworm!

They camped for the night, subdued. They had found Grey's magic, and that was wonderful. It was Magician level, and that was amazing. They could now get married, and that was best of all. But they had done harm in the testing of it, and that was bad. Way too late, Ivy wished she hadn't pushed it. There had been no need to destroy the innocent glowworm. She just hadn't thought of the consequence, despite Cheiron's warning.

In the morning, after breakfast, they discussed it—and came up with a disturbing question. It was Electra who posed it, but perhaps it had been in the back of the minds of the others too.

"How can a man from Mundania have magic at all, let alone be a Magician?"

There was the root of it. Something was fundamentally wrong, unless everything they knew about Mundanes and magic was false. Until that question was answered, they could not rest easy.

Nada assumed her snake form, and they mounted their steeds and flew back to Castle Roogna. But Ivy knew that despite their seeming victory, it was not yet appropriate to marry Grey. Magicians did not appear from nowhere, and certainly not from Mundania. She knew that her parents would insist on learning the truth, and she knew they would be right. Her quest with Grey was far from over; it had only changed its nature. It was as if they had climbed to what they thought was the top of Mount Parnassus, only to discover that it was only a ledge, and that the real peak remained as far above as ever.

12

PEWTER'S PLOY

"Please, Grey, I really didn't want to admit my ignorance there at the castle," Rapunzel said in his ear. "I mean, I understand why you and Ivy need company on this trip, because betrothed couples aren't supposed to go too far alone together, and Nada and Electra didn't care to tangle with Com-Pewter again. But why are you going to see the evil machine?"

Grey had not yet gotten used to having a tiny and beautiful woman perched on his shoulder and holding onto his earlobe with one doll-like hand. The parents had decreed that he and Ivy had to be chaperoned until they got married, which seemed to be their way of agreeing that the doubt about that marriage was gone. Ivy had met their ultimatum and proved Grey had a magic talent, with a vengeance. In fact he was now eligible to be king some day! But the parents shared Ivy's own concern about the origin of that talent. Mysteries abounded in Xanth and things that made no sense, but a mystery relating to the betrothed of a princess was a serious matter. So little Rapunzel and her similarly little husband, Grundy

Golem, were the chaperones this time; size hardly mattered in this land of magic. Grundy was riding Ivy's shoulder as she walked on the path ahead, and evidently regaling her with remarks, because every so often she giggled.

"Well, uh, it seems that this Com-Pewter is similar to a machine I had in Mundania," he said. "Actually, what I had was a computer, and all I used it for was word processing— that's the Mundane term for writing papers. I would type on this keyboard—that's, uh, do you know what a typewriter is? Um, well, then, it's like a magic pen that sort of writes the words for you; all you have to do is touch the right keys, and it sort of saves the words and then prints, uh, writes them all in one big swoop at the end."

"Mundania must be a very strange place," Rapunzel observed, kicking her feet. She had petite feet and very nice legs; he could just about see them from the corner of his eye. He understood that she had elven ancestry, so could assume the size of elves—or any other size, from tiny to huge— without changing her form at all.

"Very strange," he agreed. "Anyway, I got a new program for this computer—a program is sort of a set of instructions that tells it what to do, and—"

"Oh, the way Queen Irene tells Ivy what to do?"

"Uh, not exactly, but maybe close enough. This new program changed it a lot. It started talking to me on its screen, and uh, well, I guess granting wishes."

"That doesn't sound like Com-Pewter!" she exclaimed, tossing her hair. That was quite a trick, because her hair was as long as forever; in fact she had tied a hank of it to his pocket button as an anchor in case she should fall. The rest of it flowed out about her like a silken cloak. It was dark at her head, but faded to almost white at the end of the tresses, luxuriant all the way. Her eyes shifted colors similarly, depending on the shadow. "It doesn't grant wishes, it changes reality to suit itself."

"This, uh, program may have done the same thing. It— well, I wanted a nice girlfriend. I really, well, I was pretty.

lonely, there by myself in my room all the time, not much good at anything, and—"

Rapunzel stroked his ear with a duster formed from braided hair. "I understand perfectly. I was locked up in a tower for ages. If it hadn't been for my correspondence with Ivy, I don't know what I would have done."

"Yes, I guess you do understand! So the program, well, it claimed to have brought Ivy—"

"But she was sent by the Heaven Cent!"

"Yes. To where she was most needed—and I sure needed her! So I guess the computer was just taking credit for that when it wasn't so. But it must have known she was coming. And it did help; it made it possible for us to talk together. It was, well, like magic. Ivy recognized it as Com-Pewter. So when it turned out I had magic, she remembered that, and figured Com-Pewter must know something, so we're going to find out what it knows."

"But—but how could Com-Pewter be in Mundania?" she asked, cutely perplexed. He couldn't see her face, but the cuteness was caressing his ear like a warm earmuff on a chill day. Grundy was a lucky golem.

"That is another mystery," Grey admitted. "I thought it was a scientific program that accounted for the change in my computer, but now I recognize it as magic. So we have two problems: how can a Mundane have magic, and how can there be magic in Mundania? They may be linked, and surely Com-Pewter knows the answer to at least one of them."

"Thank you," she said. "Now I understand. Of course you must ask the evil machine. But I hope it doesn't get the better of you."

"Well, I do have, uh, magic, now, and if I can null other magic, maybe I can null Com-Pewter. So we shouldn't have much to fear."

"But if the machine knows about you and helped put you in touch with Ivy, it may know how to handle you."

"Um, yes. I'd better warn Ivy before we go into its cave." But Grey was not unduly worried because he knew that computers could not take any physical action. How could it stop him from just walking out, when its magic couldn't work on him when he didn't want it to?

He walked faster, catching up to Ivy. "Hey, Rapunzel thought of something," he said.

" 'Punzel's got a lot of thoughts in her little head," Grundy agreed. "But her hair stops most of them from getting out, fortunately."

"Unlike Grundy's big mouth," Rapunzel retorted, "which lets everything out, ready or not."

Grundy put his thumbs up beside his ears, waggling his fingers at her. She responded by sticking out her tongue at him. Again, Grey felt the gesture though he couldn't see it. This seemed to be just another incidental aspect of the magic of Xanth.

"Hey, I thought you two liked each other!" Grey said.

"No we don't," Grundy said, glowering.

"That's true," Rapunzel agreed with her teeth clenched. "But—"

"We *love* each other!" they exclaimed together, and broke out laughing.

Ivy laughed too. "I guess you walked into that one, Grey," she said.

"I guess I did," he agreed ruefully.

"They do that to anyone who hasn't known them before," Ivy continued. "Before they got together, Grundy had a loud mouth and little thought, while 'Punzel had vice versa. Now he thinks more and she talks more, and they overlap quite a bit."

"Oh, you told!" Grundy exclaimed, while Rapunzel blushed. "And you said *I* had a big mouth!"

Ivy looked flustered. "What I meant by 'overlap' was—"

Rapunzel could no longer stifle her giggle. "Gotcha!" Grundy said.

Grey stifled a grin. So it wasn't just newcomers who got teased! "But about what Rapunzel thought of—if Com-Pewter knows about me, should we just walk into his lair?"

Ivy considered. "I think Pewter wants us to come to him. I have the feeling that we shall have to do some dealing to get our information. So we have to go in. It isn't as if my folks don't know where I am, this time."

Grey realized that the King of Xanth could probably make a lot of trouble for the machine, if sufficiently annoyed. The machine surely knew that. Maybe that was enough of a backup.

"But if push comes to shove," she continued, "we can coordinate on some plan to overcome the evil machine."

"But he will overhear whatever we plan!"

She brought up her right hand, putting her two larger fingers together with her thumb in the sign for *no*.

Now he understood. Grey nodded, not making a big thing of it because he realized that someone might be magically watching or listening. They did have a secret language, thanks to that episode in Mundania. He rehearsed the signs in his mind, hoping he remembered enough to be intelligible.

They resumed their walk. "Was that a magic gesture?" Rapunzel inquired softly in his ear.

"Not exactly," he murmured. "But if you see us moving our hands when we're with Com-Pewter, pay no attention so the machine doesn't catch on."

"Very well," she agreed, perplexed.

The path was devious, but in due course they arrived at the cave of the dread machine. It seemed to be guarded by an invisible giant, but they were not affrighted. They knew that the giant was there only to stampede travelers into the cave where Com-Pewter had power.

"Hey, bigfoot, how ya doing?" Grundy called, his voice amazingly loud. Grey realized that Ivy was enhancing it for him so that he could reach the giant's distant head, up there in the clouds.

"*Aooooga!*" the giant's voice dropped down. Apparently the giant's language, like his body, was unintelligible to normal folk here in regular Xanth.

"Hey, that's great!" the golem replied. Grey remembered that Grundy could speak the languages of all living things.

"Ask him if he knows Girard," Ivy suggested.

"Hey, empty-face! Know Girard?"

A foghorn series of grunts came down. "Yes, he was a loner, always doing odd things," Grundy translated.

"That's the one!" Grey agreed. "But he's happy now."

"I'll tell him about how Girard went to the gourd." Grundy went into a series of honks and gross gutturals.

"Look, we have to get on with our business," Ivy said impatiently. "You can stay out here and chat if you want, but Grey and I have to talk with Com-Pewter."

"I'm ready," Grundy said. "Giants aren't much for conversation anyway. At least this one doesn't smell as bad as they usually do."

"I made him take a bath, last time," Ivy explained.

They entered the cave. It was dark near the opening, but lighted deeper in. They came to a chamber with polished walls, and sure enough, something very like a homemade computer sitting on the floor. This, then, was Com-Pewter.

"Doesn't look like much to me," Grey remarked. "I mean, I'm no computer engineer, but even I can see this equipment is obsolete."

"Watch it!" Grundy said. "This thing can hear you, and it can do things you wouldn't believe!"

Grey had seen enough of the golem to realize that he had respect for almost nothing. If he was in awe of this crude machine, Com-Pewter must indeed have power.

The pane of glass at the top of the assemblage lighted. WHO ARE YOU? it printed.

"I am Princess Ivy," Ivy said quickly. "I have brought my betrothed, Grey of Mundania, to talk with you."

AH, AT LAST! the screen printed.

"All we want to know is, what do you know about Grey?" Ivy said. "He has a magic talent, and—"

OF COURSE. WHAT IS HIS TALENT?

Grey had a sudden suspicion. He flashed a *no* sign to Ivy. If the machine didn't know his talent, it was better to keep it in reserve.

Ivy caught the signal. "Well, Pewter, we thought you would know. So we came to consult with you. After all, you were in touch with him in Mundania, weren't you?"

YES AND NO.

"You were *not* in touch?" Grey asked, startled. "But we saw—" He broke off, halted by Ivy's *no* sign. She was right; there was no point in telling this machine any more than they had to.

YOU SAW WHAT?

"We saw something that reminded us of you," Grey said carefully. "Can you explain it?"

I DO NOT HAVE TO EXPLAIN.

"Then we shall depart," Ivy said, turning to face the cave exit.

PRINCESS DISCOVERS DOOR LOCKED, CAN NOT EXIT, the screen printed.

A closed door appeared, shutting off the exit.

"I don't see anything," Grey said. "Come on, Ivy, let's go." He took her arm and walked to the door. As he had expected, it was illusion; they walked right through it.

A bell dinged. They turned to look back. IT WAS A BLUFF, the screen printed. I SHALL ANSWER ALL YOUR QUESTIONS.

They returned, but Ivy made a sign he couldn't interpret. He assumed it meant something like "caution." It was obvious that this was a treacherous and perhaps mean-spirited machine.

"Why does Grey have a talent, when he is Mundane?" Ivy asked.

BECAUSE HE IS NOT MUNDANE.

"But I *am* Mundane!" Grey exclaimed. "This is the first time I've set foot in Xanth. I didn't even believe in it, before!"

TRUE, the screen responded. BUT NOT THE WHOLE TRUTH.

"Then give us the whole truth!" Ivy said.

YOU WILL NOT NECESSARILY LIKE IT.

Grey exchanged another half glance with Ivy. What was this machine getting at?

"Why not?" Ivy asked after a pause.

LET'S MAKE A DEAL. TELL ME ALL YOU KNOW ABOUT GREY, AND I WILL TELL YOU ALL I KNOW.

"How can you be ignorant of what we know, if you know things we don't?" Grey asked.

I ASSURE YOU IT IS SO. I NEED TO KNOW YOUR STORY IN ORDER TO BE ASSURED OF THE RELEVANCE OF MINE. AFTER WE EXCHANGE INFORMATION WE SHALL HAVE TO DEAL AGAIN. THIS IS WHAT YOU WILL NOT NECESSARILY LIKE.

Again they considered. It seemed to Grey that if the machine tried something they objected to, like conjuring a monster, he could stop it by using his talent to null Com-Pewter himself. This would be as effective if the machine knew his talent as if it did not. Perhaps more effective, because of the psychological element.

He caught Ivy's eye again. She nodded. They would deal.

"We agree," Grey said. "We will tell you what we know, and then you will tell us what you know, with no concealment. But we make no commitment about dealing thereafter."

AGREED. START WITH YOUR LOCATION AND THE MANNER YOU CONTACTED MY EMISSARY.

Grey started in. He described his origin in Mundania, and the way he had installed the new program and then encountered a series of odd girls before meeting Ivy. He concluded by telling of his magic talent.

AMAZING! I KNEW YOU WOULD HAVE MAGIC, BUT NOT THAT IT WOULD BE MAGICIAN CLASS. PERHAPS SOME MUNDANE INTERACTION ENHANCED IT. THIS IS COMPLETELY POSITIVE.

"Your turn, Pewter," Ivy said grimly.

IT WILL BE MORE TELLING IF I DRAMATIZE THE ORIGIN.

"Do it any way you want," Grey said. "Just give us the full information."

The screen changed color. It became a picture of a dark lake in a cave, in shades of gray. Print flashed over the picture: THE TIME OF NO MAGIC.

"What?" Grey asked.

PRINCESS IVY WILL EXPLAIN WHILE I SHOW THE SCENES, the screen printed.

"It was before my time," Ivy said. "In fact, before my father's time. Something happened, and the magic of all Xanth turned off." As she spoke, the scene shifted to show limp tangle trees and bedraggled dragons, all suffering from the loss of the magic that sustained them. "I think it only lasted for a few hours, but it was awful. Xanth was dying. Then the magic came back on, and it hasn't been off since—but things weren't the same. The Gorgon had stoned a whole lot of men, and they all came back to life when the magic went and stayed alive when it returned. But the magic creatures and plants were pretty much the same. Apparently it was only temporary magic that got nulled. But the Forget Spell on the Gap Chasm took a horrible jolt, and it began to break up, and now it's gone. My father was delivered right after that; the ogres marked his birthday wrong on their calendar; they always were somewhat ham-handed."

Meanwhile the scene on the screen, which resembled nothing so much as a television movie before the days of color, had completed its scan of the devastation wreaked by the loss of magic, and returned to the subterranean pool. From this pool two figures struggled. One was a man of healthy middle age; the other was a rather pretty young woman. Others were emerging from the pool, including some monsters, but the scene oriented on these two. They seemed not to get along very well; they gesticulated as if telling each other to go away. But the man found a ledge leading up a river tunnel, and the woman followed.

Then Grey realized that there were subtitles. He moved closer to the screen with Ivy so that they could read the words, for they were in much smaller print than before, so as not to obscure the picture.

LOOK, the bedraggled woman was saying, YOU DON'T LIKE ME AND I DON'T LIKE YOU, BUT WE CAN GET OUT OF HERE FASTER IF WE COOPERATE. ONCE THE MAGIC RETURNS WE WILL BOTH BE FINISHED; YOU KNOW THAT.

The man in the picture considered. VERY WELL—WE SHALL COOPERATE UNTIL WE GET OUT OF XANTH. THEN WE GO OUR OWN WAYS.

THAT'S FINE! she agreed.

They hurried on up the river. A monster appeared like a

twisted small sphinx. I'LL RESHAPE IT, the woman said. She gestured.

But nothing happened. OH, I FORGOT! THERE IS NO MAGIC! THAT'S WHY WE WERE ABLE TO ESCAPE FROM THE BRAIN CORAL'S STORAGE POOL.

BUT WE DON'T KNOW WHEN THE MAGIC WILL RETURN, the man reminded her. WE HAVE TO KEEP MOVING OR THE CORAL WILL RECAPTURE US!

As they talked, Grey found himself getting used to the printed dialogue, and it seemed increasingly as if he actually heard them speak. The scene became real for him, as was often the case when he watched movies.

"But I'm getting tired!" the woman protested. "I'm not used to terrain like this!"

"What do you want, woman—for me to carry you?" he demanded irately. "I'm tired myself!"

"Only to slow the pace a little. Look, we can't possibly get all the way to Xanth border afoot without resting; it will be better to set a pace we can maintain so we can go farther without collapsing."

The man considered. "You are correct." He slowed the pace.

TIME PASSES, the screen said, the picture fading out. Then it showed the two emerging into daylight. They were obviously both quite fatigued. They fetched some sodden pillows from a defunct pillow bush and lay down to rest and then to sleep.

It was early morning, and evidently cold. There were no blankets, and the pillows were falling apart. Finally they embraced, not with any passion but to conserve their body warmth, and slept.

TIME PASSES.

The next scene showed the two back on their feet, bedraggled but moving better. They found stray items of food, snatching spoiling pies from bushes and eating as they traveled.

Then they encountered the Gap Chasm.

"We forgot about this!" the woman exclaimed, appalled. In

that moment in the bright daylight, she looked almost familiar, but Grey could not quite place the connection. Certainly he had known no one in Xanth then; he hadn't been alive!

"Naturally," the man agreed gruffly. "That idiot detonated the most powerful Forget Spell ever forged in it; it will be centuries before that dissipates, if ever."

The woman nodded grimly. "The same idiot who introduced Millie the Maid to the Zombie Master. I would have married him, in due course, if he hadn't been smitten by her! How could a Magician fall for a nothing like her?"

"The Zombie Master and Millie the Ghost!" Ivy exclaimed. "They did live in that time, before they came to ours!"

The man smiled. "She had a talent. She needed nothing else."

"Oh, yes—the talent of sex appeal! But she'd be just as drab as I am now, if she were here without her magic!"

The man eyed her. "Indubitably true. Now don't misunderstand me; I regard you as a bad attitude that walks like a girl, but physically you are not drab."

"Well, the same to you! Who are you to talk? Everything you touch fouls up! But you're hardly ugly, physically."

"Oh?" he inquired, annoyed. "Well, things are supposed to foul up; that's my talent. And not only are you not drab, you are in fact quite shapely, in your fashion."

"Is that so?" she demanded angrily. "You are the worst villain on the scene! But actually you're handsome!"

It was obvious by the man's sinister expression that he intended to strike back at her hard. "I would even go so far as to call you beautiful," he said with calculated affront. "Only those rags you're in detract."

She was almost speechless with rage. She tore off her remaining clothes and stood naked. "Well, now I'm out of these rags: I dare you to repeat that!"

"I repeat it," he said nastily, eying her thoroughly so as to be absolutely certain. "I had supposed that you used your talent to reshape your body to better advantage, but I know now that you came by it naturally. You can't claim the excuse of Sorceress-level enhancement."

"I'm no Sorceress!" she screamed in his face. "You think everybody is Magician level like you?"

"That is a matter of opinion. I have a right to mine. Your magic is Sorceress level."

The woman opened her mouth, but no sound came out. She jumped at him, clawing at his chest, but succeeded only in ripping away much of his own tattered clothing. Then he caught her wrists and held her helpless. "Furthermore," he said, his face close to hers, "you think you lack sex appeal, but last night when we slept embraced for warmth it was all I could do to refrain from taking advantage of you."

"Well, why didn't you?" she cried. "It's your business to foul things up! Do you foul yourself up too, so you can't even do wrong by a woman in your power?"

"I foul things up *magically*," he retorted. "This had nothing to do with magic! You have natural sex appeal; deny it as you will!"

"Well, you have it yourself, so there! You know what I think? I think that, deny it as you will, you have a fundamentally decent streak in you! Otherwise, last night—I mean it isn't as if I would have resisted!"

They stood there, chest to chest, each angrier than the other. "You female dog!" he said. "I have half a mind to—"

"So do I! So do I, you male dog!" she retorted.

"You probably wouldn't even slap me if I kissed you, you shameless creature."

"I dare you to kiss me, you hypocrite!"

Their lips met. He tried to sneer to show how little he cared; she tried to make a mush lips to show how indifferent she was. They both bungled it badly in their fury. The kiss lasted a long time, and the shameful truth was that it was a rather intense and effective example of its breed.

"Understand, I have no respect for you at all," he told her after the long moment. His hair was ruffled and his face was flushed, as if he had just been exposed to a truly repulsive experience. "I am doing this only because the sight and feel of your body overwhelms my better judgment."

"Your embrace destroys any judgment I have!" she shot

back. Her eyes were sparkling and her cheeks had what would have been rosy highlights in a color scene, as if she had just experienced something too awful to recognize. "I detest what you are making me so eager to do!"

"I will be thoroughly disgusted with myself tomorrow," he said ominously.

"I will feel totally without virtue, tomorrow," she replied grimly.

"Just to be quite certain we understand how bad this is," he said, "we had better try it another time."

"Just so we never so far forget ourselves as to make this mistake again," she agreed.

They kissed again, and sure enough, it was even worse than before. Both of them were breathless when it finished, their chests heaving as if they had been running.

"I am appalled to think that I am doing this with you," he said, holding her more closely than was necessary for support. "With anyone else it could be worthwhile."

"Well, I'm not taking this lying down," she said, disengaging so she could lie down.

He joined her. "And when I realize that we could have been making good our escape from Xanth, instead of wasting our time like this—"

"Or catching up on our rest," she added, putting her arms around him. "There has probably never been anything quite as foolish as this!"

"Especially considering that we detest each other." He drew her in quite close.

"And want nothing so much as never to see each other again," she agreed, stroking his back.

"This entire business is disastrous!"

"A complete catastrophe!"

They kissed yet again, both shuddering with the disgust they felt for this outrage.

"Say, this is getting hot!" Grundy said zestfully.

"Watch your mouth!" Rapunzel snapped, jumping down to approach him menacingly.

"Listen, hairball—" he started, meeting her.

They laughed, embracing.

Something had been nagging Grey as he watched the screen. Now he realized what it was: Grundy and Rapunzel's joke. Acting as if they hated each other—that was what this episode of the man and woman was like!

Then something strange happened. It took Grey another moment to figure it out. Color was appearing on the screen!

"I thought Pewter couldn't handle color." Ivy said.

"I didn't know Pewter could handle pictures!" Grundy said. "It was always just print, before."

"You're missing the best part," Rapunzel murmured.

Grey's gaze snapped back to the screen. "What are they doing?" he asked, amazed.

"We aren't supposed to tell you," Rapunzel said. "Ever since we joined the Adult Conspiracy."

Then the scene changed. It showed a snoozing big-beaked bird suddenly waking, as if jolted by an unexpected call.

"They're summoning the stork!" Ivy exclaimed, catching on. "And it just got the message! I never knew how it was done!"

"You are losing your innocence," Rapunzel said sadly.

The picture returned to the man and woman. They had just realized something themselves. "The magic has returned!" she exclaimed. And there, Grey realized, was the significance of the color on the screen: it signified the magic ambience of Xanth, after the blah shades of gray of the Time of No Magic.

"We did, indeed, dally too long," the man replied. Oddly, he did not look as unhappy about their dalliance as might have been expected.

"Much too long," the woman agreed, seeming no more upset about their folly than he.

"But we can still escape!" he said. "The Brain Coral should be disorganized for a time, and it can't act directly; it will have to send a message to recapture us, and that will be hard to do for a few hours."

The woman gazed out into the Gap Chasm, at whose lip they had just summoned the stork. "But it will take us days to cross this, even if we can get past the dragon at the bottom.

We don't dare use a magic bridge or even a recognized crossing region!"

"True." He considered briefly. "Perhaps we should foul up the pursuit by doing the completely unexpected: traveling south, instead of north toward the exit from Xanth."

"But then we won't escape Xanth at all! They will use magic to ferret us out, and we'll be done for!"

"Maybe not. I can exert my talent to foul up the pursuit, and you can exert yours to reshape some blankets into clothing for us. We might yet be able to sneak out before they get truly organized."

"But that means we shall have to stay together!" she said, expressing a good deal more alarm than she seemed to feel.

"It is a burden we shall just have to endure," he said, surprisingly undismayed.

"I suppose so. Just so we don't do any of this again," she said, putting her arms around him.

"Or any of this," he agreed, kissing her.

"How fortunate that we understand each other so well," she said, with a smile that might have had a hint of wryness.

"Well, we certainly made our attitude toward each other clear enough," he agreed with even less of a hint of irony.

"When you insulted me by calling my talent Sorceress level, did you really mean it?"

"Of course I meant that insult!" he said indignantly. "Do you think I would compliment you?"

She was silent, but there were tears in her eyes. It was evident that of all the insults he had proffered, that was the one that had scored most effectively. Perhaps it had been the one that caused her to make the supreme sacrifice of dragging him right down to the awful business of summoning the stork. Certainly her revenge had been effective, costly as it must have been to her self-esteem.

They walked south, away from the chasm, their aversion for each other manifesting in subtle ways, such as when he mockingly helped her over a fallen tree or when she was just as mockingly gave him the finest of the yellowberry pies she discovered. At times they waxed eloquent in their sarcasm, addressing each other as "dear" or "darling," and every so often they kissed again, just to make sure the revulsion was undiminished. A stranger might even have been fooled into thinking they felt about each other as Grey and Ivy did, so perfect was their emulation of that lamented state. It was a truly amazing performance.

Then they encountered an invisible giant. The monster was stumbling around, evidently still dazed by the recent absence of magic, and there was no telling where his clumsy foot would fall next. They fled into a nearby cave for safety.

GREETINGS, INTRUDERS, a screen printed.

The two halted, there in the cave, drawing together for mutual protection despite their dislike of each other. "What are you?" the man demanded.

I AM COM-PEWTER. I GOVERN THIS REGION. YOU ARE NOW IN MY POWER.

"I have news for you," the man said. "I am a—"

He stopped, for the woman had elbowed him. They were trying to hide their identities.

"I am about to depart this cave with my, um, wife," the man said, choking down the implied intimacy for the sake of concealing their actual feelings for one another. "I don't believe in your power." The two of them turned to go, evidently concluding that the staggering giant was a better risk than this strange device.

DOOR SLAMS CLOSED, PREVENTING EXIT, the screen printed.

A door appeared across the exit. It slammed open.

WHAT WENT WRONG? the screen demanded, appalled.

"Anything that can go wrong, will go wrong," the man murmured, smiling obscurely.

I HEARD THAT! the screen printed. NOW I KNOW YOU! YOU ARE MAGICIAN MURPHY, FRESHLY ESCAPED FROM THE STORAGE POOL OF THE BRAIN CORAL! AN EVIL MAN!

"Magician Murphy!" Ivy exclaimed. "I *thought* his talent seemed familiar!"

Murphy, glancing back, saw the print. "Curses! We shall have to destroy this thing, lest it give us away."

WAIT! I AM AN EVIL MACHINE! WE MUST POOL OUR RE-
SOURCES FOR GREATER EVIL THAN EVER!

"Now that's interesting," the woman said. "Just what is a
machine? I think I should render it into a topologically harmless configuration, just to be sure."

AND YOU MUST BE VADNE, EVIL BUT BEAUTIFUL SORCER-
ESS, ALSO ESCAPED FROM CONFINEMENT IN THE POOL.

"That's my mother's name!" Grey exclaimed. "Vadne Murphy! But she's forty years old! She's no beautiful Sorceress!"

Then he stared at Ivy, the revelation dawning.

"Not in Mundania," Ivy said. "Not nineteen years later. All
that time with no magic, getting worn down by drear existence . . ."

On the screen, Vadne pursed her lips. "Beautiful Sorceress?
This thing insults me just as you do! Maybe we should consult further with this device."

I WILL HELP YOU ESCAPE RECAPTURE IF YOU HELP ME GAIN
ULTIMATE POWER OVER XANTH, the screen offered.

"But we must flee Xanth!" Magician Murphy protested.
"We are fugitives! There is no freedom for us here! We can
not help you at all."

Com-Pewter considered, the screen pulsing gently with the
word CONSIDERING blinking in a corner. Then: I HAVE THE
PATIENCE OF THE INANIMATE. I AM PREPARED TO DEFER MY
AMBITION FOR THE SAKE OF A BETTER CHANCE OF ITS
ACHIEVEMENT. I WILL GET YOU OUT OF XANTH NOW IF YOU
WILL GIVE ME YOUR SON.

"What?" Murphy, Vadne, and Grey asked together.

YOU HAVE SUMMONED THE STORK WITH AN ORDER FOR A
SON, the screen printed. YOU MAY NOT RETURN TO XANTH,
BUT YOUR SON MAY. GIVE HIM TO ME IN EXCHANGE FOR
YOUR ESCAPE. I WILL ACCEPT HIS SERVICE IN LIEU OF YOURS.

Murphy and Vadne exchanged a glance and a half. "We
would have to stay together, even in Mundania," she said.
"Can we stand that?"

"Are you implying I can't stand as much as you can?" he
demanded. Then, to Pewter: "We are evil folk; how can you
trust us to keep that pledge?"

YOU MAY BE EVIL, BUT YOUR SON WILL BE GOOD. WHEN
HE LEARNS OF YOUR PLEDGE, HE WILL HONOR IT.

The two considered. Then, reluctantly, they made the deal.
The picture faded out.

It was only a moment, but it seemed like a generation to
Grey, as he oriented on what he had learned. His parents—
escaped criminals of Xanth! That explained so much, but was
also so difficult to accept. How could he deal with this?

"So you were brought by the Xanth stork," Rapunzel said.
"Your magic talent must have been set by your origin, even
though your parents left Xanth and you were delivered in
Mundania."

"They have a, uh different way of doing it in Mundania,"
Grey said. "But yes, I was conceived—uh, signaled for—in
Xanth, so that does explain my magic. And having a Magician
and a Sorceress for parents meant I had that level of talent
too, just as was the case with Ivy. But if they escaped at the
Time of No Magic, that was before King Dor was, uh, delivered. So how come I'm not his age?"

"No problem," Grundy said. "There's a time curtain at the
border. We can step from Xanth into any time of Mundania,
and any place of Mundania too, but Mundanes have more
trouble controlling it. Com-Pewter must have arranged for
them to step into the Mundania of more recent vintage."

I ARRANGED THAT, Com-Pewter agreed. THIS IS THE COM-
PLETION OF MY PLOT. I WAITED TO BRING YOU TO XANTH
UNTIL THERE WAS AN AVAILABLE PRINCESS FOR YOU TO
MARRY. I ADMIT THAT THERE WAS AN ELEMENT OF CHANCE
WHEN I SENT YOUR PARENTS TO THE CURRENT TIME, BECAUSE
THE FIRSTBORN OF THIS GENERATION MIGHT NOT HAVE BEEN
FEMALE. WHEN IT WAS, I KNEW IT WAS TIME TO ACT. MY
QUACKS WERE ALIGNED.

"Quacks?" Grey asked. "Oh, you mean ducks."

"So it *was* you in Mundania!" Ivy exclaimed.

IT WAS MY SENDING. I COULD NOT GO THERE, SO I SENT
MY ESSENCE. THERE WAS THAT KERNEL OF MAGIC ABOUT
GREY, EVEN THERE, SO IT WAS POSSIBLE TO ANIMATE HIS
MACHINE IN HIS PRESENCE. I DID NOT KNOW WHAT HAPPENED

THERE, ONLY WHAT ITS CAPACITY WAS. IT WAS TO ORIENT ON HIM AND MANIFEST ONLY WHEN HE WAS BEYOND THE AGE OF EIGHTEEN YEARS SO THAT HE WOULD BE RIGHT FOR THE PRINCESS. THEN I SENT THE PRINCESS TO HIM.

"The Heaven Cent sent me!" Ivy flared.

THE HEAVEN CENT SENT YOU TO WHERE YOU WERE MOST NEEDED, WHICH I PREDEFINED AS THE LOCATION OF MAGICIAN MURPHY'S SON. IT WAS INTENDED THAT YOU MARRY HIM.

"Our romance—arranged by the evil machine?" Ivy asked, appalled.

LIVING FOLK ARE SUBJECT TO CERTAIN PATTERNS. I INSTITUTED ONE OF THOSE PATTERNS. NOW MURPHY'S SON IS HERE, AND BOUND TO SERVE ME.

"I made no such deal!" Grey protested.

YOUR PARENTS DID. THEY NEVER INTENDED TO HONOR IT, AND SO KEPT ALL KNOWLEDGE OF XANTH FROM YOU SO YOU WOULD NOT WANT TO COME HERE. BUT I SENT MY ESSENCE AND THEN SENT PRINCESS IVY TO BRING YOU HERE, AND NOW YOU ARE BOUND, BECAUSE YOU HAVE HONOR YOUR PARENTS LACK.

"They have honor!" Grey said. "They were trying to save Xanth, even though they were exiled from it!"

"How do we know you're telling the truth, dim-bulb?" Grundy demanded. "Maybe they never made that deal, and you're just making it up in your pictures!"

I EXPECT GREY MURPHY TO RETURN TO MUNDANIA TO VERIFY THIS. THEN HE WILL EITHER REMAIN THERE OR RETURN TO XANTH AND HONOR THE DEAL.

Grey had the sick feeling that this was the truth. But there was still much to be clarified. "So maybe I was supposed to come to Xanth," he said. "Why was it so important that I marry Ivy? I mean, I care about her, but you don't care about either of us or about romance."

YES. YOU ARE ONLY TOOLS FOR MY AMBITION. YOU MUST MARRY IVY AND BE QUEEN OF XANTH, OR EVEN KING, SINCE YOUR MAGIC IS MAGICIAN CALIBER. EITHER WAY YOU WILL HAVE GREAT INFLUENCE ON THE THRONE OR CONTROL IT EN-

TIRELY. SINCE YOU WILL BE SERVING ME, I WILL BE THE TRUE
RULER OF XANTH. THAT IS THE CULMINATION OF MY PLOT.

Grey stared at Ivy, who looked back with the same horror
he felt. The situation was clear at last: they could go to Mundania together, or they could break their betrothal and both
remain in Xanth, or they could marry and do the evil machine's will. None of those choices was acceptable.

"Oh, I wish the Good Magician was still here!" Ivy exclaimed. "He would know what to do about this!"

HO HO HO! I GOT RID OF THE GOOD MAGICIAN AS PART OF
THIS PLOT! YOU CAN'T GET HIS ADVICE BECAUSE YOU CAN'T
FIND HIM, AND I WILL NEVER TELL WHERE HE IS!

"*You* did that?" Ivy cried, enraged. "All that mischief, all
those un-Answered Questions, just to further your foul plot?"

"I think you should put your hand on this collection of
junk and null it, Grey," Grundy said. "You won't have to
serve it if it doesn't operate any more."

THAT WOULD BE UNETHICAL, THEREFORE GREY MURPHY
WILL NOT DO IT.

Grey gritted his teeth. It was the truth.

"Oh, Grey," Ivy exclaimed, tears in her eyes. "What are
we going to do?"

YOU ARE GOING TO AGONIZE FOR A TIME, THEN VERIFY
THE ACCURACY OF MY STATEMENT, AND FINALLY CONFORM.
YOU HAVE ONE MONTH FROM THIS MOMENT TO CONCLUDE
YOUR BUSINESS AND RETURN TO ME. THEN I WILL RULE
XANTH. HO HO HO!

Grey was very much afraid that the evil machine was
correct.

13

MURPHY

"So that's the situation," Ivy concluded. "Grey's a Magician, so I can marry him, but he is bound to serve Com-Pewter, so I don't dare let him close to the throne. And even if I don't marry him, he could later become King of Xanth in his own right, and Pewter would have power. The only way we can see to stop that is for Grey to return to Mundania and stay there. Then Pewter's deal would have no force."

King Dor nodded. "Is Grey willing to do that?"

"Yes. He doesn't want to hurt me or Xanth, and he has the strength of his convictions."

Queen Irene leaned forward. "Then what of you, Ivy?"

Ivy had pondered this on the way home to Castle Roogna, and seen the stark alternatives. Either she could go with Grey and live in Mundania, or she could remain in Xanth and not marry Grey. Neither choice was bearable.

Ivy burst into tears.

* * *

But later her parents had further thoughts. "We do not know that what Pewter claims is the truth," Dor said. "We should find out."

"But how?" Ivy asked, without more than half a glimmer of hope. "If it's not the truth, Pewter will never confess it."

"Magician Murphy might, though."

"But he's in Mundania!"

"You could visit there again and ask him."

Ivy's eyes widened. The notion of living in drear Mundania was intolerable, but she could probably survive another visit there.

But still it wasn't good enough. "Why should he tell the truth? He opposes the existing order. That's why he's exiled."

"No, actually," Dor said. "He stepped out of the picture because he had lost to King Roogna. He hoped to return at some time when chances were better for him—such as when there were no Magicians available to be king. Then he could take over. But when he escaped from the Brain Coral's storage pool, there were several Magicians, so Xanth was still no place for him. Rather than remain in storage indefinitely, he fled Xanth. If he forswore his ambition to become King of Xanth, he would have no trouble here."

"But why should he forswear?"

Her father looked her in the eye. "If you were exiled from Xanth for life and were offered the chance to return if you agreed to forswear ever becoming king, would you do it?"

Ivy thought about that. "Maybe so. But it's Grey who is bound by the deal, not Magician Murphy, and it would be no good having a Magician serving Pewter, even if he never was king."

"Your mother and I have discussed this matter, and we conclude that you have three options you may not have considered. You can verify whether what Pewter says is true; and if it is not, you are all right. Or you can bring Magician Murphy back here to Xanth on condition that he serve the existing order. Or—"

"Bring him here?" Ivy demanded incredulously. "The man

who tried to overthrow King Roogna, way back when?"

"Or you can resume the search for Good Magician Humfrey, and ask him how to deal with Pewter," Dor concluded.

"How can you speak of bringing that Evil Magician back? That would just make even more mischief here and wouldn't solve any problems for me and Grey."

Her father explained. Ivy stared. "Do you really think that would work?"

"If it does not, then it may be safe to say that nothing else will."

She had to concede his point. It was a faint and devious hope, but it was the best thing available.

She would visit Mundania, and talk with Magician Murphy, and perhaps invite him back to Xanth.

They set out at dawn: Ivy, Grey, and designated chaperone Electra. The title thrilled her, and she promised to spy on anything the betrotheds might try to do together.

They rode on three fine steeds: Electra was on Donkey, who was now nicely recovered from his captivity with the goblins. Grey rode Pook, the ghost horse. Ivy rode Peek, Pook's ghost mare. The ghost colt, Puck, trotted cheerfully along beside. All three animals had chains wrapped around their barrels, for that was their nature. They had been befriended by Jordan the Barbarian some four hundred plus years before, and though they remained wild, Ivy had enhanced their tameness and they were glad to serve in this temporary capacity.

They made excellent time, trotting most of the way, but the length of Xanth was not traveled in a day and they had to camp along the north coast. The ghost horses wandered, into the night to graze; they ate ghost grass, which was invisible to normally living folk, but Ivy could hear the tiny clinks as the little chains on it rattled.

They walked down to the beach and saw the heaving sea. This was a designated camping place, so the safety enchantment was on it; no monsters or evil plants could intrude here.

But Grey started to walk down a path that crossed the magic line.

"Grey! Where are you going?" Ivy called, alarmed.

"I, uh, have to, you know," he said, embarrassed.

"But you're walking down a tangle tree path! If you cross the line and walk into the clutches of the tree—"

He smiled. "I, uh, maybe you forgot my talent."

"Ooopsy! I did forget!" she said, embarrassed in her turn. "You have nothing to fear from tanglers!"

"Uh, right," he agreed. He walked on down the path.

Curious, she watched. Sure enough, the tangler was quiescent until Grey came within reach. Then it grabbed. Its hanging green tentacles whipped around Grey's body—and abruptly fell away, limp. He brushed on through. After he was done there, he would restore the tree's magic—and if it was a smart tree, it would not bother him again.

Ivy really hadn't thought about this aspect very much, but now she realized that she was as safe with Grey as it was possible to be, because nothing magic could hurt them. That included just about everything in Xanth. Grey could nullify magic partly, or not at all, or even enhance it by the rebound effect. Thus he could use or not use magic, as he chose, to the degree he chose. He really *was* a Magician, whose power matched her own.

They were well matched in other respects, too. Grey had loved her though he did not believe that she had magic or that she was a princess. She had loved Grey though she thought him Mundane. Now each understood what the other was, and it was wonderful. Yet it was all a plot by Com-Pewter, and that made it awful. How near and yet how far!

The waves rose up ahead of her, forming odd shapes. She realized that she had been unconsciously enhancing the magic of the sea as she stood there musing about Grey. Now the water was glowing, and the spume was forming faces.

Curious, she enhanced it further. Soon a big wave took shape and held its position. Its frothy eyes stared out at her, and its little whirlpool of a mouth opened. *"Beeewaare!"* it splashed.

Ivy's own mouth dropped open. It had spoken to her!

Why would a wave try to do such a thing? Did it like being enhanced?

Electra and Donkey approached, quietly. "It's warning us about something," Electra murmured. "We'd better find out what!"

Ivy agreed. She concentrated, giving the wave her best enhancement. "Beware of what?" she called, uncertain whether it could hear or understand her. She tried to enhance its hearing and understanding, but knew there were limits.

"*Paaath oooouut!*" the wave replied. Then it collapsed back into mere water.

"The path is out?" Electra asked. "Maybe a storm washed out the dirt?"

"We should readily see that," Donkey said. "It really did not require such a dramatic warning.

"Maybe the wave isn't very smart," Electra said.

"Still, it meant well," Ivy said. She had never talked to a wave before; that sort of thing was her father's talent. Could she now enhance inanimate things too? Or had she always been able to without realizing it?

She cupped her mouth with her hand. "Thank you, Wave," she called. "We shall beware the path."

A surge of bubbly water washed up around her feet, as if licking them.

Grey returned. They gathered breadfruit and butterballs, and even found an eye scream bush with several flavors of confection.

They settled for the night. Ivy wanted to sleep beside Grey, but chaperone Electra was right there watching, eager to catch them at anything that smacked even faintly of stork. Ivy wasn't sure whether the girl was moved more strongly by duty or curiosity. She remembered how curious she herself had been about the business of stork summoning. In the last year or so she had finally succeeded in piecing together diverse bits of information and, aided by strong hints from Nada, had pretty much solved the riddle. She believed she would be able to summon the stork when the time came. But she had no intention of doing so before she got married. Now she was part of the Adult Conspiracy, obliged to hide the information from children—and Electra was still mostly a child, despite her love for Dolph and her betrothal to him.

So she piled her pillows and blankets and bedded down by herself, and Grey did likewise, though she would so much rather have hugged him to sleep.

In the morning the ghost horses returned, and they resumed their journey. Not far up the path, Peek lifted her nose and sniffed. Pook and Puck did likewise, evidently disturbed by something.

"That warning," Donkey said. "Do you think this is where the path is out?"

"It looks firm to me," Grey said. They had told him of the wave warning.

They went on, cautiously. The path was whole, entirely normal. But the three ghost horses remained skittish, which was unusual for them.

They rounded a turn—and there was a huge land dragon straddling the path. It was a smoker, with clouds of deep gray smoke wafting back from its nostrils.

Grey, in the lead on Pook, came to a sudden halt. "I thought you said this path was enchanted!" he exclaimed.

Ivy, next in line, stopped as suddenly. "It is! No predator is supposed to be able to intrude!"

The dragon formed a toothsome grin. Obviously it had another opinion.

"Well, I'll just null it," Grey said.

"Watch the smoke!" Ivy warned. "It can blind you and choke you before you get close!"

"Pook can get me there before the dragon gets its smoke really up," Grey said. "It won't be expecting us to charge it." He patted the ghost horse. "You do believe in my power?"

Pook nodded, though a trifle uncertainly. He had been told of it, but had not seen it demonstrated.

There was a roar from the rear. Ivy looked back. There was another dragon, like the first but slightly smaller. Surely the smoker's mate. "It's a trap!" she cried. "They have boxed us in!"

Electra, on Donkey, was third in line. "We'll take this one!" she cried.

"No!" Ivy screamed. "You can't—"

But now both dragons roared horrendously. Smoke billowed, for the moment masking them.

"Now!" Grey called. "While they're drawing breath!"

"But—" Ivy started, flustered.

Pook charged forward, and Donkey charged back. Ivy was left in mid-protest in the middle.

Grey disappeared into the cloud of smoke. She knew he could null the dragon if he got close enough to touch it, and at the rate the ghost horse was going they would not just touch but collide. It was Electra who needed help.

Peek, responding to Ivy's decision, whirled and galloped back. The smoke was thinning. She saw the fuzzy outline of Electra strike the dragon on the sooty snoot. The dragon blinked, shocked. But Ivy knew that Electra's charge could not knock out a dragon this size; it would only set it back a moment. Then there would be real trouble.

As Ivy reached them, Donkey was kicking the dragon's head with his hind hooves. The dragon, still jolted by the electric shock, was not moving, but the hoof strikes were only rattling its head, not making it retreat.

Still, it was an idea. "I'll enhance you," Ivy told Peek. "You turn about and deliver your hardest kick to its chin. Don't miss!"

She concentrated on enhancing Peek's power of kick. She imagined the hooves as having the same hardness as the metal chains, and the legs having enormous power. This would be some kick!

Peek turned, threw down her head, and let go with a phenomenal two-hoof kick. It connected. Ivy felt the shock; it jolted her teeth. Was it enough?

Peek's feet came down. She turned again. They both looked, and so did Electra and Donkey.

The dragon was flat on its back, its tail twitching. Peek's

double-hooved kick had flipped the monster all the way over, and knocked it out. The kick had indeed been enough.

Grey and Pook trotted up. "The front dragon is unconscious," Grey reported. "And so is this one, by the look of it."

"But how did they get on the enchanted path?" Electra asked.

"Now I think I understand," Donkey said. "The wave's warning: the *spell* on the path is out! So it isn't safe, in this section."

All three ghost horses nodded. They had known it, but had been unable to speak their knowledge.

"But the spell was set by Good Magician Humfrey," Ivy said. "He wouldn't let anything happen to it!"

"Not if he were still around," Electra said. "But he's been gone for seven years."

Ivy felt stupid. Of course the Good Magician was gone; it was Dolph's Quest for him that had introduced him to Nada and Electra, and Ivy's Quest for him that had introduced her to Grey. Now other folk could tinker with his spells with impunity. "We've got to get him back!" she muttered.

"There must be a counterspell here," Electra said. "To cancel out the path enchantment. So the monsters can get in."

"Then maybe I can null it," Grey said. "Except I don't know how to relate to it."

"I'll enhance your ability to relate," Ivy said. "Then maybe you can null it."

He shrugged. "It's worth a try."

They dismounted and took each other's hands. "You're Holding Hands!" Electra exclaimed. "I'm going to Report that!"

"If you do, I'll report that time you sneaked into my little brother's room and held his hand while he was sleeping," Ivy said darkly.

Electra looked so abashed that Ivy, Grey, and Donkey burst out laughing. One of the charming things about Electra was that she retained so much of the innocence of childhood.

Ivy concentrated on Grey's power of relation. She felt

something happening, but wasn't sure what. Then there was a moment of vertigo.

"Got it!" Grey said. "The source of the problem is over there." He walked to the side of the path. "This—bit of wood?" he asked, picking it up.

"That's reverse wood!" Ivy exclaimed. "It must have reversed the enchantment on the path, right here near it, so the dragons could get in!"

"Well, I'll null it, then."

"Don't do that!" Ivy said quickly. "Suppose it reversed your talent?"

"But we can't leave the path unprotected!"

"Just throw the wood away," Donkey suggested. "It won't do any harm if it's not in the path."

Grey wound up and hurled the wood far to the side. Immediately the three ghost horses reacted, relaxing. The two unconscious dragons stirred. Each dragged itself up and scrambled away from the path.

"Problem solved," Donkey said with satisfaction.

"But there never would have been a problem if the Good Magician were still around," Ivy said. "As soon as we settle our personal problem, we'll have to resume the Quest for him. We can't continue much longer without him."

"If we could find him, maybe he could settle all our personal questions," Electra said.

Ivy nodded. Electra had a problem that was just as serious as Ivy's own! When Dolph came of age to marry, and had to choose which of his betrothees actually to marry, he was very likely to choose Nada. Then Electra would die, having failed to marry the Prince who had rescued her from her enchanted sleep.

Unless Grey cold nullify the spell on her. Ivy pondered that. Could it represent the solution for Electra? She hesitated to mention it until she was sure. Magic did not always work the way expected, and mistakes could be disastrous.

They reached the isthmus. This was as far as their steeds could go, for magical creatures would soon perish when out of the magic of Xanth. Donkey would keep watch for their return to this spot, and the ghost horses would come at his whistle. The final station on the enchanted path was a nice one, with useful plants of all kinds and an excellent view of the changing colors of the sea. Donkey said he expected to enjoy his stay here.

The colors of the sea related to the times and places of Mundania that the folk of Xanth could go to. Scholars such as Ichabod, the Mundane archivist, and Arnolde Centaur had taken the trouble to study it and to issue voluminous reports that entirely defined it. Unfortunately, no one else was able to understand the reports. Most of what Ivy knew about the colors was that when the sea turned black, it led to the Black Sea of Mundania, where her parents had gone to rescue Grandpa Trent and Grandma Iris, ages ago.

This time they were not going to mess with the colors at all. Grey simply nulled the magic of the border, and they walked through to what was called Contemporary Mundania, which was where Grey had lived. They knew it was right, because their entry through the gourd in No Name Key had also bypassed the magical barrier.

Thus the three of them found themselves stumbling through drear brush in drear Mundania, and onto one of the paved regions called highways, though in truth they were low rather than high. Now Ivy and Electra could talk to each other, but not to Grey, because Grey had been raised with the nonsensical language of the Mundanes.

Grey demonstrated the magic of the thumb signal, to make one of the cruising vehicles screech to a precipitous halt. It didn't work very well until Ivy enhanced it slightly by hiking up her skirt to show more leg. Then a monstrous truck squealed to a stop, providing their first ride.

They let Grey do the talking, since they could not. Ivy exchanged hand signals with Grey when she needed to, and quietly pointed out the few interesting things to Electra, such as the odd boxlike buildings and colored lights that always flashed bright red when the vehicle approached.

So it went, for an interminable journey along the assorted

and confused roads of this dull realm. They found a public
sleeping place called a bus station for the night; the seats were
not at all suited to comfortable sleeping, but this was only
another evidence of the craziness of Mundanes. Ivy had to
show Electra how to use the facilities in the room for natural
functions, and the girl was appropriately awed. "How can
they use perfectly good drinking water for such a thing?" she
demanded in a whisper. "Suppose somebody forgets and
drinks it?" Ivy had no answer; there was simply no explaining
much of what the Mundanes did.

As they stood before one of the strange unmagic mirrors
Ivy was surprised to notice how tall Electra had grown. She
was now as tall as Ivy, and looked mature, too. Ivy realized
that she had been too preoccupied with her own concerns to
pay much attention; Electra would have been maturing all
along. It had taken the stark mirror that showed them standing
together to make Ivy appreciate the extent of it.

Grey got bits of wrapped food from the lighted standing
machines; he had saved some of their Mundane coins for this
purpose. Apparently the machines liked the taste of metal
better than real food and would give up their food for it. Ivy
had seen this on her last trip here, but Electra was amazed.
"When do the machines eat the food they trade for the metal?"
she asked. "Why don't they just eat the metal to begin with,
if they don't like the food?" Again, Ivy could not answer.

They slept propped against Grey on either side, his arms
around each. Ivy wondered whether this was at all like her
brother's situation, with two betrothees. Innocent Dolph
would be satisfied to marry them both, the one out of compassion, the other out of love. But the parents had said *No,
No Way, Definitely Not, Absolutely Out of the Question*, and
Never, so it seemed likely that they would oppose such a
solution. Too bad, for Nada and Electra were both so nice.

They finally reached Grey's apartment. It was hardly too
soon, for Electra wasn't feeling well. She had been eating
ravenously, never seeming to get enough, and had grown

somewhat short tempered and absentminded. She was also quite dirty, so that she hardly looked herself.

Ivy had not liked this place before, but now it was blessedly familiar. Her own room was unchanged, with plenty of Agenda's food still on the shelves. She encouraged Electra to eat what she wanted, and to clean up and don one of the dresses in the closet, so she could be presentable again. Then she went across the hall with Grey.

Com-Pewter's Sending remained; as soon as he turned the machine on, they were able to talk naturally again. It was a great relief.

SO YOU BROUGHT SOMEONE ELSE FROM XANTH, the screen remarked.

"Yes, this is Electra, our chaperone," Grey said, as Electra appeared at the door, cleaned and changed.

YES, IT IS PROPER TO HAVE AN OLDER PERSON IN THAT CAPACITY.

"Oh, she's not older!" Ivy protested. But then she took another look at Electra, and was amazed: the girl did look older, like a woman of thirty or so. She had assumed that it was dirt and wear on the clothing that had changed her appearance, but now it was clear that those things had only masked the true extent of the change. How could this be?

Grey, too, was surprised. "Electra, you're bigger and older and, uh, fuller," he said. "Your new clothing makes you look so awfully old! What happened?"

SHE IS YOUNG? the screen inquired. WHAT IS HER HISTORY?

"She's actually from about nine hundred years ago," Ivy said. "A spell fouled up, and she slept until the present, but she remained the same age until she woke. Until now."

IT WAS FOOLISH TO BRING HER TO MUNDANIA, the screen said. SHE IS NOW IN THE PROCESS OF ATTAINING HER MUNDANE AGE OF NINE HUNDRED YEARS.

The three exchanged portions of a glance of sheer horror. "Oh, Electra, we never thought!" Ivy cried. "We knew the magic folk couldn't come here—"

"It is of course my own fault," Electra said with surprising maturity. "Naturally I should have realized that this would be the case. I shall try to handle it in an adult manner."

She was older emotionally, too. She was aging in every way.

"How long before she, uh—?" Grey asked.

AT THE PRESENT RATE OF PROGRESSION, SHE SHOULD HAVE ABOUT THREE MORE DAYS BEFORE BEGINNING TO FAIL FROM OLD AGE, the screen printed.

"We've got to get her back to Xanth!" Ivy exclaimed.

"Patience," Electra demurred sensibly. "It required two days for us to reach this destination; two days should suffice for the return. We can accomplish our business in the intervening day. I see no reason to jeopardize our mission merely because of my indisposition."

"Your indisposition!" Ivy exclaimed. "By the time we get back to Xanth, you'll be an old woman! How could you marry Dolph then?"

Electra smiled with the poise of maturity. "That would seem to solve my problem, wouldn't it? Of course I would not require the child to marry a harridan."

HAVE NO CONCERN, the screen printed. IN THE RENEWED AMBIENCE OF MAGIC SHE WILL REVERT AT THE SAME RATE SHE AGED, UNTIL SHE RESUMES HER POINT OF EQUILIBRIUM FOR THAT ENVIRONMENT.

"Oh, 'Lectra!" Ivy exclaimed, much relieved. She opened her arms to hug her friend, then saw how strange the older woman looked, and fell back. This might be the same person as her friend, but it was hard to accept emotionally.

"Your reaction is perfectly understandable," Electra said tolerantly. If she was hurt, she masked it with the competence for which adults were notorious. Ivy felt very small and grubby, inside.

"We'd better, uh, go see my folks," Grey said. "They live in Squeedunk, about sixty miles from here. I went to City College because it was the closest one that gave a tuition break for state residents, but it was too far to commute. There's a daily bus, but its schedule is calculated to make it useless, and it always runs late anyway."

"But we have to do this in one day!" Ivy said.

"We could take a taxi, if I had the money, but—"

THERE IS AN EMERGENCY RESERVE FUND THAT WILL COVER THIS.

Ivy looked at the screen suspiciously. "Why are you being so helpful, Pewter? You know we don't like you!"

I AM NOT PEWTER. I AM MERELY A SENDING SENT TO DO PEWTER'S BIDDING. IT IS MY TASK TO FACILITATE THE LIAISON BETWEEN GREY MURPHY AND PRINCESS IVY, AND YOUR CONSULTATION WITH MAGICIAN MURPHY WILL ESTABLISH YOUR SITUATION. THE MONEY IS IN THE DISK MAILER UNDER MY MONITOR.

Grey looked under the screen. He found the mailer there. Behind the floppy disk was a packet of money he hadn't noticed before, hidden until he looked for it. He nodded. "This will do it."

But Ivy wasn't quite satisfied. "So, Sending, you're not the same as Pewter? What do *you* get out of this?"

DATA INSUFFICIENT.

"Don't give me that!" she snapped. "You know exactly what I mean! Bad folk never do things just because they're supposed to; they always have something to gain."

DATA INSUFFICIENT.

Electra stepped in. "What she means to say, Sending, is that it would facilitate her liaison with Grey Murphy if she had just a bit more information. She is so constituted that she tends to distrust what she does not understand, and that may prejudice her relationship with her fiancé's parents and therefore with Grey as well. Since your participation is integral, your separate input is necessary so that the mission will not be compromised."

CLARIFICATION ACCEPTED.

Ivy kept her mouth shut. Electra's new maturity was coming in handy.

"Normally each party to an agreement receives an emolument appropriate to his participation," Electra continued incomprehensibly. "What is your reward in the event the mission is successful?"

RETURN TO XANTH.

"And what is your penalty in the event the mission is unsuccessful?"

CONFINEMENT TO MUNDANIA.

Electra looked benignly crafty in the way that only an adult could. "As it happens, we are shortly to return to Xanth. We might take you with us, so that you would have no further need to gamble on the outcome of the mission for your own resolution, if you were to cooperate with us."

The screen flickered. ARE YOU ATTEMPTING TO BRIBE ME?

Again that crafty adult smile. "Parties of conscience neither proffer nor accept unwarranted remuneration. They merely come to reasonable understandings."

WHAT DO YOU REQUIRE?

"Information on how Ivy may marry Grey without being required either to support his commitment of servitude to Com-Pewter or to exile herself with him in Mundania."

I DO NOT KNOW HOW THE DEAL WITH COM-PEWTER CAN BE ABROGATED, BUT THERE IS A STRATEGY THAT WILL ACCOMPLISH THIS IF IT IS POSSIBLE. WILL INFORMATION ON THAT STRATEGY SATISFY YOUR REQUIREMENT?

Electra looked at Ivy. "The Sending is ready to deal. I think this is the best it can offer. How do you feel?"

Ivy had hardly followed the preceding dialogue. It seemed to her that neither Electra nor Sending had said anything intelligible, yet somehow they seemed to understand each other. "It will help us if we help it?"

"It will tell us what to do to get around Pewter's plot, if it is possible to get around it."

"Then make the deal!" Ivy exclaimed gladly.

Electra returned to the screen. "That information will satisfy our requirement. How may we most expeditiously facilitate your transport to Xanth?"

TAKE MY DISK.

Grey went to a small box. "The original Vaporware Limited disk is here. We can carry it with us with no trouble at all."

"But in Xanth, how will the Sending animate?" Ivy asked. "Doesn't it need a screen or something?"

THERE ARE MAGIC SCREENS IN XANTH. YOU MAY DEPOSIT
ME WITH ANY ONE OF THOSE. ONE IS IN THE ISTHMUS.

"We'll do it," Ivy agreed, pleased. "Now, what's your strategy?"

RETURN MAGICIAN MURPHY TO XANTH, AFTER OBTAINING
HIS AGREEMENT TO EXERT HIS TALENT ON YOUR BEHALF.

"But his talent is to make things foul up!" Ivy protested.

Now Grey caught on. "But he controls it, doesn't he? He
makes the side he's against foul up! And if he's against Com-
Pewter's plot—"

"*It* might foul up!" Ivy concluded. "And then we'd be all
right!"

Grey tucked the disk box into a small suitcase, and Ivy
added some Mundane clothing. Electra ate some more from
the food on the shelves. Then they set out for Squeedunk.

The Murphy's house was typical of Mundane residences:
neat, clean, and drear. Ivy wondered how they had been able
to stand it all these years. But of course they had had no
choice; no one in Mundania did. If Mundanes could escape
Mundania, they would all move to Xanth.

The taxi let them off, after Grey paid the cabbie. The dour
driver looked almost satisfied as he drove away. "I gave him
a twenty-five percent tip," Grey explained, touching her hand.
Ivy smiled just as if she understood what this was. In fact,
she was surprised that she could understand any of his words,
now that they were away from Sending's screen. Then she
realized that they had Sending along, in the disk. The machine's power was diminished, but when Ivy touched Grey
she could understand him.

They walked up the walk, and Grey knocked on the door.
A pudgy woman opened it. "Npuifs!" Grey exclaimed, hugging her.

"Hsfz—xibu bsf zpv epjoh ifsf?" she asked, surprised. "Eje
zpv gbjm Gsftinbo Fohmjti?"

"Opu fybdumz," he responded. "Mppl, Nb, uijt jt dpnqmjdbufe.
J'mm fyqmbjo fwfszuijoh."

They were ushered inside, and introduced as "Jwz" and

"Fmfdusb." Then they sat on the worn, comfortable couch, and Ivy made sure to sit right next to Grey and put her hand on his suitcase, so that she could understand what he was saying.

Grey's father was old. Ivy remembered from Pewter's pictures that Magician Murphy had been of middle age when he and Vadne escaped from Xanth, and this was nineteen years later, so his age wasn't surprising. Grey's mother was of middle age, no longer young, and had gained a fair amount of weight. It really would have been hard to distinguish this couple from any other Mundanes, but increasingly she was able to see the remnants of the folk they once had been. It was really too bad what two decades of Mundane life could do to folk.

"First," Grey said, "I have to tell you that I now know about Xanth." Both his parents stiffened, remaining expressionless; this was evidently a secret they had preserved throughout. "I know about the deal you made with Com-Pewter, and why you never told me about it. It was because you didn't want me to go there and have to serve the machine."

The parents exchanged a Mundanish glance. "Zft," the Magician said. Ivy needed no translation; he had just confirmed the thing they had come to confirm.

"But Com-Pewter didn't leave it to chance," Grey said. "It sent a Sending, who brought me Ivy, here, from Xanth. She is the daughter of King Dor and Queen Irene, and is a Sorceress in her own right." He paused. "And—she is my fiancée."

They stared at Ivy incredulously. Ivy nodded, feeling abruptly choked.

After a long moment, Vadne fumbled for a handkerchief and dabbed at her eyes. Then she stood and opened her arms to Ivy.

Ivy got up and went to her and embraced her. There was a thing about betrothals that women understood on a level men did not. The language didn't matter.

Then the language did. "Zpv—You are really of Xanth?" Vadne asked slowly.

Ivy was startled. She was speaking intelligibly! "Yes, I am. But how can you—?"

Vadne smiled. "I came from Xanth too," she reminded her, still piecing out the long-unused words. "For almost twenty years I have not dared to speak—we had to learn Mundanish—"

"Oh, of course! It must have been horrible!"

"Horrible," Vadne agreed. "Except for Grey. He was our joy, even here."

Grey was looking at them, puzzled. "Oh—he hears us talking in Xanthian!" Ivy said. "He can't speak it, without magic!"

"We never taught him," Vadne agreed. "We eschewed Xanth, so that he would never learn. But now—"

"Tell him I'll tell the rest," Ivy said.

"There is more?" Vadne asked, surprised.

"Much more."

Vadne turned to Grey. "Qsjodftt Jwz xjmm ufmm vt uif sftu, efbs," she said pleasantly. He looked disgruntled, but did not object. Probably he was dismayed to discover that Ivy could converse with his parents in a language he could not, but he realized the sense of it.

"You see, Grey helped me get back to Xanth," Ivy explained brightly. "He didn't believe in it, but he liked me, so he helped me. Then I took him in, and by the time he came to believe in magic, we, well, we were betrothed. Then we discovered he had magic himself, in fact he was a Magician—"

"Xibu?" Murphy demanded, astonished.

"A Magician," Ivy repeated. "You see, you, well, you summoned the stork for him in Xanth, so he was Xanthian, and we think maybe your going to Mundania before the stork delivered him affected his talent, so now he can null magic, even mine, so he's a Magician of Null Magic. Anyway, my folks said I couldn't marry him unless he had a talent, and so now we can marry. But we wondered how a Mundane could have a talent, and when we found out, we learned about Com-Pewter and the deal you made to get out of Xanth. But we think maybe there's a way around it."

"Wait—wait," Vadne said, seeming dizzy. "We thought he might have magic, but this—this is all so sudden!"

"So what we want to do is bring you back to Xanth," Ivy continued blithely. "Because Magician Murphy's talent— well, if he would promise to serve the existing order and foul up Pewter instead of my father—I mean, I know he wanted to be king, but that was a long time ago."

Murphy and Vadne were staring at her. "But we are banned!" Murphy said. "We would be put back in the Brain Coral's pool!"

"You weren't really banned," Ivy said. "You just thought the current folk would be mad at you, and I guess they are, because your curse really messed up my little brother, but if you promised not to do it anymore—"

"You don't understand," Vadne said. "In a fit of jealousy I turned a girl into a book, and wouldn't turn her back. That's why I'm banned."

"Oh—Millie the Ghost," Ivy said, remembering. "But she's alive now, and so is the Zombie Master, and they have twin children. I think they would forgive you, if you asked. Anyway, if Magician Murphy used his talent to make things go wrong for Com-Pewter, maybe Grey could somehow get out of that deal and then we could marry and stay in Xanth. I'm sure my father would say it's all right, because he doesn't want me to have to leave Xanth or anything. So if you will agree to come, and renounce your claim to the throne—"

"I renounced it when I fled Xanth," Murphy said fervently. "I would give anything to return!"

"And so would I!" Vadne agreed as fervently. "We have dreamed of Xanth constantly, but never spoken of it."

"But we have to go right away," Ivy said. "Because Electra here is aging and we have to get her back. She's actually fifteen years old, in Xanth."

Both turned to stare at Electra. "It is true," Electra said. "Your curse, Magician Murphy, caused me to sleep for nine hundred years or so—I never was sure about the exact count—and wake at the age I went to sleep. But now I am out of the magic, and those nine hundred years are taking effect."

"My curse?" Murphy asked. "I did not curse any children!"

"I was with the Sorceress Tapis, who opposed you on the Isle of View."

"Oh, now I remember! There were two or three girls with her, one very pretty—"

"That was Millie the Maid or the Princess; both were beautiful. I was the nothing girl."

Murphy's brow furrowed. "And you come to ask me to return to Xanth? I would think you would hate me."

"Not exactly. Your curse caused me to become betrothed to a handsome young Prince. Of course I will die if he doesn't marry me, but it has been very nice knowing him and Ivy. So I believe you did as much good for me, in your devious fashion, as evil. I really hold no grudge, though I would not want to suffer your curse again."

Murphy considered. "Would you accept my apology for the evil I did you?"

"Of course. But I am at present in a mature state; I might feel otherwise in my normal childish state."

"Then I will wait to proffer my apology until you return to that childish state, and shall meditate on ways to ameliorate the predicament you are in. Perhaps my talent can be turned to the benefit of others beside my son."

"Then you'll come?" Ivy asked, excited.

"We will both come, and ask your father for permission to stay, and suffer what consequences there may be," Murphy said. "I am sure I speak for my wife too when I say that we shall do all in our power to make amends for the mischief we have done, if only we are permitted to return and remain in Xanth."

"Then it's decided!" Ivy said. "But we must hurry, because we have only two days to get Electra back."

"We can do it in one," Murphy said. "I have a car."

"But the house, the arrangements—we can't just leave!" Vadne protested.

"Phone your friend next door and tell her the house is hers until we return. If we are accepted in Xanth, we will never return."

Vadne nodded. She hurried to the strange Mundane instrument called the telephone.

Within an hour they were on their way, the five of them piled into the Murphy's car, with some sandwiches and milk that Vadne had packed for the trip. The car zoomed along the road at a dizzying speed, in much the way the taxi had, somehow avoiding collisions with all the other cars that zoomed by in the opposite direction, almost close enough to touch.

They drove the rest of the day and didn't stop at night. Now the bright lights of the other cars flashed in the darkness, making Ivy even more nervous. But when she glanced at Electra and saw her visibly older, she knew that speed was best.

Ivy did not realize she had fallen asleep until she was awakened by a bumping jolt. "We have run out of road," Magician Murphy said. "We shall have to continue on foot."

They piled out and started walking. Magician Murphy had a flashlight, which in Mundania had the odd property of sending out a conical beam of light. They marched on into the region that was the Isthmus of Xanth, Ivy leading, because she was the one who was native to the time of Xanth they had left. That meant she could lead them back to it. If someone from another time of Xanth led, they would return to his or her time, which could be another matter.

Then Ivy heard a voice calling in the distance. "Who is there?"

That was Donkey! "Ivy is here!" she called back.

They oriented on the centaur, and soon joined forces. They were back in Xanth. Ivy felt an enormous relief; she had not realized how nervous she had been about this until they were clear of drear Mundania. How could she ever hope to survive there for a lifetime?

"But why did you bring three Mundanes?" Donkey asked. "And where is Electra?"

The middle-aged woman who was Electra stepped up to him. "I have put on some years, but I will lose them again, if you have patience."

"It *is* you!" he exclaimed, dismayed. "What happened?"

"I forgot I was nine hundred years old, in Mundane terms," she said with a wry smile. "It has been an interesting experience that I hope will soon be over."

Then Ivy introduced Magician Murphy and Vadne. "We shall have a problem, as we do not have steeds for all," she said. "We may have to break into two parties, one fast, one slow."

"My wife and I will be happy to take our time," Murphy said. "It has been so long, it will take us time to acclimatize."

"And I would prefer to wait until I am back to my normal state," Electra said.

"I will be happy to remain until you do," Donkey offered.

"Then suppose Grey and I ride ahead on the ghost horses, and the rest of you proceed more slowly down the enchanted path," Ivy said. "By the time you arrive, everything should be normal, and Castle Roogna will be prepared to receive you."

That turned out to be satisfactory to them all, and it was decided.

But first they had to deliver Sending to a screen, as they had promised. "Oh, certainly; there is an artifact of that description nearby," Donkey said. "I explored this region thoroughly while watching for your return." He led them to the place.

It turned out to be a polished slab of stone, with a deep crack at one side. Grey put the disk in the crack, and the stone glowed. Print appeared. DEAL CONSUMMATED, it said.

"But what is there for you to do, way out here in nowhere?" Ivy asked.

FIRST I MUST CAPTURE AN INVISIBLE GIANT, the screen printed. THEN I MUST PRACTICE CONTROLLED VARIANTS OF REALITY. IN TIME I MAY BE ABLE TO FASHION AN EMPIRE

AND CHALLENGE MY SIRE FOR MASTERY OF XANTH.

Ivy exchanged the remainder of her supply of glances with Grey. "Uh, how long will this take?" he inquired.

PERHAPS AS LITTLE AS THREE HUNDRED YEARS, DEPENDING ON CIRCUMSTANCES.

"Surely you can do it faster than that!" Grey said encouragingly.

NOT SO. I CALCULATED FOR OPTIMUM CONDITIONS. IT IS MORE LIKELY TO FALL IN THE RANGE OF TEN TO THE THIRD POWER TO TEN TO THE FOURTH POWER YEARS. FORTUNATELY I AM A PATIENT DEVICE.

"That *is* fortunate," Ivy agreed. "I hope my own quest is even more fortunate."

YOUR QUEST SHOULD BE RESOLVED WITHIN THE MONTH.

"Thank you, Sending," she said, pleased. But then she remembered that this was the time limit Com-Pewter had set for Grey to wrap up his other business before coming to serve. Sending must have realized this.

Then, as they rode the ghost horses on down the path, she asked Grey: "What is ten to the third power?"

"A thousand," he said. "That's one of the few things I remember from college math, which is almost as bad a course as Freshman English."

"You poor thing! But you may never have to suffer either of those torments again, if we resolve our quest within a month."

"But Sending didn't say which way it would be resolved."

"Oooops!" Her pleasure converted mystically to uncertainty. They still didn't know how to get around Grey's obligation to Com-Pewter. Their trip to Mundania had confirmed the worst, but offered them a chance to nullify it. That was all: a chance. If Magician Murphy could make something go wrong with Com-Pewter's plot.

"I hope your father's curses are as potent as they were nine hundred years ago!" Ivy said.

"I know he'll do the very best he can for me," Grey replied. "My parents—they haven't always gotten along well together, but they were always good to me. I never really understood their ways, I think, until I saw Com-Pewter's flashback scene. I only knew that despite their arguments, they had some mysterious and powerful reason to stay together. Now I know that it was their shared vision of Xanth, about which they could never speak. For me and for Xanth—they will do anything. I know that absolutely. And—"

"And you're glad they will be here," she finished for him. "So your family is together."

"I'm glad," he agreed with feeling. "Maybe my parents were evil before, but they aren't now."

"Make sure you explain that to *my* parents!" she said, laughing. But underneath she remained in a deep doubt. It was such a slender straw they were grasping at. If it failed, what would become of them?

14

PROPHESY

Grey saw that Ivy was pensive, and understood why. Nothing had been decided, and there was no guarantee. Magician Murphy's curses had evidently been extremely potent in the distant past, but this was now, not the past, and the Magician was almost twenty years out of practice. In those intervening years he had been simply Major Murphy, a Mundane office worker who earned just enough Mundane money to avoid poverty. He had been fortunate in finding an employer who was satisfied with a person with a language handicap, and fortunate in the way his efforts turned out; it was as if there were some rebound from his Xanth talent, changing the curse to good luck. But this had hardly made up for the almost complete blahness of Mundania. Now Grey understood what he had not grasped before: that the dreadful drabness of his own life was only a reflection of the much greater drabness of his parents' lives. They had known Xanth, so were aware of the magnitude of their loss. They had protected him from that awareness, but now the full significance of it was clear.

What would he do if he had to leave Xanth—and Ivy?

From time to time Grey had pondered suicide, not with any great passion, but as a prospect to relieve the inexorable boredom of his so-so existence. He had never actually tried it, not because of any positive inspiration, but because he couldn't figure out any easy way to do it without pain. So he had muddled on through, while his grades ground slowly down, feeling guilty for not doing better, but somehow unable to change it. Maybe he had been hoping for some impossible miracle to happen that would rescue him from the mire of his dull life, yet knowing, deep down, that it would never happen.

Then Ivy had come. His life *had* changed.

If he should lose her and return to Mundania alone—no, he did not have to ask what would become of him. He knew.

Anything that could go wrong, would go wrong: that was his father's talent. Could it really act in a positive manner, helping Grey by fouling up the evil machine? Grey had all too little confidence in that. But what else was there to try?

So he smiled and encouraged Ivy, and she smiled and encouraged him, but neither was fooling the other. Their happiness hung on an impossibly slender thread.

"And so that's the story," Ivy concluded. "Magician Murphy and Vadne will be here in a few days to ask your pardon for their crimes of the past, and they will support you as King if you let them stay in Xanth, and will try to help Grey get around Com-Pewter's plot. I can't marry Grey until we find that way, and if we can't find it within a month—" She shrugged.

"So you have decided to leave Xanth rather than serve Pewter?" King Dor asked Grey.

"Yes. I don't want the evil machine to use me to take over Xanth. If I had no talent of consequence, it would be bad because of my influence with Princess Ivy. As it is, it is worse, because I could do a lot of damage. Xanth doesn't need another Evil Magician!"

"We always did like you, Grey," Queen Irene said. "As we came to know you, we liked you better, and we like you best now. But what you say is true. We shall of course welcome your parents and allow them to stay in Xanth, but the irony is that you may not be able to remain here with them."

"But until that month is done, hope remains," Dor said. "Knowing the devious power of the Magician Murphy, I would say it is a significant hope."

Grey smiled and thanked them, but the gloom did not let go of his soul. Com-Pewter seemed to have it locked up tight: what could possibly go wrong with its plot when it was so close to completion? The easiest wrongness was simply Grey's absence from Xanth, and that was the one that he so dreaded.

"Somehow, some way," Ivy murmured in the hall, and kissed him. But her cheer was cracking at the edges.

Nothing happened while they waited for the arrival of the other party. Grey and Ivy picked exotic fruits in the orchard, fed tidbits to the moat monsters, made the acquaintance of the guardian zombies, peeked at the baby Bed Monster under Grey's bed (Grey was new to magic, so had a childlike acceptance of some things despite being eighteen), and played innocent games with Dolph and Nada. The castle was excellent for hide-and-seek, because it had many secret recesses that the ghosts were happy to show off when asked. According to Ivy, the castle was not as well stocked with ghosts as it once had been, because three of them had been reanimated as living folk, but it could still legitimately be called haunted as long as a single ghost remained. In short, it was almost as dull as Mundania.

Grey disagreed with her. "Xanth could never be dull!" he said. "Why, even if it didn't have magic, there's—well, look at that picture!" For they happened to be standing by a portrait in the hall, one of a number that were elegantly framed.

Ivy glanced at it. "Oh, yes, that's Mother when she was my age. She was Miss Apull on the pinup calendar. I wish I could look like that, at my age."

"You look like you," he said. "That's more than enough."

"It will have to do," she said. But she was pleased.

Then the party arrived. Magician Murphy looked improved, and Vadne much improved; both the exercise and the renewed experience of Xanth had been good for them. Electra was back to her regular form, and skipping like a child again. She hugged everyone, and even stole a naughty kiss from Dolph.

The formalities were brief: Magician Murphy formally apologized for the mischief he had done in the past, and promised to support King Dor and all his works in the future. Vadne asked to be allowed to visit Millie the Ghost at Castle Zombie so she could apologize to her for the incident of the book. Dor granted them both pardons.

"Now," Murphy said, turning to Grey. "I hereby lay my curse on the geis that is on you, my son, and wish it evil. Whatever can go wrong with it will go wrong."

"Thank you, Father," Grey said, trying to project the feeling of confidence. What a dismal hope!

"You and the Sorceress will be our guests for dinner, Magician," King Dor said formally. "Zora will show you to your suite now."

Neither of Grey's parents spoke, but Grey knew them: they were overwhelmed by the generosity with which they had been met, and could not speak. Vadne, who he now realized had resented the fact that she had never been known as a Sorceress despite having a formidable talent, would be loyal to King Dor for life because of that one remark. They followed Zora Zombie out.

Grey lingered, wanting to thank the King and Queen for their kindness to his parents. But Ivy caught his arm. "They know, Grey. Mother wasn't a Sorceress either, until the elders reconsidered. The standards have been modified. Xanth needs all the good magic it can get."

"Uh, sure," he agreed, as she hauled him off.

"You see, we also understand about good and evil magic," Ivy continued, guiding him upstairs. "Grandpa Trent was an Evil Magician, because he tried to take power before his time, and he was exiled to Mundania. But then he returned when they needed a king, and he became king, and then he wasn't evil any more. It's all in the attitude and in the situation. Now that your folks are supporting mine, they aren't evil either, no matter what happened long ago."

"But how would my folks have felt, or yours, if you and I were not engaged?"

"But you see we *are* betrothed," she said blithely. "So there's no reason for trouble between our folks, because if our children have good magic—"

"But that's presuming we can marry!" he protested. "And we can't marry if I have to serve Com-Pewter."

"I don't think you appreciate just how potent your father's magic is. I've been talking to my father, who visited King Roogna's time when he was twelve; and he met your father then, and he said that curse was amazing. The goblins and harpies were fighting, see, and—here, I'll show you on the Tapestry!"

They had reached her room. She opened the door and hauled him in. And stopped. "This isn't the way I left it!" she exclaimed, glaring at the Tapestry. "Who's been here?"

The door swung closed behind them. As it did, its hinge made a noise. "Prince Dolph!" it squealed.

"I thought so! And what is he now?"

"That fly on the ceiling," the hinge said.

Ivy grabbed a fly swatter from a drawer. "Change, Dolph, or I'll bash you into a smithereen!" she cried, stalking the fly.

The fly became a bat who headed for the window. But Ivy got there first. "Change, before I mash you into guano!"

The bat became a pale green goat, who ran for the door.

"Grey, stop that greenback buck!" Ivy called. "Null his magic!"

Grey put out a hand. The moment it touched the buck's horn, the animal became Prince Dolph.

"Ah, you'd never have caught me, if that hinge hadn't squealed," Dolph complained.

Ivy would not be distracted. "You're not supposed to be in my room when I'm not home! What were you doing?"

"Just watching the Tapestry," the boy said guiltily.

"And what were you watching, that made you sneak in here right now?"

Dolph scuffed his feet together. "Just—things."

Ivy's outrage expanded. "You were watching Nada change clothing!"

"Well, she *is* my betrothee," Dolph mumbled.

"Trying to catch a glimpse of her panties!" Ivy concluded triumphantly. "Do you know what Mother will do to you for that?"

"Don't tell! Please don't tell!" Dolph begged. "I'll do anything!"

"I'll think about it," Ivy said. "Now get out of here, you little sneak, before I enhance you into a human being."

Dolph was only too glad to make his escape.

"How can you cow him like that, when he can turn into a dragon if he wants to?" Grey asked.

"It's the natural right of big sisters. Now just let me reset the Tapestry—"

"Hey, isn't that the Goblinate of the Golden Horde?" Grey asked, seeing the picture that had been frozen on it. "I thought Dolph was watching Nada." He had some sympathy for the boy's interest; Nada was one fine-looking girl, and doubtless her panties were impressive. Grey had never seen them himself; she had lost her clothing during the episode on Parnassus.

"That's right. Obviously Dolph scrambled the weave so I wouldn't know. It was all he could do in the moment before he changed forms."

"Scrambled the weave?"

"You know—he just made a random reset of the picture, so I couldn't tell where it had been set. If he'd had more time he would have put it back the way I had left it. He's pretty cunning about that sort of thing, usually. He just didn't expect me back so quickly. He probably figured I'd take time out to kiss you in the hall for a while." She glanced at him sidelong. "Correctly. Only then we were discussing your father's curse, and I decided to show you on the Tapestry, so we came on in and caught him unawares. So this setting is pure chance. I'll just—"

"What's happening? If those are the same goblins who—"

She looked at the frozen picture more closely. "I'm sure they are. See, there's the mean old chief. But this must be years ago, because he's not quite so ugly as he was when we crossed him."

"Ouch! That means there's no chance to help their victims." For he saw that a partly of three gremlins had been captured. The goblins were just in the process of taking whatever possessions the gremlins had.

"Little chance," Ivy agreed. "I wonder how they caught those gremlins. They're usually way too smart for goblins."

"They caught *us!*" he reminded her.

"Let's play this through," she said. "Just out of idle curiosity. Then we can go on to Magician Murphy's oldtime curses."

The picture moved, the figures zipping backwards rapidly, like video tape being rewound. Then it steadied. The goblins were out of sight, and two gremlins were walking down the path.

"Oh, I see," Ivy said grimly. "The third isn't in their party. She's a—a—"

"A shill? A Judas goat? But why would she lure her own kind into a trap?"

"To save her life." They watched as the two approached the third, who was tied to a tree and gesticulating, obviously a maiden in distress.

The two hurried up to untie her—and the goblins pounced from the bushes nearby. They searched the captives, and just at the point where the Tapestry had been randomly frozen they found a scrap of paper on one. They were evidently quite exited about it and saved it carefully. Then they hauled the two off toward the hate spring and the cooking pots. The third they hustled into a cave; she would be saved for future mischief.

"I hate those goblins!" Grey exclaimed. "Can't anybody stop them?"

"It's sort of live and let live, in Xanth," Ivy said. "But I would certainly like to see them get their comeuppance."

"I wonder what was written on that paper?"

Ivy played the Tapestry back, and caused it to expand the paper. But the markings on it were incomprehensible.

"Maybe Grundy could read it," she said. "He speaks all languages, so maybe he reads some too."

"Of course that paper has probably been burned by now anyway," Grey said. "I really didn't mean to get off on a sidetrack."

"Why not? Little things can be interesting." Ivy went to the door. "Hey, Dolph!" she called.

Her little brother appeared immediately. "Anything!" he repeated worriedly.

"Go find Grundy and bring him back."

"That's it?" he asked incredulously.

"No, that's just incidental. I'm still pondering."

"Oh." Dolph became the bat and flew away.

"You're going to turn him in?" Grey asked.

"No. But I'll make him sweat for a while. He's very well behaved when he's sweating."

Soon Grundy Golem and Rapunzel were there. Grundy peered at the expanded image of the paper. "I can't quite make out what it says, it seems to be an address of some kind, but—oh, say!"

"Say what?" Ivy asked.

"That's Humfrey's writing!"

"The Good Magician's?"

"Who else? I'd know his scrawl anywhere! But of course I can't read it; he enchants messages so that only those whose business it is can read them."

"Then that's why the goblins couldn't read it!" Ivy said. "They knew what it was, but it was no good to them. But you said it's an address?"

"Probably telling where to find him if they need him," the golem said. "Those gremlins must have done him some service, so they had an Answer on tap. Too bad they never got to use it."

Ivy's eyes lighted. "An Answer!" she exclaimed.

"Don't get excited, Princess. You don't have an Answer

coming to you, and if you did, Humfrey's gone, so you couldn't get it anyway."

"But the address!" she persisted. "The magic address! That would change when he moved and always be current!"

"Of course it would," the golem agreed. "But the folk he gave it to are gone, and nobody else can read it, so what's the point?"

"*I* could read it!" Ivy said. "If I had the original paper. I could enhance its legibility and orientation, and find out where the Good Magician is now!"

The others stared at her, realizing that it was true. "And if you found him, you could ask him how to foil Pewter's plot," Rapunzel said. "Oh, Ivy, what a coincidence that you should learn of that paper just now!"

"Coincidence?" Ivy asked musingly. "No, I think it's Murphy's curse! This is just the kind of fluke that happens when that curse is operating."

Then Grey began to hope.

This time they appeared to be a party of three: a young peasant man, a pretty peasant girl, and a homely young centaur with a donkeylike hide. They were not these things, exactly, but they played their parts carefully, for their mission was important and not without risk. Had the need to find Humfrey and solve Grey's problem not been so urgent, King Dor and Queen Irene would never have permitted this excursion. But the parents had had to agree that this was their best chance.

Actually, Queen Irene had quietly approached Grey during one of the few times when Ivy was otherwise occupied, and hinted that there might be another way to deal with Com-Pewter. A sphinx might take a stroll and accidentally step on the evil machine's cave, squashing it and all inside it flat. Then there would be nothing for Grey to serve. But Grey had demurred; that would be an unethical solution, by his definition. He could not conspire so directly against Com-Pewter, who had after all made a deal with Grey's parents and fulfilled his part of it. It was Grey's own responsibility to solve his problem, whatever the outcome.

"I thought you might feel that way," Irene said approvingly. "There is an ethical dimension to power. We shall remain clear and allow you to deal with your problem yourself."

Grey had thanked her, though his prospect of success seemed bleak. The more he learned of Ivy's folks, the better he liked them.

They walked north from the invisible bridge over the Gap Chasm. This time instead of taking the enchanted path north they veered to the east, following a lesser trail that wasn't magically protected but that led to a centaur range. In fact Chester and Cherie Centaur had once lived there, before moving to Castle Roogna to tutor the young Prince Dor and Princess Irene. A few centaurs still lived there, though it was a diminishing community that was desperately in need of nubile fillies. In a past generation it had been short of centaur colts, which had led in part to the defection of Chem Centaur to another type of association. The winged centaur Chex was the result. The centaurs of this region were a good deal more liberal than those of Centaur Isle far to the south, but not *that* liberal, and neither Chex nor her dam were welcome there now. So the region continued to decline, victim as much of its conservatism as of its bad fortune. Monsters were encroaching, becoming increasingly bold despite the proficiency of centaur archers.

Peasant girl Ivy rode the centaur, while peasant boy Grey walked beside. It was evident that they were going to visit the centaur's home range, perhaps to discuss with the centaurs there some type of commission or employment. Few peasants could afford centaur tutors, but on occasion some child with excellent magic turned up, and then the centaurs could be prevailed on for instruction in the rudiments.

There were goblins not far from this region, but they had not yet been so bold as to attack the centaur community. Even goblins were able to appreciate the effectiveness of aroused centaurs; losses would be prohibitive. But the goblins did lurk, watching their opportunity. There were stories . . .

"Oh, gentle peasants!" a sweet voice called.

They looked. A slender young woman was running toward

them, her cornsilk hair flowing behind. She was so slight as to be almost transparent, but nicely contoured.

"What is it, sylph?" Ivy inquired.

So this was a sylph! Grey had not encountered one before. But of course there were a great many of the creatures of Xanth he had not yet met—and might never meet, if their quest for the Good Magician's Answer proved unsuccessful.

"Oh, kind peasants and brave centaur, surely you have come to fulfill the prophecy!" the sylph said.

"Prophecy?" Ivy asked.

"My friend, the lovely centaur damsel, is captive of an ogre who means to fatten her horribly and then crunch her bones!" the sylph explained. "According to the prophecy, only a bold gray centaur with a young human couple as companions can hope to rescue her from a fate exactly as bad as death! Surely you are the ones it refers to, for you answer the description perfectly!"

"That is an interesting prophecy," Ivy remarked. "But an ogre is a fearsome creature. What could poor peasants do against such a monster?"

"Oh, wonderful folk, I know not!" the sylph cried, distraught. "But there must be some way, for the prophecy says so. Will you not at least come and see?"

"And get our own bones crunched by the ogre?" Ivy asked. "I think we should take another path."

"Now let us not be hasty," the gray centaur protested. He turned to the sylph. "You say this filly is fair?"

"Oh, she is lovely, sir! She was a bit thin, but the ogre has been making her eat all she can hold, and now she is quite buxom, and soon she will be fat, and he will crunch her bones! I beg you, come and see her, and perhaps you can free her. She would be most grateful!"

"But the ogre!" Ivy protested. "We don't dare approach."

"He forages by day, leaving her chained. I am too frail to break the chain, indeed all normal folk are, but the prophecy says you will find the way. Please, please, come and see, while the ogre is away!"

"I think we should at least look," the gray centaur said

reasonably. One might almost have thought he had some ul-
terior interest in the matter.

Ivy sighed. "Well, the centaurs are in need of young fillies.
But we must be ready to flee at the first sign of the ogre!"

"Oh thank you, thank you, thank you!" the sylph exclaimed. "I am ever so relieved! Right this way!" She skipped
along the path ahead, her hair flouncing nicely.

They followed. Grey had kept his mouth strictly shut, not
interfering. They had just played out a little charade. They
had surveyed this matter with the Tapestry, and discovered
that the goblins had a new ploy: they used their captives to
beguile travelers into goblin ambushes and then pounced on
the hapless travelers and bore them off to the pot. The sylph
was a captive who had been promised her freedom if she
lured three travelers in for capture. Of course the goblins
would renege on that pledge, and surely the sylph suspected
it. But it was at least a hope, while the alternative was certain:
if she did not cooperate she would be dumped in the pot
immediately.

It occurred to Grey that it was about time someone did
something about those goblins. They were not nice neighbors.

The sylph led them deeper into the jungle. This was no
longer the regular trail, for there were no centaur hoofprints
on it; it was one the goblins had scuffed out for this purpose.
Goblins were good a scuffing trails, especially for a nefarious
purpose. They were making sure the prey had no chance to
escape the ambush.

Grey permitted himself a grim little smile. The goblins had
a surprise coming.

They reached a clearing. There was nothing in it except a
mound of garbage evidently left by the goblins.

The slyph turned. Tears streaked down her face. "Oh, I am
so sorry, good folk!" she said. "They made me do it!"

"Do what?" Ivy asked with simulated confusion.

"They have my child captive, my darling Sylvanie, and she
is first into the pot if I do not do all they demand, and me
too if I fail," the sylph continued. "I know it's wrong, and I
hate myself for doing it, but my man defied them and they

boiled him, and oh, I have no pride left, only I must save my daughter, and so I have done this awful thing to you and I do not beg your forgiveness, only your understanding."

Now Grey saw the goblins. They were appearing from all around, closing the net with what for them was surely delicious slowness, savoring the horror in their prey. They wanted their victims to suffer on the way to the pot.

"What is your name?" Ivy inquired.

"I am Sylvia Sylph," she replied, still weeping. "My man was Sylvester. We were just traveling through, as you were, and they caught us. We will all be cooked and eaten, I know that, but I just have to struggle through as long as I can, hoping somehow to save Sylvanie though I know I can't. Now you must suffer, you innocent folk, and I apologize abjectly for what I have done to you, but I cannot help myself."

Now the goblins ringed them closely. Grey recognized the ugly chief, Grotesk. Too bad that one hadn't landed in the Gap Chasm, back when they had last met.

"Would you help us, if we helped you and your child escape?" Ivy asked.

"Oh, yes, yes! But it is hopeless. They will never let any of us go! They are the meanest tribe of these parts. They have no mercy! They delight in torturing innocent folk. Do not go into the pool if you can possibly avoid it, because—"

"Enough, wench!" the chief cried harshly. "Leave us to our sport." The sylph was instantly quiet.

Ivy turned her face to look directly at Grotesk. "Oh goblin, what do you mean to do with us?" she asked as if affrighted.

"Well, peasant girl, I may turn you over to my lusty henchmen for their amorous sport, then let you take a nice drink from our nice pool before giving you a nice hot bath in our pot. Or maybe I'll give you the nice drink before you engage my henchmen; that could be even more interesting. As for this bedraggled centaur—" The chief's eyes widened. "Hey, I recognize this beast! The one who looks like a mule!"

"Donkey," the creature said.

"Whatever! We had you captive before, only you got away, and—and these are the ones who helped you escape!"

"Curses!" Ivy said. "They have found us out!"

"Kill them right now!" the chief cried. "All of them, the sylph slut too! Don't give them any chance at all!"

The goblins raised their clubs and spears and cocked their stone-throwing arms.

Ivy jumped off the centaur. The centaur disappeared. In its place was an immense low-slung six-legged dragon with steam puffing from its nostrils.

Grey jumped forward and grabbed the sylph by her thin arm. "Cover your face!" he said, pulling her into the center of the circle formed by the dragon's curving tail.

"The Gap Dragon!" the chief cried, terrified.

"Yes," Grey said. "He came to see you dance, chief."

"What?"

The dragon pursed his lips and touched the chief's big feet with a small jet of steam. The chief danced with pain.

Ivy poked her head over the dragon's neck. "That was just a sample, goblin," she said. "Do you know what my friend will do to you if you threaten to hurt one hair of my head?" She swept off the peasant cap and let her golden-green hair tumble out.

"You—you really *are* the Princess Ivy!" the chief exclaimed. "The dragon's friend!"

"I really *am,*" she agreed. "Now you just walk along back toward your camp, and all your minions with you, and my friend will steam any who stray."

"What are you going to do with us?"

"Well, Grotesk," Ivy said with relish, "I may turn you over to my lusty friend for his sport, then let you drink from your nice pool before giving you a nice steam bath."

"But—but—"

"Now. MARCH, frog-face!" she snapped. "Before my friend loses his patience." Her friend, of course, was not the real Stanley Steamer, but her little brother Dolph, working off his penance for spying on Nada's panties. It didn't matter; Dolph in dragon form could get just as steamed as the real dragon. After seeing what the goblins were up to, Dolph was surely just as outraged as Ivy and Grey were.

The goblins marched. The party wended its way back to the goblin camp. Whenever a goblin tried to stray, the dragon jetted steam at the seat of his pants, and he quickly danced back into place. The truth was that the goblins could have scattered, and most of them would have gotten away; and they would have done just that if any ordinary dragon had manifested. But they lived close enough to the Gap Chasm to be familiar with the dread Gap Dragon, and they were terrified of him. Their trap had been neatly reversed, and they were as helpless to escape it as they had expected their prey to be.

They reached the hate spring. Grey knew that Ivy remained angry about the way these goblins had tortured her with it before, even though that had brought about the breakthrough of their betrothal. He stayed clear, letting her handle it her way.

"Now," she said. "There is something I want from you, goblin, and I am going to get it. Are you going to give it to me?"

The chief laughed. "Take off your dress and I'll give it to you! Har, har, har!"

Ivy signaled the dragon. A jet of scalding steam shot out. It singed a group of six goblins standing by the pool. They screamed and jumped into the water.

Then they began fighting among themselves, for the water made them hate the first other creatures they saw. The water splashed, droplets striking others nearby, and they too began fighting. In very little time a dozen goblins were unconscious.

"Are you going to answer me?" Ivy asked the chief evenly.

"I told you: lie down and spread your—"

There was another blast of steam. A second group of goblins were singed into the water. Another fight broke out, finishing about ten more goblins.

"Now we can do this until all your tribe is gone," Ivy said, "if that is the way you prefer it. I suspect there is a prophecy that you will be the last to enter that pool before we get what we want. Shall we test it for accuracy?"

The chief looked at the sprawled goblins. "Exactly what is it you want?" he asked grudgingly.

"I thought you'd never ask!" Ivy said brightly. "Where is the piece of paper you stole from the gremlins?"

"*What* paper?"

More steam hissed. More goblins were goosed into the water. Another awful fray occurred.

"Oh, *that* paper," the chief said, after the fracas had died out. "We burned it long ago."

This time the dragon steamed a large group of goblins. They screamed as their skin was burned. They could cool themselves only by plunging into the water. By the time this action was done, more than half the tribe was unconscious or worse.

"In my cabin," the chief mumbled.

"Send a goblin for it."

"Go jump in the lake!" he retorted.

The steam was running low, but Ivy touched the dragon, Enhancing him, and the steam became so hot it smoked. Half the remaining goblins leaped into the pool, not even waiting for that jet to catch them. Yet more fighting broke out.

"Princess," Sylvia Sylph said hesitantly, "I will fetch it, if you wish."

"No, you fetch your child," Ivy said.

Sylvia's eyes brightened. "Oh, yes!" She hurried off.

At this point only four goblins remained standing, besides the chief. "Send a goblin," Ivy repeated grimly.

The chief grimaced. "Go, Bucktooth."

Bucktooth broke away from the diminished group and walked to the chief's hut. In a moment he returned with a box.

"Open it, Bucktooth," Ivy said.

"Princess, I can't!" the goblin protested. "It is spelled against intrusion!"

"I thought so. Open it, chief."

"Like stewed brains I will!"

More steam hissed. Two more goblins leaped into the pool. They scrambled out and attacked the two remaining goblins. The box fell to the ground. The melee ended up back in the water. Soon all four were unconscious.

"Will you let me go if I do?" the chief asked.

"I will treat you with the same compassion you have treated others."

The chief leaped at her—but the steam caught him in mid-air and blasted him back into the pool. He splashed about. "I hate you!" he screamed.

"Stay in the pool," Ivy said.

The goblin obviously wanted to rush out and attack her, but he saw the snout of the dragon covering him, and refrained. The longer he remained in the water, the worse his hatred grew, but there was nothing he could do about it. He began frothing at the mouth. Finally he waded across and out the far side and stumbled into the jungle. Grey knew that whatever creature the goblin encountered there would be in for trouble. Maybe it would be a fire-breathing dragon.

"But how can you open the box?" Sylvia asked.

Grey walked across and picked up the box. He worked the catch, and it opened. He had nulled the magic that sealed it. There was the bit of paper. He took it out and handed it to Ivy.

She inspected it. "Yes, I can see that this is spelled to be intelligible only to the person who truly needs to see the Good Magician," she said.

"I can null that spell, too," Grey offered.

"No, that might null the message along with the magic," she demurred. "The magic has to remain. But *we* truly need to see him, so I am sure it will respond to us." She concentrated on it. "Yes, it's coming clear now. He is living somewhere in—in—" She looked up, dismayed.

"Where?" Grey asked, alarmed.

"In the gourd."

There was a moment of silence. Then the dragon vanished and Dolph stood in his place. "I can go there!" he exclaimed.

Ivy gazed at him sourly. "But you're grounded, remember, until you decide between Nada and Electra. I only got you sprung today because I promised I'd keep a big sisterly eye on you all the time."

Sylvia Sylph reappeared, leading a pretty child by the hand.

"I will go into the spring now, only I beg of you, spare my daughter!"

Ivy's head snapped around. "What?"

"My punishment for what I did," Sylvia said. "But Sylvanie is innocent; please let her go."

Ivy got her composure together; it had showed signs of unraveling. "Let me explain, Sylvia: you did not deceive us. We deceived you. We knew about the prophecy trap: that you had to approach any travelers with a story about someone like one of them being in trouble so they would follow you into the goblins' trap. We have been captive of these goblins ourselves; we know what they are like. But we needed this paper, so we used you to lead us in. This is my brother, Prince Dolph, who assumed the form of the centaur and then the dragon. You know he wasn't tempted by any lady centaur!"

"Oh, I dunno," Dolph said. "She sounded sorta nice. I could have ridden on her back and used her long hair for reins, or maybe just reached around her torso to hang on while she galloped."

"Shut up." Ivy knew he was teasing her. She refocused on Sylvia. "So we bear no grudge against you. We saw how sorry you were to do it. Now you are free to go; you are captive no more."

The sylph just stood there. "But what I did—I must be punished."

Grey interposed. "Do you have anywhere to go, now that your man is dead?"

The sylph shook her head sadly no.

Ivy melted, as he had known she would. "Then you and Sylvanie will come with us to Castle Roogna."

"But my child is innocent! I beg of you—"

"To decide your punishment," Grey said. "Your daughter must be with you, but she will not be punished."

"Maybe you could give her your bed," Grey suggested.

Ivy turned to him. "My bed?"

"Sylvanie is a child. She needs a young Bed Monster. I thought maybe Grabby—"

"Who otherwise doesn't have long to live!" Ivy agreed. "Yes, of course—Sylvanie gets my bed!"

The child's eyes went huge. "My very own Bed Monster?" she piped.

The sylph almost dissolved. "Oh, thank you, thank you!"

Ivy looked over the wreckage that was the Goblinate of the Golden Horde. "I think it will be some time before this outfit causes much more trouble," she said with satisfaction.

Then Dolph became a roc. They climbed onto his gigantic feet, clinging to the talons: Grey and Ivy on one foot, Sylvia and Sylvanie on the other. The wings spread, and flapped, and they lurched into the air.

In a moment they were over the Gap Chasm. Dolph waggled his wings in a salute to the real Gap Dragon and flew on. Very shortly they were gliding down to Castle Roogna.

Grey and Ivy talked privately to King Dor, and he agreed that he would punish Sylvia Sylph by requiring her to do service at Castle Roogna as a maid for an indefinite period, during which time her child would be tutored by a centaur. The two would share a room at the castle, and the child would get Ivy's old bed. Zora Zombie would instruct the sylph in her duties.

"Such as waxing the floor!" Ivy said, laughing. "That will be terrible punishment!"

Grey smiled. Evidently the girls did not like the smell of the wax, though it reminded him of home. Maybe it was its Mundanish quality that bothered them.

Then they pondered their approach to Good Magician Humfrey. He was in the gourd; that explained why nobody had been able to find him, because the Tapestry could not track him there, and the magic mirror was limited. They were not able to understand the exact address, for the regions of the gourd had little revelance to those of waking life. The full inscription went like this:

DAMESCROFT
SILLY GOOSE LANE

LITTLE HALINGBERRY
BISHOP'S STORKFORD
HURTS
ANGLE-LAND

Grey shook his head. "I'm not sure I'll ever understand these Xanth addresses!"

"This isn't a Xanth address," Ivy corrected him. "It's a gourd address. It makes no sense to me either."

"I can find it! I can find it!" Dolph said eagerly. "The Night Stallion gave me a free pass to the gourd, remember; any of its creatures will help me if I ask, and none will hurt me or anyone I speak for."

"You just want to get out of being grounded!" Ivy accused him.

"Uh-huh! But you need me! You need me in the gourd!"

Ivy grimaced. It was true: Dolph had a special advantage in the gourd. If they wanted to locate the Good Magician at all, let alone within Grey's time limit for settlement with Com-Pewter, they had to use Ivy's little brother.

So it was decided: Grey and Ivy and Dolph would make one more excursion together, this time into the devious realm of dreams. Rather than risk it physically, they would enter the normal way: by looking into gourds growing right here at Castle Roogna. That way friendly folk could keep an eye on them and bring them back if there seemed to be a need.

Grey felt more positive than he had in a long time. His father's curse was working; already it had led to the chance discovery of the address paper, and their acquisition of it; anything that could go wrong with Com-Pewter's plot was now going wrong. If that curse held, they would find the Good Magician and get their Answer, and that could complete the disruption of the plot.

But much Xanth magic did not operate the same in the dream realm. Could Murphy's curse extend there? If not, their mission could after all prove in vain.

15

GOURD

They set up piles of pillows in the garden, each before a gourd on a vine. Dolph lay down on the center setting, with Ivy to his left and Grey to his right. They linked hands.

Nada turned Dolph's gourd so that the peephole came to face him. He had to go first to set the scene; it was individual to each person and remained at the point that person had last been, until he returned and changed it. Dolph had a standard setting that he had encountered at the time he rescued Electra. They would join him there, if they were in physical contact with him as they entered.

Dolph's eye met the peephole. He froze in place, intent on what he saw there. He would not move until some outsider broke the contact by moving the gourd or putting a hand between the peephole and his eye.

Grey went next. Ivy knew he could null the magic of the gourd if he chose, and probably he could void it at any time while he was inside the dream realm. Indeed, he could have done so during their prior adventure, had they but known it.

Maybe the Night Stallion had guessed at something of the kind, because he had sheered away from a confrontation with Grey. Ivy had wondered about that at the time, but had forgotten the matter in the press of subsequent events; now it made more sense to her. But Grey was not using his talent now; he wanted to find the Good Magician as much as she did. He froze in place.

Ivy went last. Her mother turned the gourd for her, and she too froze as her eye locked on the peephole. But she did not see this; her awareness was now within the realm of the gourd.

It was a huge building: a palace or castle, with tiled walls and thick supporting columns. Strange folk hurried in every direction, each one intent on his or her own business, glancing neither to left or right, pausing for nothing.

She was holding her brother's hand, as she had been before entering the gourd. She let go; once the scene had been set, they were all right. Grey was standing on the other side.

"What is this amazing place?" she inquired.

"An airport," Grey said.

"A Mundane bad dream," Dolph said.

Grey smiled. "Much the same thing! Airports are always rushed, and the planes are always late even though they're listed as being on time, and the baggage is a giant lottery system. So many travelers were beating the odds and keeping their bags by carrying them onto the planes that the government had to change the law, making them check their bags, and now the losses are back up to par or even beyond it. It's a bad dream, all right!"

"This can't be where the Good Magician is living!" Ivy said.

"I'll ask someone," Dolph said confidently. He stepped boldly forward. "Hey, you!" he called at a passing man.

The man eyed him with mild annoyance and rushed on.

"I thought you were supposed to be able to get help, here in the gourd," Ivy said.

"I am. But I haven't been here in a long time; maybe they don't recognize me." He tried again, this time hailing a woman. "Hey, miss!"

"Don't you touch me, you sexist!" she snapped, jerking away.

"I'm not a sexist!" he protested. "I don't even know what it is!"

"Then you're a juvenile delinquent," she said over her shoulder as she zoomed away.

"Got you dead to rights," Ivy murmured.

"This is getting us nowhere," Grey said. "Mundanes never help strangers; you have to get someone in authority. I think I see a policeman now. I'll ask him."

Dolph looked, and quailed. "That's the dread demon in blue! He chased us all over the place!"

But Grey was already stepping out to intercept the man. "Officer—may we get some help?"

The demon bore down on them. Not only was he garbed in blue, he was big and fat and looked ferocious. "Ya disturbina peace?" he demanded. "Complaints aboutya! Gonna runyain!"

"We are looking for an address, officer," Grey said. "If you could—"

But the man's beady eye had fixed on Dolph. "Hey, Iknowya! You'n that barebroad—"

"He is Prince Dolph," Ivy said indignantly. "You're supposed to help him!"

"Prince Dolph!" the man exclaimed. "Whyn'tya sayso! Whatcha need?"

"You mean you're not going to chase us?" Dolph asked, gaining courage.

"Stallion sez giveya anythingya want. Whatchawant?"

"We need to find an address," Ivy said. "Damescroft—"

"Dames? What kinda placeya think thisis?" the blue man demanded indignantly. "None a that streetstuff here!"

"Damescroft," Ivy repeated carefully. "It must be a place. The next part is Silly Goose Lane."

"Never hearda it," the man said with certainty. "No gooses here! I'll runin anyone tries it!"

"Little Halingberry?" Ivy asked, reading the next line.

"Lemme seethat!" the policeman said. He took the paper.

"Well nowonder! Yareadingit backwards! Yawant Angle-Land!"

"But I read it in the order it's listed," Ivy protested.

"Listenup, sugarplum, this's Mundania, er proximation thereof! Readfrom bottomup!"

Ivy glanced disbelievingly at Grey, but he agreed with the policeman. "That's the way Mundane addresses are read," he said. "I assumed that it was different in Xanth or I would have said something."

"This isn't exactly Xanth," she reminded him. "It's a bad dream."

He smiled. "And a bad dream in Xanth is of Mundania! It certainly makes sense!" Then he turned to the policeman. "If you will just tell us where Angle-Land is, officer, we shall be happy to go there and get off your beat."

"Well, itsa longway, butfer Prince Dolph wegotta shortcut. Taketha doorthere." He pointed with a fat finger.

"Thank you, officer," Grey said. "You have been most helpful."

They walked toward the indicated door. "He's almost decent," Dolph said, amazed. "Before, he chased us all through this place, because of Grace'l. Said she was indecent."

"But I thought Grace'l is a walking skeleton!" Grey said. "Her bare bones may be frightening, but hardly indecent!"

"Oh, when she was clothed with illusion!" Ivy exclaimed. "So she looked like a bare nymph!"

"Mundanes think bare nymphs are indecent," Grey agreed. "At least, when they go out in public."

"It certainly is a strange place," Ivy agreed.

They reached the door. Ivy put her hand on the knob and turned it. The door swung open.

The scene beyond surprised them all. It consisted of angles of every description. Some looked like thin pie slices, while others were as square as the corners of castles, and yet others were broad and dull.

"I don't see why the Good Magician would want to live here," Dolph remarked.

"Maybe it improves further in," Grey said. "This reminds me too much of geometry."

"Who?" Ivy asked.

"It's a branch of mathematics," he explained. "One of those tortures, like Freshman English, I hope never to face again."

"I can see why," Ivy said. Indeed, this looked like an awful place to live!

They stepped into Angle-Land. Some of the angles were stationary, while some moved around. Ivy almost collided with a very pretty little one. "Ooops, pardon me!" the angle begged. "Normally I see very well, for I am acute, but I'm afraid I wasn't looking where I was going."

"You certainly are cute," Ivy agreed. "Can you show us the way to Hurts?"

"You say my sharp point hurts you? Oh, I'm so sorry!"

"No, no!" Ivy said, smiling. "I said that you look very nice. You're the cutest angle I've seen here."

The angle blushed, pleased. "Well, I am supposed to be, you know. But I wouldn't want to hurt anyone."

Ivy realized that this angle's horizons were limited. "Thank you. We shall keep looking."

They went on. The next angle they encountered was relatively dull; its point would not cut anything. "Hello," Ivy said. "Can you tell us where Hurts is?"

"Duh," the angle said.

Dolph nudged her from one side, and Grey from the other. "It's stupid," the one said.

"It's an obtuse angle," the other said.

The angle heard then. "Duh, sure, I'm obtuse! I'm supposed to be. See, my point is much wider than that acute gal you were just talking to." He said this with evident pride.

"Yes, I can see that," Ivy said, and the dull angle smiled with satisfaction.

They went on. The next angle was perfectly square. "Do you know where Hurts is?" Ivy asked.

"I wouldn't think of admitting to anything like that!" it replied. "I am after all a right angle."

"But all we want are directions!" Ivy said.

"I am sure I am quite correct in declining to comment on that sort of thing."

Ivy saw that this angle was hopelessly self-righteous. They went on.

They came to a wall. "Have we run out of angles?" Grey asked, looking about.

"What do you think I am—a curve?" the wall inquired.

"Certainly not an angle," Ivy said. "You look absolutely straight to me."

"Precisely: I am a straight angle. A hundred and eighty degrees. Not a degree more, not a degree less."

"He's right," Grey murmured.

"Not at all, lout!" the angle retorted. "The last one you talked to was a right angle; I am a straight angle, as I just informed you. I deviate not an iota from my course."

"Do you know where Hurts is?"

"Do you suppose I am the straight man for your crude humor? It will never work; I shall not deviate!"

"He's *too* straight," Grey muttered.

"It is impossible to be too straight or too narrow!" the angle proclaimed.

They moved on. They came to a bend so wide it was bent backwards. "What's your angle?" Ivy inquired.

"Now that is a subject for suitable cogitation," it replied. "Whether it is nobler to suffer the slings and arrows of outrageous questions, or—"

"All we want," Ivy said firmly, "is to find the way to Hurts. Do you know it?"

"As I was saying, before you so rudely interrupted me, that is a matter for reflexion, and I am of course the one to do it, being a reflex angle. So let us consider: what is to be gained or lost by your proceeding to such a painful locale? On the one hand—"

"I'm hurting right now," Dolph said. "These angles think they're real sharp, but to me they're pretty dull."

"Philistine!" the angle shot back.

"You know," Grey said, "if puns are the way of it here,

maybe we should go for the big one: Hurts must be where the most cutting angles are."

"The ones that can hurt you worst," Dolph agreed.

They headed back toward the acute angles. "Now don't be thoughtless about this!" the reflex angle called. "There remain points to consider most carefully!"

There, in the sharpest heart of the most acute angles, was a narrow blood-stained gate. It had broken glass with sharply acute angles along its bars, and needlelike spikes along the top. They had found the entrance to Hurts.

Ivy eyed the spikes. She hardly relished squeezing through that. "You know, Grey, everything here is magic, because it's the dream realm, so you should be able to null it. But if you do—"

"Will it null the dream itself?" Grey finished. "Well, does the exercise of other magic talents interfere with it?"

Dolph became a goblin. "Not that I know of, pot-bait!" he said, true to the character he portrayed.

Ivy touched the nearest acute angle, and enhanced her so that she shone. "It doesn't seem to," she agreed.

"Then I should be able to exercise my talent here without wreaking havoc," Grey concluded. "Provided I keep it moderate." He reached out to touch the gate, carefully. "Why, this isn't glass at all!" he exclaimed. "It's illusion!"

"It's illusion *now,*" Dolph said. "You bet it wasn't a moment ago."

"It's a matter of interpretation," Ivy pointed out. "Since the entire dream world is crafted of illusion, illusions are real here. Grey just nulled out some of the glass illusion's reality."

"I'm glad," Dolph said. "When you get cut here, you do bleed. Maybe not in your real body back in Xanth, but it hurts the same."

Ivy remembered Girard Giant and his river of blood. She knew it was true.

They squeezed through the nulled gate. The shards of glass bent like leaves, harmlessly.

They were in a horrible region. This was evidently the setting for the bad dreams of those who feared pain. All around there were suffering people. Some had loathsome diseases, some had awful injuries, and some seemed to be enduring unendurable emotional turmoil. It was certain that all were hurting.

A mean-looking man wearing a black mask walked up. He carried a whip. "I don't remember ordering three more actors," he said gruffly. "Are you sure you came to the right place?"

"We're just passing through," Ivy said quickly.

"Well, there's a really bad dream coming up, with a large cast," the dungeon master said. "Maybe we'd better use you anyway. Can you scream well?"

"I am Prince Dolph," Dolph said. "I—"

"Oh, why didn't you say so! You are merely touring, of course! What do you want to see?"

"The fastest way to Bishop's Storkford," Ivy said.

The dungeon master scratched his hairy head. "We are bounded on the far side by a broad river with several good fords, but I don't recall that particular one. I can show you to the river, anyway."

"That will be fine," Ivy said.

They followed the dungeon master through the dungeon. Ivy tried to avert her eyes from the horrors of it, lest it give her bad dreams that would later bring her right back here, but it was impossible to overlook all of it. A groan would attract her attention, and she would see someone with a gory knife wound, the knife still in it, ready to hurt twice as much as it was pulled out. A sigh would summon her eye to the other side, and there would be an otherwise lovely maiden whose hair had been burned away, leaving her bare scalp a mass of blisters. Ivy knew they were all actors, only setting the scene so that the terrible dreams could be fashioned for the night mares to take, but it was so realistic that it turned her stomach anyway.

"I don't ever want to dream again!" Dolph whispered.

"I think I saw something like this in a horror movie once," Grey remarked.

"You were tortured in Mundania?" Ivy asked, appalled.

"No, I watched it for fun."

"For fun!" she repeated, shocked.

"But I didn't like it," he reassured her hastily.

"I certainly hope so!" How could she marry a man who *liked* awfulness like this? Yet she realized that there probably were Mundanes who were of that type. Just so long as they never got into Xanth!

They came to the river. The water was muddy and the current swift; anyone who tried to cross it could be swept away and drowned. Indeed, she spied a night mare picking up a just-completed dream in which a desperate girl was drowning. Ivy hoped she never suffered that dream herself, either.

"The fords are supervised by various creatures," the dungeon master explained. "I think the storks are upstream, that way." He pointed to the left. "You may walk along it until you find the one you are looking for. Keep an eye out for blood flowing into the river; it can be slippery."

"Thank you," Ivy said faintly. "You have been very kind."

"It's not my nature," the man confessed. "But for Prince Dolph, nothing is too good."

They followed the river upstream, doing their best to ignore the activities by its bank. But the activities in the river weren't much more reassuring. Grotesque monsters loomed in it, snapping their mottled teeth, and rogue winds threatened to capsize tiny boats containing helpless women and children. One section of the water was on fire, and the fire was encircling several swimmers; the more desperately they stroked to escape it, the faster the flames advanced. Another area was calm and deep; a sign said SWIMMING, and children were gleefully diving into the pool. But they weren't coming up again. When Ivy peered more closely at the sign she saw that a stray leaf had plastered itself across a word at the top, and she was able to make out the word: "no." What was happening to those disappearing children? In another place the sign was clear: NO FISHING. Naturally several people were dangling their lines in the water. What they couldn't see, because of the blinding effect of the reflection of sunlight (never mind where the sunlight came from, in this realm of dreams!), was a monstrous kraken weed below, its tentacles carefully latching onto each line. Then, abruptly, it tugged, and the fishers tumbled forward into the water and disappeared in the swirl of tentacles.

Ivy hoped she was never bad enough to have such dreams. Yet she could see that it was far better to experience the horror of the dream than the reality—and those who fished where it was forbidden might indeed get caught by a kraken. So if the dream frightened them into safer behavior, that was good. Thus a bad dream could be a good dream. She had never realized that before.

But what was the Good Magician doing here? Surely the Night Stallion had his domain well under control, and did not need any help from Humfrey. If the stallion had needed anything, he should have sent a night mare to the Good Magician's castle in Xanth to inquire. Something about this situation did not make sense.

Was it possible that the address which guided them was false? That Magician Humfrey was *not* here?

Ivy squelched that thought, because if Humfrey wasn't here, then they had no clue to where he was, and they would not be able to get his Answer, and Grey would be subject to the will of Com-Pewter. That was unacceptable, so Ivy un-accepted it. Good Magician Humfrey *was* here; that was final.

They came to the region of the fords. The first was labeled FRANKFORD, and was supervised by a man-sized sausage with little arms and legs. They passed it by.

Farther along was one marked AFFORD, where those who wished to use it had to have plenty of Mundane coinage to qualify. Then there was Beeford, strictly for the bees, and Ceeford, where everyone was looking but not touching. They passed the complete alphabet of fords, finally leaving Zeeford behind; it was being used by strange striped horses.

At last they came to the various fords that were strictly for the birds. They watched closely as they came to the Ibisford and Heronford, and finally spotted the Storkford. Here was where the storks were crossing, carrying their squalling bundles. Ivy realized that this was part of the route the storks took to reach Mundania; it must wind down to the big gourd on No Name Key, and from there they carried their babies to waiting Mundane mothers. Grey had said that Mundanes had a different way of getting babies, but naturally he was ignorant, being a man.

"But we aren't storks," Grey protested. "They won't let us cross here!"

"We can cross," Dolph said. He became a giant stork.

Ivy smiled. She went to where a pile of spare sheets was, and took a large, sturdy one. She knotted the corners together so that it formed a big sling. "Climb in, Grey," she said.

"But—" he protested.

"When at the Storkford, do as the storks do, you big baby," she teased, climbing in herself.

Double-disgruntled, he joined her. It was like a hammock, lumping them together, but they really didn't mind that too much. Dolph walked out across the ford, and no stork challenged him. Perhaps they assumed he was delivering a set of twins to a giant.

"Now we have to find Little Halingberry," Ivy announced, looking at the address as they resumed their normal forms and positions at the far bank.

"I dread to think how foolish that will be," Grey muttered.

They were at the edge of a field of assorted berries. The storks were following a path that led underground; the plants there seemed to put their fruit below. "What kind is that?" Dolph asked.

"That's a bury plant," Ivy responded. "You have to be careful about eating them, because of the pits. You don't want to fall in."

Grey looked at her as if uncertain whether their bethrothal was a good idea, but did not comment.

They passed many varieties of berries. Some seemed edible, like the red and blue berries, and some were odd, like the Londonberry. Then the heard something calling. "That's it!" Ivy said confidently. "The plant haling us!"

Sure enough, it was the halingberry plant. But it was way too large. It was the big halingberry. They looked around until they found its offspring, the little halingberry, whose voice was relatively faint. Beside that was a road, marked MAIN LANE.

"Now for Silly Goose Lane," Ivy said. She led the way

down it. She was getting the hang of this region.

There were many offshoots: Hot Lane, Cold Lane, Plain Lane, Lois Lane, Santa Claus Lane, Derby Lane, and others in boring profusion. Some of them seemed to have interesting activities at their ends, but Ivy didn't want to waste time with bypaths. Then they got to the animal lanes, and to the bird lanes. After Donald Duck Lane was Sober Goose Lane and then Silly Goose Lane.

"We're getting close!" Ivy said, relieved. She stepped onto the lane—and leaped. "Eeeeek!" she screamed, outraged.

"What happened?" Grey asked, alarmed. He hurried after her—and made his own great leap. "Ooooff!"

It was Dolph who caught on. "A silly goose—like boot rear!" he exclaimed, trying to stifle a laugh which threatened to overwhelm him. "When you get on it, you get—"

"Now it's your turn, little brother!" Ivy said grimly.

"Sure." Dolph became a wacky-looking goose and stepped forward. Naturally nothing happened to him, since this lane was intended for this species. He had outwitted it.

"Now we find Damescroft," Ivy said pretending not to be disappointed. Grey was beginning to understand why she and her brother did not always get along.

There were houses here. Soon they reached the ones labeled croft: Eaglecroft, Handicroft, Welkincroft, Manscroft, Kidscroft, and finally Damescroft.

They had made it! There before them stood a pretty cottage, with white walls and a thatched roof.

"This is the Good Magician's castle?" Grey asked.

"Nothing like it!" Dolph replied. "But you know, there are always three challenges to get in, and you have to surmount them or Humfrey won't talk to you. He's probably just as crotchety about that as he's been for the past century."

"Maybe this is illusion," Ivy said. "The challenge is to get in, when we can't see what we're getting into."

"Then let me see what I can do," Grey said. He took a step forward and stretched out his hands, concentrating.

The cottage flickered, then disappeared. In its place was a perfect replica of the Good Magician's castle as it was in

Xanth. It was of stone, with reasonably high turrets and a
moat. It looked deserted, too.

"That's more like it," Ivy said. "I don't see a moat monster,
but that's the way it is now, anyway. We can cross over the—
oops." For now she saw that there was no drawbridge over
the moat. It wasn't that the bridge had been drawn; there was
none at all.

They went to the edge of the moat. "It may be poisoned,"
Dolph said. "We don't want to risk it; Grey couldn't null real
poison."

Grey agreed. "Also, it might not be fair for me to use my
power more than once. We don't want the Magician to be
annoyed."

"I can get us across," Dolph said. He became the roc again.
They climbed onto his feet. He spread his wings and flew
across, landing on the inner ledge.

Ivy didn't say anything, but she was ill at ease. This was
too easy. The Good Magician's challenges were always chal-
lenging, while they seemed to have conquered two of them
without effort. She was suspicious of that.

They were on the ledge between the sheer castle wall and
the moat. They walked along it, seeking the entry. Normally
the main gate would be where the drawbridge crossed the
moat, but they had no bridge to orient on.

They kept walking until they had completed a circuit
around the castle. There was no gate at all.

"My turn," Ivy said. "I can get us in."

She concentrated on the impervious wall, enhancing its
state of perviousness. It became less substantial, so that water
might percolate through it, and air. It was a shadow of its
former self, looking solid but becoming illusion.

She took the hands of her companions. "We can pass
through this," she said, and led them into the wall and out of
it, inside the castle. Then she reversed the enhancement, so
that the walls returned to their normal state.

They were all the way in, now. Ivy heard footsteps. A man
turned the corner and stood in the lighted hall.

"Hugo!" Ivy exclaimed, walking toward him.

"Ivy!" he replied. "You are lovely!"

Ivy was unable to return the compliment, for Hugo was best described as homely. "You haven't changed!" she said instead, then hastily made introductions: "This is my friend Hugo, the son of Humfrey and the Gorgon. This is my betrothed, Grey Murphy. You know Dolph, of course."

Hugo nodded. "Right this way," he said. "Mom has cookies, the kind you like."

"Punwheel!" Ivy exclaimed as they followed him to the kitchen. Indeed, the smell of freshly baked cookies was drifting down the hall.

The Gorgon was there, exactly as Ivy remembered her: tall, stately, with snakelets of hair framing her invisible face. The Good Magician had made it invisible so that the sight of it would not stone those who saw it. In the dark, Ivy was sure, that face was just as solid and warm as any other. The cookies were crisp and hot, with just that bit of hardening that close proximity to the Gorgon's face caused.

"My, how you've grown, Ivy!" the Gorgon exclaimed. "You were, let me think, only ten or eleven years old the last time I saw you!"

"I'm seventeen now," Ivy said proudly. She introduced Grey, and of course the Gorgon exclaimed over the betrothal.

They ate cookies while they compared notes. The Gorgon was eager for news of Xanth, and rather missed the old castle there.

"But why are you here?" Ivy asked. "The three of you just disappeared, and we had no idea where you had gone until now."

"The Magician is on a Quest," the Gorgon explained.

"The Question Quest!" Grey exclaimed.

"Why yes; however did you know?"

Ivy explained about their sneak peak at the volumes the Muse of History was working on. "But couldn't he just take care of it right there?"

"No, this was of a preemptive nature. The Magician never was very tolerant of interruptions, and this was so important that he decided to eliminate interruptions entirely. We have not been disturbed for seven years." But there seemed to be more regret than pride in her voice.

"But we have a Question," Ivy said. "We must have the Answer before we can get married. So we tracked you down here, and we will go home as soon as we see Magician Humfrey."

The Gorgon shook her head. "I'm afraid he won't see you. He is so wrapped up in his Quest that he allows nothing to interrupt it."

"But we must have that Answer!" Ivy protested.

"I would be delighted to have him give it to you. But he just won't. He will just slide into another level of the dream realm and avoid you, without ever taking his eyes from his texts."

"But he left his texts behind!" Ivy said.

"The physical ones. He has all of them duplicated perfectly here, and all his other magic. Everything he needs for his Quest—including privacy."

"I think I could find him," Grey said. "I could null out the levels of magic illusion until—"

"No, that wouldn't make him give an Answer," Ivy said dispiritedly.

And that was it: they had come all the way here for nothing. No wonder the challenges they had faced when entering the castle had been perfunctory: the Good Magician wasn't at home to Questions anymore.

Grey nulled the magic for them as they held hands, and in a moment Ivy looked up from her gourd. They were back in Castle Roogna.

For a moment she was tempted to say they had gotten their Answer. But that would not be honest, and besides, if she could have figured out an answer herself, they would not have needed to find the Magician.

So their dilemma remained. Her dilemma, really; Grey had never had any doubt. He intended to be out of Xanth before Com-Pewter's deadline expired. It was Ivy who had to make her decision: whether to go with him to drear Mundania or remain in Xanth without him.

"Oh Grey!" she cried in torment. "I can't do either! I love you, but I also love Xanth. I can't endure without both!"

"I understand," he said. "I love you, and I love Xanth, and I know you must be together, so I will leave you."

Ivy clung to him, her tears flowing. "No, without you Xanth would be as drear for me as Mundania. I will go with you, though it destroy me."

"But I am afraid it *will* destroy you!" he protested. "That is why I know you must not go."

Then, as she clung to him, she remembered something she had forgotten. "Your father's curse! It was working! It gave us the clue to where the Good Magician was!"

"Yes, but it failed. Humfrey would not—"

"No!" she cried. "Maybe it succeeded! Only we are giving up too soon!"

"I don't understand," he said, looking at her quizzically. "We did all we could."

"No, I think we only *thought* we did all we could!" she said, uncertain whether she was experiencing a significant insight or grasping at a futile straw. "We thought we failed, but we haven't yet. Because we got on the wrong track. But maybe we can get back on the right track!"

"What do you mean?"

"I mean *the dream isn't over yet!*" she said.

"Not over?" he asked blankly. "But we exited from the gourd, and—"

"Think back," she said excitedly. "Remember how easy it was to find the Good Magician? There were exactly three challenges, and we took turns overcoming them, and we were in. And there were Hugo and the Gorgon, exactly as I remembered them."

"Yes, so you said. I hadn't met them before, so—"

"I am seven years older, but they aren't!" she continued. "They were unchanged—and they shouldn't have been. The Gorgon should have a gray hair or something, and Hugo should have been in his mid-twenties. But he wasn't. Because he wasn't real. He was from my memory—no more. Gray, I made it all up! We never found them at all!"

Gray nodded. "Unchanged—conforming to your mental images," he said, "when they should have been older. So it was a dream, not the reality."

"And the dream isn't over!" she repeated. "It side-tracked us, made us think it was over, but it isn't! We can still search for the Good Magician!"

He nodded, working it out. "I did think that the challenges weren't as horrendous as reputed. So when I banished the illusion of Damescroft, it wasn't the reality we saw, but another illusion."

"We only dreamed your power worked," she agreed. "And we only dreamed that you returned us to Xanth. *That's* the real challenge: to penetrate the illusion that we are accomplishing anything!"

He embraced her. "I'm having the illusion of kissing you," he said, kissing her.

"It's an excellent illusion," she agreed, kissing him back. "Now let's get back to business. We still have to find the Good Magician."

Grey considered. "As I understand it, we are in the realm of dreams, and everything we do here is part of the dream, but we do retain our natural powers. If I exercise mine persistently, doubting everything, like Descartes—"

"Who?"

He laughed. "A Mundane! He doubted until he could doubt no more, and decided that was the truth. I only remember him because I missed him on a test, but now I think maybe he had something. If the Good Magician is here, I should be able to find him by doubting away everything else. But since everything here is dreams, I'll have to do it carefully; and it may be tricky—and maybe it won't work at all but will just put us out of the dream with nothing."

"Try it!" she urged. "It's our only hope!"

Grey nodded. "Uh, maybe you'd better enhance me, just in case. I need to be very strong, and very accurate, so I can dismantle the dream layer by layer."

"Yes." Ivy took his hand and began the enhancement.

16
ANSWER

Grey felt the power of Ivy's magic, enhancing him. He knew that his ability to null magic was being increased. When his talent countered hers, she could not enhance others, but when hers worked on his, he had much greater power than before. If anyone could penetrate this network of deceptive dreams, he could—now.

What a pretty diversion it had been: letting them dream that their powers were working, when they weren't. Or perhaps they were, but not in the way they had supposed. He had nulled the illusion of Damescroft, only to be deceived by the illusion of the Good Magician's castle. Dolph had changed form and carried them across a moat that wasn't really there. Ivy had enhanced their way through the wrong wall. They had all fallen for it, being overconfident and too accepting.

But Ivy had caught on, and thereby saved them the excruciation of returning to Mundania. She had won the true challenge by her wit rather than her talent. Now it was his turn—and he suspected that his wit would be tested, too.

For one thing, had they really dreamed up those three challenges themselves? He doubted it. The challenges had been too pat. More likely they had been devised by someone else for the trio's benefit. That meant that the Good Magician *was* here—and only Ivy's desperation had foiled the deception. The one thing that could go wrong with it had gone wrong.

As he pondered it, perhaps better able to come to terms with it because of Ivy's Enhancement, he realized that what they had experienced could indeed be taken as three challenges—but not of the simple type they had supposed. The first could have been for Dolph: finding the address. Grey's father's curse could have enabled Dolph to handle that challenge. The second could have been for Ivy—and again, the carefully set illusion had almost by chance been foiled, as if the curse had helped her to understand its nature. The third could be his own: to ascertain the true state of things that might not be at all what they expected. Could Murphy's curse give him the open-mindedness to see what he had to see?

He certainly hoped so. There was only a week left in his grace period. His decision in the dream Ivy had just exposed had been correct: if he found no way to void Com-Pewter's claim, he would return to Mundania. If Ivy decided again to go with him—

But maybe they would not be faced with such an awful choice. The Good Magician was said to have an Answer for any Question, so if he could just locate Humfrey, all would be well. He would be glad to serve for a year, just to stay in Xanth with Ivy. Service here was better than freedom in drear Mundania. Provided it was in a good cause. Pewter's cause was evil, so he had to resist the temptation to go along with it for the sake of being with Ivy in Xanth. He hoped he still had the courage to leave both.

"That's the best I can do," Ivy said. "If I enhance you any more, you might explode." She had said it in jest, but then perhaps remembered the glowworm, and didn't laugh.

Grey concentrated on the landscape of Xanth he saw before them. He knew now that this seeming reality was illusion, the stuff of the dream. They needed to return to reality, which was the appearance of the dream.

The landscape fuzzed, then faded out. They were back before the Good Magician's castle, with Dolph beside them.

"Hey, what happened?" Dolph asked. "I thought you two were on your way out of Xanth!"

"It was part of the dream," Ivy explained. "We woke up from it, in a manner."

"But—"

"We're still doing it," she said. "Watch."

Grey concentrated on the castle. He didn't want to null too much! Slowly it fuzzed, and then it faded out, leaving the cottage of Damescroft as they had first seen it.

"Now we're back where we started," Ivy said. "But if it's not the castle and not the cottage, what is it?"

Grey focused his doubt. The cottage frayed and came apart. In its place—was the castle.

He exchanged a third of a glance with Ivy. Then he focused again.

The castle fuzzed out, and the cottage returned.

"Well, it's got to be one or the other," Dolph said.

Grey pondered, and then he considered, and then he cogitated, and finally he settled down and thought. "Maybe it's neither," he said.

"But—"

"I think we all need to blank our minds, until we expect nothing at all. Then whatever remains will be the truth."

"I can't blank my mind!" Dolph protested. "I'm always thinking about something!"

"What were you watching on the Tapestry?" Ivy asked warningly.

The cottage fuzzed. The image of something silken began to form, such as a giant pair of panties.

"My mind is completely blank!" Dolph cried guiltily.

The image fuzzed back into a formless pile of cloth, which then faded out. The cottage reappeared.

"Blank," Grey said.

"Blank," Ivy agreed.

"Blankety blank," Dolph said.

Grey focused his doubt again. He doubted that either cottage or castle was there, but he had no idea what might really be there. He kept his doubt as pure as he could, expecting nothing.

The cottage was fuzzed out. The castle tried to fuzz in. Dolph forestalled it with more doubt, refusing to be tricked by the present illusion.

An amorphous cloud developed, hovering uncertainly, unable to become one form or the other. Grey continued doubting, refusing to let it coalesce. He kept his expectations blank. Only reality would be allowed to manifest. Gradually the cloud thinned, revealing—nothing.

"Oops," Ivy said.

Grey looked at her. "But there should be *something!*"

"We're out of the dream," she explained. "You nulled it right down to nothing."

"Reality!" he exclaimed in disgust. And realized that *that* was what he had expected.

Dolph stepped forward. "What's that?"

They looked. There was a box sitting on the ground.

They walked toward the box. The landscape seemed completely barren; there were no trees or bushes, and no sunshine or cloud. It seemed to be a wasteland, except for the box.

There turned out to be three boxes, in a row, each dark and oblong and large enough to hold a man.

"Oh, no!" Ivy breathed, horrified. "Coffins!"

There had been three in the Good Magician's family: Humfrey, the Gorgon, and their son, Hugo.

"The dream address!" Dolph said, sharing her horror. "It was the way to find them—but it didn't say they were alive!"

Could the Good Magician have seen his death coming, and acted to hide himself from Xanth so that no one would know? But what was the point of that?

"To let others think he would one day return," Ivy said, her thoughts pacing his. "So that Xanth wouldn't mourn for him—or give its enemies courage."

"Enemies like Com-Pewter," Grey said, seeing it. "But now

we have undone his artifice, so that Xanth can no longer be protected even by the threat of Humfrey's return."

"Com-Pewter must have known!" Ivy said. "That's why he acted now!"

But Grey wasn't quite satisfied with that. "Why didn't Com-Pewter simply tell us Humfrey was dead, then? So that there was no chance to get an Answer?"

Ivy shrugged. "Maybe Pewter wasn't quite sure."

"And maybe it's not true!" Grey said. "Maybe we're not out of this quest yet!"

"But if they are in coffins—"

"Electra was in a coffin, wasn't she?" Grey strode to the nearest box. Now he saw an inscription on a plaque set in it. But the words were indecipherable. "What does this say?"

Ivy approached. She almost smiled. "Do Not Disturb," she read. "It's in Xanthian script. This must be Mundania, so you can't read it."

"Or something like that," Grey agreed. "Electra was in a similar state, I believe."

They checked the other coffins. Neither had a plaque. "Maybe they don't mind being disturbed," Dolph offered.

"Probably so," Ivy said. "It was always the Good Magician who was grumpy about folk taking up his time."

"Then I'm going to open this one."

Ivy was shocked. "But you can't do that! It's not nice to disturb the dead!"

"If he is dead," Grey said grimly. "I doubt it."

He put his hand to the lid of the coffin. There was no fastening. He lifted, and it came up.

A wizened little man lay within, looking just as if he were sleeping. "Hey, Magician Humfrey!" Grey said boldly.

The eyelids flickered, then the eyes opened. The lips parted. "Go away," they said.

"I am Grey Murphy, and I need an Answer," Grey said.

"Go away. I am no longer giving Answers."

"Here is my Question: how can I void the service I owe to Com-Pewter?"

"Go away," the mouth said, grimacing. "I'll give your Answer when I'm done here."

"How long will that be?"

The mouth formed a fifth of a smile. "Is that another Question?"

"No!"

"If you want an Answer, serve me until I return. Then you may have it, if you still want it. Now go away—and don't slam the lid." The eyes closed.

"There *is* an Answer!" Ivy breathed.

"But what good is it, if he returns after a year or more, and I have to leave Xanth in a week?" Grey demanded.

The Good Magician's near eye squinched open again. "No way, Mundane! You must serve until I return, without interruption, or I will not be responsible for the consequence."

"But I must serve Com-Pewter! That's my problem!"

"*After* you complete your service to me," the Good Magician said firmly. "Otherwise you forfeit your Answer." The eye closed again.

"But how can I serve you, if you're asleep?" Grey asked, hardly making sense of this.

"Go to my castle. You will find a way." The features fell into composure; the Good Magician was back in his dream.

Grey lowered the lid, depressed. Apparently there was an Answer to his problem, but unless the Good Magician returned to his castle before the week was out—which seemed unlikely—Grey would have to go home to Mundania without it. Since Humfrey had made it plain that there was no time limit on the service he would owe for the Answer, Grey would have to forfeit long before completing the service.

"The Good Magician always has a good reason for his crazy Answers," Ivy said, trying to put a positive face on it. "When the Gorgon came to ask whether he would marry her, he made her serve as a castle maid for a year before giving his Answer."

"But that's the very height of arrogance!" Grey said.

"So it seemed. But it gave her that time to work with him, so that she could change her mind on the basis of good information. When she didn't change her mind, he married her. By that time she was familiar with every aspect of the castle and his practice, so had no problem. It was really a very good way to do it, as everyone else would have understood, had they been as smart as Humfrey."

"Well, I'm not smart enough to see how having to leave Xanth before I get his Answer is going to do us any good!"

"Neither am I," she said. "But it must be so."

He let the subject drop, because he didn't want to argue with her. But his depression was back in full force. To think that there was a solution to his problem but that he could not have it because of the insensitivity of the one who had it— that was even worse than there being no solution.

They returned to Xanth. They couldn't just walk there, because they didn't know the way through this featureless region, so Grey eased up on his doubt, and the cottage returned. Then they retraced their route through the address until they were back in the airport. Then Grey resumed his doubting, and fell out of the dream.

He lifted his head from the gourd. "Cut the connection," he said. Willing hands turned the gourds, and Ivy and Dolph woke. This time it was real.

Immediately they were besieged by demands for the whole story, but only Dolph was interested in telling it. "You should have seen the guts and gore in the Hurts!" he exclaimed.

Next day they went to the Good Magician's castle. Dolph became a roc and carried them there and dropped them off, promising to return in time to take them to the border of Xanth before Com-Pewter's grace period was up. In fact, he promised to return every day, acting as courier for anything they needed; that was certainly better than remaining grounded at Castle Roogna.

The two walking skeletons, Marrow Bones and Grace'l Ossian, came along also, nominally to help clean up the castle, but really as chaperones. The King and Queen did not want to make a show of it, but they did not encourage the appearance of unseemly behavior in their daughter.

Grey could hardly blame them. At any time Ivy could change her mind and remain in Xanth, effectively breaking off their betrothal (there was a different flavor to that word, and he liked it better than "engagement") and returning to the open market. Why should they risk having her princessly reputation tarnished in this short time?

Break the betrothal—he hated to admit it, but it did seem to him that this was her most sensible course. She was a creature of Xanth, and could no more be happy for long outside it than, as she put it, a mermaid could live on land far from water. There were magic devices that could make her forget him, so that at least one of them could be happy. When he returned to Mundania, he was not going to let her go with him. What would become of him, then, without either betrothed or parents, he did not want to think about. But he knew it had to be. He refused to be the agent of Xanth's degradation, no matter what it cost him personally.

The castle was bleak and bare. The skeletons didn't mind; they were pretty bare themselves. They set about cleaning it out, and fixing separate chambers for the two living folk. Soon nice soft beds were made, though the skeletons really didn't see what was wrong with good old fashioned cold stone. Similarly they renovated the kitchen, knowing that living folk had a hang-up about eating regularly.

"But once we get it cleaned up, what else is there to do?" Grey asked as they sorted through tumbled old vials and set them neatly on the shelves. "And what's the point, fixing up a castle for someone who isn't coming back to it?" For they both knew that the Good Magician had no intention of returning soon, if ever; this service was a charade.

Ivy shook her head; she didn't know either. But at least they were together, for this brief time.

They were hard at work sorting dusty tomes when there was a disturbance outside. Marrow hurried in, rattling. Grey and Ivy looked up in alarm, knowing it took a lot to rattle the skeleton.

"A giant fire-breathing slug is charging the castle!" Marrow reported.

They went to a parapet and looked. Sure enough, the monster was steaming through the moat, causing the water to boil where the fire touched. It was of course a slow charge, for slugs were not rapid travelers, but powerful.

"We'd better flee!" Ivy said. "We can't stop something like that."

"But surely part of my service is to protect the castle," Grey said. "I mean, even if I have to leave in a few days, I might as well do the best I can while I'm here."

"But you can't even get close to that thing without getting burned!" Ivy protested.

"It does seem uncertain of success," Marrow said.

"But Marrow can get close," Grey said. "Maybe the slug is just lost. Marrow, would you be willing to approach it and ask what it wants? Can you speak its language?"

"Only if it is from the gourd," Marrow said.

"If only Grundy Golem were here," Ivy said. "He can speak any living language. If we just had some alternate way to—" Then she brightened. "Maybe we do!"

"We do?"

"Remember the sign language? Let me see if that works!" She had brought the book to the castle, in case she had to return to Mundania, where she would be dependent on this type of communication. Grey had not yet been able to bring himself to tell her of his decision that she had to remain in Xanth.

Now the slug was emerging from the moat and starting up the outer wall. It was moving at a snail's pace, but making definite progress.

Ivy leaned over the parapet. "Hey, sluggo!" she called, waving her hands. "Can you understand this?" She made the sign for "Hello": a gesture resembling the throwing of a kiss with both hands. Grey was glad he understood it, because otherwise he might have misunderstood it.

The slug paused looking up at her. Could it even see? Grey wondered; it had no eyes, just antennae.

Then the antennae moved. One extended while the other retracted. In a moment they reversed motion.

"It's answering!" Ivy exclaimed. "It knows sign language!"

"Ask it what it wants," Grey said, heartened.

"What," Ivy said, making the sign by drawing her right index finger down across her flat left palm. "Want?" She held her two hands as if clutching something, and drew them in to her.

The slug's antennae lined up, then moved forward together with marvelous slow-motion dexterity.

"Answer," Ivy translated. She had picked up a marvelous facility for this type of communication in a short time; Grey realized that she must have enhanced her own learning ability for it. Except that she had been in Mundania at the time, so her talent shouldn't have been operative. He would have to ask her about that.

She faced Grey. "It wants an Answer, but I don't know—"

"An Answer!" Grey exclaimed. "It thinks the Good Magician is back!"

Ivy grimaced. "I'll try to explain." She made the sign for conversation—the tip of one index finger moving toward the lips while the other moved from them, then reversing the motions.

The slug remained stuck to the wall, responding with its antennae. After a fair dialogue, Ivy turned to Grey. "I'm not getting through. I don't know all the terms, and it isn't awfully bright. As near as I can tell, it wants to attend a slug-fest."

"Maybe that doesn't mean the same as it does in Mundania," Grey said.

"I'm not sure what it means," she said. "But we'd better tell the slug something, so that it will go away. Otherwise it's apt to slime the castle, and its breath will set fire to the curtains."

Grey pondered. "All right. Tell it to make up a bunch of notices in slug-speak, and post them on trees and rocks and things where big slugs go. The notices will say SLUGFEST, and give the time and place. Then any interested slugs will go there at the proper time. But tell it to allow a year or two, because slugs don't travel very fast."

"I'll try." Ivy got busy with her signals. After a time the slug, satisfied, turned around and slid slowly back through the steaming moat and away from the castle.

They returned to their tome sorting. But soon there was another interruption. "A goblin is knocking at the door," Marrow reported.

"You mean pounding?" Grey asked, remembering the nature of goblins.

"No, this is a constrained, polite knocking."

"It must be a trick," Ivy said. "Let him in, then pull up the drawbridge so his henchmen can't charge after he has opened the way."

In due course they met the goblin in one of the cleaned-up chambers. "Who are you, and what do you want?" Grey inquired gruffly.

"I am very sorry to disturb you, Good Magician, but when I saw that you had returned—"

"Wait!" Grey said, embarrassed. "I'm not the Good Magician! I'm Grey, just doing a service for him." In addition, there was something odd about the goblin.

"I beg your pardon, Grey," the goblin said. "I am Goody Goblin. If I may have an appointment, I shall return at a more convenient time."

Grey realized what was bothering him about this goblin. He was being polite! "It's not that! The Good Magician isn't here right now, and I'm not sure when—"

"I am certainly willing to accept an Answer from an assistant," Goody said. "I realize that the Good Magician has far more pressing concerns than the problem of a mere goblin."

Grey was beginning to feel like a heel. "Uh, just what is your problem, Goody?"

"I seem to be unpopular with my kindred. Since naturally I would like to assume a posture of leadership, and to win the favor of a pretty gobliness, I wish to be advised of appropriate corrective action."

"Well, I'd certainly like to help you, but—" Then Grey had a bright notion. "I think you need to have a fouler mouth. Most goblins I've met are obnoxious and violent. If—"

"Oh, I couldn't be violent!" Goody protested. "That would be unsocial."

"Well, maybe you wouldn't have to actually be violent, if only you *sounded* violent. You could bluff your way through. What you need is a really foul vocabulary."

"I would be glad to have it!" Goody agreed. "May I purchase it from you?"

Grey glanced helplessly at Ivy. "No, I think you have to learn it," she said. "But I think I know where you can."

"That would be excellent!"

"Just a moment." She went to Marrow and whispered. The skeleton departed, but returned in a moment with something. Ivy set it on a chair. "Sit down," she told Goody.

"Why thank you," the goblin said, taking the chair. Because he was short-legged he had to jump up and land on it. But the moment he landed, he sailed off again. "#$*&£0!!" he exclaimed, causing the white curtains to blush pink. Something flew from him and struck the wall so hard it was embedded.

Grey caught on. She had put a curse burr on the chair!

"So you do know the terms," Ivy said, evidently suppressing her own delicate blush, for it had been quite a word the goblin had fired forth. "You just need to be encouraged to use it."

"Go to the biggest, wildest curse burr patch you can find, and sit down in the middle of it," Grey said. "I guarantee that by the time you find your way out, you will have the required vocabulary. Just make sure you remember the expressions that get you free. They can only be used once against the curse burrs, but are infinitely reusable against goblins."

"Oh thank you, kind sir and lovely maiden!" Goody said. "And what is your fee for this wonderful Answer?"

"No fee," Grey said quickly. "We're just here for a few days. Good luck."

The goblin stood up to his full lowly height. "No, I am afraid I must insist. You are doing me a service, and I must do you one in recompense. That is only fair."

Fairness—in a goblin? Now Grey had seen everything.

"Well, er, if you feel that way, maybe you should, uh, stay here a while, and when something comes up, er—"

"Excellent. I am sure there will be something."

Grace'l appeared. "Show our guest to a suitable chamber," Ivy said.

Heartened, Goody Goblin departed with the skeleton. Grey was sure he would make good among the goblins, after undertaking the corrective course.

They returned to their tomes—only to be interrupted again. This time it was a flying fan: an instrument made of bamboo that propelled itself by waving back and forth so as to generate a jet of air. Ivy was able to communicate with it by sign language, though some of this resembled a fan dance. The fan turned out to be lost, and was looking for fandom.

Now Grey had just a bit of Mundane experience that related. "Form a fan club!" he exclaimed. "Then you will be in the middle of fandom."

Satisfied, the fan flew off to find a suitable length of wood to make a club.

They were about to return to the tomes, when yet another supplicant arrived. "This is getting out of hand!" Grey muttered. "We'll never get anything done if this continues!"

"Maybe we should haul up the drawbridge again," Ivy said. "I realize that seems unfriendly, but with all these folk coming in, we'll have no rest or privacy at all if we don't limit access."

"I'm beginning to understand why the Good Magician was reputed to be reclusive and taciturn," Grey said, "if this is what his life was like before he set limits."

"You see to the one that's inside, and I'll see to getting the defenses set up," Ivy said with a smile. "Just don't do too much for her." She departed.

When Grey saw the visitor, he understood Ivy's caution. She was a lovely young human girl. "Oh Magician, please, I beg of you, I'm desperate, I'll do anything!" she exclaimed.

"Please, I'm only, uh, filling in, and I may not be able to help you," he said. "What—"

"I'm in love!" she exclaimed grandly. "But he doesn't know I exist! Please—"

Grey ascertained that it was a young man of her village she was interested in, who saw her only as a friend. She did not want to make a scene, she only wanted him to return her love. She was sure things would be fine, then. It seemed to Grey that she was correct; she was a good and lovely girl who would be good for a handsome lout like that. Just as Ivy was good for Grey himself.

"Grace'l," he said, and the skeleton appeared. "Is there a vial of love potion in the collection you have been sorting?"

"Several," Grace'l agreed.

"Bring one here." The skeletons were not always quick on the uptake, perhaps because their skulls were hollow.

She brought one. Grey presented it to the maiden. "Slip this in his drink. Make sure you are the first person he sees after he drinks. You understand? A mistake could be very awkward."

"Oh, yes!" she exclaimed. "Oh, thank you, Magician!" She flung her arms around him and planted a kiss on his nose. "But what about my service?"

"No service, this time," he said. But he realized that this aspect, also, of the Good Magician's practice made sense. Folk were too eager to get something for nothing, and were already flocking to the castle. If it was this bad on the first day, how much worse would it be on the following days? "But in the future, probably some service will be required." So that when she spread the word, it would discourage the freeloaders.

"Oh? When?" She evidently thought he meant that she would have to return to do the service.

He realized that it would hardly be expedient to call her back; she would have to do it before she left. "Uh, within the next few days. Grace'l will show you to a chamber for the night."

"That's fine," she agreed, and departed with the skeleton.

They finished the day, their tome sorting incomplete, and retired to their separate chambers after an excellent evening meal Grace'l prepared. Grey lay awake for some time, thinking about things. Now he appreciated why Good Magician Humfrey might not be eager to return here in any hurry. What were his prospects? An endless line of supplicants, each requiring attention and research, while his own work of whatever nature went undone. Grey and Ivy had been here only a day, and already the word had spread; the Good Magician had been here a century or so.

Yet he had to admit that he rather liked helping people and creatures. He was learning things, too. He had thought that all goblins were like those of the Golden Horde; now he knew better. He had thought that monsters were for fighting or fleeing, but the giant slug had only wanted advice. Each case had to be judged on its merits, and none were truly unworthy. It seemed a shame to shut them all out, when they really did need help.

But of course he could not help them. In a few days he would be gone, even assuming he had competence for this. He was a Magician, but his talent hardly applied to this sort of thing. Well, if some creatures suffered from a devastating hex or geis, as they called it, that was of magical origin, he could probably nullify it. If there was illusion, he could nullify that too, cutting through to the truth. Other cases could be handled by ordinary common sense or a little imagination. Others were amenable to the artifacts of the castle, like the love potion. So there actually was a lot that he and Ivy could do. Certainly it was the kind of thing he'd rather be doing than leaving Xanth.

But he did have to leave Xanth, because soon Com-Pewter's grace period would be over, and he would have to serve the evil machine if he were not gone from Xanth. Com-Pewter hardly cared about the welfare of individual folk. The machine would set about taking over Xanth, and Grey was aware that though his magic talent might not readily be turned to doing good, it could certainly be turned to doing evil by nulling the magic of anyone who opposed Com-Pewter. He could not allow that to happen.

How he wished it were otherwise! That his father's curse had been effective. Almost, it seemed, it had been; it had

enabled them to locate Magician Humfrey and talk with him.
But the Magician had refused to help in time. Suppose Grey
stayed in Xanth and the machine used him to destroy much
of what was good and decent in it, and then, years later,
Magician Humfrey returned? What kind of Xanth would greet
him? No, Grey had to leave Xanth; there was no other way.

Unhappily, he slept.

In the morning there was a new person approaching the castle.
It was a female figure, naked and wild-haired. A nymph?
Then Grey recognized her. "Mae Maenad!" he exclaimed.

"What could she want?" Ivy demanded. "We left her well
set up as the oracle on Parnassus!"

"Something must have gone wrong," Grey said, "I have a
feeling that plain common sense won't fix it."

Ivy glanced at him obliquely. "She was the first to call you
Magician, and you did kiss her. Do you suppose—?"

Grey laughed. "What attractive young woman would have
any interest in a nothing like me?"

Ivy's look transformed slowly from oblique glance to direct
stare. Grey realized that he was in trouble.

"Uh—" he said, with his usual social finesse.

"I'll settle with you later," she muttered significantly.
"Right now we'd better find out a way to slow her down until
we can figure out exactly what she wants before she meets
you."

A bright notion forged its way into Grey's mind. "The
Good Magician had challenges, didn't he? That didn't actually stop the people who came, but—"

"But slowed them down!" she agreed. "Until he could do
some research in his Book of Answers, and—" She broke off.

"And we don't, uh, have that book," he finished.

"We, uh, certainly don't," she said, mimicking him with a
brief smile. "We also don't have suitable challenges. The layout of this castle was different each time someone approached
it; he must have had a lot of work done between visits."

"But it's solid stone! You can't just move that around! The
whole thing would tumble down!"

Ivy pondered. "He must have had an easier way. He had the centaurs rebuild this castle, long ago. Now it occurs to me to wonder: why rebuild it, when it was already standing and only needed refurbishing? Those centaurs really worked; I saw them on the Tapestry. They seemed to have about ten different designs, and they worked on them all, but somehow it became only one castle."

"Like the dream castle and cottage, maybe," he said. "Switching readily from one to the other, according to the need, to fool intruders."

"According to the need," she echoed. "Grey, I think you've got it!"

"I do?"

"There must be a command or something to change the castle, to make it different. Something he could invoke."

Grey nodded. It was making sense! "We'd better invoke it soon; Mae is almost here."

"I'll try." Ivy took a breath. "Castle—change form!"

They waited, but nothing happened. Ivy tried other commands, but nothing worked.

"Uh, maybe since it's my service we're doing," Grey said. "I mean, it's my problem, having to serve Com-Pewter, so I'm the one who owes the Good Magician the service. The castle—well, it sorta has to cooperate, if—"

"It sorta does," Ivy agreed, mimicking him again. "Well, give it a command."

Grey turned to face the main portion of the castle. "In the name of Good Magician Humfrey, change form!" he intoned.

There was a rumble. The castle shook. Walls slid around. In a moment the platform they were on heaved, and the stones of the wall rose up high.

Grey discovered Ivy in his arms. They were no longer on a parapet, but in a cupola whose arched windows overlooked the moat. They could see the slanting roofs of the castle, different from before. The entire layout of the castle had changed.

"It obeyed me!" Grey exclaimed, amazed.

"You didn't believe your own reasoning?" Ivy inquired

archly. "That it had to cooperate, if you were to perform the service for the Good Magician?"

"I guess my faith wasn't strong," he agreed. Then he looked down again. "But we still have to deal with Mae."

"Well, the drawbridge is up, so that may slow her," Ivy said.

"The Maenads can swim; they love to bathe in their wine spring. Except for—" He brightened. "That's it!"

"That's what?"

"She doesn't like blood! Is there a vial of imitation blood in the collection? I mean, something that would—"

"Gotcha, Magician!" Ivy said. "Grace'l!"

The lady skeleton appeared. "Something funny has happened—"she began.

"All under control," Ivy said smoothly. "Is there a vial of blood in the chamber?"

"Certainly. Concentrated blood extract."

"That should do. Pour it into the moat."

The skeleton, not having much brain, didn't argue. She went off to find the vial.

They watched from the cupola. In due course a bony hand extended from a lower window. Something dribbled into the moat.

Abruptly the moat turned deep red. It looked as if the river of blood from Girard had been diverted and now coursed around the castle. There was even a wisp of vapor rising from it, as if it were hot. The Good Magician's vials remained potent!

Mae came to the brink and stared into the moat, evidently appalled. She had left the Maenads because she had no taste for fresh blood; what would she do now? Well, if her concern was less than critical, this would cause her to turn around and go back to Mount Parnassus, saving them trouble.

The woman put her hands to her face in a gesture of grief. Suddenly Grey felt like a Mundane heel. She was weeping!

The color of the moat faded in the vicinity of the Wild Woman. The water turned clear, the clearness spreading slowly outward. What was happening?

"Her tears are washing out the blood," Ivy said. "I didn't know Maenads could cry."

"Maybe true ones can't," Grey said. "I think she is surmounting the first challenge."

"And we still don't know what her problem is or how to fix it!" she exclaimed.

Grey nodded. "We're here for only a few days, but I want to do the best I can while I am here. Maybe it's a test, and if I do a good job, the Good Magician will return at the last moment and give me my Answer." It was a wild hope.

"That just might be!" she agreed. "This is certainly turning out to be more than just a castle cleaning!"

There was a shadow in the sky. "There's another one already!" he said, his heart sinking. "A roc. Neither moat nor walls will slow that down!"

"No, it's my brother, silly!" Ivy said. "We'll tell him to fetch us the Book of Answers, so you can answer Mae and send her back immediately." It was evident that Ivy remained uneager to have the shapely Wild Woman remain close to Grey for any longer than was strictly necessary. He liked that.

"You tell Dolph," he decided. "I'll figure out the next challenge. I think we can use Goody Goblin after all."

"See that you do," Ivy said darkly, and hurried off in the direction of a roof terrace.

Grey went in search of the goblin, whose chamber might not be where it had been. All the labyrinthine passages of the castle were different, but there were not a great number, and soon he did find the goblin.

"Do you know, Magician. I must have been unobservant yesterday," Goody remarked. "I could have sworn the passage was of another nature."

"It was," Grey explained shortly. "We changed the layout. Now I would like you to do me one service before you go."

"Gladly, Magician!"

"There is a Wild Woman coming into the castle. You must go down and try to scare her off. Don't hurt her, just frighten her."

"A Wild Woman? But they don't affright readily, and I am

hardly the type to—" The goblin paused, realizing something.
"I believe I saw a mirror chamber downstairs. In that I could
assume the aspect of twenty goblins. If I made faces and
moved around, I might put on a good show. But if she catches
on—"

"Then she wins the challenge, and your service is done,"
Grey said. "You will then be able to go your way with a clear
conscience."

"Excellent! I shall intercept her as she passes through that
chamber." Goody hurried down the hall.

But he still needed a third challenge. What would really
faze a Wild Woman?

Grey snapped his fingers. He searched out the maiden.
"Maiden, there is a service you may be able to perform to
acquit your debt to me."

"What would that be, Magician?" she asked, just a trifle
warily.

"There is a Wild Woman coming into the castle soon. I
want you to intercept her after she passes the goblin, and give
her a manicure and hair styling and female outfitting—a frilly
dress, slippers, and uh—" He faltered.

"Panties?" she prompted.

"Uh, yes. That sort of thing."

"Oh, yes, I am excellent at that sort of thing!" she agreed.
"But a Wild Woman—"

"You will stand athwart a locked door which bars her passage to me. She must suffer the treatment or be forever barred.
If she departs without the treatment, your debt is paid. If she
agrees to it, you will—how long would it take?"

"To do it right? Hours!"

"Perfect! When it is done, knock on the door, and I will
open it, and you may go home."

And if that didn't stop the Wild Woman, nothing would,
he thought as he went looking for Ivy. But by that time, he
should have the Book of Answers, and be able to handle her
Question. He really appreciated Humfrey's system, now.

Mae encountered the goblin in the mirror chamber. She
screamed: not in fear, but in outrage. It seemed that Maenads

didn't like goblins. She chased the first figure she saw, and smacked into the mirror. After several such smacks she began to catch on to the nature of the challenge. She noted her own reflections in the mirrors, and avoided these. Finally she found a panel in which there was neither a goblin nor Wild Woman and leaped through it, for that was the exit. She had won the second challenge, and it had only taken her an hour to do it.

Meanwhile Dolph had taken off for Castle Roogna. As a roc he could cover the distance rapidly—but once there he would have to convince King Dor to give him the volume, which was kept locked up for safety until the Good Magician's return. Ivy would have sent a note, but even so, it could take hours. Would the book arrive in time?

The maiden intercepted the Maenad. There was another screech of outrage. Almost the Wild Woman turned back— but the same flaw of character that caused her to avoid blood made her decide to submit to this transcendent indignity. The maiden started to beautify and civilize her appearance.

Two hours passed. Grey knew that the beautification could not last much longer. Where was Dolph?

Then the roc showed on the horizon. The big bird was carrying a book.

It turned out to be a monstrous volume. Grey clutched it in his arms and set it on a table evidently sized for it. He opened it—and was bewildered by such a maze of entries that he could not make any sense of them. It would take him an hour just to find his place.

The door opened. A stunning Mundane woman entered. Grey blinked. This had to be the Maenad—but what a change! Grace'l must have found a cache of supplies for this job. She was in a lovely pink dress with bows, and wore pink slippers with flowers on top, and her hair was bound in another bow with another flower. Her finger and toenails were delicately tinted, and so were her lips. Her legs were so smooth that they were surely exhibited in hose, and there was a definite suggestion of panty out of sight. She looked as if she were going to a debutante party.

She had come for her Answer, surmounting all the challenges—and he was unable to use the Book of Answers. Now what was he to do?

Her petite mouth opened, the Question incipient.

"You're beautiful," he said, partly to stave off her Question, and partly because it was true.

"You have humiliated me!" she cried. "You have made me cry, and chase a goblin, and—what?"

"You're beautiful," he repeated. "If you wish, I will null out all that magic as you stand before a mirror, and you will see that your beauty owes nothing to enchantment or nymphly arts. Any time you wish to retire from the oracle, I'm sure you could readily nab a village lout."

She considered. "Maybe I will. It has occurred to me since meeting you that there may after all be uses for men other than as food. But right now I have a Question."

He had hoped he had diverted her. Now he was in for it. "Ask."

"I am running out of gibberish to spout when I sit over the cleft. The priest says I can't be a priestess unless I have plenty of vile-sounding gibberish. How can I get it?"

His worst fear had come true: here was a Question he couldn't answer. How could a person "find" gibberish to spout when it no longer came naturally?

Then he remembered how Goody Goblin's nice language had deteriorated when he had sat on a curse burr. Suppose Mae did the same thing?

He looked at her form, and knew he couldn't recommend that remedy; it would be a defilement of beauty.

But another memory came to him: of his father, in past years, laboring over a Mundane torture known as income tax. Much of the problem had been the maddeningly incomprehensible tax manual.

"Grace'l," he said.

The lady skeleton appeared.

"Fetch the volume labeled *Revised Simplified Tax Manual*."

Soon Grace'l was back with the volume, one of the pile of dusty tomes Grey and Ivy had sorted through. He had thought that particular one useless, but had been too busy to throw it out yet.

He opened the tome. "Now I want you to look at this and try your best to make sense of it."

"A book?" Mae asked, frowning skeptically. She looked at the page. "It shouldn't be hard to blip toggle subtract twenty-eight percent of Line 114 from the total of Lines 31 and 89, whichever is less coherent, and zap fraggle Form 666 under Line 338A unless outgo is more than indicated in Supplementary Brochure 15Q, in which case fromp beezle—" She looked up. "This is sheer gibberish!"

"Precisely," Grey said. "This is *the* volume of gibberish. No one has made sense of it in centuries. Take it with you, and you will never run out of inspiration."

"Oh thank you, Magician!" she exclaimed, clutching the tome to her bosom. "And what service—"

Grey started to say that she needed to perform no service, then realized that he just might need a Wild Woman to challenge some other visitor. The Good Magician's policy of requiring a term of service was not merely to discourage applicants, but to make the system feasible. It all fitted together—now that he had spent a day, as it were, in the Good Magician's shoes. "Remain for a while," he said gruffly. "The skeleton will show you to a room. I shall notify you of your service in due course."

Then, seemingly abruptly, his time was up. They had spent most of a week putting Humfrey's castle in order and in handling the constant pleas for Answers. The Good Magician had not returned, and now it was evident that he was not going to. Their wild hope had proved vain.

Dolph was ready to change form and carry Grey and Ivy away. Marrow and Grace'l had agreed to supervise the shutting down of the castle, with the help of those who owed service. The brief restoration of Answers was about to end.

Ivy's determination to come with him remained firm. She bid a tearful farewell to the castle and the creatures of it, and would do the same as they stopped by Castle Roogna on the way to the isthmus. Forced to choose between him and her homeland, she had done him the immense kindness of choosing him, and he would always remember and treasure that, no matter how dreary his life in Mundania became. With her it would have been bearable; without her it would be unbearable. But he had to do what he had to do. He would fly with her back to Castle Roogna, then say what he had to say, in the presence of her family. He knew that King Dor and Queen Irene would understand, and would support his position. Ivy might hate him, for a time, but she did have magic alternatives.

"It's time," he said through the lump in his throat. "I wish I could stay here forever, hectic as it may be; I really like feeling useful. But I can't." That was only the half of it. This coming flight would be his last with her, and with her love.

Ivy was blinking back her tears. She took his hand, proffering silent comfort. How little she knew!

Dolph changed form. He became the roc, precariously perched on the roof. One of his huge claws happened to slip on a dead leaf on a tile; he lost his balance, and had to spread his wings to recover. The tip of one wing clipped a turret— and a flying feather was broken.

Dolph changed back. He jammed a crushed finger into his mouth. "I can't—mmph—fly with that—mmph—broken feather!" he said around it.

"You poor thing!" Ivy said with instant sympathy. "I'll bandage it."

"But how will we get to the isthmus in time?" Grey asked. He knew that no other mode of transport would be fast enough; they had depended on Dolph and had stayed just as late as they could risk it. He felt guilty for that, knowing he was playing it too close, but savoring his last moments in Xanth and with Ivy.

"Look in the Book of Answers!" Ivy said over her shoulder as she took her brother off for bandaging.

He shrugged and decided to do just that. He went to the book and opened it. Maybe there was a magic way to fix a feather instantly. He had begun to get a glimmer of the way the book was organized; it was alphabetical, but so detailed, with so many subentries and cross-references, that it was easy to get lost on the way. He looked for "Feather" and discovered such an enormous listing of types and classes and qualities of feathers that he decided it would be faster to look up "Roc" instead. He flipped over the pages, and naturally turned too many, finding himself in the S's. He started to flip the pages back, and his eye happened to light on the entry immediately by his left thumb: "Service." Curious, he read it. This, too, had many subtypes and qualifications. One he saw at the bottom of the page was "Good Magician's."

Grey paused, his hand still about to turn the page. He read that portion. ". . . that by ancient custom and practice having the force of law, service to the Good Magician, such as in payment for Answers, takes precedence over all other services of any type, regardless of their dates of inception, notwithstanding commitments that may have been made or inferred or otherwise designated, for the reason that . . ."

This was almost as obscure as the tax manual! It must have taken the Good Magician most of his century or so of life to decipher this opacity. It would have been fascinating to unravel the actual meaning of such entries, maybe sitting by a warm fireplace with Ivy in the evenings . . .

Grey had to thumb tears out of his eyes. The truth was that, despite all its confusion and frustration, this scant week in the Good Magician's castle had been wonderful. He had somehow stumbled through and managed to do some favors for the good folk and creatures of Xanth, and each case had been a separate item of education, opening his eyes to another intriguing aspect of the magic realm. But mainly he had felt so very *useful!* It had seemed as if what he did mattered to others. Never before he met Ivy had he had that feeling, and never before this castle had he had it in relation to strangers. He had felt, however foolishly, important. For these few days. He hated to give that up just about as much as he hated to leave Xanth. It wasn't just for him; it was for those he had helped, and might have helped in times to come. Had it been possible to stay—

. . . takes precedence over all other services . . .

Grey stopped still. Could that be true? Could it apply even to the service he owed to Com-Pewter?

He reread the passage, carefully, making sure he understood each part of it. It did seem to be true. And that just might mean—

"Oh, here you are," Ivy said. "Did you find a way for us to make it in time?"

"I found something else, by pure coincidence," Grey replied, excited. "I—we may not have to go!"

"Not have to go? But in another day Com-Pewter—"

"Is this book the ultimate authority?" he asked. "I mean, is there anything else that overrules its Answers?"

"No, nothing, of course. The Good Magician was always the ultimate authority on anything. He was the Magician of Information, after all. So his Book of Answers—why do you ask?"

"This says that service to the Good Magician takes precedence over any other service, no matter when that other service was undertaken. By the Custom and Law of Xanth. Which seems to mean that until I complete my service to Humfrey, I can't serve Com-Pewter. If that's true—"

"But he said he might never return!" she protested. "You'd be stuck with serving him all your life, and maybe never even get an Answer!"

"No," he said, understanding dawning like sunrise on the millennium. "I've already had my Answer. I just didn't understand it, before. Now I must serve, if need be, for the rest of my life—right here. Doing this. And do you know—"

"It's no bad thing," she finished, her confusion brightening into awe.

"No bad thing at all," he agreed.

Then they were in each other's arms, hugging and kissing and crying with relief.

Grey's eye caught sight of a magic mirror on the wall. He hadn't noticed it before, but now he saw that it was tuned to the evil machine's cave. Pewter had been watching all the time! But on the machine's screen were the words CURSES—FOILED AGAIN!

What an amazing coincidence, that he should happen on this very passage in the Book of Answers, after Dolph had by sheerest mischance broken a feather, so that—

Coincidence? Mischance? No, it was more like magic! The one thing, or series of things, that could have gone wrong with the evil machine's long-range plot to conquer Xanth—that thing had occurred, because of the nature of Murphy's curse on Com-Pewter's ploy. It was perhaps incidental that this also accounted for Grey's lifelong happiness with Ivy. Perhaps.

Grey knew better, now.

"Thanks, Dad," he murmured.

Author's Note

The prior Xanth trilogy went to nine novels, to the outrage of critics, and this one may do something similar. Don't write to me demanding the titles of future Xanths; you can figure them out for yourself if you have the wit, and I won't do it for you if you lack the wit.

I am not looking for more puns, so those of you who take this statement as a pretext to send me more pages of them will receive much the same response as those of the paragraph above. You see, I can't get these novels written at all when I have to answer hundreds of letters instead. I'm sure that those who receive letters from me are happy with them, but those who have no chance to read the next novel because I spent my time on letters may be less satisfied. If one or the other has to go, guess which one it will be?

Nevertheless, over the years I have picked up some suggestions, and here are my credits for them:

Paul Riat—suggested that Magician Murphy and Vadne escape in the Time of No Magic, and have a child in Mundania, whom Ivy later meets.

Grey Hartley—lent his name and talent to that child.

Robert Heym—suggested that a Magician be born of Xanth folk who moved to Mundania, then he moves to Xanth, thus appearing by surprise.

Matt Gay—the two-lips tree.

Rob Moreau—the sandman.

Dave Alway—first of several to note Chex's early maturity. That is perhaps only natural, for Dave is a centaur breeder from way back.

Mary "Meow" Gollihugh, David Vilendrer, and Casey "Bookworm" Bowen, for the titles to Xanths 13, 14, and 17— oops, those haven't happened yet! Unread this paragraph before you get confused.

Carla Barbee—if Ivy is king, her husband would be queen.

And for those of you who just can't wait for the next Xanth novel because you are hooked on puns, remember that there are other outlets for your illicit craving. There are Xanth gamebooks written by Jody Lynn Nye, and there are Myth-understood novels by Robert Lynn Asprin. Most of the prior puns are catalogued in *The Visual Guide to Xanth*, by Anthony and Jody Lynn Nye (the gamebook nymph), and *The Gamebook Nymph*, available soon. Finally, there is the Xanth Pin-Up Calender, with all the hot dates. Harpy reading. If those don't hold you, then perhaps you should commit yourself to a hospital for detoxification, because otherwise your case is terminal.

A Supplement
to the Lexicon
of Xanth

A

ADDRESS—Where Good Magician Humfrey can be found, if you can figure it out. See *Question Quest* for further information.

AGENDA ANDREWS—The first girl sent to Grey by Sending. She has brown hair and is excruciatingly well organized.

ANOREXIA NERVOSA—Grey's second girlfriend. She is very thin, and dieting.

B

BARON HAULASS OF SHETLAND—Guest at Chex's wedding.

BLACK PETE—Proprietor of Thieves' Isle, not to be trusted unless your memory is excellent.

BOY(1)—Witness at Grace'l's trial: doesn't like girls.

BOY(2)—Child who got lost in forest, rescued by Girard Giant. No known relation to Boy(1).

Bria—Lost brassie girl found by Esk, who gets back at him by marrying him. She can be remarkably soft when she wants to be, a trait shared by some Mundane women.

Brick Bat—Guardian of Draco's nest.

Bucktooth Goblin—One of the members of the Goblinate of the Golden Horde.

C

Calendar—The ogres run the calendars of Xanth, because they don't mind getting their fingers sticky on the dates. The months are Jamboree, FeBlueberry, Marsh, Apull, Mayhem, JeJune, Jewel-Lye, AwGhost, SapTimber, OctOgre, No-Remember, Dismember.

Centurion—Centaur who comes to the oracle for advice. He has one hundred fine arrows.

Che—Colt of Cheiron and Chex Centaur: see *Isle of View* for further information.

Cheiron—Winged centaur stallion who marries Chex. He's a handsome hunk with golden hooves and silver wings, and he really can fly.

Chex—Winged centaur filly, friend of Esk's; she has gray eyes and wings, and brown mane and hide, matching Esk to a reasonable extent. Originally she can not fly, but finally discovers the secret, and mates with Cheiron.

Com-Pewter—A magical thinking machine that plots to take over the universe. It can change reality in its vicinity to conform to its liking. In Xanth its nefarious efforts have been foiled again (curses!), but it is more successful in Mundania, where free will is less valued.

CONNIPTIONS—Nasty little things that aggravate folk to the point of rage, especially when there is already a problem.

CRI-TIC—Loathsome bloodsucking bug of Mundania.

D

DONKEY—Centaur who resembles a donkey, being small and gray, with big ears. Friend to Ivy and Grey and Electra. His talent is to change the color of his hooves.

DORIS—Curse fiend girl with nice legs.

DRACO DRAGON—Possessor of the firewater opal. His nest is in Mount Etamin, part of a constellation of mountains. Not a bad sort, if you like flying dragons.

DUKE DRAGONTAIL OF DIMWIT—Guest at Chex's wedding.

DUNGEON MASTER OF HURTS—In charge of the painful aspect of bad dreams.

DYSLEXIA—Grey's third girlfriend: a blue-eyed blonde who has trouble reading because she sees things backward.

E

ELECTRA—She substituted for the sleeping princess, owing to Murphy's curse, and was betrothed to Prince Dolph when he woke her. She's a nice girl who once had a thing about her father but now loves Dolph, despite the fact that he is three years younger than she (no father fixation *there!*), but he is betrothed to her only to keep her from dying. She looks like a child, with freckles, and her eyes are the color of wonder. Her talent is electricity: she can give a person quite a jolt. She recharges the Heaven Cent.

ENCHANTED MOUNTAIN—A replica of aspects of Xanth in the dream realm, in the form of a towering mountain. Accessed by the frankinmint plant.

ESK OGRE—Son of Smash Ogre and Tandy Nymph. A nice young man except when anger makes him ogrish. He has gray eyes and brown hair, which match the colors of his friends. His magic talent is that of Protesting: when he says no, the other party desists without always understanding why.

EUPHORIA—Grey's fourth girlfriend: hypnotically intense eyes, swirling black hair, lush figure—but she's into drugs.

EYE QUEUE—Vine with eyeballs that makes the wearer smart—or at least he thinks he's smart, which isn't necessarily the same thing.

F

FIGMENT—An illusory figure. Gina Giantess started out as one, but Girard's love made her a regular dream figure.

FIREWATER OPAL—Mela Merwoman's prize, which she needs to gain a husband. She enlists Prince Dolph's aid to recover it, because Draco Dragon killed her former husband and took the gem. One of a matched pair.

FLATFEET—Mundane demons who patrol the roads.

FRESHMAN ENGLISH—A fate worse than death, in Mundania.

FULSOME FEE—Duck-footed leader of the fee elves, who need to interbreed with others to increase their stock.

G

GALATEA—Ivory statue of the loveliest of pigs, being carved by the sculptor Pyg Malion.

GHASTLIES—Shapeless, multilegged things that spit purple venom; it is best to stay clear of them unless you happen to like purple spittle.

GINA—Invisible lady giant, originally a figment of a dream, now Girard's girl.

GIRARD—An invisible giant, trapped in the realm of the gourd, where he is visible. He was bound and bleeding for a long time until rescued by Grey.

GLOHA—Daughter of Glory Goblin and Hardy Harpy: a winged goblin girl, who participates in the festivities of Chex's wedding.

GOBLINATE OF THE GOLDEN HORDE—The meanest goblins north of the Gap.

GOODY—Goblin, unconscionably polite, cured by a session with curse burrs.

GORBAGE—Goblin, mislisted as Craven in Lexicon: father of Goldy and Glory Goblin.

GRABRAHAM—New, young, timid Bed Monster under Ivy's bed, replacing Snortimer. Grabby for short.

GRACE'L OSSEIN—Female walking skeleton, Marrow's girlfriend, with nice bones.

GREY MURPHY—Son of Magician Murphy and Sorceress Vadne, betrothed to Ivy. He has hair-colored hair and neutral eyes, and his first eighteen years were dull even by Mundane standards, but he's a decent guy. His talent is the nullification of magic.

GROTESK—Goblin chief of the Goblinate of the Golden Horde. A mean one, even for goblins.

H

HAYBERRY LONGCAKE—A delicacy. There is an inferior substitute in Mundania, using short straw instead of long hay.

HATE SPRING—Makes anyone who touches its water hate the next person seen. Used by the Goblinate of the Golden Horde to torment captives.

HEAVEN CENT—Penny piece that sends wearer to place most needed; it can be charged only by Electra.

HENRY—A deaf man who helps Ivy practice sign language.

HOARSE CHESTNUT—a tree which makes heavy breathing sounds when the wind passes.

HONEYMOON—The far side of the moon, which remains as sweet as honey and is popular with the newly married. The near side of the moon, of course, has long since been corrupted to green cheese because of the horrible sights it sees below.

HORACE—A zombie centaur: his speech is slurred and his hide may be moldy and his face wormy, but he is not too far gone, and Ivy likes him, which counts for a lot.

HUMMERS—Invisible flying creatures that annoy demons (and anyone else who hears them) intolerably. They are even worse in Mundania, especially where demons have meddled with wetlands.

I

IGNOR AMUS—Very stupid juror at Grace'l's trial.

ILLUSTRATED GUIDE TO XANTH—Like a Lexicon, only more so.

ISLE OF VIEW—Affectionate island where the sleeping princess was supposed to wait. Just speaking its name in company of the opposite sex can lead to interesting complications.

ISLES OF JOEY—Group of islands: Thieves', Beauty, Horror, Water, Fake, Food, and maybe others as yet undiscovered.

ITCHLIPS—One of the Mount Etamin goblins.

J

JODY LYNN NYE—Nymph who makes Xanth gamebooks such as *The Encyclopedia of Xanth* and *Ghost of a Chance*. Some of the punniest puns have taken refuge there.

K

KISS-MEE RIVER—Affectionate river ruined by demons, who pulled it straight, depriving it of its friendly curves and causing it to become the Kill-Me River. The same thing happened to the Kissimmee River in Florida, by no coincidence.

KOMODO LI ZARD—Guest at Chex's wedding; prince of the Isles of Indon Esia.

L

LATIA—Curse fiend crone who helps Esk. She is old, stooped, and so ugly she is able to best an ogress by using her face to curdle water instead of milk, but is a good person.

LOVE-LIES-BLEEDING MONUMENT—On Isle of View, to mark the sleeping princess, but it got stolen.

M

MAE—One of the Maenads of Mount Parnassus, a Wild Woman, who didn't fit because she doesn't like blood. She became a priestess of the oracle. Her eyes glow like candle flames when she is excited.

MAGIC MIRROR—There are a number of them, but one in particular is used by Dolph and Ivy to call home when they are away. Com-Pewter steals it for a time.

MAGISTRATE—Curse fiend official.

MAIDEN—A pretty girl who comes to the Good Magician's castle for advice about love.

MARE CRISIUM—A night mare, Cris for short.

MARROW BONES—Walking skeleton found by Esk in the gourd. Originally used to frighten sleepers in dreams, he got lost. Like all magic skeletons, he can disassemble his bones and reassemble them in assorted useful configurations.

MELA MERWOMAN—Captor of Prince Dolph; Melantha for long. She resembles a mermaid, but lives in salt water and is more voluptuous. She has no panties.

MERMAID—One of twenty lovesick mermaids in the dream realm in a scene to love a misogynist to death.

MERWIN MERMAN—Mela's dead husband: he had a difference with a dragon and got toasted at point-blank range.

METO NYMY—Juror at Grace'l's trial, with attributes.

METRIA—Demoness who annoys Esk. She has trouble remembering particular terms.

MIKE—A Mundane or barbarian (the distinction is moot) warrior with the standard huge thews, whose body Dor inhabits when he visits the 800-year-old past via the Tapestry.

MINT—A family of plants with some special qualities, as indicated by their names: spearmint, peppermint, frankinmint (smells like frankincense, only without the anger), and such.

MISOGYNIST—A man who hates women, scheduled for a horrible bad dream of being loved to death by lovely mermaids.

MOATIE—Moat monster in the Castle Roogna moat.

MONUMENT—On beach opposite Isle of View, marking King Trent's landing.

MOUNT RUSHMOST—Meeting place of the winged monsters.

N

NABOB—King of the Naga serpent-folk. His head is human, his body serpentine.

NADA—Princess of the Naga, Prince Dolph's betrothed. She can assume either human or serpent form in addition to her natural one, and is cute in all three. Dolph loves her, but she can't love him because she is five years older than he is. Close friend of Ivy's.

NALDO—Prince of the Naga, Nada's big brother. Charming and handsome in all forms: human, snake, naga.

NO NAME KEY—Where the Mundania/Xanth interface (that is, gate) is. Unlike the isthmus, this one goes through the gourd, and does not modify the time scale. Night mares and storks use it for their deliveries. Turn Key is in charge.

NONENTI-TREE—An unimportant tree, hardly worth this listing.

O

ONOMA TOPOEIA—Juror at Grace'l's trial: she looks the way she sounds.

OPPOSITE SEX—This definition has been censored, by order of the Adult Conspiracy. What would happen if a child found out which one it was?

ORACLE—A setup in which a priestess sits over magic fumes from a cleft and speaks excellent gibberish, which is then interpreted for visitors who have questions.

OXY MORON—Juror at Grace'l's trial: a stupidly clever ox.

P

PANTIES—Object of much speculation in Xanth: exactly what color are they? Boys beneath the age of consent are not permitted to speculate; it is part of the Adult Conspiracy. See *The Color of Her Panties* for further information.

PERRIN PIRANHA—Chivalrous guardian of Draco's nest.

PHLOD FIREFLY—Prince Dolph's alternate identity in dragonform: his name spelled backwards.

POLICEMAN—A blue demon in the dream realm who chases folk, yelling things like, "Sendyata tha bighouse!"

PRINCESS—Originally supposed to eat a bit of apple she carried with her and sleep for a thousand years until a handsome young prince kissed her awake so she could marry him and live happily ever after, she was foiled by Murphy's curse and had to settle for King Roogna. Electra bit the apple instead.

PUNWHEEL COOKIES—Ivy's favorite, served by the Gorgon.

PYG MALION—A pig who is a talented sculptor, carving an ivory statue of Galatea, with whom he is in love. He is a juror at Grace'l's trial.

PYTHIA—Innocent damsels who serve as priestesses and speak gibberish for the oracle at Mount Parnassus.

Q

QUICKSAND—It speeds you up.

R

REVISED SIMPLIFIED TAX MANUAL—A source of limitless inspiration for gibberish, used by Mae Maenad for oracles, and by Mundanes for annual aggravation in the month of Apull.

RIVER OF BLOOD—In the gourd, the flow from the side of Girard Giant, which caused him some discomfort.

S

SALMONELLA—Grey's fifth girlfriend. She's a great cook, but the food is contaminated.

SANDMAN—Animated sand that can assume different shapes. It puts travelers to sleep.

SEEWEED SOUP—Wholesome and nutritious, therefore the torment of children. Mela Merwoman feeds it to Prince Dolph.

SENDING—An emulation sent by Com-Pewter to introduce Ivy to Grey Murphy, part of an insidious, heinous, and successful plot to make them like each other. Similarly successful plots have occurred elsewhere in Mundania, as married folk know.

SIGN LANGUAGE—Understood by animals in Xanth, if people have the wit to approach them with it, and by a select group of Mundanes.

SKELETON KEY—Needed to find the Heaven Cent. At first thought to be an isle, it turns out to be a rib Grace'l possesses, which sounds the Grace'l note in the key of G. Female skeletons have one more rib than male skeletons.

SLUG—A giant fire-breathing slug looking for a slugfest.

SMOKEY OF STOVER—Guest at Chex's wedding, once better known in Mundane comics.

SNAGGLESNOOT OF SYNCHROMESH—Guest at Chex's wedding.

SQUEEDUNK—Grey's home town in Mundania.

SYLPHS—A family of slender elflike creatures: Sylvester (deceased), Sylvia, and Sylvanie. Sylvanie takes over Grabby, Ivy's Bed Monster, who would otherwise have perished when Ivy became adult and stopped believing.

SYNEC DOCHE—Juror at Grace'l's trial: concerned with parts and the whole.

T

TANGLEMAN—Originally a tangle tree, he was changed to manform by King Emeritis Trent when he threatened Ivy, who then befriended him. This episode was in the deleted Chapter 1 of *Crewel Lye*, which was axed because of infestation by puns.

TAPIS—Sorceress who made the Tapestry, and many lesser tapestries that enable folk to step into their worlds. She ran afoul of Magician Murphy, but survived his curse, perhaps because she was a good person.

TOTO—Wrong fantasy series; see the Land of Oz.

TRISTRAN TROLL—Scheduled for a really bad dream, as punishment for releasing a succulent girl.

TRUCULENT TROLL—A witness at Grace'l's trial.

TURN KEY—The keeper of the gate at No Name Key, where the night mares depart Xanth to carry bad dreams to Mundanes.

V

VALE OF THE VOLE—Where the voles went after they left Xanth. (For reasons unfathomable to others, they don't consider it to be in Xanth.)

VIDA VILA—Nature nymph who would like to marry Prince Dolph. She can change forms, and is diligent in the protection of her land.

VIOLENT—Originally intended for planting on a median strip between paths, this one was rejected, because they didn't want any more violents on the media. That would not have happened in Mundania.

VITAMIN F—Found on the Lost Path, and left there; it remains lost, so that folk still claim there is no such thing. It has potent F-ect if you make the right F-ort. Not to be confused with vitamin X, which is for X-perts.

VOLNEY VOLE—One of the medium larger members of the great Family of Voles, thus related to the wiggles, squiggles, and diggles. He has brown fur and gray eyes when above ground, gray fur and brown eyes when underground. He speaks normally, but all other creatures have trouble with their S's. Thus when he says "sale of the soul" they hear "Vale of the Vole."

W

WALKING STICK—Useful as a cane or as an aid in mountain climbing, because it walks by itself.

WILDA WIGGLE—Princess of the branch of voles known as wiggles, whose offspring are troublesome to the landscape of the surface. She is petite and quite attractive, for a vole.

WORM—A computer program nominally put out by Vaporware Limited. It promises a lot, if you wait long enough. It installed Com-Pewter's Sending in Grey Murphy's computer.